LEIGH CLARK

SHOCK RADIO

A TOM DOHERTY ASSOCIATES BOOK

NEW YORK

This is a work of fiction. All the characters and events portrayed in this novel are either fictitious or are used fictitiously.

SHOCK RADIO

This book is printed on acid-free paper.

A Forge Book
Published by Tom Doherty Associates, Inc.
175 Fifth Avenue
New York, NY 10010

Library of Congress Cataloging-in-Publication Data

Clark, Leigh.
Shock radio / by Leigh Clark. —1st ed.
p. cm.
ISBN 0-312-85724-1
1. Radio broadcasters—California—Los Angeles—Fiction. 2. Serial murders—California—Los Angeles—Fiction. 3. Los Angeles (Calif.)—Fiction. I. Title.
PS3553.L28615S56 1996
813'.54—dc20 96-20878
CIP

First Edition: September 1996

Printed in the United States of America

0 9 8 7 6 5 4 3 2 1

For Sue Gordon,
native and historian of
the other Hollywood,
the legendary one.

ACKNOWLEDGMENTS

Thanks to Sherry Robb for selling the idea; to Natalia Aponte for supporting the project from its inception and guiding it through to completion; to Sergeant Hundertmark of the Los Angeles Police Department, Hollywood Division, for letting me ride along on the night watch, and for explaining the details and answering all my questions; and to several people, who choose to remain anonymous, for introducing me to the backstage reality of commercial L.A. radio broadcasting.

1st MURDERER: *Let it come down!*

Macbeth

PART ONE

APPEARANCE

1

PHANTOM

The air fell on the city like the ashes of the dead.

Headlights cut through darkness on Sunset Boulevard, sweeping past graffiti-scarred walls, barred shop windows. The faintness of false dawn had begun to lighten the night sky imperceptibly, but full morning rush, with its packed traffic and choking fumes, lay more than an hour away. Tires squealed in front of the multilevel office building that housed the broadcast studios of radio station KRAS FM. A Porsche's engine roared inside the half-light of the covered parking garage, then fell silent.

On his way up to the sixteenth floor, Aaron Scott leaned back against the elevator's rear wall, watching numbers blink by on an overhead display. He glanced at his Rolex.

Three minutes until airshift.

"You're late, Aaron," a young intern whispered as she saw him step through the back security door to the station's broadcast studios. "You are *really* late!"

"Yeah."

He took a seat in his broadcast booth, in front of his console, glancing at Lisa Takashi, news and weather, Bud Bronson, sports, Tracy Cortino, traffic. They stared back at him, frowning through double panes of glass that separated their individual booths from his.

Aaron was the undisputed star of KRAS's drive-time morning show, but late starts like this set everyone's nerves on edge.

Jerry Deel, the producer, stepped into his booth.

"You're late again, guy."

"Yeah."

The digital clock above the console read 4:59:20 A.M.

His airshift began at 5:00.

"You got forty seconds—*less* than forty seconds."

"Thanks, Jerr. I can read the clock for myself."

He put on his headphones and looked out the window at brown haze smeared across a slowly lightening Los Angeles skyline.

The clock above the console read 4:59:39 A.M.

"We got your intro cart cued up, all set to go."

"That's cool, Jerr."

"You ready? Or you want someone else to start it for you?"

Aaron punched PLAY on the cart machine and pushed the slide fader forward, potting up the volume on the intro tape.

"And now," a deep voice announced, backed by rising brass, "the moment you've been waiting for! Here he is! The nastiest shock jock in all L.A.! The one, the only true terrorist of the airwaves! The Man with the Mouth! Sunset Scott!"

Brass burst into exaggerated fanfare, then cut to hammering, head-banging heavy metal chords. The needle on the VU meter bounced from a normal reading over into the red.

Aaron potted down the intro volume and brought up the instrumental lead-in for the first cut. Then he increased the volume on his microphone, switched to BROADCAST. He leaned into the microphone, an Electro-Voice RE-20, and turned his head slightly, speaking across the mike rather than straight into it.

"Go-o-o-od mornin', everybody! Another hazy, crazy morning here in L.A., glitz capital of the whole damn world. Looks like somebody just went and took a dump across the skyline. But, hey, don't choke on it. We got the edge to help you cut through the crap, right? KRAS FM. 108.5. Sunset Scott in the Morning, all mornin' long, here in the sticky heart of Hollywood. Startin' things off with— What the hell is this? Mamabangers? Yeah! Mamabangers! You heard it here first. KRAS."

The vocals opened up on the set. Aaron switched off his microphone and leaned back in his swivel chair.

"Mamabangers," he muttered. "Shit."

Jerry stepped back inside the booth. "Call-ins are pilin' up, guy. Want us to lose the crazies?"

Aaron looked up at him. "Fuck, no! You leave those crazies alone! I *eat* crazies for breakfast! I'm Sunset Scott! The one, the only true terrorist—shit, you know who I am!"

"Sure," Jerry said. "I know you're late."

"So?"

"You and Sam having trouble?"

"Leave Sam the fuck outta this, okay?"

"Sure, Aaron."

"I haven't even *seen* her for the past three fuckin' days!"

"Okay, Aaron."

"What is it, Jerr? Late start-up get to you, or what?"

"You can handle last-minute start-ups. But it's pissing off the other guys. Also, there's the competition—"

"Fuck the competition."

"You take a look at our Arbitron ratings lately?"

"Fuck the ratings."

"The ratings fuck us, guy, not the other way around. Don't ever forget that."

"Hey, Jerr? We're goddamn number *one*, okay?"

"For now. The competition's—"

"*Fuck* 'em!"

"I just don't want to see us lose our edge."

"You think *I'm* losin' it, Jerr? Is that it?"

"I don't know, guy."

He left the booth before Aaron could say anything else.

The Mamabangers cut drew to a close. Aaron got ready to pot down the music and start talking over the fade. Bill Waller, Jerry's assistant, stuck his head inside the booth.

Aaron glared up at him. "What?"

"Lisa's doing her bit on the, you know, serial killers."

"So?"

"So she wasn't sure you'd be able to, you know, like, work it in with your—jokes, and stuff."

"Of *course* I can't work it in, you lame dickhead!"

"If you could at least try," Jerry called from outside the booth, "it might help pump the ratings some."

"No problem, Jerr! I'm sure I can come up with some laugh-out-loud shit about serial killers!"

Aaron began to fade out the Mamabangers. He switched his microphone to BROADCAST and broke in over the fade.

"Okay, everybody! Sunset Scott here. KRAS, 108.5. It's a bad mood, badass morning. Our stupid assistant, Mumblin' Bill, just came over and kicked my ass on that last set. And now I'm in one goddamn bad mood. I mean, a *serious* bad mood."

Aaron motioned for Bill to come back into the booth.

"Man, why'd you dump all that crap on me? You *know* I'm in a bad mood, 'cause I got in here late again! And now you make it even worse! You just plain stupid, or what?"

Bill started to answer from outside the booth.

"Hold on, Bill! No one can understand you when you mumble like that. It's why they call you Mumblin' Bill. Step right up and talk *into* the damn mike—okay?—so we can at least hear what the hell you're tryin' to say!"

Bill stuck his head inside the booth and shouted at the microphone, "I was just, like, following orders, okay?"

"You were just followin' orders, yeah. Kiss my ass! Like you're a robot? Right? You do whatever Jittery Jerry tells you to? Jittery Jerry's the producer. I'm not even gonna *ask* him if he gave this guy any orders, 'cause Mumblin' Bill is such a total moron. Go on! Get outta here! You *mo*ron!"

Lisa broke in. "You *are* in a bad mood, Sunset Scott!"

"I'm in one hell of a bad mood! I'm ready to kick ass if any of you stupid listeners call in this morning with any stupid comments! You got that, all you morons out there?"

"Wow!" Lisa said. "It's a really bad mood Monday!"

"Damn right about that! KRAS. 108.5. Your bad mood radio station." Aaron switched to a nervous stage whisper. "That lead-in heavy enough for your story, Lovely Lisa?"

Lisa laughed. "I guess so, Sunset Scott! But you're not the only one in a bad mood this morning. The LAPD's got another serial killer on their hands, and they're not too happy about it. They've already started comparing this guy to the Nightstalker and the Hillside Strangler, two of L.A.'s most notorious serial killers. At least six murders have already been blamed on this new guy, known only as the Phantom—"

Aaron broke in. "The *what?*"

"The Phantom. You know, like the Phantom of the Opera."

"If he ever goes on the afternoon talk shows," Bud Bronson cut in, "they'll have to call him the Phantom of the Oprah."

Aaron groaned. "That was Bud the Stud, everybody, our KRAS Sports Animal. The Phantom of the Oprah! Does that really *suck*, or what?"

"Hey," Bud shrugged, "somebody had to say it."

"Get back to your sports den, you animal! And quit messin' with Lovely Lisa while she reads the damn news, okay?"

"You want to know why they call him that?" Lisa asked.

"Call who what?"

"The Phantom."

"No, not really. Okay, yeah. Tell us, Lovely Lisa, why do they call this butthead the Phantom?"

"They call him that," she said, "because whenever he attacks his victims, he always wears a white mask."

Bud Bronson jumped in again. "Who was that masked man?"

"Bud," Aaron said, "just shut up for a second, okay? Look, Lisa, how the hell do the cops know he wears a white mask? His victims describe him before they die, or what?"

"Three of them didn't die that fast."

"What happened?"

Lisa hesitated, glancing at Aaron through the double glass panes that separated them. *You sure you really want me to read this shit over the air?* she mouthed silently to him.

Aaron nodded.

She took a deep breath. "One of them, this old lady, a former actress, got cut up real bad. She bled to death in the emergency room. The other two, both young wanna-be actresses, about nineteen or twenty— He set their faces on fire. They died a few days later, in the Cedars Sinai burn unit."

Lisa stopped talking. Most of the fun seemed to have leaked from the airwaves, like helium escaping a party balloon.

Aaron glanced at Jerry, who looked more jittery than ever.

"You know, Lisa, I wish these stupid serial killers would start gettin' a little more *original.* Know what I mean? All these stupid-ass nicknames! The Hillside Strangler. The Nightstalker. The Phantom. These dickheads think they're so cute, with their stupid comic book names. Hey, look, *dick*heads! I'm talkin' to *you,* okay? All you stupid serial killers out there! Especially you, the Phantom! Get real! If you can't come up with anything more original, just go ahead and use your own sorry-ass real names, okay? Stupid dickheads!"

"Wow!" Lisa said, responding to frantic hand signals from Jerry. "It's a super bad mood Monday with Sunset Scott! Now let's check out the morning commute with Tracy in Traffic."

"Thanks, Lise," Tracy Cortino said. "Sunset Scott's not the only one in a bad mood this morning. Things are just total chaos out there on our freeways. Starting with—"

Aaron switched from BROADCAST to CUE so that he could talk directly to his producer, separated from him by two windows of double glass.

"How you like my take on the serial killers there, Jerr?"

"A little heavy, guy. This is drive-time, not '60 Minutes.' "

"So feed me a call-in! They're always good for laughs."

"We got eight on hold right now."

Aaron glanced at the video monitor next to the console.

It showed names, addresses, and phone numbers for callers holding on the lighted switchboard lines.

"Which one's the weirdest of 'em all, Jerr?"

"Number Seven, the mystery man with no name."

"He doesn't want to give us his fuckin' *name?*"

"Says he doesn't have one."

"What's he want to talk about?"

"Serial killers."

"My man!"

Aaron reached for number seven on the switchboard.

"Wait a minute, Aaron—"

"What?"

"This guy's *too* weird. Maybe we should lose him."

"Too weird is too good, Jerr. Remember the ratings?"

"Maybe you should screen him off-air first."

"Fuck, no! I'm takin' this asshole on live, man!"

Tracy moved into the windup of her traffic report.

"And now, back to the Man with the Mouth. Sunset Scott!"

Aaron punched in a seven-second station promo jingle.

Harmonizing voices chirped, "108.5, KRAS FM!"

He switched his microphone back to BROADCAST. "Okay, everybody! We got us a fresh caller here on the line at KRAS! Except we don't know what to call this dude, 'cause he ain't got no name! Yeah! So we're just gonna call him Mr. X, the Man with No Name. How's that grab you, Lovely Lisa?"

"Totally cool, Sunset Scott!"

He hit number seven on the switchboard.

"Mr. X from L.A., you're on the air with Sunset Scott."

The other end of the line was silent.

"Hel*lo*, Mr. X! Still there? Did we lose you?"

Silence.

"Look, Mr. X, if you're there, speak up. We can't *hear* you! You're givin' us too much dead air, man."

More silence.

"Okay, fine. You're just some spineless little sleaze. Don't even have the guts to say your name over the air? You just hang there on the phone and keep your coward's mouth shut? Did I get that part right? You're a real *dick*head, Mr. X! You know that? Kiss my ass, you stupid dickhead!"

Aaron reached out to punch off button number seven.

"I'm here," said the voice on the other end of the line.

Aaron's finger froze above the button.

It was a soft voice, with a hollow sound, like an echo from the past. It seemed to whisper as it spoke, with a slight impediment, as if the *m*'s were difficult.

"I'm listening," the voice said.

"Well, that's cool. You plan to just sit there and listen, and not talk? Sort of a stupid way to call in, isn't it? But then, you sound like sort of a stupid guy, Mr. X. You don't want to give us your name. You don't want to talk—"

"I'll talk." Another pause. "Oh, yes, I'll talk."

"Glad to hear it, Mr. X. You don't mind if I call you Mr. X, do you? Sort of seems to fit you—like Brand X. What happened? Mom forget to give you a real name?"

"I have no name," said the voice, "and no face."

Aaron laughed into the microphone. "No name and no face! I *love* it! The nameless and the faceless, right? Hey, Mr. X, my man? You mind if I ask you a real personal question? Are you also maybe, like, homeless, too?"

"We are all homeless, all of us, with the passage of time."

"Nameless, faceless, homeless! A triple slam! Can I ask you somethin', Mr. X.? Are you one of those weirdos we see a lot of here in Hollywood? One of the pimps runnin' hookers on the Strip? One of the crack dealers over on Selma Avenue?"

"I am part of this city. I know its ways."

"So cool, man! 'I know its ways.' Mr. Mysterious X. Is that your first name, by the way? Mysterious? Friends call you Mysty for short? As in, *Play Misty for Me?*"

"I have no name—"

"And no face either. Okay, Mr. X, let's cut the crap. You want to talk serial killers? Cool. What makes *you* an expert? You hang out with serial killers a lot? In fact, what the hell *do* you do, Mr. X?"

"I am part of this city—"

"And you know its ways. Yeah, right. This is gettin' *boring*, pal. What do you *do* with your life? Wander the streets at night? Sing? Dance? Drive a cab? Deliver pizza? Work graveyard at the 7-Eleven?"

"I have—a mission."

"The Mission! I love it! Hey, Lisa! He lives at the Mission in downtown L.A! Hey, Mr. X! You one of those guys just hangin' on the corner? Bottle of Thunderbird stuck in your back pocket? Holdin' up one of those funky brown cardboard, hand-lettered signs? WILL ROB AND RAPE YOU FOR FOOD—"

"SHUT UP!"

The voice cut with a jagged edge, like broken glass.

The needle on the VU meter jumped up over one hundred, into the red, then bounced back to normal.

"Whoa! Mr. X loses it. Mr. X gets very, very pissed!"

The voice spoke again, soft and whispering once more.

"I didn't call to amuse you. I called to share with you a sense of—my mission. To make you—part of what I must do."

"Fine, Mr. X. You haven't said what that is yet."

"I must purify this city—rid it of corruption."

"Cool, but just how do you plan to do that, man? You run a cleaning service? Ride a trash truck? Help rebuild L.A.?"

"I punish the wicked. I make them answer for the evil they have done. I bring them—judgment."

Aaron saw Jerry giving him the wrap-up signal.

He motioned his producer to stand by.

"Okay, Mr. X. I think I'm startin' to get the picture. You go after bad guys, right? Hunt down criminals? You're an undercover cop? Or part of some citizens' vigilante group, like the Guardian Angels?"

"I am alone. I need no help from others."

"Then you're a lone wolf kind of vigilante, right? Sort of like Charles Bronson in *Death Wish?* You work alone, so you have to hide your identity. That why you call yourself Mr. X?"

"That's not my name. *You* call me that."

"Hey, look, Mr. X, I gotta call you *some*thin', right? I can't just call you the Man without a Face, or Nameless, or some stupid crap like that. If you don't like Mr. X, pick a better name. What do your friends call you?"

"I have no friends."

"I believe it! What do your enemies call you?"

The voice laughed, a dry sound, like the echo of death.

"The Phantom."

Aaron's mouth dropped open, then arched into a big grin.

He looked at Jerry and raised his hand thumbs-up.

"The *Phan*tom! Well, I'll be damned! *The* Phantom? The one who's so red-hot these days, with all that slammin' prime time news coverage? The one our own Lovely Lisa just told us about? The guy who's famous all over town for wearin' a white mask? Choppin' people up, settin' 'em on fire? Hey, that's some body count you got racked up there for yourself, man! Lovely Lisa! How many people has our mystery caller killed so far?"

Lisa paused before answering. "Six—I think."

"Well, hey, listen, Phantom! I'm gonna call you Phantom from now on, instead of Mr. X, if that's cool with you? So anyway, Phantom, where'd you come up with a hard-core name like that? Rip it straight off the musical?"

"You make jokes," said the voice, "because you don't understand. But you *will* understand, in time."

"Understand what, Phantom? You? Your personality? Your childhood? You have a normal childhood, Phantom? Guess not, huh? Otherwise you wouldn't be in this line of work, right?"

"I kill because of what *they* are—what they *did.*"

"Who's 'they'? Your victims? The people you kill?"

"Their actions deserve—judgment. I judge them."

"How? With a blowtorch and a meat cleaver?"

"You mock me, because you yourself fear my judgment."

"*Me* afraid of *you?* Let's get one thing straight right now, Phantom. You're fulla crap, okay? I'm Sunset Scott, man, the one true terrorist of the airwaves! I ain't afraid of nothin' or nobody! Got that? Besides, how do I know you really *are* the Phantom, anyway? How do I know you're not just some lame dickhead out there who's decided to call in and try to suck off this whole serial killer thing?"

The voice did not answer.

"You still with me, Phantom?"

Aaron looked up and saw Jerry talking on the phone.

"You demand proof," asked the voice, "of who I am?"

"Damn straight I want proof! Tell me somethin' I don't know! Somethin' only the *Phantom* would know!"

"What if I tell you when to expect another—judgment?"

Aaron saw Jerry draw his index finger slowly across his throat in the standard kill signal—stop talking at once.

Aaron shook his head no and spoke into the microphone.

"Want to tell us who your next victim's gonna be, Phantom?"

Silence filled his headphones.

"Who's next? Someone we all know? Someone here at the station? Maybe someone like Lovely Lisa, in News and Weather?"

"Thanks a lot!" Lisa cried, fear cutting into her anger.

Aaron's laughter trailed off into expensive dead air.

The silence continued.

He reached for button number seven.

"You make jokes," said the voice, "to hide your own fear. I'll call again. Not today, but soon. Good-bye—Sunset Scott."

The line went dead.

Aaron looked up at Jerry, then glanced at Lisa, who stared back at him through the glass. He switched off his microphone to clear his throat, then put it back on BROADCAST.

"Okay, everybody! That was a KRAS exclusive! *Only* with Sunset Scott in the Morning. The *Phan*tom, L.A.'s newest and scariest serial killer! The Man with the Mask. You heard him here first. KRAS. 108.5. And you heard him promise—"

Aaron put on an echo filter and a Schwarzenegger accent.

"I'LL BE BACK!"

"So be sure and tune in tomorrow, Sunset Scott in the Morning, to find out who the Phantom's next victim will be. Who knows? It could even be you! Yes, *you* might be the next lucky winner in our Serial Killer Contest! Be the one hundred and eighth caller on our new contest line, 1-800-FEELIN'-SO-DEAD, and win an all-expenses-paid trip to eternity, one way only. Limit one prize per family, please! And now, our next song is— Hey, What the hell's this, Lovely Lisa? 'Mondo Finito.' This a new song by Madonna? Or an old one?"

"A new-old one," Lisa said, voice tight.

"Okay, everybody! A new-old song by Madonna. Or maybe an old-new one. Who the hell can tell the difference?"

Aaron shut off his microphone and potted up the song.

Jerry stepped into the booth.

"You out of your *mind?*" he shouted at Aaron.

"Problem, Jerr?"

"That caller was totally unplugged! He could've been a copycat killer! What did you screw around with him for? Why didn't you cut him off when I gave you the kill signal?"

"Because he was *funny*, Jerr. That spells R-A-T-I-N-G-S."

"We don't need ratings that fucking bad!"

"Jerr . . ." Aaron yawned. "You act like he's real."

"I don't know *what* he is! Neither do you!"

"Sure I do. He's a fake."

"You don't *know* that!"

"I've worked live phones a long time, man. I can tell real crazies from fakes. This guy's a *total* fake. Trust me."

Lisa stepped into Aaron's booth, face pale.

"Whatever he is, leave me *out* of it the next time!"

"It was just a joke, Lisa. A little Sunset Scott *shtick.*"

"I don't want some crazy person *stalking* me!"

"He's too big a dickhead to stalk his own shadow, Lisa—"

"Don't get started with me, Aaron!" Her voice rose. "I am *not* joking, okay? I do *not* want to get mixed up in this shit!"

Bill Waller stuck his head inside the booth.

"What is it, guy?" Jerry asked.

"The first calls are coming through on that Phantom thing?"

"What's the listener response like?"

"They love it," Bill said. "They totally fucking love it."

2

MEMORIES

On his way home from the station late that afternoon, Aaron stopped off at Steinberg's, a small Jewish deli in the Fairfax district of Los Angeles, across the street from an Orthodox synagogue. Steinberg's was mostly takeout, few chairs or tables. The owner, Leah Steinberg, a slight woman with gray hair, stood behind the glass-front display counter, wrapping up fish for an elderly couple.

"Nova Scotia lox," Leah said. "The best."

The older woman shook her head. "The best lox comes from Scotland. Herschel and I had some in Edinburgh last summer. Such flavor, you wouldn't believe! Now *that's* the best."

"Well, Ruth," Leah said, handing her the package, "Nova Scotia's the best you get today, 'cause it's all I got. Enjoy. And *mazel tov* on your granddaughter's engagement."

"Thank you, Leah! We're so happy for her. *Nu*, Herschel?"

"What's not to be happy?" he said, taking his wife's arm.

Ruth waved to Aaron, who entered the shop as they made their way toward the door. "Aaron! How *are* you?"

"Not bad, Mrs. Rosenthal."

"You hear our Debbie got engaged? To a doctor!"

"That's cool. *Mazel tov.*"

"He's only premed," Herschel said.

"He'll be a doctor soon enough! You still seeing the same girl, Aaron? That television reporter from On-Target News?"

"Samantha. Yeah, we're still seein' each other, I guess."

"Don't wait too long, Aaron. The good ones get away!"

"I'll remember that, Mrs. R."

On their way out, Herschel nudged Aaron's arm.

"Take your time. We're talking the rest of your life."

Aaron walked over to the glass counter where Leah Steinberg was busy straightening display items and price tags.

"Hello, Aaron," she said.

"Hey, Mom. How's the ol' deli business?"

"Not bad. Shirl called in sick today." Leah shrugged. "What can you do? Everybody gets sick sometime."

"Yeah, well, at least it's not too busy."

"Hah! You should have been here half an hour ago."

Aaron took a kosher dill from a countertop plate.

"I was still at the station, setting things up for tomorrow's show." He bit into the pickle. "It seems to take a little longer each day."

"What's to set up? All you have to do is talk dirty."

"There's more to it than that, Mom."

"Is that so?"

"Look, I know you're ashamed of what I do—"

"Who's ashamed? You're my only son. You're also very talented and I'm very proud of you. What you do with your talent's your own business. But I'm entitled to my opinion."

"You think I'm wasting this great talent of mine?"

"Anyone can talk dirty on the radio. You can do more."

Aaron reached for another pickle. Leah slapped his hand.

"I got a nice dinner packed and ready to go! You want to spoil it with all this *noshing?*"

"They're just pickles, Mom. Can't I have one more?"

"*Just* one."

Aaron took the largest off the plate and bit into it.

"Did you listen—"

"Don't talk with your mouth full, Aaron."

He swallowed. "Did you listen to the show this morning?"

"I would never listen to such *schmutz.* You know that."

"We had something a little different this morning."

"What? A new interview with a hooker? Or a lesbian?"

"Thanks, Mom."

"You do things like that on your show, Aaron."

"I thought you never listened."

"My friends listen. They tell me about it."

"Yeah, well, this morning was different. We had this guy call in who claimed to be the Phantom, the new serial killer? The one that's murdered six people already?"

Leah looked at him. "A serial killer? On a radio show?"

"Not a *real* serial killer. Just some fake who's trying to *pretend* he's the Phantom, and cash in on all the media hype."

"So did you hang up on him?"

"Are you crazy? He was good for a few laughs."

Leah put down the spoon she was using to stir potato salad.

"A poor *meshuggener* calls up pretending to be a serial killer, and you encourage him in his craziness?" She shook her head. "That's not funny, Aaron. That's cruel."

"It's just a job, Mom."

"A job can be dangerous, Aaron." She lowered her voice. "A job can sometimes even kill."

"Not my kind of job—unless I broadcast live from a hot tub and drop my mike in the water."

"Don't make jokes, Aaron."

"Look, I know you don't like what I do, because of Dad—"

Leah began to stir the potato salad again.

"Your father's work had nothing to do with why he went ahead and—did what he did."

"What kind of actor was he, anyway?"

"Not a very good one."

"I mean, what kind of roles did he play? Comedy? Drama?"

"Westerns. They made lots of those back then."

"Sorry. I know you hate even talking about him."

"He's been out of our life for such a long time, Aaron."

"He was never part of mine."

"That's just as well."

"No, it's not! I have a *right* to know who my father was."

Leah looked up at him.

"Your father was someone who never married me, and walked out on us before you were born. Then, a month later, he died in an accident. What else is to know?"

"Maybe there's pictures of him—somewhere."

"I didn't keep any. I lost touch with his family. I'm not even sure if *they* still have any."

"But if you could just tell me his name—"

"What good would that do, Aaron? You'd be like one of those poor adopted kids, looking for their birth parents. It wouldn't make you happy. Believe me."

"How do you know?"

Leah slammed down the potato salad spoon.

"Because your father's *dead!* What do you want to *do*, Aaron? Build a shrine to some dead man you never even knew? Try to honor the memory of a man who didn't even love your mother enough to want to marry her?"

Tears came to Leah's eyes. She turned away.

Aaron reached out and put a hand on her shoulder.

"Come on, Mom. Don't cry. I love you, okay?"

She wiped at her tears with a hand towel. "I guess you missed some things, growing up without a father. I tried to make up for them. I didn't do so good, but I tried."

"You did great, Mom. You're the best."

"I never told you much about your father because I didn't want you getting obsessed with someone you could never know. It's not a healthy thing, Aaron, an obsession like that."

"I'm not obsessed. I just wonder about him, sometimes."

"Become a father to your own children! That's what I want for you. Your father would want it too, if he was still alive."

"Now you sound like Mrs. Rosenthal."

"That *yenta?* Just because I want my son to be happy?"

"Sam's not ready to get married yet. Neither am I."

"You're too caught up in your jobs, the both of you."

"And jobs can kill. You already said that."

"They can, Aaron. Trust me. They can."

"You think Dad's job killed him?"

Leah looked down at the potato salad bowl. "No."

"I wish I at least knew what his *name* was."

"Why? So you could go and change your own name again?"

"You hate me for doing that, don't you?"

"No, Aaron. I don't hate you."

"It was hard enough getting hired as Aaron Scott. Aaron Steinberg would've been a real stretch."

"You're not the first Jew who had to change his name to make it in a *goyisheh* world. You won't be the last."

Leah handed him a large white paper bag.

"That's pastrami on rye, potato salad, cole slaw, *latkes*, and for dessert, apple strudel. You can heat up the pastrami and *latkes* in the microwave if you want."

"Thanks, Mom. No pickles? No green tomatoes?"

"They're in there. If you decide to go out for dinner with Sam instead, just put everything in the fridge. It'll keep."

"Thanks, but Sam's busy tonight."

"Busy with what?"

"Editing some interview she did with somebody from the LAPD. About that serial killer, the Phantom, the one my fake caller pretended to be. They'll probably run her interview at ten tonight. I'll try to catch it—if I'm still up."

"She's a hardworking girl. But don't make a habit of eating alone, Aaron. It's not good for you, or Sam."

"We eat out plenty. You should see my Visa bill."

A buzzer sounded above the door as a customer entered.

Aaron raised the white bag. "Thanks for spoilin' me, Mom!"

"Love is not spoiling, Aaron. Be careful driving home."

3

NEWSCAST

Home was a two-bedroom condo on the second floor of a two-story hillside building that overlooked the Sunset Strip.

Aaron stood in his darkened living room and stared out at the traffic on the Strip below, flowing through the night like a river of red-and-white diamonds. After a while, he turned on the room lights and closed the vertical blinds, then sat down in front of the television to eat his dinner.

He channel-surfed around for a while before switching to On-Target News. Terry Sandoval, the six o'clock anchor, with her model-perfect dark hair and smooth olive skin, sat talking to the camera. Aaron cranked up the volume.

"—still holding Los Angeles in a grip of terror, although no further victims have been added to the Phantom's toll. Meanwhile, L.A.–area residents continue to worry about how they can protect themselves from a murderer who seems to strike at random, without warning. To find the answer to this and other questions, On-Target

News sent field reporter Samantha Collier to talk with the detectives handling this case. Samantha?"

Aaron leaned forward, spilling potato salad on his lap.

The screen cut from a smiling Terry Sandoval to a blond, grim-looking Samantha Collier, gorgeous despite the grimness.

"Yo, Sam!" Aaron cried, raising his bottle of Corona.

"Terry, I'm here at the LAPD's Hollywood Station, Homicide Division, with Lieutenant Clay Brock, the detective in charge of investigating the Phantom killings."

The screen flashed to a head-and-shoulders shot of Brock.

"Lieutenant Brock, is the LAPD any closer to finding this new serial killer known as the Phantom?"

"This is a top-priority case, Samantha. A large contingent of officers have been assigned to it. But at this time, we still have nothing positive on the suspect or his whereabouts."

"What about the person calling in to radio shock jock Aaron Scott this morning, claiming to be the Phantom?"

"Shock jock!" Aaron chanted. "Shock jock!"

"We looked into that incident," Brock said, "and determined that it was not a substantive affair."

"In other words, the call turned out to be a prank?"

"Yes, that's correct."

"What about anonymous call-in tips to the police? Have any of those turned out to be helpful?"

"For security reasons, I can't go into that right now."

"What can we do, as concerned Los Angeles residents, to protect ourselves from someone like the Phantom, Lieutenant?"

"We're advising people to stay off the streets after dark, until further notice. If you have to go out, take someone with you and stick to well-lighted areas. Women who must go out alone after dark should proceed with extreme caution."

"Should they also be watching for a man with a white mask?"

"Yes. But according to eyewitnesses, the mask isn't that visible at a distance. The victims didn't seem to notice it until the perpetrator came within striking range."

"So there's nothing about the Phantom that makes him stand out in a crowd. Is that what you're saying, Lieutenant?"

"According to the eyewitnesses, he seems to be very tall."

"Like a forward for the Lakers?"

"Maybe not quite that tall. But definitely taller than average, with a heavy build."

"What about carrying something to protect yourself? Like Mace or pepper spray? Would the LAPD recommend that?"

"No."

"Why not, Lieutenant?"

Brock paused. "One of the victims had pepper spray on her person when she was attacked. It proved—ineffective."

The screen cut from Brock's impassive face to Samantha staring into the camera with a somber expression.

"The LAPD may not have all the answers they need yet, but they're determined to stop the Phantom, and his reign of terror, before any more lives are lost. As for the rest of us, all we can do is take precautions, and wait to see what the Phantom will do next. From Hollywood, this is Samantha Collier."

The screen cut back to Terry Sandoval in the studio.

"Thanks, Samantha. I'm sure we all join you in wishing Lieutenant Brock and his men good luck. In other news—"

Aaron switched to a cable sports network, where a hockey game raged in full fury. A closeup of the goalie showed a large man in a white mask, dark eyes glaring into the camera. Aaron switched to a real-life police show. A handheld camera hovered over three officers examining a motionless body on the sidewalk. He switched to an all-cartoon channel and left it there.

After finishing his dinner he tried to watch a martial arts adventure film on one of the cable movie channels but fell asleep during the first ten minutes. He awakened to the sound of a ringing telephone. A car exploded on television, scattering burning shrapnel across the street. He glanced at his watch. More than four hours had passed since he fell asleep.

He picked up the cordless phone. "Yeah?"

"Aaron?" Samantha asked. "Did I wake you up?"

"No." He rubbed at his eyes. "I mean, yeah, but so what?"

"Sorry."

"Forget it. Hey, I saw your piece at six o'clock! Pretty cool, Sam. I thought it was scheduled for ten."

"They ran it again at ten."

"Yeah, well, guess I missed that. Hey, you really put the screws to ol' General Brock of the LAPD!"

"You liked that?"

"Loved it. You could almost see the flop sweat on his face as he groped for answers."

"He was a real tight-ass, all right. Reciting canned answers, instead of just admitting nobody knows from shit—"

"You get anything to eat, Sam?"

"I grabbed a sandwich at the vending machine."

"Poor baby. You could've shared a Ma Steinberg takeout special over here with me."

"Don't make me hungry! Your mom's a great cook."

"How about dinner tomorrow night? At a good restaurant?"

"I can't promise anything, Aaron. I'm really busy."

"You can't eat out of vending machines forever."

"What have you got in mind?"

"You mean after we eat?"

"No, I mean dinner, wise-ass. Where do you want to eat?"

"How about Ca' Venezia, that new place in Santa Monica?"

"Santa Monica's out. I need to stay close to the studio, just in case this dirtbag kills someone else."

"What about Tramonto? On the top floor of Cal Pacific Savings, near Sunset and Vine?"

"Okay. But everything's off if the Phantom strikes again."

"You're really into this, aren't you?"

"It's news, Aaron."

"Or tabloid journalism."

"Hey, look who's talking! *Mr.* Shock Jock!"

"I just do comedy *shtick.* You're a real reporter, Sam."

"And the Phantom's a real monster. People are terrified by that, but they want to know the truth about monsters—how they think, why they act the way they do. That's a legitimate demand for the truth. I answer it with my reporting."

"The search for the Truth, huh?"

"You got it."

"Whatever you say. But there's one thing I don't get."

"What?"

"You know that part where you ask Brock if it's smart to carry Mace? And he says no, because one of the victims tried it and it didn't work? It sounded like he was holding out on you."

"He was. But we couldn't have used it on the air. The details are too sickening. You want to hear them?"

"Hey, this is *Mr.* Shock Jock. Remember?"

"The victim, a woman, sprayed the Phantom with pepper spray when he attacked her. It didn't stop him, or even slow him down. Just pissed him off. He took the spray from her, shot it into her eyes, blinded her. Then he shoved it up inside her— He set fire to her hair, her face, her body. They managed to keep her alive for almost seventy-two hours in the burn unit at Cedars before she finally died."

Aaron was silent on his end of the line.

"Aaron? You still there?"

"Yeah. Ugly story."

"You can see why we couldn't use it on the air."

"Yeah."

"He's a vicious bastard, taking out his anger on women."

"Yeah."

"I hope you won't keep joking about him on your show."

"Hey, wait a minute! Some dickhead calls me up, pretends to be someone he's not. I bounce some *shtick* off him, get a few laughs. He hangs up. Where's the problem?"

"What if he calls back, Aaron?"

"I bounce some more *shtick* off him! Don't worry. It won't go on forever. He'll get tired of it."

"It's not smart."

"Look, Sam. He's *not* the Phantom, okay?"

"Keep joking around with him and you might attract the attention of the real thing. You don't want to do that."

"I *don't?* My ratings would go through the fucking *roof!*"

"Aaron, we're not on the air. This is not a comedy bit. I am completely serious. You're a high-profile entertainer. Don't make yourself a target for some serial killer."

"I'll try not to."

"And remember Brock's advice: don't go out at night—"

"I just drank my last Corona. Thought I'd drive on down to the Strip tonight. Pick me up another six-pack."

"Aaron, don't joke about this."

"Who's joking? I want another beer before I go to bed! Come *on*, Sam. You think the real Phantom's gonna come lookin' for me? Just 'cause I burned his stupid ass on the air?"

"I don't know what he's going to do. Nobody does."

"So what time do I pick you up for dinner tomorrow night?"

"Make it six-forty-five, okay?"

"Whatever you say, babe. Still love me?"

"When you're not acting like a jerk, yeah, I think so."

As he hung up, Aaron glanced at the television.

A *Friday the 13th* clone was on. The screen showed a gaggle of shrieking teenagers with Jason in hot pursuit, his white hockey mask glowing like a leprous death's-head.

Aaron stood up and pointed the remote at the screen.

"Hey, Man with the Mask! Yo, *Phan*tom! You sorry piece of recycled shit! Listen up! Take this supercharged remote, and shove it up yo' fuckin' withered white asshole, okay?"

He put his finger on POWER and started to snap it off.

Just then the screen cut to a sudden close-up of Jason snarling into the camera through his white hockey mask. A savage growl burst from the set's speakers, amped to the max.

Aaron cried out and dropped the remote.

His hand was trembling as he bent down to pick it up.

He punched the POWER button, hard, but did not look at the screen again until it had turned dark and silent.

4

NIGHT WORLD

The polluted evening air lay heavy in his lungs.

A chill wind sifted the smog, invisible now against a dark, sunless sky. Scraps of waste paper, driven by the wind, rattled through the alley in back of Aaron's building, scraping across concrete. He thought he heard something else then, along with the rattling, and turned to look.

But it was nothing, just scraps of paper in the wind, and the dark sky, and smog like the scent of death in the air.

He eased his car out of the parking garage, using a remote to open the security gate, which rolled back squeaking on rusted casters, barred shadows gliding across artificial light. His Porsche 968, black like the night itself, dropped quickly down the narrow, winding road that opened onto the Strip.

A pale moon hung low over the Hollywood Hills, blurred and indistinct through the smog.

Out on the strip, traffic flashed by as if the sun had never set. Enormous iconic images stared down at him from illuminated billboards. Crowds of people, most of them young, drifted along the Strip, with hair of many colors, black leather, mostly pale skin, pierced noses, lips, nipples. Aaron gave only half an eye to the passing street parade, accustomed to it by now. Blinking lights and billboards crawled across his windshield, reflected in the curved glass.

He stopped for a traffic light.

Five young men with shaved heads and painted faces sauntered across the street in front of him. One raised a threatening fist to Aaron, mouthing something audible but incoherent. He did not have to hear it to understand what it meant.

The night belonged to them, not him.

He found parking a few spaces down from the liquor store. A young man and woman dressed in black sat on the hood of one car. Another couple danced to their own soundless music on the sidewalk directly in front of the entrance. Aaron had to step around them to enter the store.

Inside, a tired-looking black man with a gray beard bought two lottery tickets from the cashier. A kid still in his teens with long messianic hair shuffled down one of the aisles, arm draped around a thin blond girl who moved in step with him. Two skinheads with sleeveless shirts and muscles pumped by iron and steroids flipped through bondage magazines at the news rack.

The store's lighting, flat and surreal, seemed almost like an illusion, some kind of artificial daylight separating those inside from the dark world out there.

As Aaron stood in line to pay for his six-pack, a man with matted hair and grimy skin sidled up to him, holding a crude, hand-lettered sign that read STARVEN WIL WERK FOR FOOD.

Aaron tried to ignore him. The man moved in closer.

"Money for food," he whispered hoarsely, sounding as if his larynx had been cut out. His breath smelled like something left too long in the sun.

Aaron paid for his beer, then gave his change to the man with the sign, dropping coins into a dirty, outstretched hand.

"God bless you, mister," he croaked, fingering the coins.

Another homeless panhandler had stationed himself in front of the Porsche. Aaron had to pay a dollar to get rid of him.

Back out on the Strip, he floored the gas and felt the surge of the Porsche's powerful engine. He had seen enough of Hollywood at night for one night. He wanted to go home.

But he made it only a few blocks before hitting a traffic jam, one of the late-evening types that seem to materialize out of nowhere, as if through some kind of malign night magic.

"Shit!"

He slammed his hand on the steering wheel and glared at the line of red lights trailing down Sunset in front of him.

After suffering almost fifteen minutes of stop-and-slow, he turned off on a side street with an angry squealing of tires.

The tightness in his jaw started to relax as he sped south, away from Sunset. He could turn left on Fountain and drive parallel to the Strip until he got past the goddamn whatever-it-was that was causing the backup—probably some asshole changing his tire in the middle of the street.

He came to a rubber-burning halt at a stop sign, looked both ways down a dark, deserted cross street, then got ready to floor the accelerator, when, above the fine-tuned rumble of the Porsche's engine, he heard the sounds.

A woman's screams cut through the night with the jagged, ear-splitting intensity of a car alarm gone berserk. The screams erupted spasmodically, as if she was choking, or running, or fighting for her life . . .

Aaron sat there at the stop sign, engine idling, his own throat tightening as he listened to the woman's screams.

Not that it was any big deal to hear screams at night on the weird streets of Hollywood. People drank too much. They did too many drugs. They got into street corner arguments and standoffs, and sometimes real fights. Guys fought with their dates. Drag queens fought with their boyfriends.

But the screams never sounded like these.

Aaron looked down the dark street, trying to tell where the

screams were coming from. They sounded diffuse, as if woven from the fabric of the night itself, part of the black shapes of trees and houses and shadows, or the sickly orange-yellow glow of sodium vapor streetlights in the distance.

Then he heard footsteps, scraping across concrete, stepping on broken glass, scattering loose cans down the sidewalk.

He turned left onto the cross street and flipped his headlights on high beam. A cat leaped out of his way, streaking between two parked cars and across a withered front lawn.

Aaron drove slowly, his head partway out the window as he listened to the screams, and the footsteps, coming closer now.

An open beer can struck the windshield, spraying the glass with liquid and suds, flecking his face and left arm. A strong, yeasty smell of fermented hops and barley filled the air.

Aaron stopped his car and shoved open the door.

"Who the fuck's out there?"

He got out, legs weak with anger, and fear.

The beer can rolled off his hood and fell to the street.

Two figures moved into the harsh glare of his headlights.

Both wore black clothing over pale skin. One of them, tall and heavily built, chest bare under an open jacket, had shaved his broad head bald, except for a forelock of hair dyed bloodred. The other, thinner one had long hair flowing past his shoulders, gnarled and dirty, like that of a fallen angel.

"Hey!" grinned the redhead. "We fucked up his car!"

The other laughed, revealing a mouthful of mottled teeth.

"Fuckin' punks," Aaron muttered, starting to get back in the Porsche, ready to drive them down if it came to that.

"Don't make me hurt you, man!"

He looked up and saw a young black man approaching the side of his car, right arm thrust out toward him, gripping a nine-millimeter Walther PPK, an ugly-looking weapon with a snub-nosed barrel and a lethal reputation. Aaron stared at the dark hole of the muzzle as the gun moved in on him.

"I don't want to hurt you, man!" he warned. "So don't make me do it, okay?"

The left side of his mouth twisted down. The whites of his eyes burned red. He walked unevenly, with an awkward, limping, side-to-side gait.

But the hand holding the gun remained rock-steady.

"What do you want?" Aaron asked, as he tried to keep his own voice steady. "Money? The car?"

"Hey!" cried the tall redhead, squinting at the headlights, shading his eyes, bloodred forelock falling down across his fingers. "I know that *voice!* He's the fuckin' *ass*hole on the fuckin' radio! Sunset Scott! The fuckin' *shock* jock, man!"

"He's in for a shock now," said the one with fallen angel's hair, and laughed again, bad teeth flashing in the light.

Aaron's anger started to build, displacing his fear.

"Fuck you, shitheads." He glanced at the one holding the gun on him. "And fuck you too, asshole."

"Don't you *say* that to me!" The young black man limped forward suddenly, lame foot scraping across the pavement, bringing the gun muzzle right up into Aaron's face. "Don't you in*sult* me like that! **DON'T MAKE ME HURT YOU, MAN!"**

"Chill, Jabar," said the redhead. "Just hold him for us."

He drew out a hunting knife from a sheath at the back of his belt and held it up in front of him, six-inch blade bursting with reflected glare from the Porsche's headlights.

"Hold him real steady," he whispered.

Aaron heard the whispering voice in his headphones again.

I am part of this city. I know its ways.

He glanced at Jabar holding the gun on him, then at the tall one coming forward, knife out in front, bloodred forelock hanging down his forehead.

Aaron looked in the eyes of the one with the knife, and saw nothing there—except the visible form of his own terror.

I punish the wicked.

He heard it again, hissing through his headphones.

I make them answer for the evil they have done.

"Where's your mask?" Aaron blurted out suddenly. "Why aren't you wearing your fucking *mask?*"

The tall one laughed then, opening his mouth wide, stretching his lips to expose a bloodred gum line.

"Man," he said, still whispering, "I *am* the mask!"

He moved forward with the knife.

The shrill wail of a police siren pierced the night air.

Flashing red-and-blue lights burst from the end of the block as a patrol car swung into view.

"Shit, man!" the redhead muttered. "*Fuck*in' shit!"

"DROP YOUR WEAPONS," blared a speaker on top of the patrol car. "PUT YOUR HANDS IN THE AIR WHERE WE CAN SEE THEM."

"You want me to do him?" Jabar asked, moving the PPK closer to Aaron's face until the muzzle almost kissed his lips.

"Just get the fuck outta here!" the redhead shouted.

Jabar glanced at them, gun hand never wavering.

He turned back to Aaron, bloodred whites of his eyes growing larger. He pushed the snub-nosed muzzle up against Aaron's throat, shoving it into the fleshy part.

"You don't tell 'em *nothin'* about us, man!" Jabar whispered, foul breath blowing over Aaron's face. "Otherwise, you gonna make me hurt you. Bad. Right *now.* O*kay?*"

Aaron nodded.

Jabar jammed the gun into his throat until it hurt.

"O*kay!*" Aaron shouted, nodding hard. "Okay! Christ!"

"HALT!" the patrol car ordered. "STAY WHERE YOU ARE—"

Jabar gave Aaron one last bloodred glance, then turned and ran, moving with remarkable agility despite his bad leg, hopping over the sidewalk and skittering down an alley.

The patrol car screeched to a stop beside Aaron, burned rubber smell filling the night air. An overhead spotlight beamed down on the alley, turning it bright as day, revealing scattered trash and broken bottles and pieces of scrap wood.

No sign remained of Jabar or his two cohorts.

The officer who got out of the patrol car on the passenger side held a Remington M870 pump-action shotgun.

"You okay?" he asked Aaron, eyes on the alley.

"Yeah."

The officer on the driver's side got out, a Smith & Wesson .357 Magnum in one hand, ready for firing.

"They take anything from you?" he asked Aaron.

"No."

A dispatcher's voice crackled over the car's radio.

From up above came the pounding of the helicopter's rotor blades. The white shaft of the searchlight fell on nearby streets and buildings as the copter swept the area.

"Is he looking for them?" Aaron asked.

"Trying to," said the officer with the .357. "They're probably inside somewhere by now. Want to tell us about it?"

Aaron told him.

"Ever seen any of them before?"

"No."

"Get a good look at any of them?"

Aaron touched a hand to his throat where the gun had been.

"No, not really."

"You willing to try and identify them for us at a later time? Through photographs, or a lineup?"

Aaron shook his head. "Look, I can't get involved."

Both cops looked at Aaron without surprise but with a faint note of disgust, as if they had expected this.

"Want to give us your name?"

Aaron told them who he was, adding, "I really don't want to get mixed up in something like this, okay?"

"Okay, Mr. Scott," said the officer with the .357. "I'm Officer Myers. This is my partner, Officer Burns."

"Look, I don't want this being reported to the news media—or anything like that."

"You're the one who works for the media," Myers said.

"I just want to be sure about it, okay?"

"Care to file a police report?"

"No! I guess I'm not gettin' through to you guys. I don't want my name connected with *any* of this shit!"

"Okay, Mr. Scott."

Myers nodded at the Porsche's hood, streaked with beer.

"You change your mind about doing some ID work for us," he said, "we're over at the Hollywood Station, on Wilcox."

"I know where you are," Aaron said.

"You want to get your car washed," Myers said, "there's a place near Santa Monica and La Brea. Guy who runs it's name is Ramón. Tell him we sent you. He'll give you a discount."

"Thanks."

Aaron walked over to his car and started to get in.

He stopped, hand on the door, and looked back at the two officers, who stood there watching him with flat cop stares.

"Before those punks threw the beer at my car," Aaron said, "I heard these screams. Like a woman screaming. Really loud screams. That's why I turned onto this street in the first place. I wanted to find out where the screams were coming from."

Myers nodded and said nothing.

The turret on top of the patrol car revolved monotonously, bouncing red and blue and amber lights into Aaron's eyes.

"I just thought you guys should know about it. Somebody could've been trying to rape her—or something."

Myers said nothing.

"So, anyway, I just felt like I ought to let you know."

"I thought you didn't want to get involved, Mr. Scott."

Aaron's head snapped up.

He tried to shrug it off with a laugh. "Yeah. Guess so. Thanks for remindin' me, okay?"

He slammed the car door and gunned the engine, laying rubber down the length of the block.

As he turned the corner, glancing up into his rearview mirror, he saw the two cops still standing there, watching him.

5

PROPHECY

The next morning, he arrived at the station an hour early.

For a long time before his airshift began, he sat in the broadcast booth by himself and stared at the switchboard, its rows of buttons for incoming calls unlighted.

He didn't look up when his producer stepped into the booth.

"If your Phantom wanna-be calls in again today, Aaron, try to keep him on the line for as long as possible, okay?"

"Why? We got an LAPD wiretap, or what?"

"Screw the LAPD. He's ratings magic."

"I thought he scared the shit out of you, Jerr."

"Listener response is fan*tas*tic. By the way, make sure you tape him, so we can use the bits later in today's show. Or for the next few days, in case he stops calling."

"You want to make him a regular, huh, Jerr?"

"He *is* a regular, guy. The listeners love his ass."

The first few calls that morning seemed to bear this out.

"He's a happenin' dude, man. You're the greatest for lettin' him open up. Love ya, Sunset Scott! Peace!"

"You love me and you love the Phantom?"

"Love ya both, man!"

"You're a sick animal. You belong in a cage."

Aaron punched off that call and picked up the next one.

"Wendy from Venice, you're on the air with Sunset Scott."

"Oh, wow! Oh, God! I am *with* you, Sunset Scott! And I am *with* the Phantom! He knows what's comin' *down.* No one else even *knows,* man—except him and you and me!"

"Just our little secret, right, Wendy? You and me and the Phantom makes three. We'll keep it in the closet, okay?"

He broke the connection and glanced at the video monitor displaying callers on hold, then pressed number four.

"Martha from Glendale, you're on with Sunset Scott."

"Sunset Scott?" asked a slow, cautious voice.

"Yeah, Martha. Wake up, Martha!"

"I just want to say, about this Phantom thing—"

"Pump it up, Martha! Time's movin' out on us, babe."

"I just want to say, I think L.A. deserves the Phantom, and the Phantom deserves L.A. I mean, this whole city has become so—so evil! It's turned into—a city of darkness."

"A city of darkness. Three hundred sixty-five days of sunshine every year, except when it rains, which ain't often, and *you* call this a city of darkness? Thank you, Martha."

"I just want to say—"

"Can you believe these stupid callers, Lovely Lisa?" Aaron asked, punching the button to cut off Martha in mid-sentence. "What is *wrong* with these dickheads, anyway?"

"Times are weird, Sunset Scott," Lisa said.

"People are weird. Our listeners are weird. Hey, you stupid listeners out there! If any of you are *un*weird, call us, okay? Right now. Restore our faith. We know you're stupid. But we didn't know you were so damn weird!"

While he was speaking, he looked through the glass at his producer in call-screening. Jerry held up nine fingers.

"Okay, everybody! We're gonna take *one* more caller here, and he better not be weird!"

He punched button number nine on the switchboard.

"Wilbur from Sylmar. You're on live with Sunset Scott."

"Hello? Sunset Scott?"

"Come on, Wilbur! Don't go weird on me first thing, man."

"I just want to follow up on what that other caller said to you. Martha from Glendale?"

"Yes, a charming woman. What's your point, Wilbur?"

"I think maybe you were a little hard on her, Sunset Scott. And I think that's maybe because you just didn't want to hear what she had to say."

"Really, Wilbur? And what was that?"

"She wanted to warn you, and all other purveyors of filth and immorality, that judgment is coming, from the Phantom."

"Judgment for what, Wilbur?"

"Evil, filth, fornication, abomination, mocking the Lord God and His Anointed, so that when the people of this city—"

"You think the Phantom's coming to judge *me*, Wilbur?"

"The vengeance of the Lord God is swift and terrible—"

"Thank you, Wilbur." Aaron reached for the button.

"Don't you hang up on me, now."

"I'm hanging up on you because you're stupid, Wilbur. Stupid and boring, and also a hopeless dickhead, okay?"

"Don't you hang up on me, you fucking Jew bastard—"

Aaron hit the censor button on the tape delay.

"Okay, everybody. That was Wilbur from Sylmar, bringing us the news that the Phantom's coming to judge us for the way we run this radio show. How about it, Bud the Stud?"

"Maybe he's coming to judge the Lakers, Sunset Scott. Maybe they deserve it, after last night's game."

"That's Bud the Stud, everybody, our KRAS Sports Animal. And now he's gonna tell us just how bad those Lakers suck!"

"Our hoopshot homeboys ate the big one again last night—"

Aaron switched his microphone to CUE. "Jerr?"

"Yeah, guy. Sorry about that Nazi who just called in. He didn't give us any warning signs—"

"Fuck it. I don't care if he's anti-Semitic. I care if he's *boring*. Lose those other calls, would you, Jerr? They're startin' to hemorrhage shit."

"They're your fans, Aaron."

"Fuck 'em! They're the Phantom's fans. *Lose* 'em!"

"You serious?"

"Yeah, I'm serious! Disconnect the motherfuckers!"

"I'm not sure that's— Hold on."

Aaron looked up and saw Lisa talking to Jerry inside the glassed-in call-screening booth. She held a satellite-transmission printout in one hand.

Jerry got back on the CUE channel. "Aaron?"

"Yeah?"

"After I give the wrap signal to Bud, toss it to Lisa, okay? She's got a hotter than hell news lead."

"On what?"

"Our ratings superstar. He just scored again."

Aaron sat there, waiting for Bud to finish his windup.

Then he switched his microphone to BROADCAST.

"That was our KRAS sports animal, Bud the Stud, biting the lame Lakers right on the ass! But right now, Lovely Lisa in the newsroom's got somethin' even hotter for us. Hey, Lise?"

"The Lakers weren't the only ones with a bad night, Sunset Scott. Shortly after eleven last night, the serial killer known as the Phantom struck again in the vicinity of Sunset and—"

As she read the location, Aaron felt the back of his neck turn cold. He saw the tall, heavy punk with the bald head and bloodred forelock, knife blade shining under the headlights.

He switched his microphone to BROADCAST and cut in.

"Hey, just a minute, Lovely Lisa. *Where* did this happen?"

She repeated the location for him.

"Excuse me for interrupting the newscast, Lise, but *damn* it! I was practically right *there* last night—shortly after eleven, like you say. Hell, I was within *walking* distance!"

"Then you're lucky to be here with us today, Sunset Scott. An unidentified woman in the same area last night wasn't quite so lucky. LAPD patrol officers discovered her body in an alley while responding to a suspicious prowler call—"

Aaron switched off his microphone.

He heard the horrible screams again, cutting through the night air. He saw the punk with the knife and Jabar with the gun pressed hard against his throat.

He raised a hand involuntarily to his neck.

Don't make me hurt you, man!

He saw the two cops staring at him with hard cop eyes.

I thought you didn't want to get involved, Mr. Scott.

He watched the lighted buttons on the switchboard go out one by one as Bill, Jerry's assistant, disconnected the lines.

He turned his mike back on to get set for Lisa's toss.

"—and although the LAPD isn't giving out any details about the killing itself, or the condition of the body, they *are* saying that it 'definitely carries the Phantom's signature.' So they know he did it for sure, Sunset Scott. Pretty scary, huh?"

"Yeah, well, you know what I think? I think— Hey, *Phan*tom? You tuned in this early? Then listen up, you masked dickhead! I think you're a walking pile of vomit, okay? Attacking a lone woman like that. I also think you're a coward. Too scared to face anyone except a helpless victim. Too scared to call back in to this show again!"

He paused, his own voice ringing inside the headphones.

He looked over at Lisa, but she simply stared back at him from her own booth, dark eyes narrow and mistrustful.

Bud cut in and picked up the fumbled toss.

"I hope the Phantom's taking notes on all this," he said.

Aaron saw the bald head with its red forelock again, mouth stretched to reveal the gum line, grinning into the headlights.

Man. I am *the mask!*

The image vanished and everything came back into focus.

"The hell with the Phantom!" he said, moving into the microphone in his best Sunset Scott style. "He can just sweat it out during this next set. See if he can work up the nerve to call in. Meanwhile we've got— What the hell *have* we got? Oh, yeah. The Gravediggers. 'Bury My Love.' KRAS—"

He stopped in the middle of the station ID, his attention caught by Jerry's wild gesticulations from across the way.

Jerry pointed to the video monitor inside his booth.

Aaron glanced at his own monitor.

The display had been wiped clean of all names, addresses, and phone numbers—except one. On line number two, a capital **X** flashed off and on, like a pulse signal, and beside that the notation: NO HOME ADDRESS, NO PHONE NUMBER.

Aaron looked up again and saw his own reflection staring back at him from the double glass. Beyond that, Jerry gestured for Aaron to switch to CUE, all the while mouthing silently, *Don't forget to tape him!*

"Kick back, everybody! Gotta put the Gravediggers on hold for just a minute. Let 'em sit on their shovels. We got us a *hot* caller on the line! You remember how that Mysterious Mr. X called in to this show yesterday—Sunset Scott in the Mornin', KRAS, 108.5—and claimed to be the Phantom? And how you listeners all got really *down* with him? And you remember, before he hung up, how he promised us—"

Aaron flipped on the echo filter and Schwarzenegger voice.

"I'LL BE BACK!"

He turned off the sound effect and leaned into the mike.

"Well, guess what, everybody? He's *b-a-a-a-a-a-a-a-ck!*"

Aaron hit PLAY on the tape recorder, then button two.

"Phantom from Nowhere, you're on live with Sunset Scott."

Silence came from the other end of the line.

Aaron sighed. "We gonna start this crap again, Phantom? Where you hang on the line forever, givin' us dead air?"

More silence.

"You're a happenin' dude, Phantom, and you got a lot of fans here at KRAS. But if you don't open up and *talk* some, man, I'm gonna have to cut you off, okay?"

"What do you want from me?"

Aaron drew back from the microphone at the sound of that smooth, whispering voice inside his headphones. He saw the open mouth, with its red gum line, grinning into the headlights.

"I want you to *say* something! This is a *radio* show, man! You don't talk, you don't exist."

"Oh, I exist. Whether I talk or not, I exist."

"Looks like you been keepin' pretty busy since yesterday, hey, Phantom? Attacking single women on dark streets—"

"What do you want from me, Sunset Scott?"

"Look, man. Don't interrupt me when I'm—"

"Sunset Scott," the Phantom repeated slowly. "Such a childish name. A childish mask for you to hide behind."

Aaron leaned into the microphone. "Who the hell are *you* to talk about *masks*, Phantom? You *live* behind a goddamn mask!"

"But my mask is real. It forms the surface of my face. Behind my mask there is—nothing. Behind your mask is a real face, and another false name—and behind that, a real one."

Aaron paused for a second. No one noticed it except Jerry, who looked up from where he sat monitoring the broadcast in the call-screening booth.

"So, Phantom, what's behind *your* mask?"

"I told you. Nothing."

"Yeah, that's right. How could I forget? The man without a face, a name, a home. A great big walking zero, a masked nothing that cleans the mean streets of L.A. with a blowtorch."

No response from the other end.

"Still there, Phantom? Or you get your feelings hurt?"

"You ridicule me," whispered the voice. "You think perhaps I'm nothing more than a bad liar, like yourself."

"Whoa! The Phantom gets personal! He starts to diss!"

"I'm very real, Sunset Scott. As real as it ever gets."

"Yeah, real boring's more like it. You need a new handler, and some better gag writers. You're not funny anymore."

The voice spoke again, with unexpected sharpness this time.

"Let me convince you of my reality. Let me make a public prediction about what will happen before this day is over. A prophecy, if you like. A vision of—judgment."

"The Phantom's a fortune-teller? He sees into the future?"

"No. I make the future happen."

"Okay, Phantom. Hit us with your prophecy. Go for it!"

"Tonight," the voice whispered, "near one of the movie theaters on Sunset, judgment will be delivered by my hands."

Aaron's headphones felt suddenly tight around his skull.

"In other words, you're gonna kill somebody there tonight?"

"I will render—judgment."

"So when is this *judgment* of yours gonna take place, man?"

"I've told you all you need to know. Judgment tonight. A theater on Sunset. Before midnight."

"Not gonna get any more specific than that, Phantom?"

"I don't want to make things too easy for the LAPD."

"You think the cops are listening in right now?"

"The whole world is listening, Sunset Scott."

"Only because we're number one! But nobody takes *you* seriously, Phantom. Know why not? 'Cause you're a damn fake! You're no more of a serial killer than Mumblin' Bill!"

"I told you, I'm very real. You're the one who lives a lie, and speaks lies for a living. *You're* the fake."

"Kiss my ass, Phantom!"

"I'm speaking the truth. But I can do more than that. Tonight, on the streets of Hollywood, I'll *show* you the truth."

Aaron leaned forward, lips almost touching the microphone.

"So what? Even if the real Phantom kills again tonight, what's it gonna prove, fake Phantom? Just that you're some dickhead who happened to make a lucky guess!"

"I'll leave a sign for you, Sunset Scott. Look for it."

The line went dead. A dial tone buzzed in his headphones.

He looked up and saw Jerry giving him a thumbs-up.

"That was him, everybody! The Phantom! The Man with the Mask! Live, for your listening pleasure, here on KRAS. 108.5. Sunset Scott in the Morning, all mornin' long. The *only* place where you can hear the *Phan*tom predict—"

He hit the echo filter.

"MASSACRE AT THE MOVIES!"

"That's right, Slaughter at the Cinema. So all you listeners out there—especially all you *stupid* ones—listen up! If you plan on takin' in any movies on Sunset tonight, better wear a bulletproof vest, man! 'Cause that big, bad Phantom, he gone kick yo' *ass!* Yeah! And if you believe that, we got some desert property to sell you. Just dial 1-800-I-AM-SO-GULLIBLE. And now for the Gravediggers. 'Bury My Love.' Bury it deep, man, where that bad ol' Phantom can't get at it no mo'!"

Over on Wilcox Avenue, at the Hollywood Division of the Los Angeles Police Department, behind the locked doors in back of the front desk, in the large area off-limits to the general public, Lieutenant Rafael Montoya, Homicide, sat and listened to the Gravediggers sing "Bury My Love" on KRAS FM.

Montoya presented a sharp contrast to the man on the other side of the desk from him, Sergeant Francisco Lopez. Montoya and Lopez had been partners working Homicide for over four years. But Montoya was pale, overweight, and well past middle age, while Lopez was young and knife-thin, with intense dark eyes and angular, dark-skinned Indian features. Montoya favored polyester pastel shirts and ill-fitting sport jackets bought at a discount off the rack. Lopez wore only the finest handmade white cotton shirts with the most expensive Armani suits.

Montoya seemed to be meditating, eyes half-closed and far away, fingers laced over his ample midsection. Lopez sat tensed like a coiled spring.

Montoya reached out and shut off the radio.

"To believe or not to believe? That is the question."

"He could be blowing smoke up that DJ's ass," Lopez said.

"Yes, Frank. He could be."

"Or the whole thing could be a scam. Those radio stations will do anything for ratings."

Montoya nodded slowly.

"Still," he said, "I think we'd better ask for coverage."

"You want to stake out the Cinerama Dome?"

"Yes, and that new multiplex farther down the Strip."

"You think the captain will go for it?"

"Only one way to find out, isn't there?"

Montoya got to his feet and took a piece of hard candy from a glass bowl on his desk. Then he walked out of his office and down the corridor leading to the office of the Hollywood Division Commander, Captain E. L. Hammond.

As he passed the large open room where the other homicide detectives had their desks, one of them called out to him.

"Yo, Ralph! You hear that asshole on the radio? The one pretending to be your boy?"

"Every word of it, Tom."

"Next thing we know, he'll claim *he* was the one who chopped up the fuckin' Black Dahlia!"

"Could be."

Inside Hammond's office, Montoya took a seat.

They had known each other for years, going back to the days when both were rookies right out of police academy.

"So what is it, Ralph? Something new on the Phantom?"

Montoya told him what he needed.

As Hammond listened, a frown settled over his face.

"What makes you think he's the real thing?"

"He feels real, Ed."

"The famous Montoya intuition, eh?" Hammond shook his head. "Sorry, Ralph. I can't assign that many plainclothes officers to something like this. What if it all turns out to be nothing more than a practical joke by a crank caller? I *could* let you have a few uniformed officers, if that would help."

"No good, Ed. I don't want to scare him away from the scene. I want to be ready for him, if and when he shows."

"Then it looks like you're shit outta luck, ol' buddy."

"But what if this prediction he made comes true, Ed? What if he kills someone tonight, near a theater on Sunset?"

"You really think that could happen, Ralph?"

"Going strictly on the famous Montoya intuition—yes."

6

ALARM

Samantha Collier looked tense as she walked out of the On-Target News studios on Sunset, about half a mile east of the high-rise that housed the KRAS station.

Aaron glanced at his watch as she came over to him.

"Whoa, seven-twenty! Whatever happened to six-forty-five?"

"Don't get started, Aaron."

"Hey, Sam, just kidding! I love to rag other people when they're late, 'cause Jerry's always on *my* ass whenever—"

He stopped, noticing her tenseness.

"Sam . . . You okay?"

"Just great."

"You *look* great."

She let out an angry breath, blowing back a strand of hair.

"I look like shit!"

"Sam, what's wrong?"

"You parked close?"

"Sure. Right over—"

"Let's get out of here. I'll tell you on the way."

But she said nothing more until they had parked again, in Aaron's space beneath the KRAS building, and walked across the street to California Pacific Savings.

As they rode the elevator to the top floor, he said, "This is the same building that girl jumped off of a few years back. Remember? Jesus, was she a mess when she hit the ground!"

"Thanks, Aaron. I needed to hear about that tonight."

He watched her as she watched the floor numbers flash across the overhead display, their own images reflected in the mirrored walls of the elevator car.

"What's wrong, Sam?"

"Nothing."

"Bullshit. *Some*thing's bothering you."

"I had to do a field report on that new Phantom killing."

Aaron saw the grinning mouth under the headlights again.

"Was it worse than the last one?"

"I don't even want to talk about it."

"What did he do? Shoot pepper spray up her twat again?"

The elevator doors opened just then, and an older couple waiting to go down got the full benefit of Aaron's last remark.

Sam closed her eyes.

Aaron cleared his throat and tried to smile at the couple.

"We were—rehearsing a bit, okay? Know how that goes?"

The older couple eyed them warily, and stepped well to one side in order to let them exit the elevator car.

"Nice timing," Sam muttered, lips barely moving.

"Hey, I didn't know the fuckin' door was ready to open!"

The hostess led them to a table beside a wall-to-wall picture window, one that commanded a sweeping overhead view of Hollywood at night. Solid rivers of light blazed down Sunset, the Strip, and Hollywood Boulevard. Scattered lights dusted the Hollywood Hills like jewels left glimmering in a magic forest.

"View's the best part of this place," Aaron said.

"Hmm," Sam replied, studying her menu.

"It's been four days, Sam. You miss me?"

"I've been busy as hell, Aaron."

He opened his own menu, scowling at it.

She laid down hers.

"Now what's wrong?"

"You're supposed to miss me," he said, without looking up.

"Aaron—"

"I missed *you*, goddamn it!"

She looked at her menu again, without reading it.

"My field report this morning started out a lot like the last one. Show up at the location. Wait around for at least an hour. Get stonewalled by Brock's men. Finally talk to Brock himself. Find out he doesn't have much to say, and most of it's off the record anyway. Except—"

"Except what?"

"Except this time, he decided to *show* us why they couldn't give us anything we could use." She put a hand to her forehead. "Aaron, it was like something from a slaughterhouse. I didn't know a human body could *hold* that much blood. And she was cut into so many pieces—"

She started to choke. Aaron reached out for her.

"You don't have to talk if you don't want to, Sam."

"I've already *started*, okay?"

He withdrew his hand.

"She had one of those little pocket alarms on her. What do they call them? Pocket Protectors?"

"Something like that."

"She managed to set it off before he got to her. That's what alerted the neighbors, the ones who called the cops. By the time they got there, they found— He'd slit open her throat, stuffed the pocket alarm inside, set it off again. Then he closed her throat back up."

She looked at Aaron, her eyes filling with tears.

"It was h-horrible!"

"You guys ready to order yet?" asked their cheerful young server, an anxious smile on her face.

"Give us some more time," Aaron said.

He put a hand on Sam's arm.

"Sorry you had to look at that shit."

She shook her head. "The worst thing is, it's not just some isolated tragedy. It's going to happen *again*, Aaron! The cops don't know *any*thing! They don't know who he is, or why he's doing this. They don't even know what he *looks* like!"

Aaron saw the grinning mouth again, the red gum line.

Man, I am *the mask!*

"I heard he called in to your show again today."

"*Heard?* Jesus, Sam! I thought you tuned in occasionally."

"I was busy—"

"Yeah, sure." Aaron snorted. "He called in again."

"And threatened to kill someone near a theater on Sunset?"

"Yeah, that's right."

"And you played along with him?"

"I did not 'play along' with him! I fuckin' trashed him!"

"Why do you keep *doing* it, Aaron?"

"Ratings. Jerry says the listeners are really into this."

"It's a long way to stick your neck out, even for ratings."

"Sam, he's not the Phantom. He's just some sick asshole. After the way I got in his face today, he won't call back."

"There must be a reason why he keeps calling you."

"He likes to hear the sound of his own voice on the air."

"He's bonding with you, Aaron, forging an emotional tie."

"Bullshit!"

"Did he say anything personal to you this time?"

"Hell, no! Only thing he said was—"

I'll leave a sign for you, Sunset Scott.

Aaron picked up his spoon, then put it back down.

"He said he'd leave me a sign. Told me to look for it."

"He's trying to personalize your on-air relationship."

"I don't have any fuckin' *relation*ship with him! And he's not gonna leave any *sign*, because nothing's gonna *happen* tonight! He's just a lot of bullshit talk. That's all!"

He crossed his arms on the tabletop.

"He's not the only one I don't have a relationship with."

"Stop it, Aaron."

"Stop what?"

"Let's not get into this tonight."

"What do you want, Sam? To keep up the on-and-off shit for another six months, maybe another year? Then break up, because there never was any damn commitment in the first place?"

She pretended to read the menu.

He reached out and jerked it away from her.

"Hey! What the hell—"

"You want to wind up like everyone else in this town?"

"Give me back my menu, Aaron."

"Living single, too scared to say you *love* someone?"

"Aaron, this is a public place, okay?"

He handed her back the menu.

She tried to read it, then put it down and sighed.

"We have been over this so many times. I think I love—"

"You *think?* Thanks a lot, Sam!"

"I don't *know* for sure, and I'm not going to lie about it."

"Yeah. The search for the Truth. How could I forget?"

"What I *do* know, right now, is that my career comes first."

"So? You've already got a career."

"But it could go anywhere, if things start to happen. I could be transferred to New York, DC, maybe even Atlanta."

"Or get moved up to the anchor desk at On-Target."

"I can't count on that."

"Okay, fine! I'll transfer *with* you, all right?"

"Aaron, you can't do that."

"Why not? 'Cause I'm not searchin' for the Truth?"

"It's a different kind of broadcasting. Shock radio—"

"I'm not just a shock jock, Sam. I can do other things."

"Sure. But they'd keep you here, too. Movies. Sitcoms."

"Just don't want a guy who's not after the Truth, huh?"

"No. I don't want to get married then divorce because of career conflict—or have to give up my career to stay married."

"I already *said* I'd give up mine!"

"No, Aaron. For right now, no."

Their server returned, still cheerful, but cautious.

"You guys ready to order yet? Or you need some more time?"

"We're ready," Aaron said. "You got any lasagna?"

"I'm so sorry. We just ran out."

"I knew it! Okay. How about spaghetti with clam sauce?"

"One *pasta alla marinara?* And to drink?"

"Let's wait and see what she wants first."

The server turned to Sam. "And for you?"

"I think—"

The beeper on her belt went off, startling the server.

"Wow, that's some beeper!"

Sam shut it off and took out her cellular phone.

"Excuse me, I have to call my studio."

The server smiled. "I can give you some more time—"

"Don't bother. If it's what I think, I won't be eating."

"Then cancel my order, too, goddamn it!"

Aaron balled up his napkin.

"You could still eat," Sam said, dialing the number.

"Look, Sam. If we can't even have *dinner* together—"

She held up her hand for silence and listened carefully.

"No," she said, "I'm close. I can get there right now."

As she put the phone back into her purse, her eyes seemed somewhat glazed.

"What is it?" Aaron asked. "Another Phantom victim?"

"Victims."

She looked at him, the glaze gone from her eyes.

"A movie theater, on Sunset."

7

SHOWTIME

Jessie De Santis looked up from where she scooped popcorn behind the concession stand and glanced at the lobby clock of the Cinematheque, a six-theater multiplex near the Sunset Strip.

"Yo, Jessie!"

She looked across the lobby and saw Cameron Chaffey, a skinny kid with the stupid maroon vest, white shirt, and black pants they all had to wear. He carried a flashlight in one hand.

She frowned at him. "What?"

"Did you check the exit doors?" Cameron asked.

She dropped her mouth open and pointed a finger at herself. "Like, it's suddenly *my* job to check them?"

"I think some guy just sneaked into number four."

"Wouldn't the alarm, like, go off if they forced the door?"

"It should. But the alarms are broken on six and four."

"Oh, that's cool! That is totally cool! Some geek can, like, sneak in here from off the street whenever he wants?"

"Where's Bax?"

"How should *I* know?"

Cameron turned and headed for theater number four.

"Tell Bax I'm checkin' it out. Okay, Jess?"

"Don't call me Jess, you little dweeb!"

She heard gunshots from theater four and her heart jumped.

Then she remembered that they were showing an action thing in there and she knew the gunshots must be from the movie.

But what if some guy really *had* sneaked into number four by forcing the exit door? What if he was weird, or something? Who was going to tell him to get out? Not Cameron, that's for sure. Cameron wouldn't scare anyone over the age of five.

Sometimes she wished there were more people working the night shift, like right now. Aside from Cameron and herself, who was there? Just the projectionist, some really old guy who had to be at least twenty-eight and kept to himself upstairs most of the time. And, of course, good old Bax, who was a real hunk and all, but sort of stuck on himself. He was probably in the rest room now, jerking off with the latest copy of *Penthouse.* Guys did disgusting things like that if they got by themselves. Jessie knew. She had three brothers.

One of the double doors to theater four opened.

She drew back from the concession counter.

But it was just some kid, climbing the red-carpeted stairs to the rest rooms on the second floor.

Jessie placed her hands on the glass countertop and let out a deep breath. The heavy smell of reheated popcorn filled the air around her. Outside, muted traffic hummed along the Strip.

More shots rang out from theater four, accompanied this time by squealing tires and racing engines. Her heart beat faster for several seconds before resuming its normal rhythm.

God, she wished this shift was *over!*

What was taking Cameron so long in there, anyway?

She tried not to think about the guy who might have forced his way into theater four, though it remained lodged in a corner of her mind like a dark, obscene thing, whispering to her.

Then she thought of something that made her flesh crawl.

She listened to KRAS, but mainly in the evening, when the DJ known as Nightman worked his seven to twelve midnight airshift. She thought Sunset Scott was the coolest, even though she didn't get to listen to his show much. But her best friend, Kimberlee, had told Jessie all about the Phantom.

—promised to, like, kill someone near a theater on Sunset?

That's just what Kimberlee had said when Jessie talked with her this afternoon, before leaving for work.

Her heart beat faster now and refused to slow down.

God, what if that was *him* Cameron noticed in theater four?

Or what if he was in theater six, and no one even *saw* him?

Her face felt tight, as if she might start crying.

She reached for the phone behind the concession stand.

The door to theater six opened, banging against the wall.

She looked up, startled.

"Hey, Jess!"

Bax Dawson swaggered across the lobby, stocky and overbuilt from too many steroids, flashlight swinging in one hand.

"What's up, girl? Where's Cameron?"

"He—" She raised a hand to her throat.

Bax walked up to the concession stand and leaned on it.

"You okay, Jess?"

She nodded. "Cameron thought maybe someone sneaked in the exit to theater four? So he went to, like, check it out."

"No shit? How long's he been in there?"

"About—"

The door to theater four opened.

They both turned and looked in that direction.

Inside theater four, Cameron moved down the left aisle, letting his eyes adjust to the low light. He switched on his flashlight, checking the rows as he went. But that really pissed off the customers, so he didn't do it for long.

On screen a van exploded, sending reverberations across the speakers in the theater walls. An action hero ran toward the burning wreckage, firing dozens of shots from a nine-round automatic pistol without once changing clips.

Cameron's eyes had adjusted to the darkness now, and he could see easily by reflected light from the screen. All the customers seemed to belong there. Kids sprawled across their seats, eating popcorn, drinking sodas. Older couples sat there with the stiffness adults seemed to grow into as they aged.

Then he saw him, sitting by himself, three rows back from the front, off to the extreme left-hand side, a place where nobody ever sat if there was any other choice.

But it might be the first choice of someone who had entered the theater by forcing his way through an exit door.

Cameron stepped into the third row and moved toward him.

He looked big and sat hunched forward, wearing a black sweatshirt with the hood pulled down low over his head so you couldn't see his face. He had on black gloves, the thin kind race car drivers wear, and faded jeans.

Cameron came to within four seats of him and stopped.

He should shine the light on him and ask him to leave.

But this guy could be an overgrown gangbanger from South Central or East L.A., totally into that Look-At-Me-Funny-And-I'll-Kick-Your-Fuckin'-Ass-Or-Maybe-Kill-You shit. You didn't want to piss off someone like that for no good reason.

The hooded man got up and started for the side aisle.

"Sir!" Cameron called after him, shining the flashlight on him, its beam outlining his broad back beneath the sweatshirt.

"Excuse me, sir!" Cameron started to follow him, moving across the rest of the third row and toward the far side aisle.

"Down in front, butthead!" someone yelled from the back.

"Yeah, dude! We're tryin' to watch the fuckin' show!"

The hooded figure kept moving up the far aisle, next to the theater wall, not looking back at Cameron.

He didn't seem to be running, but he was moving *fast.* Cameron had to push it just to keep up with him, panting for breath. He shined the flashlight on his back again.

"Sir, wait!" he called out. "I need to talk to you!"

The hooded figure ducked around the partition separating the double entrance doors from the theater auditorium.

"Shit!" Cameron muttered, and broke into a run.

If the asshole made it out of the theater and across the lobby before anyone could warn Bax to stop him, he'd be gone. Cameron poured on the speed.

He heard the entrance door bang open and ran even faster.

By the time he got out into the lobby, the hooded figure was already racing up the stairs, two at a time.

"Bax!" Cameron yelled, pointing to the running man, who had almost reached the top of the stairs by now. "That guy snuck into four through the exit! When I went up to him, he jammed!"

Bax sprang from concessions and made for the stairs.

"Chill, man!" he called back to Cameron. "I'll get him!"

"What do I do?"

"Wait there with Jess, okay?"

Cameron walked over to concessions, puffing hard to catch his breath. His face was flushed and the clip-on bow tie that was part of his uniform hung lopsided from his neck.

Jessie looked at him with wide and frightened eyes.

"What did he *do*, Cameron?"

"He ran! I went up to him and he fuckin' ran. Shit!"

"Did you see his face?"

"It was dark in there, Jess."

"Did he have on— Was he, like, maybe wearing—a mask?"

"A *mask?* What kinda shit is that?"

Upstairs, Bax caught sight of the hooded figure on a narrow set of stairs leading up to the projection room. Bax sprinted for the stairs, charging up them. He could see that the fucker had almost reached the door to the projection room.

"Hey, dude!" Bax called after him. "Wait *up*, okay?"

The hooded figure stopped.

Bax, gasping for breath, closed the short distance between them as the man with the hood started to turn.

"Need to talk to you, dude!" Bax panted.

He kept on turning, until he stood facing Bax, and the night manager could see clearly what lay beneath the hood.

"My assistant, he said—"

Bax's voice shut off, like a downed radio signal.

The mask looked filmy, or blurry, as if you *ought* to be able to see through it, but for some reason or other could not. It was as if nothing existed beneath the hood except for a translucent blankness, and two dark eyes, receding into the void, and a slit where the mouth should be, like a gill flap on the pale, smooth skin of a fish.

Bax realized then how tall this guy must be, towering above him, and Bax was tall for his age, almost six-two.

The Phantom stood looking down at Bax, his shoulders barely rising and falling beneath the black sweatshirt, winded hardly at all by the race up two flights of steep stairs.

His black-gloved right hand dropped down behind his back, so quickly that Bax might have imagined he saw it move. One moment it was there, the next it was not.

He brought it out again and slashed Bax across the eyes.

At first the pain did not even register. Bax only knew that he could not see, and that panicked him. He wondered if maybe the masked asshole had smeared something in his eyes. He felt warm liquid running down his face and into his open mouth.

Then he felt the pain.

The Phantom slashed Bax across the throat, with a backhand cut this time, severing the right and left carotid arteries, laying both jugular veins wide open. Blood pulsed from Bax's neck, spattering the walls of the narrow stairwell.

Bax dropped his flashlight and fell down onto the dark red carpeting of the stairs, clutching at his throat with one hand, the other arm twitching spasmodically, eyes slit open, blood soaking the hand that held his throat.

More blood gushed from his neck, spilling down the stairs like a tiny, bright red waterfall, dropping from tier to tier.

Bax's legs began to jerk violently. His heels started drumming against the stairs. His body stiffened and his back arched. Another large volume of blood burst from his neck and he grew rigid, then lay absolutely still.

When the door to the projection room burst open, Jim McCauley's head jerked up from his comic book.

"Hey, what the fuck! Somethin' wrong down there?"

The figure in front of him looked as if it could have stepped out of the page he had just been reading. Tall stature, broad shoulders. Black hood. White, blurred mask.

"Somethin' wrong?" McCauley asked again, coming forward.

Behind him, the reels of the projector revolved steadily, pulling film through the gate at a constant twenty-four frames per second. Down below, amplified gunshots exploded on-screen.

The hooded figure raised a black-gloved hand.

McCauley felt something wet and slick squirt into his face.

He closed his eyes and raised a hand to protect himself.

"Hey, fuck you! Cut it out, okay?"

But the shithead kept squirting it all over his hair and T-shirt. As McCauley stepped in to take a swing at him, a tongue of flame flickered in the darkness of the projection room, igniting the gasoline. It caught with a brightness that lighted up the whole room, casting the Phantom's gigantic shadow on the opposite wall, making it flicker with the flames.

McCauley screamed.

He staggered around the projection room, groping with his burning arms for something to stop the pain.

Down below, special effects flames raced across the screen.

McCauley tripped over the chair he had been sitting in and fell against the projection machine. One of his fiery arms brushed against the film as it entered the projection gate and burned straight through it.

The moving images dropped off the screen in the theater below, leaving only a glaring white emptiness.

Angry customers began shouting at the projection booth.

The flames that burned through the film feeding into the projection gate crawled up to the main reel itself. After a few seconds, it went up like an oil refinery, spraying new flames over the already-burning body of Jim McCauley. He began to run and leap around the room, a blazing Nureyev.

A black-gloved hand reached out for the switches on the wall of the projection room—the ones that controlled the lights in the theaters and the rest rooms and the lobby—and pulled down the master switch, throwing the Cinematheque into darkness.

Cameron Chaffey, in number four, had been trying to lock the exit door when the lights went out. Just before that happened, he had noticed flames in the projection room window. Thinking he must have imagined it, he had just started to look up again when everything suddenly faded to black.

He turned on his flashlight to make an announcement.

"Ladies and gentlemen!" he shouted. "Could I have your—"

No one could hear him above the chaos.

"Ladies and gentlemen—"

"Turn the fuckin' lights back on!"

"Could I have your attention—"

Someone threw an empty jumbo popcorn tub at him.

Upstairs, as the Phantom came down from the projection room, he stepped on Bax Dawson's head. The face bones collapsed with a crunching sound. He bent over to pick up Bax's flashlight from a puddle of congealing blood.

Jessie screamed when the lights went out.

But when she heard the customers shouting and screaming inside the six theaters, like members of a rioting mob, real terror made her mute. She knew there had to be a flashlight somewhere behind the concession stand, but where *was* it? She groped for it in the dark, reaching into the shelf beside the cash register, where she thought it should be. She felt several objects she could not identify, including something soft and squishy that made her shudder. When she touched the hard plastic cylinder of the flashlight, she grabbed for it. But her nerves were shaken and she knocked it off the shelf, down to the carpet.

"Shit!" she hissed, getting down on her hands and knees.

She did not notice the other flashlight, beam on high, gliding swiftly down the broad central staircase, across the lobby, and into theater number four.

Inside theater four, Cameron was beginning to have some success with the angry, frightened audience.

"—temporary power failure."

"Turn the lights back on, asshole!"

"If you would please try and remain calm—"

"Or give us our fuckin' money back, dude!"

Cameron noticed the other flashlight then, shining out from the back of the auditorium. He lowered his own light and walked toward the blinding white circle.

The audience members turned their heads and shifted in their seats to follow him, temporarily lulled to an angry murmur by this new visual distraction.

"Hey, Bax!" he called out in a low voice. "What happened up there? Power go out? Or did Jim turn it off?"

He had almost reached him by now, the intense radiance of the flashlight beam obliterating everything else around it.

"Bax? What's wrong, man?"

Cameron raised a hand to shield his eyes from the light.

The beam seemed to jump then, from left to right, like a bouncing blip on a video monitor.

Cameron, not at all sure now if this was really Bax, raised his own flashlight and pointed it straight on.

He saw the black hood, the white mask beneath it, the black-gloved hand holding the heavy nine-millimeter Parabellum MAB P15 automatic pistol—just before it went off.

The bullet took him full in the chest, blowing a wound canal through his heart and left lung, then exiting his back, where it struck an audience member in the face. Cameron pitched backward, arms flopping loose beside him, flashlight dropping to the carpeted aisle, blood spraying across the beam of the other flashlight in a fine, rose-tinted mist.

The cries of the man hit behind him were drowned out by the terrified screams of the audience, shrieking now like demons in a pit as the flashlight beam swept over them slowly and the Phantom began to fire at random into the crowd.

Some dived behind their seats. Others scrambled out into the aisle, making them easy targets in that dark shooting gallery. The wounded dropped to the floor or fell across their seats. Fourteen more shots rang out, following the one that had killed Cameron. But they sounded nothing like the amplified gunshots that had been echoing from the auditorium speakers. These shots started out almost like muted pops, then bounced back off the theater walls with the ear-shattering, mind-numbing force of exploding artillery shells.

The Phantom stuck the flashlight under one arm, ejected the empty clip from the MAB, inserted a full one, and continued firing into the crowd.

Some screamed for mercy in the darkness. Others prayed. Still others crept down the floor space between the rows, moving on their hands and knees through scattered popcorn and spreading pools of blood, only to find themselves out in one of the aisles, caught in the blinding glare of the flashlight beam, shot down as they tried to scramble to their feet.

Even after the Phantom stopped shooting and left theater four, his gunshots seemed to ring out in the darkness, along with the screams of the wounded and the terrified.

Out in the lobby, Jessie finally found the flashlight.

She dialed 911 and asked for the police in a barely audible voice. Then she crouched behind the concession stand, listening to the sounds of slaughter inside theater four.

At one point it got so bad that she covered her face with her hands and wept like a frightened child.

When the gunshots suddenly stopped and the door to theater four banged open, she looked up and saw a flashlight beam move across the lobby and up the central staircase.

"Cameron!" she whispered. "Bax!"

Fearful of calling any louder, she watched from behind the counter as the beam crossed the mezzanine and disappeared into the door on the right, the one leading to the men's rest room.

She got up and turned on her own flashlight, and walked out into the lobby, toward the stairs. She ascended them on trembling legs, terror gripping her like an iron claw.

When she reached the mezzanine her heart was pounding so hard she could actually hear it in the darkness. She took a deep breath to steady herself and moved forward.

Her flashlight beam fell on the dark wooden door and the letters MEN.

She pushed open the door, stepped around the blocking partition inside, flashlight beam advancing into the darkness ahead of her. She swept it over the urinals, the stalls—

The beam came to rest on a long row of sinks, and stopped.

Her fear gave way to astonishment, then to anger. She could not be*lieve* this! Some prick with a hood, some too cool wanna-be gang-banger, had decided to choose now, of all times, to come up here and tag the mirror with graffiti!

He leaned into the mirror as he wrote on it with an oversize marker, felt tip head squeaking across the glass.

His flashlight rested on a counter near a sink basin, low beam reflecting off the mirror. From somewhere in the darkness came the sound of running water.

"Hey, ex*cuse* me?"

He turned toward her, letting her see the mask.

"Oh my God—"

She backed off, reaching behind her for the door.

He moved toward her.

"You keep away from me!"

He grabbed hold of her arm, the one with the flashlight.

She started screaming.

He brought it down hard on his raised knee, breaking it backward at the elbow. The bone snapped with a cracking sound.

The flashlight fell from her hand, bouncing on the tiles.

Her scream dropped to a low, guttural moan.

He shoved her headfirst into one of the sinks. Her face smashed against the porcelain, breaking teeth loose from her gums. She screamed again as she fell on her shattered arm. Collapsing over the sink, she looked down and saw her own blood, bright red under the beam of the other flashlight, trickling down the sides of the porcelain basin.

He jerked her up from the sink by her hair and threw something into her face. She shut her eyes. It felt cold, intensely cold. She opened her eyes, blinking back the numbing cold, and saw herself in the mirror—face covered with some kind of white foam, everything *steaming*, tendrils of smoke rising from her face like fog in a low-budget horror movie.

She howled in fear and despair.

Then the cold turned suddenly to searing, unbearable heat, burning into her eyes and face like fire.

She screamed again, pleading hoarsely with him, begging him to do something, anything, to stop the pain.

Then, when it got really bad, she just screamed.

8

THE SIGN

Before they could get a clear view of the Cinematheque, the traffic ahead of them slowed to a crawl.

Farther up the street, turret lights flashed from patrol cars and ambulances blocked off the Strip.

"Stop the car," Sam said. "I'm getting out here."

"Sam, we're still two blocks—"

"Stop the *car*, Aaron. Now."

"All *right!*"

She got out, slamming the door behind her, and crossed through stalled traffic to the sidewalk, where she started walking in the direction of the Cinematheque.

"Hey, Sam!" Aaron called through a rolled-down window.

She glanced back at him, without slowing down. "What?"

"Watch yourself! This could be a hostage situation."

"It's not," she shouted back.

"How do *you* know?"

"Positions of the vehicles. This isn't a SWAT Team standoff. It's a body bag count."

"Where do you want me to meet you?" Aaron called after her.

But she was out of range by then, or pretended to be.

Aaron watched as she kept walking up the street, until she disappeared from sight among the crowds lining the Strip.

Fifteen minutes later, after parking three blocks away on a side street, he found himself stopped by a police cordon that had been drawn around the block containing the Cinematheque.

"Look," he said to one of the officers on the cordon, "my girlfriend just went in there. I'm supposed to be with her."

"Sorry. We can't let anyone through."

"Bullshit! How did *she* get through?"

"I don't know anything about that."

"Look, she's with the media! Hell, *I'm* with the media!"

He got out his wallet, flipped to his driver's license.

"See? Aaron Scott. I do the drive-time shift on KRAS FM. Sunset Scott in the Morning."

The officer studied the license photo, then Aaron.

"My kid brother listens to you. How much you make?"

"Not enough. Can I get through now?"

"Sorry. Nobody's allowed through."

Muttering to himself, Aaron put away the wallet and looked past the cordon to see if he could spot Sam.

At first he thought she must be part of the phalanx of reporters and cameramen surrounding Lieutenant Brock of the LAPD. When he failed to find her there, he looked again, straining to see past paramedics carrying out the wounded on stretchers and the dead in body bags and firefighters rushing in and out of the Cinematheque, everything intensified by the pounding of news camera helicopters overhead.

Then he saw her, over to the left, near the lobby entrance, talking to two guys who looked like plainclothes cops, one short and fat, the other tall and dark.

"Hey, Sam!" he yelled across the cordon, waving to her.

She looked up in his direction. The cops looked too.

"It's *me!*" he pointed to himself. "I can't get *through!*"

"Keep it down," ordered the officer on the cordon.

"Hey!" Aaron turned to him. "Do I have free speech here?"

"Long as you keep it down."

Sam started talking to the two plainclothes cops again.

Aaron sighed. At this rate, he could be here the rest of the night, standing outside the goddamn cordon.

Sam pointed to him. The tall, dark plainclothes cop started walking in his direction. Aaron could see his dark Indian eyes and Armani suit, and wondered who the hell this guy was supposed to be.

"Busy night," said the plainclothes cop.

"Yes, sir, Sergeant Lopez," said the officer on the cordon.

Lopez turned to Aaron. "You Aaron Scott?"

"Yeah. I've been tryin' to get past—"

"Come with me. Let him through. Montoya's orders."

"Yes, sir, Sergeant Lopez."

"Hey, thanks for gettin' me in," Aaron said.

But Lopez had already drawn ahead of him, walking fast with long, athletic strides. Aaron had to sprint to catch up.

When they reached Sam and Montoya, the older homicide detective glanced at Aaron with tired, heavy-lidded eyes.

"Aaron Scott?" he asked.

"Yeah. Thanks for gettin' me through. You wouldn't believe what parking's like out there."

"I'm Lieutenant Montoya, Homicide. This is Sergeant Lopez, also of Homicide."

Aaron offered his hand, but no one made a move to take it.

"You two guys work for him, over there?"

Aaron pointed to Lieutenant Brock, surrounded by reporters.

"No, Aaron," Sam said. "Lieutenant Montoya's the one in charge here. Lieutenant Brock works for *him.*"

"But on the news report last night, you said—"

"I was misinformed, okay?"

"Lieutenant Brock handles media coverage on this case," Montoya explained. "He talks to the reporters."

"So you're really in charge of finding the Phantom?"

"Yes."

"How come you decided to talk to Sam about it now?"

"We're not speaking for broadcast," Montoya said.

"That's what *you* think. You don't know Sam. Right, Sam?"

"Everything's off the record," she said.

"Then what the hell are we doing, wasting—"

"You're the one they want to talk to, Aaron."

He turned from her to the detectives, his mouth open.

"Mr. Scott," Montoya said, "when the Phantom called you during this morning's show, did he say anything to you that was *not* broadcast? Anything off the record?"

Aaron started to answer, then stopped.

"You guys *listen* to my show?"

"For the past two days, we've been taping it."

"No shit? In that case, you heard me hang up on the fucker over the air, right? He didn't call back. And he's *not* the Phantom, anyway, which I'm sure you guys know by now."

"He said he'd kill tonight, near a theater on Sunset."

"Lucky guess. Besides, he said *near* a theater on Sunset, and this is—"

Aaron watched the paramedics bring out another body bag.

"We wouldn't expect him to give exact details, Mr. Scott."

I don't want to make things too easy for the LAPD.

He saw the two paramedics who had brought out the body bag go back inside the theater, tension visible in the way they held themselves. In the distance, sirens wailed as more ambulances made their way up Sunset, toward the Strip.

"How many people did he kill in there, anyway?"

"We'd like to show you something. It may help convince you that the man who's been calling in to your radio show these past few days is exactly who he claims to be."

Aaron stared at Montoya, then at Lopez.

Overhead, news camera helicopters pounded into the night.

"Coming with us, Mr. Scott?"

"Yeah. Sure. Why not?"

They mounted the steps to the Cinematheque entrance and passed through another police cordon, this one set up to keep ambitious cameramen from sneaking unauthorized shots.

Inside, the extent of the Phantom's depredation became clearer. The lobby had been converted into a temporary morgue. Dead bodies, chalked and photographed inside the auditorium, had been brought out into the lobby to be bagged then transported to the ambulances.

Five more bodies lay in the lobby, awaiting removal.

Sam leaned forward to examine the corpses.

"Jesus," Aaron said. "How many did he kill?"

"We're going up those stairs," Montoya pointed, "to the men's room on the right. Along the way you'll see some marked-off evidence areas. Don't step in them."

As they ascended the central stairs, they saw two paramedics coming down with the corpse of Jim McCauley, the projectionist, charred and blackened to the point where his features were barely recognizable as those of a human being.

The distinctive smell of burned human flesh filled the air.

Sam flinched, but did not turn away.

"Jesus," Aaron muttered, turning his head.

The inside of the men's rest room had been marked off into different sections with raised barriers of wide yellow tape reading POLICE LINE—DO NOT CROSS. Several homicide detectives dusted sink basins for prints. Others took blood samples. Two paramedics bent over what seemed to be a girl's body—if you could tell anything about what it had been from a face like that. The face was covered with large purple blisters that obscured its features and form, like makeup for a monster from outer space.

A homicide detective snapped a Polaroid photograph.

"What the hell is *that?*" Aaron asked.

"Liquid nitrogen," Montoya said. "It's kept frozen to about 320° below Fahrenheit. It burns into flesh like a powerful acid, eating it up. Until they finish with the autopsy, we won't know whether he threw it on her while she was still alive. But given the Phantom's usual M.O., he probably did."

Aaron swallowed. "Is that what killed her?"

"No. He slit her throat. She bled to death before she could die from the shock of liquid nitrogen in her face."

"What happened to all the blood?"

"Apparently, he caught most of it in one of those basins."

"Why did—"

"He needed it to finish his sign."

Before Aaron could ask what he meant, Montoya nodded at the large, wall-to-wall mirror hanging above the porcelain sinks.

Aaron turned and saw the message scrawled across the glass.

SUNSET SCOTT

I KEEP MY PROMISES. DO YOU?

THE PHANTOM

The message itself was in black marker, with a line drawn through three letters, PRM, right before PROMISES, as if the writer had caught his error, crossed it out, and started over.

SUNSET SCOTT and **THE PHANTOM** were written in blood, dried now to a brittle, rust-colored brown.

Aaron, stomach burning, heard the whispering voice again.

I'll leave a sign for you, Sunset Scott. Look for it.

He stared at the message scrawled across the mirror, not even noticing his own reflection staring back at him.

He looked long and hard at the sign.

Sam grabbed his shoulder.

"Aaron? You okay?"

"Yeah." He turned to her. "I'm cool."

"Mr. Scott," Montoya began, "the Phantom said he would leave you a sign—"

"He told me to *look* for one!" Aaron snapped. "So what? A sign could be anything! Just another lucky guess. That's all. Or maybe the real Phantom happened to listen in and heard what the fake Phantom said. Who the hell knows? Not me. I just run a radio show from five to nine every morning. I don't work a hot line for serial killers!"

Aaron turned away, trying not to look at the mirror.

"It might be mere coincidence," Montoya agreed. "But this man who calls himself the Phantom is fast, smart, and very careful. He doesn't leave many clues, Mr. Scott."

"Your guys are finding fingerprints, aren't they?"

Aaron nodded at the detectives dusting sinks for prints.

"Maybe. We haven't picked up any from his other crime scenes. He probably wears gloves, a precaution most killers overlook. Like I said, he doesn't leave many clues—except for the one he left here for you, Mr. Scott."

"He didn't fucking leave it for *me!*"

"You don't have to shout, Aaron," Sam said.

"Who's *shouting?*"

He turned away from her, and from Montoya and Lopez, and stopped at a yellow tape barrier. POLICE LINE—DO NOT CROSS.

"Excuse us."

Aaron looked up, then stepped back to make way for two paramedics as they carried Jessie De Santis's corpse out of the rest room, blister-ringed sockets staring up at him from where her eyes had been.

He walked back to Montoya. "Look, am I under arrest?"

"No."

"Am I being held for questioning—anything like that?"

"No. All we ask is that you reveal nothing of what you've seen here over the air, or in private conversation with anyone except Miss Collier. Other than that, you're free to go."

"Cool. In that case—"

"Of course," Montoya said, "there *are* some questions we'd like to ask—unless you'd rather not answer them."

"Questions about *what?* You taped the last two shows! You heard everything that asshole said to me!"

"Last night," Lopez said, stepping forward, dark eyes on Aaron, "two patrol officers arrived at the scene of what seemed to have been an aggravated assault, in the vicinity of—"

As Lopez continued, Aaron saw the mouth with the red gum line, grinning into the Porsche's headlights.

Man, I am *the mask!*

"At that time," Lopez said, "you refused to press charges."

"Damn right! I didn't want it reported, either!"

"The patrol officers had to file their internal reports."

"Fuck their internal reports!"

Lopez stared at him.

"You didn't tell me about this, Aaron," Sam said.

He looked away from her.

"You also refused," Montoya said, "to identify your assailants—either by reviewing photographic files or by observing suspects in a lineup."

Aaron saw the young black man again, Jabar, and felt the gun muzzle pressed hard against his throat.

You don't tell 'em nothin' *about us, man!*

He felt his fear rising, along with anger and indignation.

"What gives you the right," he asked Montoya, "to go around and fuck up other people's lives like this, huh?"

"Mr. Scott—"

"I am *not* part of this shit! I do not *want* to be part of it! If you think I *am,* then, pal, *you're* full of shit, okay?"

"Mr. Scott—"

"I'm a radio jock who runs a drive-time show with call-ins. *One* of my call-ins happened to be this fuckin' weird-ass from hell who thinks he's the Phantom. He could've picked John Wilkes Booth or Lee fuckin' Harvey Oswald! He just *happened* to pick the Phantom. That's all I *know* about it. That's all I'm gonna *say* about it. That's—Fuck it! I'm outta here!"

He headed for the rest room door, then stopped.

"Want to come with me?" he asked Sam. "Or stay here?"

She looked at him.

"You told the investigating officers," Lopez said, "that you heard a woman scream, just before your assailants attacked you. The Phantom killed someone near that same location, at about the same time you were there. You're part of this, Sunset Scott, like it or not."

"Fuck you!" He pointed a finger at Lopez, then Montoya. "Fuck *both* of you, and your fuckin' hard-core attitude! You got enough evidence to arrest me? *Go* for it! Just *do* it, man! Otherwise, get the fuck outta my life! And leave me the fuck alone!"

He turned and stalked out of the rest room, head lowered, tearing through the yellow police tape that blocked his way.

He was already down the steps of the Cinematheque and through the police cordon, heading for the Porsche, before he realized that he had left Sam back there in the rest room, along with the two homicide detectives.

9

PERSONAL

He gripped the steering wheel harder than necessary as he made his way up crowded side streets, cutting a wide detour around the tied-up traffic in front of the Cinematheque. The hell with Sam. She could get a ride back to the On-Target lot from one of the cops, probably from that tall lonesome Indian. Who the hell did those assholes think they were, anyway? Working him over like some punk off the street.

I keep my promises. Do you?

He swallowed, forcing down fear at the back of his throat.

It was already a long night, a wasted one, and he had to get up at four-fifteen tomorrow morning if he wanted to make it to the studio on time. He should go home and go to bed.

He drove to the Rakehell Club instead. The Rakehell was one of those upscale topless places that differed from the downscale kind mainly in terms of how much they charged for admission and how often they swept the stage. The Rakehell was so far upscale you actually had to buy a membership. Sam had given him trouble about renewing his last year, but the hell with her.

He drove up in front of a dark brick building with a sedate striped awning above the entrance and let the valet park his Porsche. Inside, he showed his membership card to a kid with a ponytail who called him Mr. Scott. Then he pushed his way through a glass-beaded portiere, swaying with reflected light, and took a seat in a dark leather armchair near the stage.

A dancer, doubling as a barmaid, breasts pumped full of silicone, came over to him, leaned down, and kissed him on the cheek, exuding a mixture of perfume, tobacco, and peppermint.

"Hi, sweetheart," she gushed. "You want a drink?"

She put down a cocktail napkin on the table next to him.

"Yeah, bring me a Guinness."

He looked up at the stage and watched a dancer with breasts the size of ripe melons and areolas large as tea saucers go through her gyrations, eyes closed and mouth open, feigning the swoon of erotic ecstasy.

Aaron recognized the music pounding from overhead speakers.

The Gravediggers. "Bury My Love."

He smelled perfume and peppermint again, and felt a light hand on his left shoulder, then a wet kiss on his right cheek.

"Hi, sweetheart," lisped one of the dancers who had just finished her set and was out collecting. "You see me dance?"

"Yeah." He reached for his wallet and took out a five.

She dropped it in her yawning cleavage. "Thanks!"

Aaron glanced around the room, at the men sitting in shadows and half-light near the stage, like himself, and at the ones in the back, entirely creatures of shadow. He didn't see anyone he knew, and wouldn't have said anything to them if he had. You came to a place like this for the same reason you went to the cheaper ones, to letch in solitude.

But it wasn't working for Aaron, not tonight.

He watched a young girl with pale skin, smooth and supple, like sculpted white marble, offset by large dark nipples. But he didn't really see her, not the way he was supposed to. He saw instead the dark, empty sockets in Jessie De Santis's face, ringed with purple blisters, and the message on the mirror, with his name and the Phantom's written in the dried blood of a dead girl lying on the rest room floor.

Revolving lights flashed on and off, turning the room into a spectrum of disassociated colors. The Gravediggers howled from the speakers, hammering home their heavy, metallic chords.

He paid for his stout, tipping five for another wet kiss.

Inside the garage beneath his building, he parked in his assigned space. As he turned off the car's motor, he could hear the security gate rolling shut behind him—so slowly it would allow anyone standing nearby enough time to slip into the garage unobserved before the gate closed. He had never noticed that before, had never even thought about it.

He thought about it now as he sat in the car and looked at the dark corners of the parking garage, the places where pallid light from the overheads did not quite reach. He got out, hair and clothes reeking with secondhand smoke from the Rakehell Club, and set the Porsche's alarm. The usual brief, high-pitched electronic squeak rewarded his efforts.

But after it stopped, it seemed to become another, different sound, or to engender one, as if the second sound had become an echo of the first. He stopped and listened. The sound came again, sharp and quick, like metal scraping against metal. He stood there, car keys in one hand, alarm remote in the other, staring past the white, sickly light of overhead fluorescents into the dark corners, the places where the shadows were.

The metallic sound came again, followed by a new one—the muffled, gritty scraping of a rubber sole across concrete.

"Hey!" Aaron called out to the shadows. "Who's there?"

No one answered.

Aaron strained to listen, but he could hear nothing now, except the distant hum of traffic from Sunset down below, and closer in, the grinding of a car's engine as it labored up the grade, and closer still, the persistent beating of his heart.

"Hey! Who the fuck's back there?"

It felt good to say that, to let out some of the anger, and the fear, building inside him since the Cinematheque. But the words were hardly out of his mouth before he realized the danger of having said them. Whoever was back there in the shadows didn't want to be seen. So just yell at him a little, right? Force the fucker's hand. Jesus! He might be a car jacker. People got *killed* for their cars these days!

Someone was definitely back there, no doubt about it. Aaron could not see into the shadows, but he could feel what was there. Someone stood in the darkness, watching him, someone who could afford to be patient, because he had all the time in the world, and this was *his* game, and he knew it.

Disparate images flashed through Aaron's mind. The mouth with the red gum line, grinning into the headlights. Jabar with his frightened eyes and the muzzle of his automatic pressed up against Aaron's throat. The mirror with its message and the two names, his and the Phantom's, scrawled in blood.

He could feel the dampness on his forehead, despite the cool night air, and he knew that he was sweating, his own sour odor mixing with stale tobacco smoke from the Rakehell Club. He still could not see into the shadows, but he thought he could see an outline of something, a darkness within the darkness.

He stood there next to his parking space, uncertain whether to go or stay. If he moved, would that provoke a reaction? If he didn't move, would *that* set off something? His hand involuntarily squeezed the button on the remote.

His car alarm went off with a whoop, making him jump.

"Shit!" he muttered, shutting it off.

He looked into the shadows again. No new sounds came from there. The shadow within the shadows did not move.

He turned and started for the narrow gate that let foot traffic in and out of the parking garage. He saw the bodies in the lobby of the Cinematheque, shot down in cold blood by a madman with a mask, and he felt a sharp pain cut into his chest. His first thought was heart attack, but he knew what it was.

Fear—of the unknown, darkness, death.

When he reached the gate and opened it, he thought he heard a sound from the far side of the garage—someone shifting position, getting ready to move, or shoot.

He stopped and looked back into the shadows. Then he walked through the gate and banged it shut behind him. He moved faster than usual, taking the stairs to his second-floor condo two at a time.

As he put his key in the lock, he heard the gate to the parking garage squeak open, then bang shut, followed by the sound of footsteps running off into the night. Several seconds passed before he looked down at the gate and the sidewalk leading away from it. Whoever had run out of there had disappeared—probably some punk hiding in the garage, trying to work up the balls to car-jack somebody. Just that. Nothing more.

Once inside, he threw the dead bolt, checked it twice, then turned on most of the lights, from the harsh kitchen fluorescents to the muted track lighting in the living room. He got out a bottle of tequila from under the sink and poured himself three stiff fingers and knocked it back. It took effect almost at once, working him over with its raw, cactus-brewed potency. It seemed to flatten out his nerves and slow down the rapid beating of his heart. He walked into the living room with the empty glass in his hand and stared out his picture window at the lights below—but not at the lights of Sunset Boulevard. They reminded him, tonight, of the Cinematheque. He stared instead at the lights beyond Sunset: the flatlands of Hollywood, stretching south to Melrose, to Beverly, to Wilshire, and beyond.

The Phantom's domain.

He frowned to himself. What kind of shit was that?

His phone rang. The empty tequila glass dropped from his relaxed fingers and tumbled to the carpet in slow motion.

"Shit—"

It was probably Sam, calling to tear into him for not waiting around to drive her back to her car.

He grabbed at the cordless phone.

"Yeah?"

No one answered on the other end.

"Sam?"

His voice sounded distant, blurred by too much tequila.

"Sam? Is that you?"

He heard a sudden, hissing intake of breath.

"You saw my message, didn't you, Sunset Scott?"

It was the same whispering voice he had heard inside his headphones that morning—but he wasn't wearing headphones now.

"*Now* do you believe I'm real, Sunset Scott?"

He pulled the cordless phone away from his head and held it out in front of him, staring at it, as if what he saw might somehow help him understand what he heard.

"Do you believe I am who I say I am, Sunset Scott?"

"Fuck you," he whispered.

He put down the phone and backed off from it, as if it had become a sentient thing, with the power to harm.

"Shit . . ." He ran a hand through his hair and stood there, staring at the phone where it sat on top of a counter separating the living room from the kitchen.

Maybe if he turned off the phone—

Maybe if he changed his number—

The phone rang again.

Aaron's heart seemed to leap inside his chest, then come down hard, hammering fast, with a crazy rhythm. He backed farther away from the phone, terror taking hold of him, like a child's fear of the dark. If he didn't answer it, then he wouldn't hear the Phantom again.

If he didn't hear him, he didn't exist.

He knew that was bullshit, all of it.

Still, he didn't pick up the phone.

He stood on the other side of the living room, back pressed against the picture window, staring at the phone as it continued to ring, giving out its rhythmic string of electronic chirps.

How long he stood there he did not know. But at last fear turned to self-disgust, then anger.

He snatched the cordless phone.

"Yeah?"

He snarled out the word, a challenge more than an answer.

No one spoke on the other end.

"That's right. *Go* silent on me, you motherfuckin'—"

"Aaron?"

He heard his mother's voice—cautious, somewhat concerned.

"Mom! Is that you?"

"Of course it's me. Who did you think it was?"

He sat down hard on the couch.

"I don't— Look, I'm sorry. I just had a crank call."

"Who was it? Jeffrey Dahmer?"

Aaron tried to laugh.

"No, look. I'm sorry. It's been—one of those days."

"Did you get to see Samantha?"

"Yeah, sort of."

"What's with the *sort of?*"

"We went to have dinner at Tramonto, but something just—came up. Like I said, it's one of those days."

"Don't start skipping meals, Aaron. You need to eat."

"Thanks. I'll try to remember."

"You sound tired. I better let you go."

"No! Don't hang up!"

He reached out a hand, as if trying to grab hold of the electronic thread that connected them, spanning the darkness of the world outside and all the horrors it contained.

"Is something wrong, Aaron?"

"No. I just— Hey, you just called. Why not talk?"

10

CALL-IN

When he got to the radio station the next morning—even earlier than the day before—he found a woman who looked like a field reporter waiting for him in the glass hallway outside his broadcast booth, along with a television cameraman, the camera on his shoulder bearing the logo for On-Target News.

"Hey!" he said, not quite awake. "What the fuck is this?"

The cameraman turned on a floodlight and aimed the camera at him. The woman stuck a handheld microphone in his face.

"We can't use that on the air," she said, "but we want you to say something about the Phantom, and the prediction he made on your show yesterday morning—"

Aaron recognized her now, Bonnie Redfield, one of Sam's rivals at On-Target News, a field reporter who usually covered the hot criminal trials. "Reporting from the Criminal Courts Building, *this* is Bonnie Redfield—" That one.

He pushed past her.

"Excuse *you!*" she cried.

He took a swipe at the camera lens, but the cameraman, his reflexes quick and ready for this sort of thing, stepped back in time and went on shooting. Jerry Deel appeared in the hallway.

"Aaron, what's wrong?"

"You tell me, man. What *is* this shit?"

"A million bucks' worth of free publicity! After the Phantom's prediction yesterday, we're hot, guy!"

Aaron glanced at the cameraman, still filming everything.

"Yeah? Tell him to turn that fuckin' thing off!"

"Aaron!" Jerry came forward. "They just want a story on you and the show and the station. This is solid gold for us!"

"We'll talk about it—*after* he turns off that shit."

"Aaron—"

"Tell him to turn it *off*, man. Or someone's gonna be *wearin'* it shoved sideways up their fuckin' asshole, okay?"

The cameraman backed up again, but this time found himself at a dead end, against a shelf of tapes, with no way out.

Aaron moved toward him, a no-nonsense look in his eye.

"Okay, Aaron." Jerry said, then turned to the cameraman. "Shut it off for now, would you?"

The portable floodlight went out, leaving the hallway with its normal lights looking dark by comparison. The cameraman took the camera off his shoulder and stood there, waiting.

Bonnie Redfield put away her handheld microphone.

"We just want to do a story on you," she said. "We need some pickups of you coming into the station, then some shots of you working the board, and then a short interview."

Jerry nodded. "That's reasonable, Aaron, isn't it?"

"Look, I don't want any of that behind-the-scenes shit, okay? You want to shoot me workin' the board *while I'm on the air*, that's cool. Otherwise, forget it."

"This is a news story," Bonnie said. "You're news."

"I'm a radio personality, babe. You want to interview me like a celebrity, you got it. But fuck your this-is-how-he-sets-up-an-airshift shit, 'cause you ain't gettin' it."

"Aaron," Jerry said, "On-Target News is offering us lots of big bucks publicity for free. I repeat, *for free*. I think it would be a good idea to sort of, like, cooperate with them."

"*You* cooperate with 'em, man."

"After the Phantom delivered on his prediction to you last night," Bonnie said, "the viewers want to know more about you—who you are, how you work your show. I think they have the right to know that."

"Search for the Truth, huh?" Aaron asked, remembering Sam.

"I wouldn't go that far, but viewers do have rights."

"Why didn't On-Target send Sam over here to do this?"

Bonnie smiled. "This isn't Samantha's kind of story."

Aaron walked away from her, back toward his booth.

He stopped at the door and turned around, glancing back down the glassed-in hallway at her.

"It's not my kind of fuckin' story either. But the only way we do it is *my* way. Deal?"

Jerry stepped forward. "Aaron—"

"*You* stay outta this. Well, Bonnie? Deal or no deal?"

"Deal," Bonnie said. "But I'll remember this, Aaron."

"You do that, babe," he said, and stepped into the booth.

The first three hours of that morning's show proved uneventful but tense. The On-Target field crew got on the nerves of the other announcers—Lisa, Bud, and Tracy—while Aaron fought Bonnie every step of the way. Three hours' filming yielded not quite that many minutes of usable tape. Aaron kept moving out of the frame, ruining close-up after close-up. When the cameraman tried to use a wider angle to show him working the console, Aaron turned his back to the camera or spoke away from Bonnie's handheld microphone. Finally he threatened to walk off the show if Jerry didn't ban them both from his broadcast booth.

During a twenty-minute commercial-free set of back-to-back hits, Aaron switched his microphone to CUE and joked off the air with Lisa, Bud, and Tracy, ignoring Jerry and Bonnie.

"You think the Phantom will call today?" Bonnie asked.

Laughing at something Lisa had just said, his headphones on, Aaron pretended not to hear her. Jerry cleared his throat.

Bonnie walked over and pulled the left earphone away from his head, then bent down and spoke clearly into his left ear.

"I said, you think the Phantom's going to call in today?"

Aaron whirled around in his chair, grabbing her wrist.

"Don't you *ever* touch my fuckin' headphones again!"

She tried to pull her wrist free, but he gripped it harder.

"Want me to take your fuckin' mike away from *you?*"

"If you don't let go of me right now," she said, "I'm filing a sexual harassment suit against you *and* this station. And with an asshole like you, I can make it stick."

He glared at her, but kept his grip on her wrist.

"Let go of her, Aaron," Jerry said quietly. "Now."

He released the wrist, throwing it back at her.

"Get her the fuck outta here!" he screamed at Jerry.

"Okay, Aaron."

"And *keep* her the fuck outta here!"

Jerry leaned down next to him, speaking rapidly in a low voice. Aaron took off his headphones.

"—need to cooperate with these guys, whether we like them or not, okay? I don't want to have to drag Chuck into this—"

Charles J. Davis, Jr., was KRAS's general manager.

"Is that a threat, Jerry?"

"No, Aaron. It's reality."

"Just keep her off my fuckin' back, okay?"

"I'm trying, Aaron. But you've got to try, too. Be nice to her. At least don't *fight* with her, for Christ's sake."

As Jerry stood up to leave, Aaron glanced at the digital display above the console—8:27:49.

"We've only got half an hour before we wrap this fucker, Jerr. Our wanna-be's not gonna call in again today."

He turned his chair back to the console and bent over it, blocking Jerry, and Bonnie, from his peripheral vision. He stared at the slide faders and moved one of them forward, potting up the on-air song, just to have something to do.

Then he happened to look at the call-screening booth across the way. Bill Waller held up a piece of paper with a message in crude hand-lettered capitals.

LINE THREE **X**

Aaron glanced at the video display to his left.

Line number three had a blinking **X** beside it, along with the notation NO HOME ADDRESS, NO PHONE NUMBER.

He stared at it, pulsing like a cursor on the screen.

The images came in a rush this time, flashing across his consciousness like close-ups from a heavy metal horror video.

The dead girl on the rest room floor, face disfigured by purple blisters, dark sockets where eyes should be. The names written in blood on the mirror, his and the Phantom's. The open mouth with its red gum line, grinning into the car's headlights.

Man, I am *the mask!*

His own reflection staring back at him from the living room window, cordless phone gripped in one hand, as the whispering voice came through loud and clear on his own private line.

Now *do you believe I'm real, Sunset Scott?*

His eyes moved slowly from the blinking **X** on the video display, down to the lighted button number three on the switchboard panel. He felt his chest moving in and out, breath catching like stray filaments in his throat.

He reached out a hand toward the button.

"Aaron!" Jerry called. "Don't shut him off! Take it!"

"Is that *him?*" he could hear Bonnie asking.

He felt the glare and the heat as the cameraman switched on the portable floodlight. He saw the twin warning lights flash on and off above his console, indicating that the last song of the back-to-back hits set was drawing to a close.

He adjusted his headphones, switched his microphone to BROADCAST, and began potting down the volume on the song as he broke in over the fade.

"And there you have it! The Slashers. 'Rip Open My Heart.' Windin' down twenty minutes of stopless hits, here on KRAS, 108.5, Sunset Scott in the Mornin'. But we gotta stop it now, dudes and dudettes, put the ol' chokehold on it, 'cause guess what? He's back again! *Every*body's favorite caller—"

He switched on the echo filter and gave the Shadow laugh.

"THE MAN WITH THE MASK!"

Man, I am *the mask!*

He faltered for a second. His voice seemed to dry up. His mind went blank, except for the image of that grinning mouth with its red gum line. He was a professional, with enough on-air experience to handle something like this. But he recognized it for the terror it was. He tried to turn it to anger, to hatred, to use it against the whispering voice waiting for him there on line number three.

"Okay, everybody! Here he *is!* On KRAS. 108.5."

He could hear the cameraman stepping in close, framing him in wide angle as he reached out to hit button number three.

"Phantom from Nowhere, you're on live with Sunset Scott."

Silence filled his headphones.

"Hey, what the hell is this? The Phantom hangs up on us!"

Moving fast, he reached for line number three again.

"What a shame! But when yo' lose it, yo' *loses* it!"

He glanced to his left, where Jerry stood waving his arms, signaling for him not to disconnect the call.

"Can't you stop him from doing this?" Bonnie asked.

Aaron grinned at her and flipped her his middle finger.

Then he brought it down on button number three.

"Don't hang up on me," said the whispering voice.

Aaron stopped, the familiar voice hissing inside his headphones, his middle finger unsteady above the button.

"Hey, masked bro! What's up? We thought maybe you did the ol' chicken crap there. Lost your balls and *bailed* on us, man."

"I'm not afraid of you, Sunset Scott," said the voice. "*You're* the one who hung up on me."

For an instant the terror returned. He saw himself staring at his own reflection in the picture window again, the dark streets of Hollywood lying beyond it, like the land of the dead.

Then the anger took over.

He moved into the microphone, turning his head to the left, so that he stared straight into the camera lens as he spoke.

"Yeah, I hung up on you, man. You wanna know why? 'Cause you're a boring, stupid-ass fraud! Got that? You're a *fake!* You made a lucky guess, you pathetic suck-off. That's all it was! The real Phantom—who's a butt-kissing coward, by the way—slaughters a bunch of innocent people in a movie theater. And *you* want to call up and take credit for that crap? Kiss my ass! You fake imitation of a scum-sucking fraud!"

He stopped to take a breath, and thought he heard dry, hollow laughter on the other end of the line.

"Are you afraid, Sunset Scott? I think you are. I can't see the fear in your eyes, but I can hear it in your voice."

"Fuck you, asshole!" Aaron shouted into the microphone.

He heard Jerry gasp in horror behind him. Saying *fuck* over the commercial airwaves was a heavy FCC offense. A radio station could lose its license.

Aaron hit the tape delay, turning his outburst into several seconds of expensive dead air. He shut off his microphone, took a deep breath, then switched back to BROADCAST.

"Hey, *dick*head!" he screamed in his best Sunset Scott over-the-top style, yelling sideways across the microphone. "I ain't afraid of you, man! Want to know why? 'Cause I'm Sunset Scott, the only true terrorist of the airwaves! And you're just a limp dickhead! You pathetic Xerox imitation of the real thing! In a Phantom look-alike contest, you wouldn't even place third!"

He paused, listening to the silence on the other end.

He reached out to disconnect line three.

"But you know I'm real, Sunset Scott," said the whispering voice, "because I said I'd leave a sign for you, and I did. You saw it. You saw the names written in blood. You saw the first three letters of the word *promises* crossed out, as if I'd made a mistake. But I don't make mistakes, Sunset Scott. I did that on purpose, so you'd know for sure. The police haven't released that information yet. Even *I* couldn't have found out about it unless I was there last night with you and the police, and that girl from the television news. Or unless I kept my promise to you, and did what I said I'd do."

Aaron wasn't even listening to the last part of it. The terror changed to a dull, numbing fear, as he realized that what once seemed false had somehow become real, like a stuffed rattlesnake turning suddenly alive and slithering in his hands.

He wiped his hand across his mouth.

"Yeah? So what? I don't give a damn what kind of crap you try to unload here over the air, Mr. Wanna-be Phantom! I still say you're a fake and a fraud, okay? Just a lot of funky-smellin' butt gas comin' out the wrong end, man!"

"You're putting on a brave front, Sunset Scott. You're pretending I'm not real, when you know—"

"Eat my shorts, Fake Phantom! Kiss my ass! You play with yourself when you make these calls, you masked moron? Is that what you're doin' right now, playin' with yourself?"

"I'm not playing with anyone, Sunset Scott. *You* are. But that's going to stop. I can see I'll have to make this more—personal. I may have to pay a visit."

"You threatenin' to come down here to the station, Fake Phantom? Let's *do* it, man! Come *on!* Don't forget to wear your stupid mask! Better yet, wear *two*, so you'll have one to hide behind when I rip the first one off your phony, kiss-ass face!"

The needle on the VU meter bounced over into the red as Aaron screamed into the microphone. It dropped back to normal range, even slightly below normal, into the mud, when the soft, whispering voice came on the line again.

"I don't want to pay a visit to the station—not yet."

Lisa looked up from the news booth, eyes wide with alarm.

Even Bud and Tracy looked up. But Aaron saw none of these things—only an open mouth, grinning into his car's headlights.

"I don't want to spoil the—purity of our conversations, Sunset

Scott. I won't pay a visit to the station, not just yet. I think I'll stop by the Steinberg deli instead, and pay a visit to the woman who runs it—"

Aaron punched button number three hard enough to make the *snap* audible inside the booth and over the air.

"Whoa, everybody! Looks like we just lost the Fake Phantom there! Probably started to choke on all those butt gas fumes! Yeah! But you're still hangin' with Sunset Scott, here at KRAS, 108.5. So let's get down and dirty with *another* twenty stopless minutes of back-to-back hits, commercial-free! Startin' off with the Public Offenders and 'Nasty in Yo' Face.' *Right* after these words! Keep it on KRAS, man!"

He slammed two commercials into the cart machine, followed by the twenty-minute song tape, and jabbed the PLAY button. Then he jumped up from his chair, making it swivel.

He grabbed the receiver from the switchboard, hit a button for an outside line, dialing the number to Steinberg's so fast that he screwed up and had to do it again.

Jerry stepped into the booth.

"Aaron! Why did you cut him *off* like that, guy?"

The incessant buzz of a busy signal droned in his ear.

"Shit!" He slammed down the receiver. "Goddamn fuckin'—"

The cameraman zoomed in slowly on him for a close up.

Aaron pointed his finger straight into the lens.

"Get that fuckin' shit outta my face, man!"

"Aaron!" Jerry shouted. "I'm *talking* to you!"

He went for the cameraman and got him this time, knocking the camera to one side, and the cameraman along with it. He shoved his way past Jerry and out into the hallway.

Bonnie flattened herself against one wall, holding both hands out in front of her.

"Don't you *touch* me, you crazy, fucked-up son of a bitch!"

He brushed past, not even looking at her, and ran down the hallway, heading for the exit door that led to the elevators.

"Aaron!" Jerry called after him. "Where are you going?"

He turned as he hit the exit door. "I'll be right back!"

"Who's supposed to run this show while you're gone?"

"The carts'll take it to sign-off, then Alonzo's on."

Alonzo Gore worked the next shift, Alonzo at High Noon.

Jerry stepped out into the hallway.

"*Aaron!*"

But Aaron was gone.

11

DELIVERY

He gunned the Porsche through stop-and-go traffic.

Rush hour was still winding down and would be for another hour, turning the major boulevards of Hollywood into gridlocked parking lots. When he finally got off Sunset, he was able to make better time down the side streets, until he had to turn on to Fairfax and hit the brakes again.

All the while he tried to keep his mind on the things he could see in front of him. The steering wheel. The speedometer. The shiny black surface of the Porsche's hood, reflecting the buildings and the trees and the other cars as they passed by in a stroboscopic blur.

Anything to keep the other images at bay.

The dead girl with the purple blisters bubbling up from her face on the rest room floor. The corpses laid out in the lobby.

The mouth with the red gum line, grinning under headlights.

I think I'll stop by the Steinberg deli—

He slammed on the brakes as someone slowed down in front of him for no goddamn reason. He hit the horn and the asshole flipped him the finger. He honked again, but it did no good. The traffic was locked. There was no way out.

He ran a hand through his hair, damp with sweat, and took a quick, deep breath, coughing on it in the midmorning smog.

Where had the Phantom called in from?

A private phone, in some flophouse somewhere?

A pay phone on the street, tagged and vandalized?

How close had he been to Steinberg's when he called?

How close was he *now?*

He tried to turn them off, but the questions kept racing through his mind, along with the other images, starting up all over again, flashing across his inner vision in graphic, detailed, technicolor virtual reality.

When he got to Steinberg's, the spaces in front were full, as always, so he parked two blocks down, then got out and ran like hell, almost colliding with a Hasidic father and son, walking back slowly from morning services.

He burst into Steinberg's, startling a man on his way out.

Behind the counter, Shirley Landau looked up in surprise.

"Aaron! How are you?"

"Where's Mom?"

"Out."

"Out *where?*"

He walked up to her and slammed his hands on the counter, rattling plates of lox and gefilte fish beneath the glass.

"Aaron, what is wrong?"

"Where the hell did she *go*, Shirley?"

"Out! She went out to make a delivery. You want to wait half an hour, maybe forty-five minutes, she'll be back."

"Why did *she* make the delivery instead of you?"

"Because she felt like it! How do I know? She said to me, 'Shirl, I'm going out to run a delivery,' and then she did."

"*Who* called in that delivery, Shirley?"

"Aaron, I don't know! There were customers in here. I was busy. I'm busy now—not that I don't enjoy talking to you."

"Shirley, this is *very* important. Can you find out what name the guy gave who called in for the delivery?"

She sighed. "Aaron, I don't need this aggravation—"

"Also his phone number? And his address?"

"His number? His address? What are you? A cop?"

"God*damn*it, Shirley! This is important!"

"All right, all right! We can find out."

She moved over to the cash register and picked up a thick wad of receipts, skewered on an old-fashioned spike.

"Let's see." She thumbed through them. "Takeout, takeout, takeout, takeout— *Aha!* Delivery. Abraham Kornfeld. One small bowl of borscht, no sour cream. One onion bagel with low-fat cream cheese. One piece whitefish. You happy now?"

She flourished the receipt in front of him.

He snatched it from her.

"Aaron!"

He glanced over his mother's scrawled handwriting.

"You're sure this is the one, Shirley?"

"Yes, I'm sure! Now give it back to me."

"This has the address. Why didn't Mom take it with her?"

"Maybe she wrote it down on another piece of paper?"

"This address is somewhere in West Hollywood."

"That must be where Abe Kornfeld lives. Now give it—"

"I'll be right back with this, Shirley, okay?"

He rushed from the counter, receipt clutched in his hand.

"Aaron! We need that for our records!"

The bell jingled as he pulled open the door and left.

He drove through West Hollywood like a bat out of hell, startling gay couples walking their dogs and gay young men sipping cappuccinos at sidewalk cafés and elderly Russian Jewish émigrés arguing with one another on street corners.

He took a corner on two wheels, laying rubber from one block to the next, accelerating instead of braking.

Aaron glanced at the address again, receipt rattling in the wind from his rolled-down window. It looked like Kornfeld lived in a house instead of an apartment. But that could be a setup. The whole god-damn delivery could be a setup.

I think I'll stop by the Steinberg deli—

That part had been a lie. He hadn't stopped there.

But maybe he had called in instead, pretending to be Abraham Kornfeld. The Phantom didn't always do what he said. He said he'd kill someone *near* a theater on Sunset, not massacre a whole morgue-ful of them *inside—*

He saw Kornfeld's address and hit the brakes.

Tires squealed as he came to a jolting stop.

It was a house, all right, a classic California bungalow.

He stuffed the receipt in his pocket, got out of the car, slamming the door behind him, and walked up the cracked sidewalk to the wooden porch, the sun hot on the back of his neck, heart beating rapidly. He pressed the doorbell and heard it ring inside with a distant, muted two-tone response. White lace curtains, darkened by smog, hung across the small front window. Inside, behind the smudged lace, he could see nothing but darkness, and his own reflection staring back at him. He shifted impatiently from one foot to the other and waited for the sound of footsteps coming to the front door.

But no footsteps came.

He rang the bell again, leaning on it this time, aware of grime on the panels of the wooden door and on the blue plastic of empty water bottles on the unswept surface of the porch.

When no one answered his second ring, he pounded on the door, giving vent to his anger, rattling the wood in its frame.

Then he stopped and listened, but heard nothing—except the rapid beating of his own heart, the hum of distant traffic.

I think I'll stop by the Steinberg deli—

He felt cold sweat on his face.

—and pay a visit to the woman who runs it—

"Shit!"

He ran around to the side of the house, glancing in the windows, but they were all dark and curtained, like the one in front. He kept running, his breath coming in loud chuffs, back to the rear of the house, with its unfenced yard, parched and full of weeds, the withered remains of a garden along one side.

He hammered on the back door, rattling the doorknob as he pounded on the wood, gasping for breath like a hundred-meter man who had just broken the tape.

A shadowy figure appeared behind the window glass.

The door opened.

He stepped back from it, chest heaving.

"Aaron! What are you doing here?"

His mother squinted at him in the bright morning sunlight.

"Mom—" he gasped. "You're still— Are you—okay?"

"Yes, I'm fine. But what's wrong with *you?*"

"I came— I brought—"

He dug into his pocket and pulled out the receipt.

"Shirley gave— She gave me— This!"

Leah took it from him. "My God, Aaron. We need this for our records. Why did Shirley give it to you?"

"I thought— I thought that—"

"Here. Come inside and catch your breath, before you die of a heart attack on Abe Kornfeld's back doorstep."

His eyes took several seconds to adjust to the low light inside. Once they did, he could see shelves and cabinets in a small, dark kitchen, an elderly man in a wheelchair, neck thin and stringy like a starving bird's. He blinked at Aaron through lenses that must have been half an inch thick.

"Abe, my son Aaron. Aaron, Abe Kornfeld."

"Running, *nu?*" Abe Kornfeld said slowly. "Always running, these days. What I want to know is, what's to run for?"

Aaron nodded, still panting for breath, and tried to smile.

"Pleased to meet you. I—thought you were someone else."

PART TWO

ILLUSION

12

CONSOLATION

A pale moon rode high in the night sky over Hollywood, looking down on a dark, mostly silent world.

The evening chill kept most windows closed. Occasional cars strained up the narrow road from the Sunset Strip.

Someone walking along the sidewalk in front of Aaron's condominium building would have heard his, or her, own footsteps ringing out in the still night air, and not much else.

The sudden knocking at the front door startled him.

It broke the silence inside his condo, absolute except for electronic chatter from the television on low volume, tuned to a science fiction epic about mutants from another dimension. He roused himself from a semitorpor, brought on by three bottles of Corona, and made his way across the living room to the door.

It wasn't until he almost reached it that he remembered the Phantom's whispering voice, and with it, the terror.

I may have to pay a visit.

This morning had been a ruse, a big joke, a nothing.

Tonight might be the real thing.

The knocking came again, right in front of his face, and scared the hell out of him, making him jump back from the door.

When the knocking stopped, he looked through the peephole, but whoever was out there had managed to stand back beyond the range of the fisheye lens. He hesitated for a moment, wondering if it was safe to open the door. But what else could he do? Call the cops? Call his mom?

Angry with himself, he unlocked the door—opened it.

Sam stood on the small covered porch, blond hair framed by the night sky, shoulders hunched against the cold.

"Sam—"

"I'm sorry about what Bonnie Redfield did this morning."

"Jerry says she's threatening to sue the shit out of me."

"She won't sue. That's just talk." Sam looked up at him. "But I want you to know I didn't have anything to do with it. It was all Bonnie's idea. I wouldn't ever do something like that to you, Aaron."

"Sam, forget it, okay? I knew you weren't part of that bullshit. But is this why you came over here, just to tell me?"

She nodded. "Yeah."

He reached out and grabbed her, kissing her hard, feeling himself stiffen as he pressed into her leather jacket.

"Aaron—" She pushed him away. "I'm freezing to death out here! Could we maybe go inside and do this?"

He ushered her through the doorway. As he closed the door behind her, and locked it again, she looked around the condo.

"When's your cleaning woman coming in again?"

"Never." He stifled a Corona belch. "She's gone for good. Jammed on back to El Salvador."

"You need a new one, then. This place is a mess."

"Thanks, Sam."

"Should I lie about it?"

"Hell, no. Search for the Truth, always. Want a beer?"

"No. You drink it for me."

He put his arm around her and rocked her from side to side.

"Can't afford to, babe. Don't want to take the *edge* off my performance—if yo' knows what I means!"

She squirmed in his embrace. "Let go, Aaron. I didn't come over here just to fool around."

He released her and followed her out into the living room.

"What *did* you come over for? To search for the Truth?"

"You think that's a real big joke, don't you?"

"As pursued by assholes like Bonnie Redfield, yeah, I do."

"I *told* you I had nothing to do with that—"

"Okay, babe, okay! I believe you. Have a seat."

He sat down on the couch and patted a cushion beside him.

"What's that?" she asked, pointing at the television.

"I don't know. Some UFO-type shit, with space monsters."

"Mind if I shut it off?"

"Be my guest."

He looked at her sitting next to him and thought how cool it would be to have her here like this every night, so that if he went out into the kitchen to get another beer, and then came back, she'd still be there, waiting for him.

Her black leather jacket almost matched the couch.

"Take off your coat, Sam. Stay a while."

"It's cold in here, Aaron."

"I'll turn up the heat."

"No, don't. It's probably just me."

He went over and cranked up the thermostat ten degrees.

"I didn't get to hear your show this morning," she said.

"You didn't miss much."

"But I heard the audiotape Bonnie made, and saw some of that video trash she did." Sam paused. "That was horrible, what he said about stopping by your mom's. Bonnie said you left the station right after that. She was still there when you called back later and said your mom was okay. I'm sorry I didn't call you about it, Aaron. But I was so busy—"

"Forget it. She was okay. It was just a practical joke."

"Some joke."

"Yeah, well, the Phantom's got a strange sense of humor."

"So now you think it really *is* the Phantom?"

"Come on, Sam. Let's not stir up that shit again. I don't know for sure who the fuck he is, or *what* he is. But if he's not the Phantom, then he's the Phantom's twin brother, or the Phantom's old man. Someone who knows a lot about him."

"He seems to know something about you, too."

"Drop it, Sam, okay? I don't want to get *into* this!"

"It's the truth, Aaron, whether you like it or not. How did he know about your mom's deli?"

"Sam—"

"You ever talk about her place on the air?"

"Shit, no! What do you think I am? Crazy?"

"Who else knows at the station? Lisa? Bud? Bill?"

"Just Jerry—and he's probably forgotten about it."

"Then how did the Phantom find out?"

"I don't *know!* Jesus! Would you back off with the third degree, already? I might as well get fucked over by the cops!"

"You've been thinking about that, haven't you?"

"What?"

"Going to the police."

He stared at the blank television screen.

"I never thought I'd say this, Sam, but why don't you just, you know, leave—go home."

"No problem." She got up from the couch.

"No, don't!" He grabbed her hand. "It was just a *joke!*"

"It wasn't funny."

"I do a lot of jokes in a day. Some of them really suck. Jesus, Sam! Would you please sit down again?"

They both sat down, leather squeaking beneath them.

"Okay, I admit it. I've thought about going to the cops. That shit with my mom really freaked me out."

She started to speak, but he raised a hand.

"I know. If I want to sit here and *think* about it, why not just go ahead and *do* it. Right?"

"Wrong. I don't think you should go to the police."

His forehead wrinkled into a frown. "What?"

"Aaron, I've been thinking about this a lot. The police can't help you. We both know that now."

"We *do?*"

"Yes!"

"You sure as hell talked with 'em long enough last night!"

"I wanted to find out what they really knew about the Phantom—what they'd be willing to talk about, off the record. It took a while for them to open up. They weren't in a real friendly mood right after you left."

He cleared his throat.

"Sorry about that. And sorry about not driving you back to your car. I hope someone gave you a ride."

"Sergeant Lopez drove me back."

"The tall lonesome Indian?"

"He's a nice guy."

"Yeah? So what did you learn from him and that fat cop?"

"Nothing."

"Come on, Sam. They have to know *some*thing!"

"They do. They know what he does to his victims—the kind of horrible shit we saw last night. They know he wears a mask. They *think* they know how tall he is. They know he's right-handed, which really narrows it down. But they don't know *who* he is, or why he's killing people, or what he's going to do next—"

She stopped and looked at him.

"That's why they can't help you, Aaron."

"I was thinking about it more for my mom than myself."

"Aaron, they can't give her a twenty-four-hour security guard. They won't even do that for women who are being stalked by crazy ex-husbands or jealous boyfriends."

"So what do you suggest? I just sit here and wait for him to call in with another threat against her? Or you?"

"I warned you not to encourage him in the first place."

"Well, *thank* you, Dear Abby! Thanks for your fucking excellent advice! But since I'm already up to my ass in shit, what do you think I should do about it *right now?*"

"I think we should go find him by ourselves."

His mouth dropped open. He got up, then sat down again.
"Sam, are you on dangerous drugs, or what?"
"I'm serious. I think we should look for him on our own."
"*How?* You just said the LAPD can't even do that!"
"There's a reason he's calling you like this, Aaron."
"Yeah? And what's that?"
"He wants to be found."
Aaron started to laugh, then stopped.
"He wants to be found, Aaron—by you."
The phone rang.
Aaron jumped up from the couch. His chest rose and fell as he stared at the cordless phone, ringing on top of the counter that separated the living room from the kitchen.
Sam watched him from where she sat on the couch.
"He's called here before, hasn't he?"
He looked at her.
The phone continued to ring.
"You better answer it, Aaron."
He stared at the phone.
"Here," she said. "*I'll* answer it."
"Fuck if you will! Stay right there."
He snatched up the phone.
"Yeah?"
He heard only the static of an open line.
"Fuckin' crank caller—"
He put the phone back on the counter.
"He *has* called here before, hasn't he, Aaron?"
He looked up at her. "Yeah! He called last night! So fuckin' what? Want me to get his number? Call him back?"
"Don't you see now why the police can't help you?"
He walked over to the window and stared at the darkness that covered Hollywood like a shroud.
"This is why we have to find him ourselves."
"Just shut up for a minute, Sam, okay?"
"You won't make it go away by not talking about it."
He turned around. "*If* we find him, it'll be a *big* news story, right?

That's what this is really all about, isn't it? Getting you an anchor desk at On-Target, or maybe even your own afternoon talk show!"

She looked back at him from the couch.

"I never said I wouldn't report it—but it's more than just a news story for you, Aaron. We *have* to find him, before—"

"Before *what?*"

"Before he finds you."

13

LINEUP

"My mom's the one I'm worried about."

Aaron sat in a straight-backed chair, facing Lieutenant Montoya and Sergeant Lopez of the LAPD inside a small room with whitewashed walls and a closed door. Fluorescent lights buzzed overhead. Montoya sat with hands folded across his ample stomach. Lopez leaned forward in his chair, the predatory alertness of a jungle cat in his dark eyes.

"Of course," Montoya said.

"I was wondering if maybe you guys could, you know, provide some kind of protection for her?"

"That's not a service we offer, Mr. Scott."

"I don't mean a twenty-four-hour guard, or anything like that. I just wondered if you could maybe have someone keep an eye on her business and the apartment building where she lives? It's not that far from her deli."

"You need to contact a private security firm for something like that, Mr. Scott. We could give you a referral."

"Cool! You can *refer* me! But you can't protect my mother—not even when a serial killer threatens her *life!*"

"We try to be proactive in regard to crime, Mr. Scott. But there's a limit to what we can do. Especially—"

Montoya exchanged glances with Lopez.

"Especially when members of the general public are so—reluctant to get involved."

"Look, I'm *here*, okay? I *said* I'd help—"

"But we can't help you, not the way you want to be helped."

"Okay, fine. If you can't, you can't."

"Are you still willing to help us, given that?"

"Is there an echo in this place? Am I repeating myself? I said I'd help, so I'll help, okay? Want me to sign something to prove it?"

"No. But could you convince your station manager to let us install monitoring devices on your incoming phone lines?"

"So you can trace the Phantom when he calls me again?"

"Yes."

Aaron shrugged. "I don't know. Chuck's a little spooky about outsiders screwing with our equipment. I could *ask.*"

"Good. If we get the okay to monitor, we'll have to make sure that, when the Phantom calls in again—"

"Which may not be real soon. He didn't call this morning."

"Yes," Montoya said. "Now that he has your home number, there are other ways to contact you. But he *will* call the station again. You can count on that."

"How did he get my number anyway? It's unlisted."

"It's not difficult to do, if you know how."

"You mean there's *legal* ways to get it?"

"No," Montoya said, changing the subject. "When he calls in again, we'll need some time to trace him."

"How much?"

"Five minutes, at least. Ten to fifteen would be better."

"Want me to just keep him on the line? *Schmooze* with him?"

"Yes."

"You got it, man. I'll jerk him along."

He tried not to see the mouth with its red gum line grinning into the headlights, or hear the whispering voice.

I don't want to spoil the—purity of our conversations—

"But we need help from you now, Mr. Scott."

Aaron looked up, blinking to dispel the vision.

"We want you to look at some photographs of recent robbery and assault suspects, to see if any match those who accosted you three nights ago."

"When they stopped your car," Lopez said, "you were close to where that woman's body was found."

Aaron heard her screams again, cutting through the cold night air, and saw the three of them under the headlights: the fallen angel, with his bad teeth and long hair, Jabar sidling up to him, dragging his crippled leg, automatic gripped hard in one hand, and finally, the grinning, whispering mouth.

Man, I am *the mask!*

"Also," Montoya said, "we'd like you to look at a lineup."

"Wait a minute! *Live* suspects? Who can look back at *me?*"

"Don't worry," Lopez said. "You'll be standing behind a two-way mirror. They won't be able to see you."

Aaron felt Jabar's gun pressing into his throat again.

You don't tell 'em nothin' *about us, man!*

"I don't know about this—"

"Mr. Scott," Montoya said, "we wouldn't ask you to do it if we didn't think it was important."

"All *right!*" Aaron got up from his chair, feeling the whitewashed walls close in on him. "Let's fuckin' *do* it!"

"And this one—"

Aaron blinked at the Polaroid photograph under the glare of a hooded lamp. He had no idea how long they had been looking at these things, but he had a headache, and his eyes itched.

"No." He shook his head. "Never saw him before."

Lopez put another photograph in front of him.

"This one?"

"No."

"Or this one?"

"No."

"Or this—"

"No. Could I go take a leak?"

"We're almost finished," Lopez said, placing another Polaroid in front of him. "How about this one?"

Aaron sighed. "No."

"Or this one?"

"No. Not even close."

"And how about—this one."

Lopez snapped down the photograph like an ace of diamonds.

Jabar's dark face stared up at him from the grainy texture of the photograph, hostile and defiant.

Don't make me hurt you, man!

Aaron could see the bloodred whites of Jabar's eyes and the snub-nosed muzzle of the automatic, and hear the sound of his crippled foot as it scraped across the pavement.

He started to rise from the chair when he felt Lopez's hand on his shoulder in a steel-hard grip.

"Take your time. Look at it carefully."

Aaron swallowed and stared at the photograph.

"Is this one of them?" Lopez asked, his voice low.

He felt the automatic against his throat.

You don't tell 'em nothin' *about us, man!*

"Is he one of them?" Lopez repeated quietly.

Aaron nodded. "I—think so. Yeah. Yeah, that's him."

"Which one?"

"I'm—not sure."

"The one with the knife? The gun? The long hair?"

"Look, I'm not really sure."

"Were they all black?"

Aaron looked into Lopez's dark, faintly mocking eyes.

"Okay! He was the one with the fuckin' *gun*, all right?"

Lopez picked up the photograph and marked it with a pen.

"Sorry this took so long," Montoya said. "You can use the bathroom now, if you still need to."

"Are we finished?"

"With the photographs, yes. The lineup is next."

"You mean I have to go through this shit all over again?"

"No. The lineup shouldn't take as long."

"How do you know?"

"Because one of the suspects is the same man you just identified in that last photograph."

Aaron got up from the chair. "He's *here?* Now?"

"We have him in custody. We had good reason to suspect he might be one of the three. We thought you'd pick him."

"You *thought*— Then why the fuck didn't you just *show* it to me in the first place? Instead of saving it for last?"

"We had to be sure."

The lineup room had an elevated stage where the suspects were illuminated from below by glaring footlights.

Aaron sat behind a two-way mirror, shoulders slumped forward, watching as the suspects filed onto the stage.

"Turn to your right," commanded an officer below the stage, "then face straight into them lights."

His voice carried into the observation room through a small speaker in the ceiling. Aaron looked up at it.

"Can they hear us out there?" he asked.

"No," Lopez said.

"You sure about that?"

"Yes. It's a one-way speaker."

Aaron turned back to the suspects. He looked them over slowly, one by one, until he stopped at a pair of dark, angry eyes, the whites bloodred. They stared back into his own eyes as if they could see past the glare of the footlights, straight into the observation room.

"You sure they can't see us in here?"

"Yes," Lopez said. "Which one is he?"

You don't tell 'em nothin' *about us, man!*

"Him." Aaron pointed. "Third from the left."

"You sure about that?"

"Yeah. I'm sure."

"He's the one who held the gun on you that night?"

"Yeah! Yeah! How many times do I have to say it?"

"Would you be willing," Montoya asked, "to testify against him in a court of law?"

"Fuck, no! I identified him for you. Isn't that enough?"

"Did he threaten to kill you," Lopez asked, "if you identified him, or any of the others?"

Aaron's head snapped up. He turned toward Lopez.

"Who the fuck's the one that got arrested? Him or me?"

Lopez whispered something to Montoya, then left the room.

"What did they arrest him for?" Aaron asked.

"Rape," Montoya said, "and mayhem. The victim was a drag queen. He mutilated him with a straightedge razor."

Aaron watched as two uniformed officers took Jabar over to a metal chair, not far from the two-way mirror where Lopez stood waiting for him, cool and intense in a gray Armani suit, dark eyes taking in everything.

"We're going to question him," Montoya said. "He can't see you in here, or hear you. You're completely safe. But if you'd rather not watch—"

Without waiting for an answer, Montoya left the observation room, appearing moments later on the other side of the two-way mirror, near Lopez. Jabar sat on the metal chair, hands on his knees, bloodred eyes glancing from Lopez to Montoya, then over to the two-way mirror, fixing his gaze directly on Aaron, as if he knew he was in there.

Aaron felt a raw chill as he looked into those eyes.

He thought of leaving, and got up from his chair, turning toward the exit. He sat down again, unable to take his eyes off Jabar, as if staring at a caged animal that had threatened his life once, and could do so again—if ever he became uncaged.

Lopez repeated the facts of the assault on Aaron for Jabar, speaking in a terse, clipped manner.

"You pulled a gun on him," Lopez said.

"That a lie, man," Jabar muttered, looking away.

"You the only one of the three that had a gun?"

"I didn't have no fuckin' gun!"

"You plan to shoot him? Or just scare him a little?"

"I *said*—I didn't have no fuckin' *gun!*"

"We have a witness who says you did."

Jabar looked up at Lopez. "Then *he* a fuckin' lie, man!"

He turned and stared hard into the two-way mirror.

"Who your witness, huh? He sittin' back there behind that fuckin' mirror now? Like this some kinda freak show?"

"You used a razor on your boyfriend," Lopez said.

Jabar's head jerked up. "He wasn't no fuckin' *boy*friend!"

"Why did you use a gun two nights ago?"

"I told you, man! It wasn't *my* fuckin' gun!"

Lopez looked over at Montoya, who stepped forward, his wrinkled pastel shirt and cheap polyester tie in stark contrast to his partner's lean, intense Armani presence.

"Mr. Wilkins," he asked, "just who is it you work for?"

"I don't work for *no*body, man. Just myself."

He spoke with the same defiant contempt he had used on Lopez, but he sounded uneasy now, as if Montoya had somehow shifted things to more dangerous ground.

"Maybe I wasn't clear," Montoya said. "I didn't ask *if* you work for someone else. The answer to that is obvious—to you, and to me. We both know you're employed by someone. The only question is, who?"

"I *told* you, man! I don't work for *no*body—just me."

Montoya nodded thoughtfully.

"It wouldn't be the Phantom, would it?"

Fear entered Jabar's eyes, and Aaron felt a vindictive thrill at seeing him squirm.

Jabar laughed, but it came out wrong, with a hollow sound.

"You think I work for *him?* Man, you so fucked-up—"

"He wouldn't be very happy, would he," Montoya said, in his quietest tone of voice, "if he found out that you told us you worked for him. He might become—unpleasant."

"Man, *fuck* you! I tell you I don't *work* for him!"

"So," Montoya continued, as if unaware of Jabar's mounting terror, "it wouldn't be a good idea just to turn you back out on the street again—not if a rumor went along with you, that you told us everything you do for the Phantom."

Jabar sprang to his feet, head twisted to one side, right hand raised toward Montoya in a threatening gesture.

"You do that to me, man, and I swear by Allah—"

"Well," Montoya said, with a tired sigh, "that's just what we *will* do—unless you start cooperating."

Jabar lunged at Montoya, but Lopez stepped in front of him, hands raised, dark eyes hard and penetrating. Jabar, master of false intimidation, was smart enough to recognize the real thing when he saw it. He glared at Lopez, then sat back down.

"We want to know," Montoya said, speaking very quietly, "about his arrangement with you."

Jabar looked up at him, bloodred eyes hooded and dangerous.

"I tell you, man, and that devil with the white mask, he tear my fuckin' heart out and *eat* it! Then he kill you, too!" He glared with hatred at Lopez. "And you, too! And *you*—"

He turned to the two-way mirror with a basilisk glare.

"Sit there behind that fuckin' mirror, think you so fuckin' safe—Mr. *Wit*ness! Man, he kill you, too! But he save you for *last.* 'Cause he know who you *are!* Man, he *know!*"

14

SURVEILLANCE

"Sunset Scott?"

"Yeah, babe. Who's this?"

"Serena from Montebello."

"Yo, Serena, baby! What's up?"

"You still, like, do song requests? Or just Phantom stuff?"

Aaron laughed.

"Feels that way sometimes, huh? This show's become the Phantom's home away from home—even though that limp dickhead hasn't called in for two days now! But hell yes, we still play the hits! We're KRAS FM, everybody! 108.5. The jumpin' powerhouse of L.A. rock! What you want to hear, babe?"

"The Corpse Eaters. 'Devour My Love.' "

"Serena, baby! You must be psychic! That's the *first* of our very next set of stopless hits! Is that too hot, or what?"

"That's hot."

"You bet your booty, it's hot! Red-hot! Twenty minutes of the hottest hits, commercial free! Startin' with those bad ol' Corpse Eaters, chompin' right into your heart. KRAS."

He switched from BROADCAST to CUE, then shoved in a twenty-minute tape.

"We got more calls on hold here," Bill Waller said, coming into his headphones over CUE. "What do I do with 'em, Aaron?"

"Lose the fuckheads."

"Just dump 'em?"

"Yeah, Bill. Just flush 'em down the fuckin' toilet. Then get your ass over here. I need someone to watch the board for me while I go talk to Chuck and Jerry."

"But what if the Phantom—"

"He won't. Fuckin' pussy's wimped out on us, man."

Aaron knew why the masked freak wasn't calling—because of his visit to the cops—but no use telling Bill about that.

"But what if—"

"Just *do* it, Bill, okay? Get the fuck over here."

Aaron walked out into the hallway where Jerry stood in deep consultation with Charles J. Davis, Jr., general manager.

Chuck Davis was a tall, imposing African American with the aloof air of a Wall Street CEO. He dressed in custom-made suits imported from a tailor on Savile Row, rarely softening that image for the looser, wilder world of rock radio broadcasting. How he had ever gotten into the business in the first place was a mystery to all who knew him.

Farther down the hallway stood Sergeant Tom Kelso, telecommunications specialist with the LAPD, the man who had come to put in the equipment for wiretapping the phone lines.

"I'm not sure about this, Aaron," Chuck said.

"I'm not sure, either," Jerry added, "especially about its possible effect on the ratings."

"Yes," Chuck agreed, nodding. "Our listener share for the morning show has been good this week."

"Very good," Jerry said.

"We don't want to risk jeopardizing that, Aaron."

"This doesn't have a damn thing to do with ratings, Chuck."

"How do you know?" Jerry demanded.

"Because it only affects the *phone* lines, man. It won't cut into the broadcast. It just lets the cops trace the call, and find out where it's comin' from. That right?"

This last comment was directed at Kelso down the hallway.

"Correct," he said. "The surveillance equipment won't have any effect on broadcast sound quality. No static or background noise. You won't even know it's there."

"What about the Phantom?" Jerry asked. "Will *he* know?"

"Not unless Sunset Scott here decides to let him in on it."

Aaron turned to Kelso.

"When Montoya told me about this yesterday, he said I should keep him on the line for at least five minutes, but more would be better. How far do *you* want me jerkin' him out?"

"That's hard to say. All depends where the call—"

"Wait a minute," Jerry interrupted. "I think we're jumping the gun. We don't even have a green light on this thing yet. Right, Chuck?"

The general manager frowned.

"There *are* some First Amendment problems."

"Chuck!" Aaron said. "What's with this First Amendment shit? They won't control what we *say* over the air! They just want to find out where the hell he's *callin'* from!"

He turned to Kelso again. "Right?"

"Correct."

"I understand that, Aaron," Chuck said. "But I still don't like the idea of *inviting* the LAPD to wiretap us. There's the First Amendment problem, and then the privacy problem. Maybe I'd feel differently if they had a subpoena—"

"Can you come up with one?" Aaron asked Kelso.

"There's no real probable cause."

"No *cause?* What the fuck kind of cause do you *want?*"

"It's a legal term. Probable cause. We can't actually prove that it's the Phantom making these calls."

"You think he's *not?*"

"We wouldn't be interested in tracing him if we thought that. But we can't prove it. And we'd have to be able to do that if we wanted to get a subpoena forcing Mr. Davis here to install the surveillance equipment. With a situation like this, the ball's entirely in your court."

"Maybe we should sleep on it," Jerry said. "It's not like we have to make a call on this today, or even tomorrow."

"Yes," Chuck nodded, "maybe we should do that."

Aaron looked hard at both of them, especially Jerry.

"You guys even *want* this asshole caught? Or would you rather see him stay loose? So he can kill some more people and send our fuckin' listener share right through the roof?"

"Aaron," Jerry said, "we all want to see him caught."

"Yeah, Jerr? Just not too soon, huh?"

"We're not even talking about that right now."

"You bet your ass we are! Hell, *I'm* lettin' 'em put this wiretap shit on *my* home phones. Know why? 'Cause he's callin' me there, and I want it fuckin' *stopped!*"

Chuck and Jerry exchanged glances that made it clear this was the first either of them had heard about calls at home.

"What are you guys waitin' for? Until he calls one of *you?* Or comes down here to the station? How long before it's more than just another goddamn ratings game?"

"Look, Aaron," Jerry said, "I know you're still upset about what happened yesterday, about that thing with your mom—"

"Leave her *outta* this, okay?"

"Maybe," Chuck said, clearing his throat, "if it involves security, we might be better off going ahead with it for now."

Jerry closed his eyes.

"It's not as if we can't change our minds at some later date, if we decide to." Davis turned to Kelso. "Right?"

"Correct. We put in the equipment. You decide you don't like it, all you do is tell us to take it out, and it's out."

"How long will the complete installation require?"

"About two hours."

"And it won't affect the broadcast?"

"Sound quality, not at all. I *will* have to tie up your incoming lines for about fifteen minutes at one point."

"What if the Phantom decides to call in then?" Jerry asked.

"Man," Aaron said, "this is the second day in a row that putz hasn't called! We can't take him now, not during the twenty-minute set. After that, there's only a few minutes left before wrap-up. You think he'll call *then?*"

"What if he does?"

"He'll call back. He's a sound bite pig."

Jerry shook his head.

"Chuck, it's your station and they're your ratings—"

"And it's my decision. I've just made it." He nodded to Kelso. "Proceed with the installation."

"Yes, sir."

After Chuck excused himself to return to a budget meeting, Aaron grabbed Jerry's arm.

"Hey, man! *Número uno* scores again!"

"Go ahead and gloat, Aaron. You always get your way."

"Hey, Jerr! I'll make it up to you. When this set ends, I'll say somethin' *guaranteed* to make him call back tomorrow."

"Like what?"

"Just listen."

As the last song died down, Aaron broke in over the fade.

"You got it! The Dead Fetuses and 'Afterbirth of Love'! Windin' up twenty stopless minutes of the hottest hits anywhere in L.A.! Here on KRAS FM, 108.5. Sunset Scott in the Mornin', all mornin' long. But we're almost ready to shut it down now and call it a day. Alonzo Gore just stepped into the broadcast booth here at KRAS, ready to shred yo' *mind* for the next five hours with Alonzo at High Noon. Yo, Alonzo! What's up, man?"

Alonzo Gore, wearing a head of wild hair, looked over from some carts he was sorting through.

"Your listener share's up, thanks to the masked man."

"You know it, baby! KRAS, 108.5, the only place where you can hear the Man with the Mask go one-on-one with the Man with the Mouth, Sunset Scott in the Mornin', every mornin'—except, hey!

That dickhead didn't even call in today, or yesterday. Lovely Lisa! Did he call in while I was out takin' a dump during that last commercial-free set?"

Glaring at him for a toss this late in the show, Lisa flipped on her mike. "Not that I know of, Sunset Scott."

"Bud the Stud?"

"Not unless he left it on my voice mail. I better check."

"Well, I'll be damned! No calls on hold now, either."

Aaron glanced at the video monitor next to the console, which flashed a TEMPORARY SERVICE INTERRUPTION message, caused by Kelso's installation of the surveillance devices.

He leaned into the microphone, getting close.

"Yo, Phantom?" He started off soft, his voice gliding over the mike head. "The Masked One. O Mysterious Mr. X! You listenin', man? 'Cause I want you to pay real close attention now. I want to tell you straight up what I think about you, for not callin' in here to KRAS for the last two days, okay?"

Aaron paused, deliberately creating expensive dead air.

Then he screamed into the mike, lips almost touching it.

"COWARD!"

The needle on the VU meter shot over into the red, bouncing against the right-hand side of the scale.

"Scum-suckin' *coward!* You don't have the *balls* to call in to this radio station again! You know why? 'Cause if somebody comes back at you—just once—all you do is *fold!* Just like the limp dickhead you really are! Kiss my ass, Phantom! Nobody's afraid of you! You said you'd stop by here and pay us a visit, right? So let's *do* it, man! Or if you're too scared, just tell me where you want to meet, and let's just *do* it! But let's quit screwin' around, okay? Let's get it *on!* The Clash of the Drive-Time Titans! Sunset Scott versus The Phantom! *Mano a mano,* for the World Heavyweight Nasty Mouth Title! Yo!"

Aaron paused, and took a deep, exaggerated breath.

"But you know what, everybody? It ain't never gonna happen. You know *why?* 'Cause the Phantom's yellow! Yellower than ever, since he just peed all over himself in fear. He'd call in right now, but he can't talk with all that spit dribblin' down his chin. We got to face it, everybody! The Man with the Mask just can't handle the Man with the Mouth!"

Aaron signed off, then slipped a station promo tape into the cart machine and pressed PLAY. As he got up to vacate his seat for Alonzo Gore, he glanced at Bill Waller, staring back at him from the glassed-in booth across the way, mouth wide-open.

"Man," Alonzo said, "you just tore the dude a new asshole."

"Just a wake-up call. He's startin' to slip away on us."

"Whatever." Alonzo adjusted his headphones. "If he calls in when *I'm* on the board, I'm hangin' the fuck up."

15

AFTERIMAGE

A knock sounded on the closed door and Montoya stepped into the small room where Lopez sat working. The heavier man's cheap polyester shirt looked cheaper and more wrinkled than usual, and his weariness showed in the way he moved. But the slight flicker of a tired smile on his face told Lopez, who rarely smiled, that something had gone well.

Lopez shut off the tape.

"That *pendejo* Jabar Wilkins open up yet?" he asked Montoya.

"Yes."

"Say anything worth listening to?"

"Maybe."

"Talk about working for the Phantom?"

"No. He still won't admit to that."

"But you think he works for him?"

"In some minor but important way, yes."

"He give you anything to ID the Phantom with?"

"You never can tell. What have you got there?"

"Some new shit from Kelso. A series of calls to the radio station, spaced ten minutes apart, starting exactly ten minutes after Scott's come-on at the end of his broadcast this morning."

"What happened when they picked up the calls?"

"Silence, then a disconnect, then a dial tone."

"Every time they picked up?"

Lopez nodded. *"Cada vez."*

"But the calls kept coming in, ten minutes apart?"

"Like clockwork."

"Interesting."

Montoya took two pieces of cellophane-wrapped hard candy out of his pocket and offered one to Lopez, who turned it down with a quick shake of his head. Montoya kept one piece for himself and put the other back in his pocket.

"Of course," he said, unwrapping the candy, "whoever it was didn't stay on the line long enough to let Kelso trace him?"

"No, but he called enough times that Kelso could pin down a general location—the main switchboard of a resident hotel."

Montoya dropped the piece of hard candy into an ashtray on Lopez's desk, where it rolled around like a pinball.

"He was calling from a hotel?"

"Yeah. Some flophouse on Franklin."

"You wouldn't happen to have the address?"

"Yeah. Kelso couldn't nail the exact number, but he got the hotel address through the switchboard. Lucky for us, huh?"

Lopez picked up a piece of paper and handed it to Montoya, who took it from him and studied it carefully.

"Very lucky . . ."

"Qué pasó, Ralph? You got a funny look on your face."

"I do?"

"Yeah. What did that asshole tell you?"

Montoya did not answer right away. He stared at the paper with the hotel's address for several seconds.

"He told me something that might prove—useful."

"What?"

Montoya took out the other piece of candy and unwrapped it, cellophane crackling as he crumpled it into a ball.

"He gave me an address."

"No shit! *His* address?"

"He wouldn't say. He referred to it as 'our place.' "

"His and the Phantom's place?"

"Possibly. He wouldn't say."

"He could always be lying about it."

"Yes, he could be."

"And if he is, what good does a fake address—"

"It's the same one Kelso got for the hotel on Franklin."

Montoya laid down another piece of paper on the desk in front of Lopez, who leaned forward, snatching it up.

"Son of a bitch! We got ourselves a fuckin' *match!*"

"Yes," Montoya said, "it seems that way."

The Hotel Comadre, a six-story building with salmon-colored stucco exterior, sat at the intersection of narrow Franklin Avenue and a larger, busier street. It was the residence of choice for drifters, drag queen hookers, small-time crack dealers, and other hard types who attracted the occasional attention of LAPD patrol officers. The desk man was new. In a place like the Comadre, they always were.

"You got someone who looks like this?"

Lopez showed him a computer-generated sketch, a full-face view of the assailant with the shaved head and dyed red forelock, based on Aaron's description. The desk man, his own dark hair cropped close to the skull, a scruffy goatee smudging his chin, glanced at the sketch, then shook his head.

"Things change fast around here, man. Know what I mean?"

"You'd remember this guy," Lopez said.

"Like, maybe I'm not sure, okay?"

"We want you to be real sure. Take your time."

"Look— You guys got a warrant or somethin' like that?"

"We don't need one. We're not ready to arrest anybody."

"I mean, it's not like they pay me to remember all the assholes who check in and out of this place."

"We don't want to hear about all of them. Just this one."

"I *said* I'm not sure, okay?"

The desk man pushed the sketch away from him.

"What's your name?" Lopez asked.

"I have to tell you that?"

"You don't have to tell us anything—yet."

"Scally, okay? Ned Scally. You happy now?"

"Ned." Lopez picked up the sketch. "Why won't you tell us whether the guy lives here or not? A simple yes or no. That's all we're looking for."

"I *told* you I don't—"

"You haven't told us why. That part's starting to bother me. Makes me wonder if maybe you're mixed up in this, somehow."

"Man, I ain't mixed up with *no*body's shit, okay?"

"Sure, Ned. But I wonder— Why cover for him?"

"Hey, look! I don't cover for *no*body, okay? You two guys think you can just walk in here—"

"All we want," Montoya interrupted, speaking slowly, in a quiet, nonthreatening voice, "is to go up there, knock on his door, and talk to him. Nothing more than that. All we want you to do is tell us which door to knock on."

Scally stroked his goatee and studied the sketch.

"We know you're busy," Montoya continued. "That's why we don't want to waste your time, standing here, talking. But we've already wasted *our* time, driving over here. We want to talk to *some*one. You understand that, don't you?"

Scally looked up slowly, light from a naked overhead bulb reflecting off his rimless lenses.

"If I tell you, then you go up there and tell *him?*"

"No. We just talk to him. Then we leave."

"I don't want *nothin'* to do with this asshole, man."

"We understand."

"I don't want *none* of this shit comin' back on me!"

"That can be arranged. Which room is he in?"

"I don't want him findin' out I told you, then comin' down here, lookin' for me. That's one fuckin' scary dude up there!"

"Which room is he in, Ned?"

Scally hesitated, like a man who wanted to make a confession—wanted it badly, needed it—but feared the sound of the words coming out of his own mouth. He turned away from the detectives, his face cast into obscure shadows and half-lights by the angle of the overhead bulb.

He gave them the room number.

By the time they reached the sixth floor, Montoya was wheezing as he tried to catch his breath. Lopez, on the other hand, seemed entirely unaffected by the climb.

Only two bare bulbs glimmered from the ceiling fixtures of the sixth-floor corridor. The shadows seemed darker, deeper than those on the lower floors, as if they contained a third dimension that was as much a part of the physical reality as the torn wallpaper or the stained carpet, or the scarred wooden doors.

They walked down the hall, into the shadows, aware now of traffic noises rising from the intersection six stories below.

A thick red line had been scrawled along one wall, sharp and jagged, hooked with spikes and dips, like an enlarged electrocardiogram of a tachycardia episode.

The line came to a stop near a battered wooden door with the number Scally had given them. Single words, possibly names, written in spidery, illegible capital letters, had been cut deep into the dark surface of the wood.

"Calling cards," Lopez muttered.

Montoya nodded, and stepped to one side of the door.

Lopez did the same, drawing a nine-millimeter Beretta from the shoulder holster inside his jacket.

He reached across the scarred wood to knock on it.

The knocks resounded inside the room. But Lopez could hear no response—no footsteps creaking across the floor, no hand drawing back a chain lock or turning a doorknob.

He knocked again and called out, "Police! Open the door."

Again, no response.

"Break in?" Lopez whispered to Montoya.

"Yes, but don't overdo it, Frank."

Lopez had been called before more than one LAPD review board for excessive force in suspect arrests.

"And watch yourself," Montoya added. "The lights are out."

Lopez took out a thin black flashlight and turned it on.

Then he rushed the door, hitting it with his left shoulder. The wood, old but solid, shuddered for a moment before the dead bolt tore loose with a loud, cracking sound and the door gave way. Lopez stumbled into the darkness, hurled forward by his own momentum, overturning a chair with a startling crash.

He whipped the narrow beam of his flashlight toward the chair, aware now of the anxious sound of his own breathing.

Montoya searched along the edge of one wall for a switch.

A naked bulb came on overhead, in the ceiling's center, casting weak light about the room. Aside from the chair that Lopez had hit, the room contained hardly any furniture. A worn-out writing desk, the relic of a long-forgotten yard sale, stood back against the far wall. Two unattached stereo speakers, one with a front grille kicked in, sat on the hardwood floor. A stained mattress sprawled diagonally across a corner.

The room stank of rotted food and desiccated excrement, human or animal, possibly both. The sash of one window, high and narrow, had been pushed up partway, letting in the cool, polluted night air, along with the sounds of Hollywood street life after dark.

Lopez put away his flashlight and walked over to the desk. On the wall above it, someone had thumbtacked a collection of Polaroid snapshots. Several displayed different views of the building that contained the KRAS studios. One was a long shot of Aaron's condominium building. Another showed the body of a recent Phantom victim, the woman who had been killed near the side street where the three punks had stopped Aaron's car.

Lopez let out a sharp breath.

"We need to get crime lab over here," he said.

"Yes," Montoya agreed. "They have work to do."

Lopez noticed a black Touch-Tone telephone near the back of the writing desk. He reached for it.

"No," Montoya said. "We want them to look for prints."

"That's the phone he used to make those calls today."

"Probably."

"That asshole won't leave any prints for us, Ralph."

"Maybe not. But let's let crime lab look first, okay?"

Lopez took out a pen and notepad and copied down the phone number. Montoya looked over the rest of the room.

"Interesting," he said.

"What?"

"That."

Montoya nodded to a gathering of articles cut from trade newspapers and magazines, thumbtacked to the opposite wall—all dealing with Aaron Scott or some aspect of his career. Below the articles, just above the baseboard, someone had used the same red paint that defaced the outside corridor to write a large, two-word message across the bottom of the wall.

JUDGEMENT DAY

The letters were bold and slightly sprawling, with *judgment* spelled the British way—the way Ben Jonson spelled it in his eulogy on Shakespeare—with an *e* after the *g*.

Halfway between the message and the articles, someone had tacked a map of Los Angeles to the wall, with the Hollywood area highlighted in pale yellow marker. Red Xs had been made at various points on the map, one of them near the street where Aaron had been attacked four nights ago.

Lopez walked over to the wall and stared at the message, the map, then the articles.

"*This* is where he's been keeping himself for the past few days, making those fucking calls."

"Possibly," Montoya said.

"Possibly? Shit. He was *here*, Ralph. You can *feel* it."

Like the faint afterimage of something that had been inside a place long enough to leave its own mark, the sense of the room as a psychic repository of some kind was so strong that it would not have surprised either man to turn back to the desk and see him sitting there, receiver to one ear, head shaved bald, except for the bright red forelock.

"We just missed him," Lopez said, turning to his partner.

"Yes," Montoya agreed, "but not the physical evidence."

"Fuck it. I don't want evidence. I want his ass nailed to the backseat of a cruiser."

"You might want to take a look at that."

Montoya pointed to the sill of the open window.

"What is it?"

They found a self-adhesive yellow note that had been marked with a blue felt tip pen. Lopez bent down to read the message, written in almost-perfect, carefully formed cursive letters.

Are you here to render judgement? Or be judged?

Lopez frowned. "What the fuck does *that* mean?"

The bullet broke the glass with a hard, chipping sound, like an insect clawing its way out of an ossified chrysalis. A star-burst pattern radiated across the glass, crackling softly. The pane fell from the sash in slow motion—small slivers, long, jagged shards.

A gunshot sounded, floating up from somewhere down on the street below, almost like an afterthought.

Lopez pushed Montoya out of the way, dropping to one knee. He shoved the barrel of the Beretta through the shards of glass and fired twice, in quick succession. The reports echoed out over the late-night streets of Hollywood, cutting through the drone of traffic.

The gun down below fired back. More glass shattered from the window, falling into Lopez's hair and down the back of his Armani jacket. The bullet had come closer this time, but Lopez had been waiting for it, and saw the flash from the weapon's muzzle, inside the shadows between two apartment buildings across the street.

He locked on that spot and fired four in a row.

"Francisco!" Montoya called out to him. "*Basta!*"

A third shot came back from below, a wild one. Lopez could hear it hit the Comadre's thick stucco exterior.

A dark figure, shapeless in shadows, dropped back into the tight passageway between the two apartment buildings. Lopez fired three more shots.

The room stank of cordite. Tendrils of smoke curled from the Beretta's muzzle. Lopez stood up, away from the open window, broken glass crackling underfoot. An old-fashioned neon sign glowed in a liquor store window on the other side of the intersection, six stories down. Cars had pulled over at the sound of gunshots. Drivers got out and looked up at the top floor of the Comadre. Lights came on in apartment building windows across the way.

Lopez shoved the Beretta back into its shoulder holster.

"If the *pendejo* hadn't run, I would've *got* him!"

"A few shots too many, Frank," Montoya said.

"We were set *up!*" He gestured angrily at the photos on the wall, the red letter sign. "We were fuckin' set up!"

"Yes," Montoya said, "it seems that way."

16

BLOOD

As they passed the Jacuzzi, on their way across the enclosed courtyard to Sam's Studio City apartment, steam clouds rolled off the surface of the bright, still water.

"How hot do they keep this fucking thing?" Aaron asked.

"About a hundred, I guess."

"Want to hop in and switch it on?"

"You didn't bring a swimsuit with you, Aaron."

"Fuck that. Who needs one?"

"Hey, I *live* here! I have to see these people every day!"

"Well, excu-u-u-u-se me, Miss Modesty!"

"I'm just not into exhibitionism, okay?"

"Not even inside, where you're only exhibiting for me?"

"Inside's different."

He kissed her hard, arching her back out over the water.

"Aaron, stop it! You're drunk."

"We're *both* drunk."

Something dark brushed against Samantha's leg and she drew back with a startled cry, then smiled. She stretched out her arms toward a small, dark shape crouched near the water's edge.

"Aaron, look! Isn't he sweet?"

A black kitten, halfway to cathood, stepped up to her leg and began to rub his head against it, purring loudly.

"The son of the Black Cat," Aaron said.

"He's so sweet! Yes you are, aren't you?"

She leaned over and stroked his dark fur.

"Aaron, you like cats, don't you?"

"Not enough to adopt one, no."

"Aw, come on! I'd take him myself, but they don't allow pets at this complex."

"They don't allow them where I live either."

"Bullshit! You live in a condo."

"*I'm* the one who doesn't allow them."

"But he's such a sweet little guy! Aren't you?"

"Let's go, Sam. The longer you wait, the harder it'll be. Just say good-bye to him, then get on with your life."

"I wonder if anyone's fed him, Aaron?"

"Someone's always feeding stray cats."

"But what if nobody has?"

"Then *I'll* feed the little fish-eating bastard—later."

"Is that a promise?"

"Come *on*, Sam! Before we get too sober for sex."

The minute they got into bed, he thrust inside her. She gasped and arched her back, head turned sideways, eyes closed. Aaron pumped away at her like a madman. The wine, the steam from the spa—everything seemed to rush to his head, driving him into a wild, Dionysian frenzy.

Sam began to groan in time with his thrusting.

They had been going at it for a while when she cried out.

"Shit!"

"What's a matter?" he mumbled, still deep into it.

"God*damn* it! My fucking *period* just started!"

He glanced down to see himself pumping rhythmically in and out of her, shaft slick with dark red blood.

"Don't sweat it, babe," he whispered. "It's cool."

"Hurry up and come, Aaron! Or just get out!"

"What's the rush? It's a turn-on."

"Not for *me!* Get *out!*"

"Sam, what's wrong—"

"It reminds me of those cut-up body parts I had to look at! It reminds me of the Phantom!"

Afterward, after they changed the sheets and took a shower, Sam sat on the bed wearing fresh panties, a tampon, and a white T-shirt. Aaron stretched out beside her, naked, head propped up on one arm.

"At least you could take off the shirt," he said, "so I could get a better view."

"We're not doing it again tonight, Aaron."

"You never know. If you took off—"

"No!"

"Or maybe if you changed into one of your fancy broadcast news suits? I've always had this crazy fantasy about humping you while you were wearing one of those."

"Aaron, grow up."

He grinned at her. "How you like that hot sex, eh?"

"It was okay."

"O*kay?* It was great!"

He sat up and lifted her shirt, exposing erect nipples.

"Aaron—"

"Just looking."

"Put down my shirt—"

He began to pull on her nipples, stretching them.

"I do *not* want to have sex again, Aaron! If you get me turned on, I am going to be so pissed—"

"You're beautiful when you're pissed."

The phone rang, a shrill electronic flutter.

"I need to answer that, Aaron. Let *go!*"

He released his grip and she hopped off the bed.

"Where are my blue shorts?"

"You don't need shorts to answer the phone, Sam."

"If it's someone from the studio, I could be on for hours! I don't want to stain a chair with this— They were *here* just a few minutes ago! Where the fuck *are* they?"

The phone continued to ring.

"*There* they are!" She picked them up from a far corner of the room. "Who put them there?"

"Don't look at me. This is your place."

She stumbled as she pulled on her shorts, phone still ringing in the background.

"You're sexy when you get dressed too fast. Especially with your shirt pulled up over your boobs like that—"

"You could answer the phone! Instead of just *lying* there!"

"It's probably that bitch from On-Target, Bonnie Redfield, or some other pain in the ass. Let the machine get it."

As if on cue, Sam's machine caught the call.

Its greeting message echoed through the apartment.

"—not here right now. But if you leave a message, I'll get back to you as soon as possible. Bye!"

She ran for it, tugging at the zipper to her shorts.

A long beep was followed by a voice—one that whispered.

Sam stopped, hand above the receiver.

"I know you're there, Sunset Scott."

In the other room, Aaron leaped out of bed.

"I wonder why you're not picking up the phone. I heard you talk about cowards the other day, on the radio—"

He came out into the living room, still naked, and walked over to the phone.

"But we know who the real coward is, don't we? It's so easy to be brave in daylight, with no one else on the line—"

Sam reached out to disconnect the call.

"Don't!" Aaron ordered her.

"—when you're talking only to the air, and yourself—"

He grabbed the receiver.

"Listen, asshole—"

"Why, Sunset Scott! You worked up enough courage to *answer* the phone. I'm surprised. I'm very surprised."

"Why don't you go fuck yourself?"

The voice laughed—a harsh, contemptuous sound that forced Aaron to hold the receiver back from his ear.

"How childish of you, Sunset Scott. Do you really hope to drive me away with playground insults? You called me a coward on the air the other day. You dared me to call in. I did. But you weren't even listening. Only your friends the police were listening, trying to trace my calls—"

Aaron clutched the receiver. How the hell did *he* know about the wiretap? That black punk, whatever the fuck his name was, the one behind the two-way mirror— He couldn't have told him. The police still had that son of a bitch in custody. Didn't they?

"Jesus—" he breathed.

"Ah, good! First the curses, then the prayers. You're a frightened man, aren't you, Sunset Scott? You're frightened because you're alone now, on your own, without the help of your lackeys at the radio station or your friends the police."

"How did you get this number, fuckhead?"

"Your friends the police aren't the only ones who can play games with the phone lines. Wherever you go, Sunset Scott, I know where you are."

"You don't know shit." He started to hang up.

"Don't leave just yet, Sunset Scott. I don't think you understand. I know where you *are*, right now. You feel secure because you think I'm just a voice on the phone, but you're wrong. Open the front door and take a look at that whirlpool spa in the center of the courtyard. You should be able to see it easily from where you are."

"What do you mean?"

"Just open the door, Sunset Scott. You'll see."

He looked over at the front door, framed by potted plants.

"Unless you're afraid," the voice continued. "Unless you're afraid to step outside that door and face reality, because all your life you've lived with illusions—"

"Shut the fuck up."

He walked over to the door and unlocked the dead bolt.

"Aaron," Sam whispered, "what is it?"

He opened the door, leaning out just far enough to see down to the Jacuzzi.

Someone had turned on the whirlpool. The swirling waters of the spa, lighted from beneath by submerged floodlights, were cloudy with blood. Severed limbs and slashed entrails and bits of black fur bobbed on the surface of the foaming water, making it look, at that distance, like something in a witch's cauldron.

He closed the door and locked the dead bolt carefully.

"Aaron! What *is* it?"

He walked back to the desk and picked up the receiver, breathing hard into the mouthpiece.

"Did you like my surprise, Sunset Scott? Think of it as a gift from me, to you—and your girlfriend. You were down there not too long ago. It could have been either one of you, or both. Instead, it's just some homeless animal, a small sacrifice to your arrogance and carelessness."

"You twisted piece of shit—"

"Your fear is beginning to bore me, Sunset Scott. It always comes out the same way: cheap, little-boy toughness—"

A sudden gasp made Aaron look up.

Sam stood in front of the open front door, looking down at the spa, hands to her mouth.

"*Close* it!" he screamed at her. "And *lock* it!"

"Yes, Sunset Scott. Tell her to lock all the doors, and all the windows, and draw all the curtains tight. You never know who might be outside, watching, even as we talk."

He felt the receiver on his chin, slick with his own sweat.

"Where are you calling from?" he asked.

"I thought your friends the police were working on that. Ask them. Later. Right now, I want you to listen to me. I can find you, wherever you go. If I can't call you at the radio station, I can call you here, or at your home, or at your mother's home. If I can't call you, I can still talk to you, face-to-face. Are you listening to me, Sunset Scott?"

"I'm here."

The line went dead—silence, followed by the hollow buzzing of a dial tone. Aaron looked up at Sam, standing in front of the closed and locked door, her face pale.

"Still want to go out and find him, Sam?"

She gave a small cry and turned away.

The phone rang again.

Aaron jumped back from it.

It rang four more times before he could pick it up.

"Yeah?"

Samantha could hear the voice on the other end, but not the words. She saw Aaron's face retreating into shock.

"Was it him again, Aaron?"

"It's the cops, down at KRAS."

"*What?*"

"The Phantom finally paid his visit."

17

IN-STUDIO

It's on *fire!* It's burnin' *u-u-u-u-u-u-u-u-p-p!*"

Lance Trebizond screamed into the microphone, in the style for which he had become famous as Nightman.

"That was the Arson Squad with 'Hearts on Fire!' Burnin' through the night like a canyon blaze in a Santa Ana wind! And you're hangin' with Nightman, King of the Nighttime, here at KRAS FM, 108.5. Home of the hard, the radical, the mindless—"

He pressed PLAY on the reel-to-reel and a prerecorded phone conversation began to broadcast over the air, sounding exactly like the real, live thing.

"Yo, dude! You're hangin' with the Nightman!"

"Nightman?"

"What's up, dude?"

"I want to, like, do a request—"

"Yeah? Well, like, what you got in mind?"

Much of the show was prerecorded this way. While the songs were playing, Lance would take call-ins, joke around with the callers, try to get something usable, then edit the tape, cutting out the boring crap and the taboo words.

"—sing the jingle for us."

"Huh?"

"The *jingle*, dude! You know—108.5, KRAS FM!"

"Aw, man. I can't sing!"

"You want the concert tickets? You sing!"

"108.5—"

"Hold on, dude! You gotta take a *big* mouthful of water, or soda, and *then* you sing!"

As the caller gargled his way through the jingle, Lance lighted a cigarette and looked out the window at the lights of Hollywood, glittering like a mirage in the dark night sky. It was hard work, doing a night shift like this, with all the call-ins, always talking with some stoned kid, splicing the tape and rewinding it, rocking it by hand to cue it up.

As the prerecorded caller hung up, Lance started a new song, then punched another button, picking up a new, live caller.

He switched the reel-to-reel from PLAY to RECORD.

"You're hangin' with the King of the Night!"

"Ooo, Nightman!" squealed a young girl, about fifteen.

"Yo, baby! What's up?"

"We think you're so—"

Screams and giggles burst from other voices near the phone.

"Yeah, babe?"

"We think you're so—cool!"

"And you don't even know what I *look* like, baby!"

"Oh, God—"

"You want to find out?"

"Oh, *God!*"

"Well, to start with, I got this long, shoulder-length hair, and this killer face, and this hunk's body—"

The first part, about the hair, was true.

"—and this tattoo that goes all the way down to my—"

* * *

Downstairs, in the lobby of the KRAS building, Ernie Soto, a uniformed security guard in his early twenties, sat at a console in front of the main entrance, trying to talk his girlfriend out of breaking their date for tomorrow night.

He failed to notice the image, tall and dark, that appeared suddenly on the multiple video screens of his security monitor.

The intruder made his way over to a bank of elevators lining the west wall and pressed the UP button.

Soto noticed him then on the monitor—a tall figure, clothed in black, leaning forward, hand on the button.

He turned in his swivel chair.

"Shit! No, not you— Look, I gotta hang up. I'll call you right— What you mean you won't be there? Fuck! I got me a fuckin' problem here. Call you *back*, okay?"

He slammed down the receiver and got up from his chair, unclipping the cellular phone on his belt with one hand, feeling for his holstered nine-millimeter Browning automatic with the other. As he walked toward the elevators, he punched the button that automatically dialed the security company he worked for.

"Dispatch," answered a woman's voice.

"This is Soto at Sunset. I think I'm gonna need backup."

"You looking at a confrontation?"

"I got an asshole that sneaked in here somehow."

"Have you approached him yet?"

"I'm about to. But he looks big. I need backup, okay?"

"We're short on backup tonight—"

"Cool! Totally cool."

"But keep me on line as you approach him."

"Whatever."

He looked even bigger close up, back turned to Soto as he waited for the elevator. Broad shoulders filled out a black leather jacket. A large, dark hat covered his head and neck. He wore black gloves. Probably a wanna-be rocker with an appointment at one of the recording studios upstairs, but he had to follow the rules, just like anyone else.

"Hey, my friend! You got to sign in at the front desk before you go upstairs. That's the rules."

The guy did not move.

Soto slowed down. This guy was standing still, very still, but different from the way you saw most guys stand in front of an elevator, with their slump-shouldered, fucked-over, end-of-the-day exhausted look. This guy stood tall and still, like a wrestler, or a fucking dancer.

Soto could hear the open line to dispatch crackling on the phone in his hand, and outside, the shouts and laughter of drunks leaving the bar at the back of the building.

"Hey, my friend! You got trouble hearing?"

Soto reached out and grabbed hold of the guy's shoulder.

There was no muscular response, no sudden jerking away of the arm. It was like touching something dead, hard, unyielding beneath the black leather.

A chime sounded above one of the elevators.

The intruder turned suddenly, so fast Soto felt the breeze from the movement.

The guy had no face—or a blank spot where a face should be, as if someone had rubbed out a face from a drawing with a dirty eraser and left a blurred white image in its place.

Soto began to understand, but it was too late.

He fumbled for the holstered gun as he raised the cellular phone to his mouth. A black-gloved hand smashed the side of his head, knocking him into the open elevator car. Sharp pain cut through his skull and the world flashed white.

Something hit his arm with the force of an iron bar, snapping the bone like dry wood. He screamed as the cellular phone flipped out of his hand. He felt the other arm being twisted around behind him, then broken backward at the elbow. He opened his mouth to scream again, but this time the pain made him vomit.

As the doors to the elevator closed, he stood there, broken arms dangling loose, vomit spilling from his mouth.

The cellular phone lay in the center of the lobby floor, the voice of the dispatcher echoing against the elevator doors.

"Soto at Sunset. Are you still there? Over."

Inside the elevator, Soto fell to his knees, crying out at the pain in his shattered arms. One eye was blinded by red flashes, like optical fireworks. But he could still see well enough to make out the white mask staring down at him, pale and indistinct, like a full moon blurred by smog.

The black-gloved hands reached down and grabbed his head, lifting him to his feet, sending new pain shooting through his skull and broken arms.

"Don't—" he gasped. "Don't hurt—"

Strong thumbs poked into his eyeballs, pressing down hard on them, gouging them out of their sockets.

Soto screamed. Aqueous humor dribbled down from his crushed eyeballs and into his open mouth.

Lance leaned back from the console and gave himself another cigarette break. He had enough shit on tape to carry him through to the next twenty-minute set, and during that time he could get what he needed for the rest of his airshift.

"—repeat after me: Nightman rules the night—"

"Nightman rules the night—"

The girl on the tape, around sixteen, began cracking up.

"Lydia, baby! You gotta get *serious* about this!"

"I'm so nervous, Nightman!"

"Let's try it again. Nightman rules the night—"

"Nightman rules—"

" 'Cause he's got such a big, hard—"

She started giggling again.

"Come on, Lydia! 'Cause he's got such a—"

" 'Cause he's got such a—"

"—big, hard—"

"—big—"

She spluttered into helpless giggles.

"—such a big, hard—microphone. Got that, babe?"

He blew out a cloud of smoke. It wasn't bad, for what it was worth. But who listened to this shit, except stoned kids? He took a mouthful of cold coffee, then spit it out and looked around for the gofer. About his only job was to keep the coffee hot, and he couldn't even do that. Asshole was always off somewhere, drinking coffee or stuffing his fat face with takeout food.

Lance saw the streaks on the glass wall then—dark red, runny, with bits of shit sliding slowly down the surface, like someone had accidentally flipped a pizza into the glass but hadn't gotten around to cleaning it up yet.

"—twenty minutes of stopless hits, the hottest and the rudest in all L.A.! Only on KRAS FM, 108.5! Only with Nightman, the King of the Night!"

He pressed PLAY, then began talking over the instrumental lead-in to the first song.

"We got tickets to give away here tonight and they're *f-r-e-e-e-e*, baby! Yeah! Just be the twentieth caller during our twenty stopless hits! Right here! Right now! Hangin' with the Nightman! 108.5. KRAS."

He switched off his mike and got up from the console.

He would just have to go get his own fucking coffee. And maybe leave a note for Jerry Deel in the morning, to fire that fuckhead gofer.

"Don't get up," said the voice, "just because of me."

"*Now* you show up. Where the fuck's my—"

But even as he said it, and even as he turned toward him, he knew something was wrong. The voice was wrong, for one thing. The gofer was a fat kid from somewhere up north of Sacramento, with a high-pitched whine to his voice. This voice was deep and raw and whispering. And what it said was wrong, too. The gofer would never say—

Don't get up, just because of me.

He saw the black jacket, the wide-brimmed hat, the black gloves, and the white mask, holes for eyes, slash for a mouth, looking down at him from what seemed a great height against the shadows and half-lights of the broadcast booth.

He knew who this was now, and what the pizza sauce smears on the glass wall really meant. . . .

But he said, "Who the fuck are you supposed to be?"

"A visitor. Someone who has come to pay you a visit."

If he could have made it, Lance would have just run for it—out the broadcast booth, down the glass-walled corridor, into the main hallway, left to the EXIT stairs—

But the Phantom blocked his way.

No question that's who it was. He looked like some fucking psycho. He *was* a fucking psycho. Lance didn't know how he had even gotten in here. The doors were all locked from inside. The gofer wasn't supposed to let anyone—

He remembered the blood smears on the glass wall.

Then he looked down at the hands, black-gloved but empty.

Maybe he hadn't come in here to kill anyone else. Maybe he just wanted his shot at a little airtime, a chance to answer some of that shit Aaron Scott had been hurling in his face.

And now a reply from our in-studio guest, the Phantom!

Thanks a lot, Scott, for sending this fucking nightmare my way, you fucking asshole! Why couldn't he come in here tomorrow morning, on *your* fucking airshift?

He sat down again, slowly, trying to smile at the monster standing over him. Maybe, just maybe, he could talk him out of whatever he had come here to do. Let him say what he wanted to say over the air. Fucking *help* him say it.

"Sorry, man. Got an airshift to finish up here."

"You don't seem to be broadcasting now."

"Yeah, but that's 'cause—" His throat closed up on him. He swallowed hard to clear it. "I got about fifteen minutes of precarted songs to go, okay? Then I start in again."

The masked figure said nothing.

"But I can start talkin' sooner, if you want. Fuck, I can break in right now! Say somethin' over the air. *You* can say somethin', if that's what you want to do."

"How?"

"Just flip this little sucker here—the one that says CUE?—over to BROADCAST. Then you're on. Want to try it?"

"I have nothing to say."

"Hey, that's cool."

From somewhere—inside his black leather jacket, behind his leg—he drew out what looked like a small meat cleaver or straightedge razor, lights from the console reflecting off its polished blade. The blade looked slightly damp, as if it had been used recently, then wiped dry.

Lance felt his guts turn liquid. He knew what he was in for now. Talking wasn't going to save his ass. He was going to wind up just like that fat little fuck of a gofer—pizza smears on a long glass wall.

Without thinking about it, without giving himself time to clutch, he reached suddenly for the emergency button on the console, the one that alerted security downstairs, then called the Hollywood LAPD.

The cleaver dropped, its polished blade cutting through skin and muscle, tendon and bone, lopping off Lance's hand at the wrist as neatly as a butcher slices off a side of beef.

He sat and stared at his severed hand, a vital part of him mere seconds ago, now a separate entity, index finger still extended in the act of pressing the emergency button. He watched as blood began to pulse from his mutilated wrist, spurting out across the console, sending up small bursts of sparks as the liquid interfered with the board's electronic circuitry.

He cradled his ragged wrist and began to howl, blood leaking through the fingers of his one remaining hand.

"You goddamn fuck— You cut off my fuckin' *hand!*"

The gloved hands yanked his arms backward, forcing from him a high, frightened shriek. The sharp, ripping sound of electrician's tape was followed by the binding of Lance's bleeding wrist to the one good hand behind him, then by the strapping of his body into the wheeled swivel chair where he sat.

"What—" Tears rolled down his cheeks. "What are you—"

"I'm giving you your one chance at immortality."

The whispering voice seemed to be coming from some hidden source inside the booth, as if the mask was nothing but a phantasm, a mocking illusion.

"I'm going to offer you as a—sacrifice."

"Oh, God, no! God, Jesus, fuck, please, *no!*"

The Phantom rolled the swivel chair into the console, so that Lance was forced right up against his microphone.

"But I'm going to do it—live."

He switched the microphone to BROADCAST.

Then he moved in on Lance's face with the cleaver.

18

CLEANUP

When Aaron arrived at the KRAS building, what he saw there looked like the night at the Cinematheque.

The police cordon, the black-and-whites, the ambulances, the gridlocked traffic, the jostling, neck-craning crowds—only this time he got through and Sam didn't.

"You Aaron Scott?"

"Yeah. Let me show—"

"I don't need to see any. Follow me."

Sam started to go with them.

"Sorry, ma'am. Station personnel only."

"I'm with On-Target News."

"She's also with me!"

"Station personnel *only*. Lieutenant Montoya's orders."

"This is bullshit—"

"Just go, Aaron. I'll wait here."

He looked at her, then followed the officer through the cordon and into the lobby, where a forensic team was busy taking photographs, collecting blood samples, dusting Soto's cellular phone for prints. Most of the activity seemed to be centered on an open elevator car with a yellow POLICE LINE—DO NOT CROSS tape stretched across the entrance. The officer took Aaron over to Lopez, who stood near the elevator.

He nodded to Aaron. "It didn't take you long."

"I wasn't far away. What happened?"

"He took out a security guard."

Lopez pointed to the inside of the elevator car.

Aaron peered over the yellow tape.

The walls were streaked with blood, an action painting in red. Soto's body sat slumped in one corner, limp and lifeless, broken arms at impossible angles. His eyes were two hollow sockets. Drying blood crusted over slashes to his face. Black blood oozed from a gaping wound in his neck and spilled down the front of his uniform, pooling on the floor of the elevator car.

Aaron turned away.

"Played with him some on the way up," Lopez said, "then slit his throat before they got to the sixteenth floor."

"What did he do up there?"

"Let's go up and you can see for yourself."

"Did he try—"

"But why don't we use a different elevator."

The glassed-in hallway connecting the broadcast booths was crowded with another forensic team, and Montoya, unwrapping a piece of hard candy.

"Glad you could make it on such short notice, Mr. Scott."

"Hey, it's not every day I get a call from the cops—right after a serial killer hangs up on me."

Lopez glanced at Montoya.

"He called you tonight?" Montoya asked. "At home?"

"At Sam's. We're buddies now. He calls me everywhere."

"Did he mention—"

"Can we cut to the chase? Who's fucking *dead* in there?"

"Follow us, Mr. Scott."

As they moved down the hallway, Aaron stared at the dried blood on the glass and the pieces of matter stuck to it, like insects in amber.

He felt a hand push into his chest and looked down.

"Watch out there. Don't step on him. He's evidence."

A forensic investigator held him back from the corpse of the fat-faced kid who gofered for Lance Trebizond. The corpse lay curled fetuslike on the carpeted floor, great dark wings of blood sweeping out from it on either side. The top of the head seemed to have caved in and the face looked pushed out, as if someone had stuck a hand in behind the skin and shoved.

Aaron stared at it.

"Smashed his head open," Lopez explained, "using a blunt, heavy object, swinging it with full force."

"What's that stuck on the wall, along with the blood?"

"Brains."

Aaron looked at them, embedded in the blood.

"Is that what happened to Lance?" he asked Montoya.

Forensic investigators moved slowly in the background, passing through barred shadows and half-lights like sea creatures trapped inside an aquarium.

"The Phantom spent a long time with him," Montoya said.

"What are you talking about?"

"He broadcast his torture and mutilation over the air."

Aaron started to say something, then stopped.

"He killed him live, Mr. Scott, in the broadcast studio. He killed him slowly, and kept the microphone turned on for most of that time."

"How did you—"

"We taped it. We've been taping KRAS twenty-four hours a day, ever since the Phantom started calling in to your show."

"You just *sat* there and listened to Lance *get* it?"

"We weren't even listening, at first. Were you?"

Aaron stared at him.

"After some listeners called and alerted us, we got here as soon as possible. By then, of course, he was already gone."

Aaron headed for Lance's broadcast booth, shouldering his way past forensic investigators.

He almost ran over Jerry Deel.

"Aaron—" Jerry grabbed his shoulder.

"Excuse me, Jerr. I gotta see what happened."

"Don't go in there, guy! You'll just make yourself sick."

"I'll take the chance."

He pulled loose from Jerry's grip and stepped into the booth, craning his neck to see past more forensic investigators and uniformed officers.

The smell hit him then. He had noticed it out in the hallway, but thought it must be coming from someplace else—like the backed-up stool in the john that the DJs had to use during airshifts. But now that he was inside the booth, he could tell that the smell was coming from in here: shit and piss and puke, mixed in with other raw smells, dying smells, the stench of death throughout them, and permeating all the smells, the sickly sweet, gagging odor of burned human flesh.

He started breathing through his mouth, looking for Lance's body. He could not find it at first. He glanced at the floor, near the console, below the window that looked out over the Hollywood skyline. Lance's swivel chair had been pushed in against the console, a bunch of old rags on top—

He looked again. The bunch of old rags *was* Lance.

What was left of him, anyway.

The top layer of skin had been stripped from his head, exposing muscles, nerves, arteries—like one of the plastic Visible Heads that science nerds used to put together back in high school. Hollow sockets gaped where eyeballs should have been, the way they did in the guard's head downstairs. But these eye sockets seemed burned, blackened around the edges, as if someone had set fire to them, after gouging out the eyes.

The rest of the body had been burned, too—not burned to ashes, nothing like that. Just a touch of inflammable liquid on the surface of the skin, followed by the flick of a disposable lighter. Then lots of screaming and twisting around, taped into the chair, and a hell of a lot of intense, annihilating pain.

Lance Trebizond's flayed head stared sightlessly at him, like a gargoyle perched on a vampire's tomb, lips cut back from long, grinning teeth.

Aaron became aware of the sweat on his own upper lip.

"Excuse us." A forensic investigator brushed past him. "We need more room to work on him here."

Aaron backed away, anger flushing his face.

"What are you gonna try next?" he asked. "A little CPR?"

The investigator gave him a tired look.

"You're one of those radio personalities, right? So that's supposed to be funny, right? Some kind of joke?"

"Fuck you," Aaron said, and walked out of the booth.

He moved down the hall on rubber legs, careful this time not to step on the gofer's corpse.

Jerry stood blocking his way, along with Chuck Davis, a man who looked as if his entire career had been put on hold.

"Where do you think *you're* going?" Jerry asked.

"Home. I've seen the show."

"You can't just *leave* like this!"

"What do you want me to do? Help clean it up?"

"Aaron— Is Sam downstairs, waiting for you?"

"What the fuck does that have to do with it?"

"She's a reporter."

"So?"

"Look, Aaron." Jerry sounded desperate. "You have to help us. We need to keep a total news blackout on this. We've *got* to—until we can figure out what to do with it."

Aaron started to laugh.

"A news *black*out? Are you serious, man? By tomorrow night this shit's gonna be *every*where!"

"No," Chuck said, "it's not—not if we try to contain it. We need your help, Aaron."

"In other words, you don't want me to tell Sam about this?"

"No, we don't."

"Dream on, Chuck! She's gonna *know!* And if she does a story on it, she won't be the only one. Man, *I'll* probably be talkin' about this on my show tomorrow morning!"

"Aaron," Jerry cried, "no!"

Chuck took a deep breath. "We would prefer—"

"*Fuck* what you prefer! A friend of mine—okay, just some guy I *knew*, some guy I *worked* with—gets peeled and charbroiled by a maniac, right after that maniac calls *me!*"

Every head in the hallway looked up.

"And you want me to make like nothin' ever fuckin' *happened?* That's what you want? What you *really* want?"

"Aaron—"

"Well, fuck you! It's not gonna *work* that way!"

He pushed past Jerry and Chuck, out of the hallway and into the main corridor.

Jerry called after him, but Aaron did not look back.

Lopez caught up with him, pacing his agitated stride.

"That was a hard thing to see back there."

Aaron said nothing.

"Montoya wants to ask you a few questions about the Phantom's phone call tonight—"

Aaron pushed the DOWN button for the elevator.

"Do I *have* to answer them?"

"Technically, no."

"Then Montoya can go fuckin' ask someone *else.*"

A chime sounded and the elevator doors opened.

Aaron stepped inside an empty, mirrored car.

"You seemed upset back there," Lopez said, stepping in with him. "You sounded pissed-off."

Aaron scowled at his own reflection in the mirrored wall.

"Want to do something about it?" Lopez asked. "Or just keep feeling pissed-off and impotent?"

Aaron glanced up into the mirror and saw Lopez's reflection staring back at him.

"What have you got in mind?"

"It's not anything we can talk about in public."

"That means you want me down at the police station?"

"Yes."

"So Montoya can ask his fucking questions after all?"

"Yes."

Aaron watched the display count down the numbered floors.

"You think there's any way to stop him?"

"There's always a way. We just have to find it."

Aaron crossed the lobby, investigators still hard at work on Soto's body inside the other elevator car. He walked out the main entrance, into a crowd of reporters and cameramen, with outthrust microphones, rapid-fire questions.

"You're Aaron Scott, aren't you? Sunset Scott?"

"Can you tell us what happened up there?"

Aaron scanned the faces in the crowd, looking for Sam.

"Who killed Lance Trebizond, the DJ known as Nightman?"

"Can you describe for us what you saw up there?"

But Sam was nowhere to be seen.

"Excuse me," he said, starting to push through the crowd.

"Do you feel any sense of personal responsibility for what happened up there?"

Aaron stopped and turned toward the questioner.

"Do you feel that what you said to the Phantom on your show might have led in any way to Lance Trebizond's murder?"

He looked into the hard eyes of Bonnie Redfield, On-Target crime reporter, handheld microphone angled to catch his every word, cameraman beside her, at the ready, lens aimed straight at Aaron's face, framing it in tight closeup.

"Do you think you helped kill him?" Bonnie repeated.

Aaron stared at her as the cameraman moved in even closer.

Then he turned and walked away, pushing through the crowd.

On a narrow street next to the KRAS building, beneath the orange glow of sodium vapor lights, kids from the local clubs gathered along the sidewalk, crowding toward the police cordon, hoping to see blood.

Aaron walked past them, away from the KRAS building, up a steep incline that, followed far enough, would lead him into the Hollywood Hills.

He passed a group of night people, a breed apart, unconcerned with the commotion at the KRAS building, too deep into the dark rhythms of their own subterranean world to care. One of them, a young girl, leaned her bald head back against a stucco wall, cigarette between her teeth, smoke curling out of her nostrils like incense from a stone god's mouth.

A guy with nose rings turned toward Aaron.

But Aaron looked slightly dangerous tonight, not to be messed with, and the guy with the nose rings seemed to sense this and let him pass.

He was coming up on Hollywood Boulevard, walking fast. If normal people were out anywhere on the streets tonight, he could not see them—just more isolated groups, standing like icons beneath the lights, still and silent. One group clustered at the mouth of an alley, not far from the boulevard. A dazzling light shone down on them. Aaron had to blink twice before he could see the On-Target News cameraman, portable light above his head, and Sam, holding out a microphone toward some young guy with dirty, shoulder-length hair and, even at that distance, mottled, malformed teeth.

He recognized the fallen angel, dark companion to the other one with the shaved head, forelock dyed blood red, lips pulled back over grinning gums.

Man, I am *the mask.*

"Sam!" he yelled at her. "Get *away* from him!"

He started running toward them.

The fallen angel glanced up and slipped into the alley with the quickness of thought. Aaron broke through the crowd of media groupies, jostling Sam and her cameraman, running headlong into the darkness of the alley.

He stopped.

The fallen angel slithered down the alley, back to one wall. At the farthest end, faintly illuminated by a distant street light, stood a tall, motionless figure, his skull smooth and hairless in a barely visible silhouette.

Aaron stood there as time hung suspended like smog in the heavy air. Then the figure turned and seemed to disappear into the imageless landscape of the night.

19

NIGHT RIDE

Almost an hour later, at the Hollywood Division on Wilcox, he found both homicide detectives waiting for him.

"We appreciate this," Montoya said, as Aaron walked with them down a wide corridor that led to the back of the police station. "It's already been a long night for you."

"Which way to your office?"

"We thought you might like a ride instead."

"What the fuck—"

They reached the end of the corridor and stepped outside, where Lopez opened the door to a black-and-white patrol car.

"Where are we going?"

"No place special," Montoya said, climbing into the front seat, then motioning for Aaron to get in back.

Aaron looked at the standard-issue Remington M870 pump-action shotgun holstered on the front dashboard next to Lopez, who had already taken his place in the driver's seat.

"Do I have to guess? Or do I get some clues?"

"Certain persons are interested in your whereabouts," Montoya said. "Interested enough to follow you."

"Bull*shit!* Nobody followed—"

"Did you tell him you were going there tonight?"

He heard the whispering voice from Sam's answering machine.

I know you're there, Sunset Scott.

"You think he followed me?"

"Or had someone else follow you. Yes."

Aaron turned around and looked out the back window of the patrol car, where he saw nothing, except shadowy figures moving on the other side of Wilcox, and beyond that, the low buildings and harsh electric lights of Hollywood.

"If he tries to follow us now," Montoya said, "we'll know."

Lopez pulled out of the parking lot and headed north on Wilcox. Then he turned east on Sunset.

Aaron told them about the Phantom's phone call, and about the dismembered black kitten, floating in the spa.

"He's starting to make it more personal," Montoya said.

Aaron's head snapped up.

He heard Sam again, in his apartment the other night.

He wants to be found, Aaron—by you.

"The obvious signs are there, Mr. Scott."

"Look, I get lots of weird call-ins on my show—"

"But this one's different. He's stalking you. By phone, at first. Then, in person, shadowing you."

"I told you I didn't see *any*one—"

"You wouldn't, not if he's good. And he is. Also, he may not be the one who's doing the actual stalking. He may have had someone else follow you tonight."

Aaron saw the fallen angel again, caught in the glare of the On-Target floodlight, bolting from the scene at first sight of Aaron, running back inside the alley—back to where the Phantom stood waiting, tall and silent.

He looked out the side window at the bright lights of Sunset Boulevard, his own reflected image staring back at him.

A dispatcher's voice crackled from the two-way radio on the dashboard, reporting a robbery in progress.

"Want to go check that one out?" Lopez asked Montoya.

"No."

"Look," Aaron said, "something else happened tonight—"

He told them about the incident in the alley. Montoya betrayed no emotion as he sat there and listened, boulevard lights passing across the back of his head.

"You're sure about this?" he finally asked.

"Positive. That fucking little weasel with the long hair, and the other one—"

He saw the grinning mouth again, under the headlights.

Man, I am *the mask.*

Aaron stared at Lopez's hands on the steering wheel, the M870 holstered on the dashboard beside it, the boulevard itself extending into infinite lights and darkness.

"We need your help, Mr. Scott," Montoya said.

"For what? Another lineup?"

He saw Jabar again through the two-way mirror.

"No. This time we know who we're looking for." Montoya unwrapped a piece of candy. "We need your help to set him up."

"You want to use me as fucking *bait?*"

"You're already bait," Lopez said.

Aaron turned to him angrily.

"He's right," Montoya said.

Aaron leaned back against the seat.

He saw Lance Trebizond again, the flayed head grinning at him with its long, lipless vampire teeth.

"So what do you suggest?" he asked Montoya.

"His calls to you are growing more frequent, more personal, his approaches more dramatic. He wants to meet you, Mr. Scott. One way or another, he *will* meet you."

He wants to be found, Aaron—by you.

Aaron glanced out the back window at the dark streets and bright lights, the glittering unreality of the night world.

"Don't worry," Lopez said. "Nobody's following us."

He slumped back down into the seat, feeling sorry for himself now, and afraid.

He waited for Montoya to go on, but the detective simply sat there, sucking on a piece of hard candy, cracking it between his teeth.

"How do you want me to do this? Invite him out to lunch?"

"We want you to provoke him again, to challenge him on the air, the way you did the other day. Dare him to meet with you—somewhere, anywhere."

"And then let *him* decide where?"

"It has to be that way. Serial killers must feel that they, and only they, are in control of whatever happens in their lives. They have to think that they are, anyway."

"But what if he wants to meet me in—"

He saw the alley again, the tall figure in silhouette.

"Whatever he offers, take him up on it."

"Easy for *you* to say!"

"It won't be anyplace dangerous, or anywhere you might feel threatened. He wants you to show up. He *wants* to meet you."

"What if he asks about the police?"

"He will."

"What do I tell him?"

"There will be no police. Only you, and him."

"Is that *true?*"

"No uniformed officers will be on the scene."

"Just me and the Phantom?"

"Sergeant Lopez and I will be there, too, undercover. But he doesn't need to know that."

Aaron remembered the carnage at the Cinematheque, the guard in the elevator car, and Lance Trebizond, taped tight to the chair in front of his own console.

"Think you two can take him, alone?"

"Sergeant Lopez is an excellent shot."

"What if something happens to him?"

"I have a gun, too. I know how to fire it."

Aaron drew a long, uneven breath.

"What if I just decide to say—fuck all this?

"That's your choice. Then you leave the matter of the meeting—time, place, circumstances—entirely up to him. You can postpone it. But you can't avoid it. Because there *will* be a meeting. You can count on that."

I can find you, wherever you go.

He heard the voice again, hollow, whispering, over the phone, at Sam's place, just hours ago—it seemed days—echoing inside his head like a death rattle.

If I can't call you at the radio station, I can call you here, or at your home, or at your mother's home.

He raised a hand to the side of his face and began to massage it slowly, where it seemed to have gone numb.

If I can't call you—

—if you change your number, or don't answer the phone—

—if you try to ignore me, or pretend I don't exist—

—I can still talk with you, face-to-face.

A dispatcher's voice crackled from the radio up front.

"We have a body in a used car parking lot."

Lopez took one hand off the wheel and punched in some numbers on a small computer keyboard attached to the radio. The exact location of the incident appeared on the video display.

"Not far from here," he said, glancing at Montoya. "Want to drive by and check it out?"

"Not unless—"

"Attention, Lieutenant Montoya," the dispatcher continued. "If you're listening in, Lieutenant, the boys who found this one say it's got the masked man's signature all over it."

"In that case," Montoya said, "we'd better go."

20

PLAYGROUND

By the time they reached the scene, four other patrol cars had already arrived ahead of them, turret lights flashing blue and red and amber off the chain-link fence that enclosed an inner-city elementary school playground.

The night air seemed cold to Aaron as he got out of the car, smog cutting deep into his lungs, burning them like an iron brand. He looked through the chain links at the dark, squat school buildings, bursts of light from the revolving turrets bringing them forth into sudden relief, then dropping them back into darkness. The concrete playground, and everything around it, seemed deserted, forgotten.

All the action was taking place in front of the fence.

Uniformed officers gathered around a body sprawled across the sidewalk, one arm reaching out to the curb, a leg pushing against the chain links of the fence itself. Aaron followed Lopez up to the body and looked down. He tried to turn away the instant he saw it, but there was a compulsion to this horror revealed by heavy-duty, handheld flashlights.

She was a woman somewhere between first youth and early middle age. The attack had been fast, brutal, the knife work slashing and crude. Blood flowed across the sidewalk in abstract patterns, pooling underneath the chain-link fence. On the other side, more blood spilled over the edge of the curb and down through a metal grating, dripping into the storm drain below. Under the glare of the flashlight beams, the blood looked bright red, almost phosphorescent, against the pinkish gray of eviscerated intestines, the ocher yellow of exposed fat.

Aaron took a quick breath and closed his eyes.

He saw the restaurant again, the one where he and Sam had tried to have dinner the night of the Cinematheque murders, and she had talked about viewing the remains of the Phantom's latest victim, earlier that day.

He heard her speak, saw her raise a hand to her forehead.

Aaron, it was like something from a slaughterhouse.

The smell of fresh blood rose from the sidewalk below.

I didn't know a human body could hold *that much blood.*

Nausea began swirling in the pit of his stomach.

And she was cut into so many pieces—

"You okay?"

He swallowed his sickness and opened his eyes, and found himself looking into Lopez's dark eyes.

"I'm— Yeah. I'm cool."

"You get used to these things, after you've seen enough of them," Lopez said. "But at first, it's hard."

"When did he—" Aaron nodded vaguely, trying not to look at the atrocity beneath the flashlight beams. "After he killed Lance? Or before?"

"After."

"How do you know?"

"The blood," Montoya said, looking up from an examination of the corpse. "It's still fresh. That's why it's flowing so freely. The coroner's office will fix the exact time of death, but this one is of very recent vintage. Possibly taking place at—oh, about the time we started our drive tonight?"

He turned for confirmation to Lopez, who merely nodded.

"Strictly a hit-and-run slasher attack," Montoya continued. "No time for finesse on this one. Move in on the victim, make your marks, then move out again, fast as possible."

"Why did he kill again so soon?" Aaron asked. "After just finishing with that security guard—and Lance?"

Montoya looked at him, but did not answer.

"Did he think we'd *find* this shit? Did he *know* we would?"

"Hey, Lieutenant!" a uniformed officer called out, walking back from some point farther up the sidewalk.

Aaron grabbed Montoya's arm. "Did he know—"

"Maybe." He turned to the officer. "Yes?"

"We can't find any blood trails."

"You checked carefully?"

"We didn't lick the sidewalk. But we went over it step by step. *Nada*. Your boy's a wiper."

Aaron turned to Montoya. "A wiper?"

"Someone who wipes the murder weapon thoroughly and doesn't leave a trail of detectable bloodstains."

"What do you call *that?*" Aaron pointed to the sidewalk.

"Primary bloodstains. We're talking about secondary stains, the kind that—even in minute amounts—leave a clear trail to indicate which direction the murderer went in fleeing the scene of the crime. Most criminals don't have the presence of mind to clean a weapon, not on a hit-and-run job."

"How did he know we'd find—this?"

"I don't know that he did."

"You said—"

"I think he *might* have known. I don't pretend to understand how his mind works. But this murder taking place so soon after the others tonight, and our just happening to be in the vicinity—" He paused, then asked Lopez, "How far are we from the radio station at this point?"

"About three miles."

"Too much of a coincidence," Montoya said. "I stopped believing in coincidences a long time ago, Mr. Scott."

A uniformed officer asked Montoya to look at something.

"This may take a few minutes," the detective said to Aaron. "If you want to, you can get back in the car. It's warmer in there."

"I'm okay."

"Or if you'd rather come with us—"

"No, thanks."

As Montoya and Lopez walked back toward the corpse, Aaron turned and looked through the chain links at the dark school playground. Swing sets and jungle gyms stood stark and unattended, like metal skeletons in the night. The playground seemed permanently empty of life, as did the buildings and the walkways between them.

He noticed it then, beside a distant building, the one farthest back from this side of the playground. He couldn't see clearly at such a distance, and at night, but he knew that the figure standing there now was the same one he had seen in the alley—silent, motionless.

"Hey!"

Aaron grabbed the fence and shook it.

"Hey, *ass*hole! You wanted to see me? I'm *here!*"

He shook the fence harder, making the chain links rattle.

Several officers looked up from the corpse on the sidewalk.

Lopez came over.

The figure remained motionless, dark against the distant school building, a black shadow on a black wall.

"Come on over here, man! Let's have it *out*, one-on-one!"

Aaron's voice carried across the empty playground, against background noise from the traffic on Sunset.

"Hey, masked man! You're not *afraid* of me, are you?"

The figure stood watching, then withdrew into darkness.

"Son of a bitch—"

Aaron gripped the chain links, wedged his right foot into one, left foot into another, and began to climb. The fence started rattling fiercely, groaning beneath his ascent.

He could hear Lopez yelling for him to come down, but he continued to climb. He was panting for breath and his arms were shaking by the time he reached the top. Down below, Lopez started up the fence after him.

Aaron began climbing down the other side, into the empty schoolyard. He misjudged the distance and dropped several feet farther than he meant to, landing hard on one ankle, twisting it. He gritted his teeth and looked at the distant building where the dark figure had been standing mere seconds ago. Barely visible now, receding from sight, like a bright image fading on the retina, the figure moved down a covered open space between the building and the one next to it.

Aaron began to limp in that direction, determined to see him once again, to catch a glimpse of the shaved head and red forelock, the exposed gum line and mocking grin, as if to fix that image, to verify its absolute reality, was a most important thing just then, perhaps the most important of all.

Lopez leaped from the top of the chain-link fence and came down lightly, with the grace of an acrobat.

He caught up to Aaron in two quick strides.

"What did you see back there?" he asked in a low voice.

"Him."

"Who?"

"The Phantom!"

"You sure?"

"Yes!"

Lopez grabbed him with an iron hand.

"Stand back. Let me make the collar."

"I want to *see* him!"

"You'll get to—if it's really him."

Without another word, Lopez drew a nine-millimeter Beretta and rushed into the darkness, moving quietly across the concrete surface of the playground. Aaron limped after him, trying to catch up, but Lopez was already at the far building by now, then into the open space between that and the other building, following the Phantom wherever he had gone.

By the time Aaron reached the far building, Lopez was walking back slowly toward him, Beretta pointed down.

"I told you to stay back there."

"I had to see—"

"Then come over here and look."

Lopez took a compact black flashlight from inside his suit jacket and shined it on the wall of the building facing the open walkway. Spray-painted graffiti popped into sharp focus beneath the flashlight beam. Most of it was gang tagging, tribal signs of urban scavengers. But one message stood apart from the others. It had been done with broad, sweeping strokes, using some kind of expensive, permanent marker rather than cheap spray paint. Unlike the gang tagging, the letters in this message were clearly written and could be easily read.

SUNSET SCOTT
ARE YOU STILL AFRAID?

Aaron felt the air leave his lungs.

Lopez pivoted with the flashlight, aiming it down the walkway, moving it quickly from corner to doorway to rooftop, anywhere someone might duck or hide. But the light revealed nothing except the physical decay of an urban schoolyard, crumbling piece by piece.

"It was *him*," Aaron said.

"Or someone trying to look like him."

"Bullshit!"

They walked back to the fence on the other side of the playground without speaking. Lopez and another officer pulled the bolts on the main gate and removed it so Aaron could get out without climbing. Then they replaced it, the whole operation taking no more than a few minutes. The gate, when replaced, looked as if it had never been touched.

"You don't want to do things like that, Mr. Scott," Montoya said to him. "It's not safe. Besides, it's our job."

"*I'm* the one he calls!"

"He's more than a simple irritant. He's unpredictable and extremely dangerous. You don't want to play games with him."

"Does it *look* like I'm playin' some fuckin'—"

He caught sight of the dismembered corpse on the sidewalk again and his voice came to a sudden stop, like a radio switched off in mid-sentence. He realized then, as if for the first time, the madness of his recent actions, the dark consequences encircling his every move now in a twisting skein of fate.

"You need to get off that foot," Montoya said, changing the subject, "or you won't be able to walk on it tomorrow."

"*Look!*" Aaron turned to him, limping. "That deal we talked about? Where I help set up this son of a bitch? I want to *know* the details. I want to hear them *now!*"

21

SETUP

Aaron tried to sleep, but after more than an hour in bed with his eyes wide open, watching numbers change on his clock radio, he got up and drove back to the KRAS studios.

The police were still working in the downstairs lobby, but only a skeleton crew by then. All the media people and most of the crime scene groupies had left.

On the sixteenth floor, he made himself some coffee, then went into his own broadcast booth and sat down at the unlighted console, Styrofoam cup steaming in one hand.

Jerry Deel knocked on the frame of the open door.

"Mind if I come in, Aaron?"

"Would it make a difference if I did?"

Jerry sat down on the chair reserved for in-studio guests.

Without looking at him, Aaron asked, "Where's Chuck?"

"Left about forty-five minutes ago."

"Where did he go? Home to write a suicide note?"

"Not funny, guy."

"Hey, it's my *job*, Jerr! It's what they *pay* me to do! Be *funny*—no matter fuckin' what."

He reached out and pushed a slide fader forward, pulled it back down, then repositioned it where it had been before.

"We still on the air?" he asked Jerry.

"No."

"What did you do? Send Mindy home?"

Arminda Romero ran Mindy at Midnight, the midnight-to-five shift that segued into Aaron's own morning show.

"You broadcastin' dead air instead of Mindy, Jerr?"

"That's right."

"FCC's gonna be righteously pissed."

"We already contacted them about it."

Aaron leaned back in the swivel chair, drumming his fingers on the console. He looked at Jerry, who sat hunched over, staring at a blank television monitor, the one that usually displayed the names and addresses of call-ins.

"Never figured it would turn out like this, huh, Jerr?"

"What do you mean?"

"Him! The ol' mas' man! Remember how we practically *prayed* that the fuckhead would keep callin' in, so it'd boost our listener share? Jesus, did we get what we wanted, or what?"

"Our listener share's gone through the roof."

"Then why you no *smile*, mon?"

Jerry looked up from the blank screen.

"It's a four-star cluster fuck. Sure, we own drive-time now. But after what happened tonight . . . The FCC could shut us down any day now. We can just sit around, waiting for that to happen. Or we can shut down on our own—"

"Bullshit. You know why he did this, don't you?"

"Did what?"

"Shredded Lance like a fuckin' bad check!"

"I don't know anything right now."

"He did it to send *me* a message."

Jerry frowned.

Aaron got up from the swivel chair and gave it a spin.

He began pacing back and forth across the narrow broadcast booth, limping slightly.

"He got his *feelings* hurt. He got pissed when I wouldn't take his calls yesterday, or whenever the fuck that was."

"Is this your idea? Or something the LAPD came up with?"

"*Mine!* You think I get my ideas from *cops?*"

"So what are you trying to say? That you could've stopped him from coming down here by taking his calls?"

"Fuck, yes!"

"And now you're going to start taking them again?"

"You bet your fuckin' ass, I am!"

Jerry shook his head.

"I don't know if that's a good idea, Aaron. The risk factor's just gone way up on this thing."

"Hey, Jerr, *I'm* the one whose ass is hangin' out over the edge! If the Phantom comes down here again lookin' for anyone, it's gonna be *me* the next time!"

"I don't know, Aaron."

"Well, man, I *do!*"

"You haven't had much sleep tonight, guy. Sure you can run things this morning? Or you want someone to cover for you?"

"I'm pumped, Jerr! I'm pissed! I'm *ready* for the fucker!"

But Jerry did not think Aaron looked ready.

He thought he looked scared.

For the first two hours of Sunset Scott in the Morning, everyone seemed to call in—except the Phantom.

Bill Waller screened most of the calls off the air, losing the losers, putting the faithful on hold, letting Aaron pick the ones he wanted and play them the way he saw fit.

"I think what happened, Sunset Scott— I think you got to expect it when you don't show no respect."

"What the hell are you talkin' about?" Aaron grabbed the neck of his microphone. "You're not makin' any sense, man! Respect who? The Phantom? Are you *serious?*"

"You don't show no respect, things'll happen."

"Yeah, you bet they'll happen, dickhead! Like *this!*"

Aaron punched off the call, letting the dial tone buzz over the air for a few seconds before muting it.

"Hey, everybody! That was another world-class dickhead out there, lettin' us know it's *our* fault that someone came in and smoked the Nightman last night. Yeah, that's right! It's *our* fault! Hell, it's the *Night*man's fault! Blame the damn victim! Isn't that the way it goes? If I get killed, it's *my* fault! I *made* the killer do it! Can you believe that crap, Lovely Lisa?"

"No way, Sunset Scott!"

But as she said it, she extended her middle finger, plainly visible through the glass, just to let him know what she thought of tosses like that.

Aaron gave her a silent mocking kiss and flipped her a finger in return. He glanced at Bud Bronson, who watched him from the sports booth with that wary look hard-core gamblers get just before the roulette wheel starts to spin.

Everyone was on edge this morning, not just Lisa. No one wanted to be connected with anything said about the Phantom over the air. If Aaron intended to keep trashing him, that was his business—as long as he didn't include anyone else.

"What do *you* think about all this, Bud the Stud?"

"I think it's time," Bud said, "for a sports wrap-up."

"Cool, man. You do that. You go ahead and wrap it up."

As Bud started on the statistics, Aaron switched his microphone from BROADCAST to CUE.

"Got anything on those fuckin' phone lines yet?"

Bill Waller winced at the sound of Aaron's amplified voice booming inside his earphones.

"He hasn't called in, Aaron."

"I want to know when he *does*, man!"

"We know that—"

"You lie to me about this, I'll take 'em *all* on live!"

"No one's lying to you, Aaron."

Jerry stood beside Bill in the call-screening booth.

Also in the same booth, but farther off, as if trying to keep his distance, Chuck Davis stood by himself, Savile Row suit slightly rumpled, white broadcloth shirt soiled, a look of stoic resignation in his eyes.

Tracy Cortino, in the traffic booth, had made it clear even before the broadcast began that she wanted no part of Phantom banter. She sat there with earphones clamped tight to her head, frowning at Aaron, as if daring him to toss her something.

Interns and gofers stood at various points around the studio, watching Aaron through the glass wall, unable to go on with their own work—waiting, like witnesses to a multicar pileup, for someone to bring out the next body.

Aaron switched his microphone back to BROADCAST and cut in on Bud as he neared the end of his sports wrap-up.

"Okay, everybody! That was Bud the Stud, our KRAS sports animal, with the best and the baddest from the athletic arenas of Southern California. But you know what? The hell with it! I mean, yeah, sports is God, okay? But screw it! 'Cause we got a different kind of game goin' on here at KRAS FM, 108.5, the spot on your radio dial for—"

Aaron flipped on the echo filter. "MIDNIGHT MASSACRE!"

Jerry and Chuck looked up at the same moment, as if neither could believe what each had just heard.

Aaron flipped off the filter. "That's right, everybody! We got us a player out there on the mean streets of Hollyweird. He's cut himself some mighty fancy moves, but we know he's got more tucked away up his sleeve. And we're just sittin' here now, at KRAS FM, 108.5, waitin' for our player to make *another* move. Waitin' for him to do *some*thin'—unless maybe there's nothin' for him to do 'cause he just *lost* it. Lost his steel-plated *cojones.* Dropped 'em on the cement last night at the school playground. Remember *that*, Mr. X?"

Jerry signaled from behind the glass wall for Aaron to switch to CUE and talk to him inside the call-screening booth.

Aaron pressed the button on the cart deck and put a tape in play. Heavy metal chords slammed through the speakers above the console. The glass wall seemed to vibrate with the sound.

"But while we're waitin' to see if he can even *find* his *cojones* and figure out how to glue 'em back on, let's get into some b-a-a-a-d music. The Annihilators! 'End of the Road'!"

He switched to CUE. "Yeah, Jerr?"

"What the hell do you think you're *doing* in there?"

"Trying to get him to call."

"He came in here last night and *killed* someone!"

"Yeah, Jerr, I remember."

"You're taunting him! You're *daring* him to come in again!"

"I just want him to call, Jerr."

"I'm replacing you for the rest of today's show, Aaron."

"You're *what?*"

"Sleep deprivation. That's what you're suffering from. Go home and go to bed. Get some sleep."

Aaron stood up and stared through the double glass.

"Fuck you, man! And fuck your sleep-deprivation shit!"

"Don't make this any worse than it already is, Aaron."

"If I walk out of here, that's *it!* Understand?"

"Aaron—"

"I'm not crawlin' back on my fuckin' hands and knees!"

"Listen to me—"

"And if I go, so does the Phantom and so do your fuckin' ratings—right out the fuckin' door! So, tell me again, Jerr. Tell me to go home and go to bed and get some sleep. O*kay?*"

Jerry stared back at him through the glass wall, looking as if he just might tell him that, as if it might be worth it.

But he said, "If you think you can handle it—"

"What *is* this shit? If I think I can— I *am* handlin' it, man! I'm fuckin' in control! *Total* control!"

He stared at Jerry, at the other announcers in separate booths, at the interns and gofers, standing around, watching.

Then he sat back down at his console.

"Aaron?" He heard Bill's voice inside his headphones.

"Yeah, *what?*"

"He's on the line."

A capital **X** blinked on and off beside line number nine, a white icon against a dark background, like a quasar pulsing in the heart of deep space. Beside that, the notation glowed with ominous familiarity: NO HOME ADDRESS, NO PHONE NUMBER.

Aaron shut down the Annihilators in mid-chord with one hand, switching back to BROADCAST with the other.

"*Wake up*, everybody!" he screamed into the microphone. "We got us a call-in! A mystery caller! The mysterious Mr. X! The Man with the Mask! L.A.'s own homeboy made good, the lovely and talented *Phan*tom—here, for your listening pleasure, on KRAS FM, 108.5, more *electrifying* shock radio! This is the one, everybody! The one who managed to reattach his *cojones* after dropping them near the swingset on that dark ol' playground—just a little in joke, there, a little private diss for my bro, the Phantom. Hey, I mean, he's, like, almost my cohost on this damn show, right? Sunset Scott and the Phantom, broadcasting from deep in the heart of Hollywood, high atop the KRAS building, overlooking scenic Sunset and Vine—"

The others watched him through the glass wall, waiting to see just how far he would go, wondering what would happen when he brought the Phantom on live.

Jerry glanced at the switch on the call-screening console, the one that could shut down the entire broadcast and replace it with prerecorded music or public service announcements.

He made a gesture of reaching for it.

His eyes met those of Chuck Davis, who shook his head no.

Aaron jabbed at button number nine on his console.

"Mysterious Mr. X! The Phantom! The man with no name and no phone and no home—you're on *live* with Sunset Scott!"

Silence filled his headphones.

Aaron laughed into the microphone. "This is the same *shtick* we go through every damn time, me and the Phantom. I bring him on live, okay? Then he *bails* on me. Just sits there, givin' me all this damn dead air—"

"You think you're running this, don't you, Sunset Scott?"

It was the same voice, soft and whispering, but with a new asperity to it this time, a hoarse impatience.

"Hey, man! Long time no hear! I thought maybe—"

"What would your listeners say, if they could have seen you last night, Sunset Scott? Running down alleys, chasing shadows. Limping across schoolyards, hunting bogeymen. What would they think if they could have heard the *fear* in your voice—"

"Listen, butthead! I ain't afraid of *nothin'!* I'm sure as hell not afraid of some dickless wonder like you!"

"You're very afraid, Sunset Scott. I can hear the fear in your voice right now. Last night, I could *see* it—"

"Hold on, man. Mr. X. Mr. Mysterious Phantom. The man without a name. The voice without a face. Aren't you startin' to get a little bored with this cat-and-mouse crap?"

"I don't understand—"

"I'll bet you don't. You'd be happy to keep playin' this brain-dead game forever, wouldn't you? Where you call me up here whenever you feel like it and hang up whenever you want. And you never have to put your cards down on the table or your money on the line because it's just a *game*, isn't it, Phantom? A damn game, where it never gets real and that's fine with you, 'cause you don't ever *want* it to get real. Just like phone sex, only not as much fun, right, dude?"

"You're the one who's not real, Sunset Scott."

"Yeah, I know. We've been over it before, man. But it's just words, that's all. Just talk."

"What happened to Lance Trebizond wasn't just talk."

For a moment Aaron's stage presence faltered and he felt the terror of last night, smelled the burned flesh lingering in the air, saw Lance's charred, mutilated body taped into a swivel chair, not that different from the one he sat in now.

Some of those watching through the glass wall turned away then, because they felt it too, and knew that what was happening now was not just another bit, a staged confrontation, but the real thing, a kind of madness, a dance with death.

"Lance got caught with his pants down. Not me. You know where I am. I know where *you* are. We're like two evil twins, you and me.

Two different halves of the same twisted zygote—"

"You're stalling for time, Sunset Scott. You're trying to help them trace me, aren't you?"

"Trace *you?* Who? The FCC? The competition?"

"The police."

"This is a radio show, pal, not a police station."

But at that very moment, inside the Hollywood Division on Wilcox, telecommunications specialist Tom Kelso sat hunched over his audio monitoring equipment, running an electronic trace back along the line the Phantom was calling in on, trying to pinpoint the precise location of the phone he was using to make the call.

"Just a little longer, Sunset baby," Kelso said to himself.

"Who the hell would want to trace *you,* anyway?" Aaron yelled into the microphone, glancing at the digital readout on the console clock. "You think you're so damn mysterious! But you're *not,* okay? You're probably callin' from somewhere right here in Hollywood. Maybe from one of the pay phones down in the lobby. Or maybe from the Fatburger down the street. Man, you're so lame and predictable! You should go into early reruns!"

"I'll talk to you again, Sunset Scott."

Aaron froze at what he knew was the Phantom's sign-off.

He leaned forward suddenly, moving into the microphone.

"Let's lose this crap and cut to the chase, Mr. Not-Very-Mysterious X! You're always makin' threats to drop by here, to pay me a visit. Right? So put your damn money where your damn mouth is! Let's *meet* somewhere, man! Let's have it *out! Mano a mano!* Face-to-face! You name the time, the place, the date, the refreshments, the cover charge! If you're ready, Masked Man, *I'm* ready! O*kay?*"

Aaron waited, trying not to breathe into the microphone. If the Phantom hung up, it would be all over for right now. He would have to wait again for another call, with the LAPD standing by, unable to do anything but wait along with him.

"Where?" asked the whispering voice.

"*Any*where, man! Any damn place you want!"

Silence filled the other end.

Fearing he had lost him, Aaron pushed it to the limit.

"Unless you're *afraid* of meetin' me, Phantom! Unless you want to spend your whole damn life watchin' from the shadows—"

"We don't have time for this," the Phantom interrupted. "Meet me at your private club, Sunset Scott. The one you're so fond of. Your lonely little boys' club. The one you stopped by the other night, on your way back from looking at my sign on the mirror of the rest room in the Cinematheque."

Aaron felt the words pass through him like a fever chill.

He saw the sign again, written in blood, and the girl's face—blistered, purple, swollen beyond human recognition.

Aaron's throat seemed to go dry on him. "What—"

"Eight o'clock. Tomorrow night. Good-bye, Sunset Scott."

PART THREE

IMAGO

22

TRACES

Tom Kelso walked into the cramped office occupied by Montoya and Lopez.

"We got it!" Kelso said, waving a computer printout.

Montoya took it from him and examined it.

"A pay phone on Sunset, near Vermont," Kelso said, "not far from the hospital."

"Very good," Montoya said, without looking up.

"I'll go check it out," Lopez said, heading for the door.

"He'll be gone by the time you get there."

"I know. But maybe he's left something behind this time."

Montoya looked up from his desk. "Frank, no."

Lopez stopped and turned around in the doorway.

"That a direct order, Lieutenant?"

"Yes."

Kelso cleared his throat.

"If you don't need me for anything else, sir—"

"Good work, Tom. That's all for now."

After Kelso left, Lopez walked back inside the office and stood facing Montoya, who was unwrapping a piece of hard candy.

"Why don't you want me going over there, Ralph?"

"This trace report tells us what we need to know."

"It tells us *shit!*"

"Exactly. It tells us he made the call from a pay phone in Hollywood. But we already know he's calling locally."

"Now he knows, too, thanks to Scott's fuck-up on the air."

"Aaron Scott's not a trained criminal investigator. We can expect him to make mistakes. That's not our problem. Our problem is everything we still don't know about the Phantom. We don't have any real psychological fix on him. Rushing over to a pay phone he recently vacated isn't going to help us much. What it *might* do instead is alert him to the fact that this meeting with Scott is a police setup."

"That's going to be one bitch of a stakeout. The Rakehell Club's not your average tit bar. Sal Esposito runs it with big money from Vegas. He likes to give the place a high-class veneer. He'll shit bricks if we ask to stake it out."

"Probably so. But he'll cooperate. Esposito owes us."

"Why? We pay him off?"

"Not exactly. It was more a matter of mutual cooperation. He helped us, but we helped him even more."

"Think he'll remember it?"

"Oh, yes."

"So we get to spend a night with Esposito's bouncers, waiting for the Phantom to show. I'd rather take my chances trying to bring him down as he hauls ass from a pay phone."

"You won't catch him that way, Frank. He's too fast and too smart. What this setup might give us—*if* we're lucky—is our first chance to see him, to sense the way he works."

"And if he doesn't show?"

Montoya shrugged. "Nothing changes."

"If he *does* show, he might get to Scott before we do."

"There's always that possibility."

"So then we set a piss-poor trap, wasting our only bait."

"I don't think he'll kill him—even given the chance."

"Why not? The famous Montoya intuition?"

"Something like that."

The radio station was flooded with calls after Aaron's on-air agreement to meet with the Phantom. Even with help from all the interns and gofers, Jerry and Bill couldn't keep any of the phone lines open.

"Fuck it!"

Aaron punched off a line he had been trying to use.

"What do I have to do to call out of this place? Go downstairs and use one of the goddamn pay phones in the lobby?"

"Don't waste your time, man," Alonzo Gore said. "They all got long lines stretched out in front of 'em. You really started things jumpin'."

Alonzo sat inside the broadcast booth with Aaron, waiting for a twenty-minute set to wind down, so that Aaron could sign off and Alonzo could start up his own airshift.

"*Fuck* it!" Aaron got to his feet.

"They find anyone to replace Lance yet?" Alonzo asked.

"I don't think anyone's exactly applied."

"There's always *some*one lookin' for a night shift."

"Not here. Not unless he's seriously suicidal."

A breathless intern came in, a note in one hand.

"Aaron?"

"Yeah, what?"

"You got two important calls. One from Sam. The other—"

"What line are they on?"

"They're not. We had—"

"What the fuck you mean they're not? *Why* not?"

"We can't keep anybody on the line. The lines are—"

"You asshole! Don't come here and tell me shit like that!"

"Jerry said—"

"*Fuck* what Jerry said!"

"Easy, man," Alonzo said. "She's just doin' her job."

"Some job! Who's the other call from?"

The intern wiped at her eyes.

"The other call's from your mother."

"Jesus! My own mom can't even get through!"

"You're lucky, man," Alonzo said. "They *always* put mine through, even when I'm in the middle of a shift."

The phone lines were still jammed when Aaron left the KRAS studios early that afternoon. Curious listeners wanted to know. Where was the meeting with the Phantom going down? Was it free? Or did you have to pay? Was there going to be live television coverage? Where could you go for T-shirts and hats?

The lack of sleep was starting to hit him now. As he drove through Hollywood, heading west on Sunset, the whole world seemed subtly distorted by the Phantom's malign presence, as if viewed through a strange, prismatic evil. Fronts of buildings did not stand true. Billboards seemed to slant outward. Side streets ran at wrong angles up into the Hollywood Hills. Doorways and windows looked cubist in their misalignment.

Beneath the traffic sounds he heard the whispering voice.

Eight o'clock. Tomorrow night. Good-bye, Sunset Scott.

He gripped the steering wheel harder.

When he stopped by Steinberg's on Fairfax, he saw several bearded Hasidic men eating lunch with their hats on, and an older Russian Jew at the display counter arguing with Shirley Landau about something, but no Leah Steinberg.

"The pastrami," the Russian said. "It's too much fat."

"Look," Shirley said, "I don't cut it off the cow. I just sell it. You don't like the too much fat? Go complain to the *shochet,* not me. Aaron! What's wrong? You look like you just saw a ghost!"

"Where's Mom?"

"She tried to call you at the radio station."

"I know that. Where *is* she?"

"Gone. She went home early."

"How much I got to pay for this fat?" asked the Russian.

"A minute, okay?" Shirley turned to Aaron, lowering her voice.

"Look, I think she's upset about something. She's looking almost as bad as you. You two have words?"

"No. It might've been something I said on the air."

"The radio show?"

"Yeah, maybe."

"You got to watch what you say, Aaron. Leah don't listen, because she knows what type show it is. But her customers! Do *they* ever listen. This morning, it's all they talk about. How you're going to meet with some *meshugge* murderer—"

"Did she go straight home, Shirley? Is she there now?"

"Did she show me her schedule? Do *I* know?"

"Okay, Shirley. Thanks." He turned to leave.

"Aaron?"

"Yeah?"

"This murderer *mishmash*. It's some kind advertising?"

"Yeah, Shirley. That's all it is."

She shook her head as she watched him leave the deli.

"*Nu*," said the Russian, "how much costs all this fat?"

Leah Steinberg lived in a small, eight-unit, two-story apartment building in West Hollywood built sometime during the twenties. It had a beige stucco exterior with black wrought-iron window bars, red tile roof, and other Spanish Colonial features. Leah had lived there for years in a two-bedroom unit that was semiofficially rent-controlled. Aaron, who had grown up there, found his usual parking space in the back alley.

After ringing the doorbell, then knocking on the door, he used his key to let himself in.

"Mom?" he called, stepping in from the outside hall and closing the door behind him. "Anybody home?"

The living room was decorated with potted plants and fresh flower arrangements, as usual. Early afternoon sunlight streamed in through a tall, old-fashioned window, making a distorted oblong on the flower-patterned carpet. Aaron walked slowly through the living room, savoring the strong sense of familiarity he always felt whenever he came back here. It still seemed more like home than his own place, even though he had been gone for almost ten years now.

He was getting ready to go hunt in the refrigerator for something to eat when he happened to glance at the hardwood dining table and stopped.

A letter of several pages lay to one side on the polished tabletop. It had been unfolded, but apparently had spent many years folded inside an envelope, for the pages would not lie flat. Aaron walked over and picked it up. The paper felt stiff and brittle, its original white hue now a tarnished ivory yellow. The black fountain pen ink had turned a kind of sepia. The letters were formed with the old-style cursive hand that schools used to teach before the Second World War.

My dearest Leah, the salutation read.

Aaron folded the letter, aged paper crackling as he did so. He never read his mother's mail. He seldom had the chance. Leah was an orderly person. She kept the books at Steinberg's and her private life in the same way. Letters were opened and read upon receipt. Bills were placed on her work desk for payment, greeting cards on the mantelpiece for display. Personal correspondence was filed away.

So what was this old letter doing here on the dining table?

Aaron hesitated several long seconds, the letter half-folded in his hands, debating whether to put it back down where he had found it or open it up and read it. He started to put it down, then unfolded it and began reading.

My heart yearns for you, and for what will soon be ours.

Aaron frowned as his eyes moved over the faded words.

I know now that any time spent away from you is time lost forever, and I hate the very thought of it.

Who the hell was *this?* Who wrote it?

Aaron shifted the brittle pages, turning to the end of the letter to find the author's name. As he did so, he skimmed over stray lines and phrases.

. . . *count the hours and the minutes until I return* . . .

. . . *no matter what the bastards at Panopticon* . . .

. . . that whatever happens, I will never leave you . . .
. . . our happiness, and that of our child . . .

He found the closing on page four, the last one, squeezed down near the bottom, as if the writer had wanted to use every spare inch of available space.

Yours forever, loving and faithful to the end,
Your own,
Mick

The closing itself was written in the formal cursive hand used throughout the letter, but the signature was formed with large, swirling loops, the dot over the *i* an extended circle, as if the writer's emotion had surged into the act of signing his own name, making it a statement of dramatic intensity.

"Enjoying yourself?"

Aaron looked up, dropping the letter.

"Mom!" He picked up the letter from the table again.

Leah Steinberg stood in the open doorway to her apartment, a plastic grocery sack in each hand.

"I—" Aaron began. "I didn't—"

"You never used to read my mail when you were a kid."

Leah walked across the room, put down the sacks beside the table, and grabbed the letter from his hands.

Aaron offered no resistance.

"So what makes you want to start doing it now?"

"I didn't think— I didn't know it was yours."

"Don't give me such *chozzerai!* Suddenly you can't read?"

"Who's it from?"

"Somebody I used to know."

She turned from the table and walked toward the kitchen, letter clutched in one hand, held close against her breast.

"What's his name?"

"You didn't get that far?"

Aaron followed her into the kitchen.

"Okay! I did! Sue me! His name's Mick. Who *is* he?"

"Was. He died a long time ago."

Aaron stopped in the middle of the kitchen, afternoon sunlight flooding in from the window over the sink.

His mother stood facing him, letter held to her breast.

Aaron's mouth had gone dry. He could hardly speak.

"That's from my father, isn't it?"

Leah said nothing.

"Mick. That was his name, wasn't it?"

She held the letter out in front of her.

"I should have torn this up a long time ago."

She made a gesture of starting to do so right then.

"No!"

Aaron moved forward, reaching for the letter. She pulled it back from him, and held it close to her breast once again.

"My father wrote that! I have a right to read it!"

"I thought you already did."

"I *started* to. I read the first few lines. Then I skipped to the end to see who wrote it. Then—you came in."

Neither spoke for almost a minute.

"It was a love letter, wasn't it?"

"I don't want to talk about this, Aaron."

"He knew you were pregnant with me, didn't he? When he wrote that part about 'our child'—"

"I *won't* talk about it!"

She turned her back on him, holding the letter close to her with both hands, leaning forward slightly, as if wounded.

Aaron came up to her slowly.

"What's so terrible about it? It's a letter where he says how much he loves you. Is it wrong for me to read a letter where my father tells my mother he loves her?"

Leah turned around suddenly. Startled, he stepped back.

"This—"

She held out the letter, like a symbol of what was wrong.

"This was written by a man who's *dead*, Aaron! It can't change anything. It'll *never* change anything. Not now."

She started to cry. He went over and put his arms around her. He did not try to take the letter.

He did not even look at it.

When she stopped crying, she wiped at her eyes. Then she walked out of the kitchen, down a short hallway to the first room on her right, the one that served as her bedroom. The second one, now a combination workroom–guest room, had been Aaron's bedroom when he used to live there.

"I don't want you coming in here to try and see where I'm putting this, okay?" she called to him from her bedroom.

"Don't worry. I won't read it without your permission."

Leah came back out into the kitchen, pulling her cardigan sweater up close, a haunted, faraway look in her eyes.

"What the hell's Panopticon, anyway?" he asked.

"It was one of the cheap studios he worked for."

"The one he worked for most of the time?"

"He's dead, Aaron. Let the dead bury the dead."

"What made you get it out and look at it again?"

Leah did not answer. Aaron went over to the refrigerator and opened the door. He surveyed its contents, then took out a cold *latke* from a covered Pyrex bowl.

"Don't get started *noshing*, Aaron—"

"—or I'll spoil my appetite. Don't worry. I don't have much of one to spoil."

He sniffed at the *latke*, then put it back inside the refrigerator and closed the door.

"You're worried about that meeting with the murderer," Leah said, "the one they call the Phantom."

"I've thought about it."

"Aaron, don't go! Let someone else go in your place."

"Sorry, Mom. But I really don't have that much choice at this point. Not after what happened to Lance Trebizond—"

"He's a serial *killer*, Aaron! My God, he *kills* people. If you meet him face-to-face, he could kill *you!*"

He came up to her and put his hands on her shoulders.

"Look, Mom. I'm not supposed to tell you this— Hell, I'm not supposed to tell anyone. If I tell you, you can't tell anybody. Not Shirley. Not even your favorite customers—"

"I can keep a secret, Aaron."

"When I meet him—*if* he shows up—I won't be alone. The police will be there with me. They won't be in uniform. But they'll be there."

"You still have to be careful, Aaron."

"I'm always careful."

She went to the stove and began fixing something for him to eat. As he watched her work, he thought of the letter hidden away in her bedroom somewhere, probably in that chest of drawers next to the bed, and for a while even the Phantom's dark presence seemed to diminish slightly, overshadowed by the greater mystery concealed in the next room.

23

MOVING IMAGE

Aaron tried to call Sam back at On-Target News, but he kept reaching her voice mail instead of her, and after leaving three messages, he gave up.

She returned his calls late in the evening as he dozed in front of his television set, tuned to the Miss Nude Aerobics USA Pageant on cable.

He fumbled for the phone. "Yeah?"

"Aaron?"

"Sam! I tried to—"

"Can you come down here to the studio?"

"Tonight?"

"Yes."

"Jesus, Sam. It's—" He looked at his watch, then leaned back on the couch. "It's almost eleven o'clock!"

"I wouldn't ask if it wasn't important."

"What is it?"

"A video I want you to see."

"A *vid*eo? Jesus! Can't it wait till tomorrow?"

"It's a video of that kid I interviewed last night. The one with the strung-out hair? And that other one, the one you said was back there in the alley, with the shaved head—"

Aaron sat bolt upright on the couch. "Where are you?"

"In a screening room. But I'll meet you in the lobby."

"Give me fifteen minutes."

The lobby of the On-Target studios contained a bank of television sets along one wall, all tuned to "On-Target News at 11," the highest-rated late evening newscast in Los Angeles. Samantha sat in front of the multiple screens, a cellular phone to one ear. She got up when she saw Aaron, breaking off the conversation with whoever was on the other end.

"You in this one?" he asked, glancing at the screens.

"Yes, but it's nothing. Just some fire in Glendale. Come on." She put away the phone. "Screening room's this way."

She led him through a series of security doors, exchanging pleasantries with various guards on duty. Aaron followed her, limping down the length of a carpeted corridor.

"Where did you get this tape?" he asked.

"I'll tell you inside the screening room."

"What's all the top secret shit for, Sam?"

"You know what they say. Even the walls—"

Just then a door to the side of them opened and Bonnie Redfield stepped out into the corridor. Her eyes came into sharp focus at the sight of Sam and Aaron.

"Samantha! You're working late tonight!"

"Woman's work is never done, Bonnie."

"And what brings your famous boyfriend down here with you?"

Aaron glared at her, but said nothing.

"Something to do with the Phantom, I'll bet. Right?"

"Good guess, but no cigar," Sam said. "We're here to check out some stock footage for a few sound effects Aaron needs."

"He couldn't send over a technician to get that?"

"No, he couldn't."

"Mind if I come along and watch?"

She smiled and tried to make it look sincere.

"Yeah, Bonnie," Sam said. "We mind."

"What if I decide to tag along anyway?"

The smile had a cutting edge to it now.

"It's a private party, Bonnie."

"You're not making friends this way, Sam."

"I've got all the friends I need."

Bonnie glanced at Aaron.

"I'll bet," she said.

She turned her back on both of them and stepped into the room she had emerged from, slamming the door behind her.

"Bitch!" Aaron shouted at the closed door.

"Forget her," Sam said, starting down the corridor again. "Hurry up. I want to get there before anyone else does."

She noticed his limp then.

"What happened to your foot?"

"Twisted my ankle. I'll be okay."

"How did you twist it?"

"Jumping off a school playground fence."

"Jumping off—"

"I wanted to get a better look at him."

"Who?"

"The same asshole that's on your goddamn tape."

She said nothing more until they were inside the screening room, about the size of a cramped classroom, with five rows of permanent seats facing a seventy-inch Mitsubishi Big Screen.

"What were you doing chasing him across a playground?"

"I saw him there—watching us."

"Us?"

"Me and the cops. I was with the cops, okay?"

"Why didn't they go after him?"

"They did. One of them did. The tall dark Indian. I was trying to keep up with him."

"I thought we agreed," Sam said, "that if you decided to go after the Phantom, we'd do it together."

"*I'm* not goin' after that son of a bitch!"

"Yes, you are. You're just taking someone else with you."

Aaron gave a disgusted snort, then sat down in one of the chairs in the first row.

"Start the movie, Sam."

"Where are you meeting him tomorrow, Aaron?"

"Look— I can't tell you that, okay?"

"Why not?"

"Because you'll want to be there, too."

"Of course I will. *Where* are you meeting him?"

"God*damn*it, Sam! This is the cops' show, not mine!"

"He doesn't want to see them. He wants to see you."

"It's not like they'll be standin' there with their fuckin' uniforms on! It's more like an undercover operation—"

"I don't think he'd care much if I was there. But if the cops are, he'll try to kill them. He may kill you, too, accidentally, when the shooting starts.

"For*get* it, Sam! The cops are runnin' this one. I have to play it their way. They'll *get* the asshole. He's not fuckin' Superman. They'll get him, and that'll be it. Now where's this stupid video of yours?"

She took a cassette from inside her blazer and fed it into the VCR connected to the Big Screen.

"Where'd you get it?" Aaron asked.

"Someone mailed it here anonymously, no return address."

"And you just went ahead and *opened* it?"

"That's right."

"It could've been a letter bomb!"

"It looked like a cassette."

"Who do you think sent it?"

"The kid with the strung-out hair."

The screen filled with electronic static, then several seconds' worth of blue leader, speakers hissing as it moved past the playback head. Then the screen flashed color, action, noise. Whoever had handled the camcorder for what they saw now must have been drunk, or stoned, or in some way physically incapacitated. Images jerked around on the screen, bobbing in and out of view. A party of some kind seemed to be in progress. Laughter, chatter, music, squeals, and background noises came together in the kind of undifferentiated sound smash that only an omnidirectional camcorder mike can produce. The images were dimly lighted, jumping in and out of darkness, illuminated fitfully by bursts from cigarette lighters, sputtering matches, and track lights hanging from the ceiling at odd, disjointed angles.

The video camera panned spasmodically across a room, jerking to an awkward halt to focus on a young girl, somewhere in her late teens, topless, breasts flopping loose from side to side, dark nipples blurred by the motion, as she gyrated her way through some sort of private dance routine.

"What *is* this?" Aaron asked. "A homemade porno flick?"

"A club video. The kind they shoot at very private clubs on the Sunset Strip, places like The Viper Room."

"Where River Phoenix cashed in his chips?"

"Right."

"That where they shot this?"

"No. This was shot at another club. The Meat Locker."

"Sounds like a fun place."

"Keep watching."

The camera panned lopsidedly over groups and couples moving through the darkness. It tilted down to catch couples lying on the floor on futon pads, then jerked up and panned back in the direction along which it had already traveled, coming to a stop once again on the topless girl, framing her in close mid-shot this time, the image relatively stable. She had stopped dancing now and stared straight into the camera lens, bare breasts jutting out below. Her eyes stared blankly at the viewer, pupils constricted to pinpoints.

"What's she on?" Aaron asked.

"Heroin."

"You sure?"

"You'll get to watch someone mainlining it in a minute."

The camera panned down to focus on the girl's bare breasts. Each nipple had been pierced with a large gold ring. They dangled from her breasts like misplaced earrings.

"Ouch!" Aaron said. "That's gotta hurt."

"That's the idea. Body piercing's all about pain."

The camera panned farther down to the girl's crotch, where she was unzipping her jeans. She wore nothing underneath. She wriggled out of them, then pulled back her dark pubic hair to reveal labia pierced with three separate sets of jewel-encrusted gold pins.

As the camera focused on this, a fully erect penis poked into the right side of the frame, a gold ring dangling from its uncircumcised foreskin.

"Jesus!" Aaron cried. "What *don't* they pierce?"

"The more intimate the better."

"How do they even do it with all that hardware on?"

"Watch this."

Aaron leaned forward to get a good view of the outsized sexual organs on the Big Screen. But the camera suddenly whip-panned away, flashing across patches of light and darkness until it came to rest on a tilted-angle view of a boy, anywhere from sixteen up, injecting a hypodermic needle into the underside of his forearm. The arm had been tied off above the elbow with a strip of elastic rubber, a junkie's tourniquet. The boy grinned, mouth hanging open, straight dark hair falling in his eyes, as he drove the needle home.

"He's just a goddamn kid!" Aaron said.

"But if you look, he's not the youngest one there."

"Is everybody doing heroin on this tape?"

"Most of them—if you sit through the whole thing."

"No thanks. I've seen enough dope and pierced tits."

"Just wait, Aaron. Your favorite stars are coming up."

The camera swung in a sudden arc, running the images together in a whirling, continuous blur. It stopped on a jagged mid-shot of the fallen angel with his strung-out hair, one of Aaron's three assailants. He was laughing, mouth open wide, revealing his bad teeth, eyes squeezed shut.

Aaron leaned forward in his seat. "Son of a bitch!"

"That's him, right?"

"Yes, that's him! The fucking little shit—"

The fallen angel stopped laughing and said something, but whether because he was stoned or because the sound was at the wrong level, nothing intelligible came through. He moved from mid-shot to closeup, walking up into the camera lens, stretching his bad teeth across the full expanse of the Big Screen.

The camera moved again, snapping to the left, then jerking to a halt to frame a doorway and a figure leaning against it like a threshold guardian. Behind him, the lights of another room glimmered fitfully in the distance. Shaved head, red forelock, round face, hollow eyes—all these things were clearly visible, and instantly recognizable.

"Goddamn," Aaron whispered.

The face on the screen smiled, stretching its lips to reveal small, widely spaced teeth and a bloodred gum line.

"That's it?" Sam asked. "The face behind the mask?"

"Yeah—"

Aaron stared at the face on the screen in front of him, trying to fix it with the hoarse, heavy voice he had heard whispering through his headphones earlier that day.

Eight o'clock. Tomorrow night. Good-bye, Sunset Scott.

"He doesn't look old enough," Sam said.

"What?"

"The Phantom's voice sounds old. At least the few times I heard him, it sounded old—not nursing home old, but older than that kid up there."

"Well, that's *him*, goddamnit!"

"Whatever you say, Aaron."

Up on the Big Screen, the object of this attention turned his back to the camera, presenting a shapeless wedge of dark-jacketed shoulders. He moved through the doorway and closed the door behind him. The camera rushed up to the closed door and stayed there, moving over the doorjamb and doorknob with microscopic precision, as if looking for some sign, some clue, some visible presence he had left behind.

"That's it?" Aaron asked.

"For now, yes."

"What do you mean 'for now'?"

"He comes back in later. Sort of drifts in and out."

"Along with more pierced tits and kids shooting up?"

"Sure."

"Shut it off, Sam. I've seen enough."

"You sure that's him?"

"Fuck, yes, I'm sure! I've seen the asshole more than once. And the very first time I saw him, he said—"

Man, I am *the mask.*

"What did he say, Aaron?"

"He told me—what he was."

Seeing the face again, bigger than life-size on the seventy-inch Mitsubishi screen, brought back other images. The girl with her eyes burned out by liquid nitrogen. The guard in the bloodred elevator. The woman on the sidewalk in front of the schoolyard fence. Lance Trebizond, taped tight into his announcer's chair.

Aaron understood then, as if for the first time, that the one who had done these things was more than a mere phantom, a whispering voice, an illusory white mask.

He had his own real face, his own dark eyes.

And he was going to meet him, face-to-face, tomorrow night.

24

CHECKOUT

The LAPD arranged a meeting with him the next day, right after his airshift ended at 9:00 A.M. Aaron took the call inside his announcing booth. It was Lopez.

"Want me to drive over to the—"

"No," Lopez said. "Not here."

"Where?"

"You know that hot dog wagon, on Vine near Selma?"

"The one that's usually on Sunset, in front of the bank?"

"It's on Vine today."

"You want me to meet you *there?*"

"How long will it take you?"

"From here? It's just downstairs and around the block."

"How long?"

"Five minutes, if the elevator's slow."

"I'll be waiting."

* * *

He found the hot dog wagon where Lopez said it would be, with Lopez standing in front of it. The detective wore jeans, leather jacket, and aviator-style sunglasses. He was ordering a hot dog as Aaron approached.

"I thought you just wanted to meet here. You hungry?"

"We want it to look real, *amigo*, in case he's watching."

Aaron glanced over his shoulder at the traffic building on Vine and the pedestrians moving along both sides of the street.

"What do you want on yours?" Lopez asked.

"Uh—mustard, relish, no onions."

Lopez paid for the two hot dogs, then handed Aaron his.

"Come on," he said. "We can walk while we eat."

"Are you kidding? I can't eat mine like this!"

"Then carry it with you."

Lopez moved down the sidewalk, biting into his hot dog.

Aaron had to push to keep up with the cop's long strides.

"The most important thing," Lopez said, swallowing, "is to follow your regular routine to the letter. Change nothing. Whatever you do when you go to this place—where you sit, what you order to drink—do the exact same thing tonight. If you usually look around a bit and scan the other customers when you first walk in—"

"I don't."

"Then don't do it tonight. We'll be there, before you. But *don't* look for us. Don't try to fake it, either. No glancing out of the corner of your eye, or pretending to watch some stripper when you're really checking to see if we're there. This one's too smart to fall for amateur crap like that."

"You think he'll know it when I walk in?"

"He could be sitting right next to you."

A piece of hot dog seemed to stick in Aaron's throat.

"You think he won't be wearing his mask?"

"I don't know what he'll wear."

Aaron saw the face from the videotape last night, framed by shadow and half-light, smiling into the camera.

"Whatever he does—or doesn't do—that's our problem. All you have to do is show up."

"But what if he doesn't show?"

"Then he doesn't show."

Lopez took another bite of his hot dog, chewing it vigorously as he crossed Selma against the light. A van driver leaned on his horn. Lopez ignored him. He seemed to be accustomed to eating street food on the run. Aaron hurried to catch up with him, mustard dripping down his fingers.

"What if he asks me to go outside? Or step into the rest room with him for a few minutes?"

Aaron paused, remembering the dead girl on the floor of the Cinematheque rest room, dark purple holes instead of eyes.

"Do I just go with him—or what?"

"We'll already be moving in on him by then."

"But if he's as smart as you think, he could be wearing a wig. He could look like anybody. How will you know it's him?"

"We'll know."

"You want me to wear a wire, so you can record us?"

Lopez smiled hard as he ate the last of his hot dog.

"This *pendejo*'s been recorded enough. We don't want any more tapes. We just want to take him down. But that's not your problem. All you have to do is go in there and wait for him to approach you. We'll do the rest. And we'll do it fast."

Aaron looked at a smear of ketchup on Lopez's hand and saw the blood splashed across the walls of the elevator, the guard's body slumping sideways, eyes gouged out, throat slit.

"Eight o'clock tonight, *amigo*. Don't be late."

Aaron lifted his head, stung by the implied accusation, wondering if maybe Jerry had been complaining to Lopez and Montoya about his late arrivals at the radio station.

"What makes you think I'll be late?"

"And don't get cute. That's what gets people killed."

* * *

Later that morning, shortly before noon, Aaron turned into the driveway of what looked like a group of decayed office buildings and warehouses clumped together on a side street off Melrose. The usual graffiti scarred the outside walls. Some of the windows on the upper floors had been broken.

A guard in a cheap rented uniform got up slowly from a stool on the left-hand side of the driveway. He was an older man with a heavy pot gut and weak, squinting eyes.

"Excuse me," Aaron said, leaning out his rolled-down window. "Is this where the Panopticon studios used to be?"

"No, this here's Post-Tech Sound Labs."

"I know that. But did it *used* to be Panopticon?"

"Oh, Panopticon," he said, as if hearing that word for the first time. "Now you goin' *way* back. This place ain't been Panopticon for more'n thirty-five years now."

"But this is where the studios *used* to be?"

"Sure. Studio A was right over there."

He pointed with a gnarled, arthritic finger.

"Did you used to work here then?" Aaron asked.

"Nope. I was stationed in Korea 'bout the time Panopticon closed down for good. Then, after I got out, I signed up with the L.A. County Sheriff, but that didn't last long—"

"Is there anyone who still works here who used to work here back when it was Panopticon?"

The guard rubbed the stubble on his chin thoughtfully.

"Well, let's see now. No, he came on after they turned it into a storage lot. You know they used to store the costumes from some of them other studios here for a while? Some of the big ones, too. MGM, Twentieth—"

"Sure. So nobody's still here who was here back then?"

"Nope. Nobody that— Wait a minute, now. Johnny was around back then. Old Johnny Moffet. He's even older'n I am, and that's pretty darn old. Why, just last year—"

"Where can I find him?" Aaron asked.

"Works at the commissary, washin' dishes. That's the one thing never *has* closed down around here. The commissary. People got to eat. So they keep that old commissary—"

"How do I get there?"

"Just drive down to that red building over there and take a left. You can't miss it. It's the one with the awning out front, and all the chairs and tables—"

"Thanks." Aaron started to drive off.

"Wait a minute! You can't park without a permit!"

Aaron slammed on his brakes.

"Where do I get one?"

"Just fill this out."

He filled out the permit application, then drove off before the guard could get started again. He parked in front of a low, ramshackle wooden building that looked as if it might have been part of a Western set at one time.

He found Johnny Moffet out in back of the commissary, hosing down greasy grill racks in a narrow alley.

"Johnny?" he asked, walking up to him.

"Who wants to know?"

Johnny Moffet had a hard, thin old man's face, lined with deep wrinkles that must have been caused by too much smiling years ago. Water from the hose splashed noisily onto the concrete surface of the alley.

"My name's Aaron Scott. I do a morning radio show on KRAS FM. I use the name Sunset Scott when I'm broadcasting." He paused. "Maybe you've heard of me?"

Moffet coughed deep in his chest, bringing up a mouthful of phlegm. He spit it out on the concrete, where it washed away with the torrent from the hose.

"I don't listen to the radio much."

"Cool. I wonder if—"

"Except for sports. Football. You broadcast sports?"

"Not really."

"Then I haven't heard you."

He turned his attention back to the grill racks.

"They tell me you used to work here," Aaron said, "back when this place was still Panopticon."

Moffet looked up suddenly, his thin face harder than ever.

"Who told you that?"

Aaron hesitated. "The guard—the one out front."

"Floyd? Old Floyd Trask. Got a mouth on him, don't he?"

"Is it true?"

"What? All that horseshit old Floyd told you?"

"About you. That you used to work at Panopticon."

Moffet went over and gave the spigot handle several hard, fast turns. When the flow of water stopped, he coiled up the hose, wrapping it around the spigot. Then he took out a crumpled pack of unfiltered Camels from his shirt pocket. He offered one to Aaron, who shook his head. Moffet fished out a bent cigarette and lighted it with a match from a matchbook advertising one of Las Vegas's more budget-conscious casinos.

"Yeah," he said, spitting out loose ends of tobacco. "I used to work here. Once. A long time ago."

"Did you always—" Aaron gestured vaguely at the racks.

The hardness flashed in Moffet's eyes again.

"Did I always have this kind of job? Washin' shit off grease racks? That what you tryin' to ask?"

Moffet coughed out a lungful of smoke. Some of the anger seemed to dissipate along with it. He looked past Aaron, down toward the other end of what had once been a busy studio lot.

"Used to be an AD. Assistant Director, to you."

"Did you always work here at Panopticon?"

"Hell, no. I used to work for some *real* studios. Warners' back in the late thirties, early forties. My name was on some of the biggest movies they ever put out. Nobody noticed it, but it was right up there. John S. Moffet, Assistant Director."

"Why did you leave?"

Moffet spit out some more loose tobacco ends.

"Fuckin' Jack Warner accused me of bein' a goddamn commie."

"Were you?"

Moffet gave him a look that made Aaron step back a little.

Then he drew deep on his cigarette and exhaled another lungful of smoke, coughing slightly as he watched it drift in the air. Up above a raven cawed loudly, large and black, perched on the edge of a decaying studio rooftop.

"What does it matter, after all these years? Hell, give it enough time, nothin' seems to matter. Anyways, I starved for a while after that, but I never scabbed, by God. Then I got on with Twentieth. Worked for 'em a year or so before fuckin' Darryl Zanuck fired my ass. Then I got on here."

"Panopticon did mostly B-pictures, right?"

Moffet laughed, revealing a mouth full of tobacco stains.

"B-pictures? C-pictures, more like it! Maybe even Z-pictures. We scraped the bottom of the bottom of the goddamn barrel. Even did some television there at the end. Sold shit for gold. But it was still the movin' pictures. Best job in the whole wide world. Bunch of boys—and the crew *was* mostly all male back then, except for maybe the script girl and the coffee girl—bunch of us workin' together, drinkin' hard, playin' hard, the way boys will. But after it was all over, we *had* somethin'—somethin' that would *last.* Not much really lasts, you know, not even football. But movies do, by God. People go into these video stores today, check out some Warners' thing from the early forties, and by God that's *us,* fifty-some years later."

"Did you ever get to direct?" Aaron asked.

"Direct? Shit! Only way an AD ever gets to direct in this town is politics. I was never much good at that."

"Did you ever get to know any of the actors here?"

"Hell, yes. Actors, extras, stunt men. Knew 'em all."

"You ever know one named Mick?"

"Mick who?"

"I don't know his last name. Just Mick."

Moffet frowned, not in anger this time, but in serious concentration, as if moving back into the dead and buried past.

Overhead the raven cawed again, hoarse and grating.

Moffet raised the cigarette to his lips, then put it down.

"Mick! Of course— Mick Grady."

Aaron's heart skipped a beat at hearing that name.

"Sure, I knew Mick. But he wasn't really an actor."

"What was he?"

"Sometimes an extra, or a bit player without no lines. But mostly he was a stuntman. Panopticon made lots of action pictures. We always needed stuntmen."

"I heard he worked in a lot of Westerns."

"Who didn't? It's what the public wanted to see back then. Westerns. So it's what we gave 'em."

"What kind of guy was he?"

"Mick? Like most stuntmen, I guess. Tall, good-lookin', hard-drinkin'. Good-natured sort of fella."

"But not enough talent to be an actor?"

Moffet snorted smoke out his nose.

"Talent? To be an actor? Shit! Actin', directin'—not much difference. All a bunch of fuckin' politics."

"I heard he got killed in an accident."

Moffet looked up at him. "I heard the same thing."

"Do you know how it happened?"

"No. It was on a location shoot. I wasn't there."

"Did he—"

"Excuse me. I gotta get back to work."

Moffet threw his cigarette into a pool of standing water.

The burning tobacco hissed sharply, then went out.

25

STRIPTEASE

The Rakehell Club seemed the same as always when Aaron drove up to the entrance that night, shortly before eight. The awning still stretched out over the front door, sedate and old-fashioned, with broad, conservative stripes.

Only tonight, for some reason, they looked like fangs.

The valet parking attendant greeted him as usual, held the door while he got out. The other attendants stood watching—polite, smiling, deferential. They seemed to be paying closer than ordinary attention to him. Nothing obvious, just something he noticed on an almost-subliminal level.

Inside, it grew more obvious.

The kid with the ponytail, the one who usually greeted him at the door, was nowhere to be seen. In his place stood a short, heavy man with shiny flat hair and an Armani suit that must have set him back an easy thousand. Two ox-faced bodyguards waited in the shadows behind him, their muscles pumped to cartoon dimensions by free weights and steroids, straining the seams of their cheap, off-the-rack suits.

"Hi, there," the short man said, stepping forward and offering Aaron his hand. "I'm Sal Esposito."

"Cool. I'm—"

"Where you want to sit tonight, Mr. Scott?"

Aaron stared at him, wondering how he knew his name.

"Close to the stage? Halfway back? You tell me."

"I usually sit close to the stage."

"Then that's where you sit tonight."

Esposito snapped his fingers at the two hulking bodyguards.

"Make sure Mr. Scott's comfortable, next to the stage."

He turned back to Aaron, smiling with his mouth only.

"You need something, you let them know. They don't get what you want, you let *me* know. Okay?"

"Sure."

Aaron moved through the glass-beaded portiere and into the Rakehell's main room. He took a seat in one of the dark leather chairs near the dance stage. Rock music pounded from speakers overhead, hard and bass-heavy. Revolving lights flashed in his eyes, scattering reflected patterns across the stage floor and the large mirror that formed its back wall.

Everything felt the same as usual.

Except it didn't. It seemed as if the other customers were watching him. He wanted to turn around and check things out, reassure himself that it was all in his mind. But he remembered Lopez's warning from earlier in the day.

No glancing out of the corner of your eye—

As he took his seat in the leather chair, he noticed one of the bodyguards standing back from the stage. He hadn't heard anyone move through the jangling glass beads of the portiere behind him, but there he was. He realized then, as if for the first time, how dark the main room was, what lights there were were placed carefully to give the illusion of clear vision without its substance. Everything seemed to be in shadow, even the dancer up on the stage, a thin blond with jutting silicone boobs and a twitching butt, hands moving slowly over her sleek body, image doubled in the wall-to-wall mirror behind her.

You couldn't really see things in here. You couldn't tell who was sitting next to you, who was standing behind you—not even how many people there were inside the room with you.

A hand came down on top of his.

He jumped, muscles contracting. It was a small hand, with artificial spike nails, costume jewelry rings, and lots of clearance sale cologne.

"Oh!" said the high, hard voice. "Did I scare you?"

He looked up past the silicone cleavage and into small eyes squinting from a face framed with brown, frizzed-out hair.

"You see me dance, sweetheart?"

"Sorry, babe. Just got here."

She leaned over to place the traditional kiss on his cheek.

He put a hand on her shoulder, stopping her.

The skin felt cold, as if someone had just thawed her out.

He took out a five and handed it to her.

"Hey, thanks!"

She dropped it down her cleavage, shaking the frizzed hair.

"You want a drink, sweetheart?"

"Yeah. Guinness."

Aaron watched the act on stage with unusual concentration.

He didn't want to think about why he was there, what he was waiting for, whether Lopez and Montoya were actually in the room with him, whether they could move fast enough—

He watched the thin blond go through her dance, which consisted mainly of an autoerotic rubdown, slim hands moving over her smooth stomach and inflated breasts, caressing her nipples, dark areolas stretched huge and flat by all the silicone. Her body wasn't as good as Sam's, but it reminded him of Sam's, and he felt himself getting hard. He kept his eyes on her slow, smoky moves, not looking away even when the dancer with the frizzed hair came back with his Guinness and they did the standard kiss on the cheek and five-buck tip.

The bottle of Guinness felt ice-cold and comforting in his hand. Up on stage, the thin blond smiled at him, then blew him a phony, pouty-lipped, come-fuck-me-baby kiss.

He raised the bottle to his lips and took a healthy swallow of dark, sweet stout.

"Don't get drunk," said the voice. "We have to talk."

He almost choked on the Guinness.

It was the same whispering voice he had heard so many times before over his headphones, but it sounded different now, coming through live. There was a growl to it, a low-register rumble, perhaps caused by the fact that it was necessary to talk louder than a whisper in order to be heard above the steady, pounding rush of hard rock from the speakers overhead.

He could not make himself turn toward that voice—not yet.

He stared hard at the bottle of Guinness in his hand, as if that had something to do with it.

"Are you afraid to look at me, Sunset Scott?"

He was very afraid. But he turned anyway, and looked.

A large man sat at the table next to him, shoulders slumped forward, hood from a black sweatshirt pulled down low over his forehead. He wore dark blue jeans and black Doc Martens, or maybe running shoes—it was hard to tell which in the shadows. He wore black workout gloves, the kind with the fingers cut off at mid-knuckle. But his own fingers, sticking through the gloves, looked dead white beneath the uncertain lights, almost phosphorescent, like ghost fingers glowing in the dark.

The table next to him had been empty when he first came in and sat down. Aaron *knew* that. He remembered glancing in that direction as he took his own seat. What sat there now had just moved in, without apparent sound or motion, like something materializing out of the shadows.

He swallowed, the Guinness sour in his mouth.

"You're early, Sunset Scott."

"You said eight."

"Yes, I did. But you're often late, aren't you?"

"Want me to leave, and then come back in half an hour?"

The man in the hood did not answer.

Aaron regretted the words the moment he said them. It was the kind of smart-ass remark he tossed off all the time, without even thinking about it, just some standard radio *shtick.* But this was not radio. He sensed the physical menace of the man sitting at the table next to him—not just his size, but his power, like a pressure-sensitive bomb, timed and set, waiting to go off at the wrong touch.

The Phantom continued to sit there and say nothing.

Rock music hammered down from the speakers overhead. Flashing lights revolved on the stage. The blond undulated through the movements of her self-caressing dance, reflected in the dark mirror that stretched from one wall to the other behind her. But it all seemed to be happening at a separate distance, like a performance viewed through a filter of soundproof glass. It was as if a magic circle had been drawn around them, and nothing else existed inside the main room except for himself and what sat there at the table next to him.

The Phantom sat without moving, as if sculpted from dark stone. With the hood drawn over his head, it was impossible to see his face. He looked like some street person who had wandered in from the cold, or a drug dealer seeking anonymity. An untasted bottle of beer sat on the table in front of him.

Aaron wondered whether one of the dancers had come up and tried to give *him* the old five-buck kiss on the cheek.

He took another stiff swig of Guinness, hardly noticing the taste or the chill as the liquid went down his throat. The alcohol buzz seemed to blunt some of his fear.

"Why don't you show me your mask?"

The hooded man sat slumped forward over the table, staring down at his own bottle of beer.

"My listeners will ask me that, you know. They'll say—"

"You like to watch, don't you, Sunset Scott?"

The Phantom lifted his hand and gestured toward the stage, where the blond was winding up the fake orgasm finale of her act, slim hands pulling on the nipples of her silicone breasts.

Aaron drew back at the Phantom's sudden movement, as unexpected as a statue's coming to life. His hand looked huge, extended like that, fingers poking through the workout gloves, white and glowing. Aaron stared at them, and saw that they were white gloves, worn beneath the black workout gloves. Gloves within gloves. Wheels within wheels.

Was there a mask behind the mask? Aaron still couldn't see anything inside the hood, except for a glimmer of something white and vaguely phosphorescent, like the other gloves.

"You talk to people, Sunset Scott, but only through a microphone. You separate yourself from your coworkers by walls of glass. You have a girlfriend, but you spend most of your time watching her on television, along with everyone else. And you come here to watch women pretend to masturbate for your own private sexual gratification—"

"Look, masked man," Aaron said, turning in his chair, anger overcoming his fear, "my sex life's entirely cool, okay?"

"You're afraid of real life, aren't you, Sunset Scott?"

"What the fuck you call *this?*"

He slammed down the Guinness on the table in front of him.

The Phantom turned partway toward him, and he could see something white and insubstantial within the shadows of the hood, like a pale blur where a face should be.

"This," he said, "is only a game, Sunset Scott."

"Oh yeah? Then you're playin' it along with me, pal."

"No, I'm not. Not at all."

"*You're* the one who asked me to come here—"

"Do you think I don't know you brought them with you?"

Aaron, ready to say something, stopped, mouth open.

"Do you think I'm a fool, Sunset Scott?"

This one's too smart, he heard Lopez say.

"Do you think I don't know where they are, right now?"

"Look," Aaron began, "nobody came here with—"

"Don't lie to me. Don't make it worse than it already is."

And don't get cute, he heard Lopez again, walking down Vine with a hot dog in one hand. *That's what gets people killed.*

"Don't you think I know that everyone in this room is looking at *us* right now, not her?"

He gestured again toward the thin blond dancer.

"Do you think *they* can protect you, Sunset Scott?"

"Just don't try anything in here, man. You'll be sorry."

The Phantom laughed then—a low, unpleasant sound, with an unexpected depth of malice to it. He turned suddenly and leaned toward Aaron, bringing the mask into full view.

Aaron pulled back instinctively, grabbing for the Guinness bottle with his left hand, but knowing it was useless, an empty gesture, his fingers cramping around cold glass.

He tried to find his voice. "Look—"

"*You* look."

He could see the mask clearly now, but there was nothing clear to see. It seemed diaphanous, a veil floating over a lumpy, irregular surface—not a face, but something else. He could see the dark holes where the eyes must be, a glimpse of something inside the slit that served as a mouth. He remembered the hollow sockets in the skulls of his victims, eyes burned out by fire and liquid nitrogen, gouged out by main force.

"I could kill you before *they* knew what was happening."

Aaron turned his head to one side as the Phantom's breath blew over him like the winds of death.

"And they couldn't do a thing to stop me."

The Phantom drew back abruptly, the mask in half-shadow beneath the hood once again. Aaron felt his own breathing moderate. He relaxed his cramped grip on the Guinness bottle.

"But I haven't come here to kill you, Sunset Scott. I could do that whenever I wanted to, wherever I chose."

The Phantom drew himself up to his full seated height, slumping no more, and looked down on Aaron, who felt the arm of his own chair cutting into his back.

"I came here to show you something—to show them all."

With what seemed one movement, quicker than thought, the Phantom got to his feet and leaped onto the stage, where the thin blond dancer was still taking her bows, a remnant of discarded costume clutched tight against her silicone breasts for modesty's sake.

Continuing the movement, he turned to the audience, grabbed the girl's arm with one hand, pulled out a seventeen-inch Uzi submachine gun from beneath his hooded black sweatshirt with the other—everything so fast it appeared instantaneous, black-gloved hand empty one second, holding the Uzi the next.

Had it been any slower, Esposito's bodyguards would have gunned him down. They drew their own weapons from inside concealed shoulder holsters and took aim as he leaped onto the stage. But the Phantom started shooting first, spraying the bodyguards and the audience members with full-automatic fire at the rate of 950 rounds per minute.

Esposito's bodyguards took it in the chest, nine-millimeter Parabellum bullets knocking them back over tables, down to the carpeted floor. Bottles blew off racks behind the well-stocked bar as bartenders dived for cover, glass shards flying everywhere. One of the dancers doubling as a barmaid got hit in the jaw. She dropped her tray of drinks and began screaming, mouth full of blood.

Aaron scrambled beneath his own table, ice-cold Guinness spilling on his head. He never felt it. Bursts of automatic fire from the Uzi went off above him like strings of cherry bombs, deafening reverberations bouncing off the walls.

The thin blond dancer, spunky despite her size, began kicking at the Phantom, swiping at him with acrylic nails.

"You fuckin' *shit!*" she screamed. "Let *go* of me!"

She caught the edge of the hood and pushed it back, revealing most of the mask. Her next swipe might have caught that and ripped it right off. But the Phantom threw her away from him with a sudden backhand jerk, hurling her headfirst into the wall-to-wall mirror behind them. The glass shattered in a star-burst pattern, radiating out from where her head hit like filaments of a jagged spiderweb. Blood and brains dribbled down the surface of the cracked glass. The dancer's body hung motionless, held by the sheer force of impact. Then gravity took over and it slid down to the stage floor, along with the blood and brains.

The main room echoed with cries from the wounded, screams from the scared-shitless, reverberations from repeated bursts of automatic fire. The sound system took a direct hit, along with Esposito's bodyguards. Only static hissed from the speakers. Most of the revolving lights had been shattered by wild fire.

Aaron, on his knees beneath the table, hair stiff with drying stout, cursed Lopez and Montoya, mumbling to himself as machine gun fire exploded overhead.

Where the fucking hell *were* they?

One of the dancers, crossing the main room on her way to the john when the shooting started, had taken cover during the worst of it and somehow managed to avoid getting hit. Now, scared to death, and damp in the crotch where she pissed herself, she hoped that maybe this was a good time to make a break for it. She knew where the exit doors were behind the stage. She could find them, even in this fucking, black-ass darkness. And the shooting seemed to have stopped for a while. *Maybe* it had stopped. Her own ears felt like they were plugged up with wax from the thunderous reverberations, louder by far than the shots themselves. Who could hear any fucking thing right now?

She crawled across the carpet of the main room, stifling a squeal when one hand landed in something wet and sticky and she felt it move. She kept crawling, past overturned chairs and tables, across glass shards that cut into her hands and knees. It hurt like holy shit, but she wasn't stopping now, no way, not until she was around the fucking stage and into the back dressing rooms and out the fucking emergency exit door.

She was crawling along the side of the stage when a hand grabbed hold of her upper arm, almost crushing it, and yanked her up to her feet and then up onto the stage, knocking off one of her spike heel dancing shoes—all of it happening so fast she had no time to react, not even to scream.

She could see him now, a great menacing shape, dark against the darkness, and within his own darkness a ghostly luminescence, like surf breaking under moonlight.

"Oh fuck please don't hurt me! Jesus God please fuck *no*—"

She saw the knife then, long as a ninja sword, blade glittering beneath the direct beam of an overhead track light.

She started to scream.

Aaron, beneath his table, heard her screams and thought it was the same dancer the Phantom had grabbed when leaping onto the stage—the thin blond, blond no more, head red and pulpy now, like a watermelon run over in the middle of the road. He wondered if he should try to run for it, now that the Phantom was busy, or just stay down here and sweat it out, praying for help from those two fucking, double-crossing, asshole cops.

Above him, the screams came to a sudden stop.

Aaron remained below the table on his hands and knees. He could feel his heart pounding inside his chest. If his ears hadn't been temporarily deafened by the bursts of automatic fire, he could have actually heard it beating, a frightened sign of life beneath the shadow of death.

The table flew up and away from him, kicked back by the Phantom's heavy-booted foot. It crashed into another table behind him, shattering wood and glass, splitting the frames of leather-covered chairs. Aaron crouched on his hands and knees, immobilized by fear, unwilling—unable—to move or look up.

"Look at me, Sunset Scott."

Aaron remained as he was.

"*Look* at me."

He looked up.

A hoarse cry escaped him. The Phantom held the dancer's head by its thick brown hair. It had been severed crudely at the neck. Arteries and muscles, along with a jagged bit of bone, hung down below the neck. Blood fell in irregular, slopping drops, like water from a turned-off hose.

Aaron saw the knife in the Phantom's other huge hand, its blade long and broad enough to be used for combat, or decapitation. He carried the Uzi under one armpit, crushed against his side by the same arm that held the head.

"Take a good look, Sunset Scott."

He thrust the head forward, into Aaron's face. It looked slightly shrunken, drained of blood and life force. The eyes seemed shriveled, the mouth distorted by fear, like the haptic features of an Expressionist mask.

The Phantom's own mask had become a blank white wall, a barrier beyond which nothing human could pass.

"Take a *good* look. This could be your girlfriend, the one on television. This could be anyone you care about. This could even be you, Sunset Scott."

The Phantom plunged the knife down into the dance floor, where it struck with shuddering force. In the same instant, almost as if by magic, a butane lighter appeared in his hand. He flicked it on. A jet of flame pierced the darkness. He ignited the dancer's long brown hair. Flames snaked up the curled tresses. A slightly sweet, sickening stench filled the air.

"Here." He tossed the burning head Aaron's way. "Catch!"

Aaron raised his arms to protect himself. The head on fire, a blazing Medusa, bounced off his elbow, singeing his leather jacket, then dropped to the carpet, where it began to smolder as flames ate into scalp flesh.

Gunshots rang out from the back of the room, near the ruins of the bar—pistol shots, squeezed off in rapid succession.

The glass of the wall-to-wall mirror, shattered initially by the blond dancer's head, began to explode behind the Phantom, shards bursting with the force of shrapnel. He presented a poor target, a dark figure in deep shadow, transfixed by track light beams, dropping like lances from the ceiling. Most of the unseen gunman's shots went wild. But one came close enough to tear the hood back from the Phantom's head.

With a deep-throated growl, he fired Uzi bursts into the darkness. Return fire came back at him. One of the bullets showered him with glass fragments from the disintegrating mirror. Another ricocheted off the Uzi's muzzle.

The Phantom got off one more burst, then turned and ran for the side curtains leading to the dressing rooms and the emergency exit at the back of the building.

Gunfire continued from the darkness, tracking him as he sprinted across the stage, shattering more mirror glass, tearing at the red velvet curtains as he vanished through them.

Aaron caught a fleeting glimpse of the back of the Phantom's head, now that the hood was down—hairless flesh, scarred and discolored, vilely misshapen, as if it had melted, then hardened into something repellent and nonhuman.

Aaron turned and saw gunshots flashing in the darkness, then the knife-thin form of Lopez. He leaped onto a stage front table, passing by Aaron in a blur of motion, then onto the stage itself and through the red velvet curtains.

Aaron got to his feet and pulled himself up on the stage, wincing as a piece of glass cut into the palm of his hand.

"Shit!"

He felt blood leaking from his hand as he ran across the stage. Someone called out his name from the chaos of the main room, but he kept going—through the red velvet curtains, into a dark corridor. He stopped, uncertain which way to go next, until he saw the EXIT sign at the far end, letters pale green and glowing in the darkness. He made his way to the sign and found a door with a bar release. He pushed on it and stepped outside, into the alley at the back of the Rakehell Club.

He heard gunshots echoing back down the alley, and the whine of bullets ricocheting off metal and concrete. He dropped to the pavement, then looked up.

At the far end of the alley Lopez pursued the Phantom, firing shots from the Beretta as he ran. The Phantom, at least thirty yards ahead, turned occasionally to fire back a burst from the Uzi. Neither man, shooting wild, had much chance of hitting the other, but Lopez was slowly closing the distance between them. The Phantom, realizing this, came to a full stop and turned to face his pursuer, getting off an extended burst of automatic fire. Lopez dropped and rolled, flattening his body against the side of the alley. But even as he dropped, he fired one last shot, and that one found its target.

The Phantom howled like a maddened beast, pain and rage breaking forth from behind the mask. He grabbed at his leg above the knee. Blood flowed through gloved fingers down the length of his blue-jeaned leg, iridescent scarlet under the pale orange glow of a sodium vapor streetlight.

He backed toward the end of the alley, limping on the wounded leg, squeezing off more rounds of automatic fire, pinning Lopez flat against the side of the alley. He limped around the corner, out onto the main boulevard that ran parallel to the Rakehell Club. Lopez got to his feet and went after him.

Aaron stood up, hand throbbing where he had cut it on the glass. He stumbled toward the end of the alley, coughing as he ran, pavement hard and obstinate beneath his feet. He heard tires squealing out on the boulevard, followed by gunfire, then the honking of horns. He stopped at the mouth of the alley, listening for more gunfire. Hearing none, he turned the corner.

Lopez stood far down the sidewalk, the Beretta held in one hand. In the other he raised his LAPD badge for the benefit of frightened bystanders crowding in around him. Traffic had come to a dead stop on the boulevard. Curious drivers leaned their heads out rolled-down windows. Impatient drivers hit their horns. An uneven trail of blood stretched down the sidewalk, coming to a stop near Lopez.

From the looks of things, none of it belonged to him.

Aaron pushed his way through the crowd gathering around the detective. When they saw the blood from the cut on Aaron's hand, most of them stepped back.

Lopez looked at him with a flat cop stare.

"What happened?" Aaron asked.

"I told you not to get cute."

Lopez put his badge back inside a rumpled Armani jacket.

"I saw you hit him. Where did he—"

Lopez grabbed Aaron by the shirt collar and slammed him back into a storefront window, not as hard as he could have, if he had been really trying, but hard enough to thump Aaron's head solidly against the safety glass.

"Hey!" he cried, more in surprise than pain.

"Police brutality!" someone shouted. "I'm a witness!"

Lopez turned and pointed the Beretta at the guy.

He ran, along with the rest of the crowd. More shouts and a few threats rose over the honking from the boulevard. Lopez ignored it all, turning his attention back to Aaron, who glanced uneasily at the barrel of the Beretta, thin tendrils of smoke still curling from its blue steel muzzle.

"You get cute, you get killed. Under*stand?*"

Aaron nodded. "Sure."

"Don't *ever* run after a suspect fleeing the scene. *I'm* paid to do that shit. You're paid to talk about it—later."

"Okay. But what happened?"

"He got away." Lopez let go of Aaron's shirt collar and replaced the Beretta in a custom shoulder holster beneath his jacket. "Had a pickup waiting for him. Black cargo van, no plates. He got in. He got away."

"What were you and Montoya *doing* back there? You said—"

Lopez looked down at the trail of blood along the sidewalk.

"We fucked up."

26

MESSAGE

Hours later, he drove home through the dark.

Darkness engulfed him, gathering above streetlights and electric signs, shrouding his passage through the city. Night was his world now, more real than sunlight, the place where he lived, along with the Phantom.

At the police station, different anonymous officials had questioned him at great length. He was not allowed to see Lopez or Montoya, or find out why they no longer seemed to be in charge of the investigation.

Arriving home, he fully expected the Phantom to call.

He wouldn't have been at all surprised, unlocking the front door to his condo, to hear the phone start to ring at that very moment, greeting him from the darkness within. The Phantom seemed wired to him now, plugged into his every move, dark heart beating in perfect synchronization with his own.

Why shouldn't he time his calls to the running second?

But the phone did not ring. The rooms of the condo remained silent and dark. He didn't feel like another beer just then—he still had lots of dried Guinness in his hair—but he got a Corona out of the refrigerator anyway, along with the remains of a two-day-old sandwich, approaching calcification. He snagged a bag of chips from the cabinet above the stove and went out to the couch to see what was on television.

As he sat down, he glanced at his portable phone, lying on the television next to the remote, and dared it to ring.

But the phone just sat there.

He took a handful of chips and sipped at the beer.

Everything still seemed unreal, washed by the blood and violence of the Rakehell Club, stained white instead of red, pale as the Phantom's own luminous mask, staring at him from inside the black hood like a radioactive death's-head as he stared back at it, all the details and complexity of his whole life collapsing into the simple outline of a blank, white mask.

I could kill you before they knew what was happening.

He had been at a monster's mercy, saved by his grace alone.

And they couldn't do a thing to stop me.

That was true. The cops couldn't save him. The cops, as Lopez said, had fucked up—given up, dropped out of the picture, leaving only the Phantom, and himself, a forced player in a game he could not control, or understand.

The phone rang.

He dropped the chips, spilling some of the beer.

The phone rang quietly—long, fluttering chirps—but the sound dug into his brain like the repeated bursts of automatic fire and the screams of the wounded and the dying.

He got up from the couch, scattered chips crunching underfoot, and walked toward the ringing phone—moving automatically, unaware of either time or place, knowing only that this was his destiny, and to try to avoid it, not to answer it, would be futile, a child's defiance in the face of death.

He reached out a hand toward the ringing phone.

It stopped.

He stood there, hand outstretched, heart pounding inside his chest, room swaying slightly from side to side, like the stage floor of the Rakehell Club, awash in blood, floating in the echoing darkness down a silent river of death.

He picked up the phone.

The dead sound of a dial tone buzzed in his ear.

He put the phone back down and looked around the room, as if to reassure himself that it was still there, and he was still alive, despite the darkness, and the death.

He noticed the answering machine then, on the desk across the room. The red light blinked on and off to signal a new message. Of course. There it was. The Phantom had called earlier, and left his comments on tape.

Aaron went over and punched PLAY. The beep sounded sharply. He took a swallow of Corona to steady himself for the sound of a whispering voice coming at him from the speaker.

"This is John Moffet. We talked this afternoon, at Post-Tech Sound Labs? Used to be the old Panopticon Studios? Anyways, I been doin' some thinkin'—about Mick Grady. The guy you should really be talkin' to, the one that worked with stuntmen the most, is old Moe Edelstein—"

Aaron searched desperately for a paper and pencil.

"Moe used to be what they call a production manager nowadays," Moffet continued, on tape. "Back then they just called 'em unit supervisors, or some such bullshit. Anyways, he's the one who handled the stuntmen. Saw how much they got paid for each stunt on each picture. Saw that they *got* paid, which didn't always happen. If you ran short of money at the end of a job, you always screwed the stuntmen—"

He finally found something to write with.

"—but Moe's the one to go see. You can find him out there at the Home. The one in Woodland Hills, for retired actors and movie people? Anyways, thought you might like to know about ol' Moe. If you do go out there, tell him I said hi. We wasn't good friends or nothin', but we did used to work together."

27

ARMED AND DANGEROUS

The handguns lay in rows beneath the glass, strong fluorescent light gleaming off blue steel barrels.

"Any of these here would do the trick," the gun shop owner said, flipping through a key ring, trying to find the right one to unlock the glass case.

"What's the best?" Aaron asked.

"They're all fine guns."

"Okay, but which one would *you* recommend?"

"You each need a gun, right? For personal protection?"

He looked at Sam, standing next to Aaron.

"I guess so," she said, not sounding very convinced.

He reached inside the case and lifted out a handgun.

"SIG-Sauer P220 automatic."

"German?" Aaron asked.

"Swiss. That's what the SIG stands for. *Schweizerische Industrie-Gesellschaft.* Swiss Manufacturing, Inc."

"It says 'Made in Germany' right there."

"They manufacture some in Germany. They're still Swiss."

Aaron looked at the price tag attached to the trigger.

"Eight hundred bucks! Jesus."

"You're paying for the workmanship."

"I don't want to hang it on my wall!"

"It's not just for looks. The way they fit this barrel, it's got about the best accuracy of any handgun you can buy."

"How many bullets does it hold?"

"Nine rounds, nine-millimeter Parabellum."

"Para-what?"

"Parabellum. More powerful than regular nine-millimeter."

Aaron held the gun in his hands, feeling its weight.

"Will it—do the job?"

The owner looked up from where he was locking the case.

"Depends. You want it just for personal protection?"

Aaron glanced at Sam, who simply returned his stare.

"What if the guy we're worried about is—big?"

"What you got there's no pop gun. Nine-millimeter round might not stop a big man dead in his tracks, but it'll slow him down. Hit him enough times, or in the right place, and you'll kill him dead enough—if that's what you're tryin' to do."

Aaron nodded. "Okay. What about for her?"

"You like to see somethin' different, ma'am?"

"That looks a little heavy."

"I got one here that's more compact, and almost as good."

The owner unlocked the glass case again and took out a snub-nosed automatic with P9S HECKLER & KOCH GMBH OBERNDORF/NECKAR stamped along its short barrel.

"HK P9S," the owner said, handing it to her, "a beautiful piece of workmanship. Small enough to fit a lady's handbag, but plenty lethal in the right hands."

Sam held the gun gingerly, as if it might bite.

"Does it have the same bullets," Aaron asked, "the Para—"

"Nine-millimeter Parabellum, yes sir, and a magazine capacity of nine rounds, same as the SIG."

"You like it?" Aaron asked her.

"No. It gives me the creeps."

Aaron read the price tag, then turned to the owner.

"Six hundred. It's a deal. You take credit cards?"

"Visa. MasterCard. American Express. Discover."

"Cool. We'll go with these two. Put it on my Visa."

"Not so fast. There's the small matter of a marksmanship certificate, and the fifteen-day waitin' period."

Aaron sighed, as if he had been expecting this.

"Look, we're sort of in a hurry, okay?"

"Everyone's in a hurry."

"I mean, we're not planning to do a bank job, or knock over a convenience store, or anything like that, but fifteen days—Jesus! We could buy it on the black market faster than that."

"Then maybe that's what you'll have to do."

He took both guns and went over to put them away.

"Look— We're willing to pay a little extra."

The owner looked up, key to the glass case in one hand.

"You tryin' to bribe me?"

"It's not exactly a *bribe*—"

"How much?"

"Well, let's see. If the total comes to—"

"Fourteen hundred," Sam said, "plus tax."

"Right. So how about—oh, maybe—two thousand?"

The owner shook his head and put the key in the lock.

"Some mighty tough penalties for breakin' that law—"

"Okay, fine! How about twenty-two hundred?"

"Twenty-eight hundred and you got yourself a deal."

"Twenty-eight *hundred?* That's *double* the original price!"

"Take it or leave it."

Aaron stared at him, then turned to Sam.

"This is your idea," she said.

"Okay! Put it on my goddamn Visa!"

"Can't use a card for somethin' like this. Have to backdate the receipt. I'll need cash."

"I don't carry that kind of cash on me!"

"Most people don't."

"God*damn*it! Now I have to go to the bank! Come on, Sam!"

"Aaron, are you sure this is necessary?"

"Yes! For *both* of us. Come on!"

The owner watched them walk toward the door of his shop.

"I don't know what you two need them guns for," he said.

They stopped.

"I don't want to know. But I'll tell you this much. The fifteen-day waitin' period's just for the cops, to run a records check. You two don't look much like crooks to me. But the marksmanship certificate, that's for your own protection. So get some practice with these things. There's target ranges all over the place. Learn how to do it right. A gun's no toy. And shootin' someone with it's no game."

When they returned to Aaron's condo later in the day, he carried a plastic bag with the guns in their separate boxes, and another box of nine-millimeter Parabellum cartridges.

"I still think this is totally insane," Sam said.

"You weren't *there* last night. You didn't see him."

"For this much money, you could hire a bodyguard."

Aaron remembered Sal Esposito's two ox-faced henchmen, their bullet-riddled bodies sprawled across the floor of the Rakehell's main room, dark red blood soaking into the carpet.

"Yeah, bodyguards."

"Makes more sense than guns we don't even know how to use."

"Look, Sam—nobody stuck a cut-off head in *your* face! Nobody threatened to kill *you*, and the people you love!"

He dropped the plastic bag in the middle of the floor.

"Careful, Aaron!"

"The safeties are on."

She came over and put her arms around him.

"I'm sorry. I know it was bad last night. But you won't make it any better by overreacting."

"*Who's* overreacting?"

He broke free from her embrace and went over to the black leather couch and sat down hard.

Sam sat down beside him.

"The police couldn't stop him, Aaron. *They* had guns."

"The cops can't do shit."

He got up and checked the front door, finding it closed but not locked. He pushed the button on the doorknob, turned the dead bolt, then slid the security chain firmly into place.

Sam watched him from the couch.

"After what you said about him on your show this morning—making fun of his face, and the way he got shot—"

"I let him have it, didn't I? And the fucker didn't even call in after that!"

"What were you trying to do, anyway?"

"Show him I'm not afraid."

He took the SIG out of the box and gripped it with both hands, the way he had seen Lopez do it last night—running up onto the stage, firing at the Phantom. He took aim at an imaginary target across the room and squeezed the trigger.

"Pow!"

"Aaron! Don't play with that! It's loaded!"

"Who's playing? Besides, the safety's on."

"*Aaron!*"

"You know, I could've been one hell of a cop."

"Aren't you in enough trouble already?"

"We've got to go to a target range and get some practice."

"I thought you wanted to look at the video again."

He lowered the gun, then put it back in its box.

"Let's roll the sucker. You got it with you?"

"I still don't know who sent me this tape," she said.

"Who else? Mr. Masked Asshole himself."

"But why would he send it to *me?*"

"Vanity. To show off his real face behind the mask."

"Except now you don't think it's the same face—"

"I'm not sure. That's why I want to watch it again."

He fast-forwarded through the jerking, handheld images from the Meat Locker—the topless girl with the pierced nipples, the boy mainlining heroin—until he reached the image of the tall figure standing in the doorway, skull shaved bald, except for the forelock of dyed red hair.

Man, I am *the mask!*

It was the same face he had first seen grinning at him under the headlights of his Porsche, the one he knew for certain belonged behind the Phantom's mask—until last night.

He took it off fast-forward and resumed normal speed.

They watched as he stood in the doorway, staring into the camera lens, a creature of half-shadow and strange backlight, a blank expression on his round, pale-moon face, ominous and childlike at the same time, red forelock startling in its intensity, like bright blood on dead flesh.

"What makes you think it's not him?" Sam asked.

"I'm not sure it's not."

"He never took off his mask last night."

"No. But I saw the back of his head, when the hood fell down. The mask didn't cover that part. And what I saw didn't look *any*thing like this guy's face from the front."

"What you said about it on your show this morning—how it looked like the Swamp Thing's head? Or someone who got caught at ground zero in Hiroshima? Was it really that bad? Or were you just exaggerating?"

"It was worse than that. You couldn't believe how bad."

The image on the television screen twitched like a nervous tic, jumping from side to side and up and down, as the unknown operator of the handheld camcorder jerked and pulsed to his own internal rhythms, driven on by designer drugs, or perhaps even darker demons.

Sam looked away and put a hand over her eyes.

"Aaron, this is giving me a headache."

"So don't watch."

"What are you *looking* for? This guy has a normal face! It's not disfigured or melted—or anything like you said."

"I don't remember for sure from the last time we saw this, but I *think* there's a part where he turns around—"

"And?"

"I can see what the back of his—wait! There he goes!"

As the image twitched and a jumbled mix of screams, laughter, shouts, and music spilled from the speakers, the figure in the doorway turned around, apparently in response to something someone said to him. And as he turned, he revealed the back of his skull, shaved smooth as a baby's bottom.

Aaron pressed PAUSE, freezing the picture.

They stared at the blurred image on screen, like something from a dark Impressionist painting, the back of the head pale and featureless, a void turned inside out.

"There's nothing wrong with his head, Aaron."

"Fucking *make*up," he muttered.

"Maybe the light in that strip joint made you see things."

"I *know* what I saw!"

"Then you didn't see *him.*"

Man, I am *the mask!*

"I *know* it's him!"

"You can't have it both ways, Aaron."

"It *has* to be some kind of makeup."

He sat on the couch, the remote gripped tight in one hand.

"You want to keep watching this?" Sam asked.

"It *has* to be! There's no other explanation!"

"Or do you want to turn it off?"

He grabbed Sam and kissed her hard on the mouth, pushing her back against the black leather couch.

"Aaron!" She struggled to break free.

He kissed her harder, and moved his hand down between her legs. Her struggles turned into a different kind of motion.

"I told you to stop—" she said, her voice thick.

He kissed her harder, pulled up the sweater she had on, unfastened her bra. He fixed his mouth on one of her nipples, then the other, kissing, sucking them, biting them lightly, making them swell up hard and large, areolas shriveling around them, straining against the taut skin of her breasts.

She pushed him away, breathing hard.

"Want to go into the bedroom?" she asked.

"No."

"You want to do it *here?* On the couch?"

He tore off her clothes, and his, then spit on his hand and moistened the swollen head of his cock, and slipped it into her hot, willing dampness. She began to claw at his back as they writhed on the couch, sweating flesh squeaking against black leather. Her hand jerked out to one side on an especially deep thrust and knocked the remote off the coffee table. It flipped onto the carpet, changing channels as it fell.

The television screen blared into life.

"And it does all *that?* For *only* $29.95?"

Sam arched her back, swollen nipples pointing skyward.

"Yes, Martin! It's the *ideal* all-in-one kitchen helper! It does *everything* you could *ever* want it to! And *more!*"

Sam started gasping for breath.

"It chops and shreds—"

"Oh God, Aaron!"

"It slices and dices—"

"Oh God!"

"It whips and grinds—"

"God!"

Afterward, they sat huddled on the couch, Sam's sweater thrown over her naked shoulders. The infomercial had moved on to another product: an all-purpose miracle degreaser.

"And it gets off *all* the grime, *all* the time!"

"Could we turn this shit off?" she asked.

"Sure."

"I've got to get going, Aaron."

"Now?"

"It's almost dark. I have a lot of unfinished work back at the studio—thanks to your Dirty Harry shopping trip."

"Any of it that's important?"

"Yes! I may have to do a field interview."

Aaron reached over and took her hand in his.
"Don't go, Sam."
"Aaron—"
"Stay with me tonight."
"Aaron, I can't! I've got to get back to work."
"Call in sick. Go in early tomorrow morning."
"I don't even have any *clothes* over here!"
"Wear the ones you have on—or used to have on."
"Aaron, no."
"This is important, Sam."
"Why?"
"I don't want to be alone tonight. Can't you under*stand?*"

28

DEFAMED

And now, for all you cheap stupid listeners out there—and I mean you *real* cheapskates, the ones that hang on to your quarters till they grow *mold!* Here's an insurance company right outta your wet dreams! The blue light special of insurance companies! Offering the guaranteed *cheapest*, coupon-clipping, end-of-season, going-out-of-business, day-after-Thanksgiving, everything-must-go auto insurance you ever heard about in your whole damn cheap, pathetic lives!"

Aaron shoved a prerecorded spot into the cart machine.

"Easy on the sponsors, guy," Jerry said, standing inside Aaron's broadcast booth. "We're starting to lose some of them—after what happened the other night."

"Bunch of dickless wonders, Jerr. Fuck 'em!"

"We need the advertising dollars. And go a little easier on the listeners. We're starting to lose some of them, too."

"*Fuck* 'em, Jerr! They'll come back. They'll *all* come back! 'Cause we're number *one!*"

"You have a good night last night, Aaron?"

"The best, man! Great sex at night! Great sex in the morning!" He started to belt out his own improvised version of "Ain't We Got Fun." "In the mornin', in the evenin', ain't we got *sex!* Yeah!"

Bill Waller came in during this musical interlude, glancing first at his boss, then at Aaron.

"Sounds like Sam's starting to stay over," Jerry said.

"You know it, man!"

"You guys getting married," Bill asked, "or what?"

"None of your fuckin' business, you little ass-kisser!"

Bill whispered something to Jerry, who nodded quickly, as if he did not want Aaron to see. But Aaron did. He also saw Alonzo Gore, with his massive profusion of hair, coming down the glass hallway toward the broadcast booth.

"What the fuck's Alonzo doin' here this early?"

"He comes on after you, Aaron."

"Not for two fuckin' hours! What *is* this, Jerr?"

"We need to talk, guy."

"About what?"

"Your cart's almost over," Bill said, nodding at the two flashing lights on top of Aaron's console.

"Fuck you!" he snapped back, and switched his microphone to BROADCAST. "Okay, you pathetic cheapies! I hope you were payin' attention there, findin' out all about that cut-rate auto insurance. 'Cause now it's time to kick back and kick butt and get *crazy!* Yeah! We got us *another* twenty-minute set of back-to-back, stopless hits! Startin' things off with Ultimate Violation and 'Penetrate My Heart.' 108.5. KRAS."

He slammed the twenty-minute cassette into the cart machine, pulled off his headphones, and spun around in his swivel chair to face Jerry and Bill, and now Alonzo Gore, who had just stepped into the booth.

"Now what's all this shit about, Jerr?"

"Aaron—" Jerry cleared his throat. "We know you're a little

stressed, because of what happened the other night—"

"Don't get started on that, man."

"—and we thought—"

"Who's 'we'? You and Chuck? Then why don't you just go ahead and *say* so? And cut through all this bullshit?"

"We thought," Jerry continued, barging straight ahead, hoping he could get it said before being interrupted again, "that maybe it would be nice—"

"Nice? What's with this *nice?"*

"We want you to take some time off, Aaron!" Jerry snapped it out. "Take some time to relax, unwind, get your head back together, think over what's happened—"

"My head's cool. Whose goddamn idea is this? Chuck's?"

"Chuck and I discussed it, informally. We both think it would be good if you took some time off. Alonzo here can fill in for you while you're gone."

Alonzo raised a hand. "Yo!"

"You puttin' me on suspension? Is that it, Jerr?"

"No, Aaron. We're only talking a few days."

"Because of what happened at the Rakehell Club?"

"We can't afford any lawsuits, guy."

Aaron sat there in his chair, looking at them.

"Fire me, Jerry. Or put me on suspension. Okay?"

"Aaron, we don't want to do either one."

"Then get out of here!"

He jumped up from the chair and pointed to the door.

"All three of you! Get the fuck *outta* here!"

Alonzo raised a hand. "Peace, man. I'm gone."

"Out! All of you! I got a fuckin' *show* to do!"

Jerry edged toward the door, Bill behind him.

"You still have a twenty-minute cart in there," Bill said.

"I'm cuttin' it fuckin' short! *Move!*"

He slammed the door after them, then went back to his chair and replaced his headphones.

"Whoa, everybody! Our twenty-minute set of stopless, back-to-back hits just came to a stop there, didn't it? That's 'cause we got us some major calls on hold and we're not waitin' one second longer before we take 'em on *live!*"

As he reached out to press a button for one of the incoming phone lines, he looked up at the call-screening booth across the way, and saw Bill pointing to his own earphones.

Aaron switched to CUE.

"What the fuck do *you* want, gearhead?"

"Those calls aren't screened yet."

"So? I'll screen 'em on the air."

He switched back to BROADCAST and pressed number three.

"You're on live with Sunset Scott, man!"

"You don't sound as scared as you looked the other night."

It stopped Aaron cold for a few seconds, coming out of nowhere like that, without the usual dead air intro, followed by the usual snide but courteous opening remark. There was an edge to the whispering voice this time, as if it held real anger.

He glanced at the others behind their glass walls—Lisa, Bud, Tracy, Bill and Jerry in the call-screening booth—all of them staring uneasily at him, as if the Phantom's very voice carried a contagion that could spread.

"Hey, masked man! Long time no—"

"We can dispense with the formalities."

The voice was angry all right, good and pissed-off.

"Hey, Phantom! I'm glad you called in, man. After yesterday I was startin' to wonder if I hurt your feelings. Or if maybe you didn't like my description of your ugly head—"

"I want respect from you. I de*mand* it."

"Respect for what? For bein' a masked butthole who shoots innocent people and cuts off their heads, and waves 'em around in public like party balloons—"

Jerry, inside the call-screening booth, shook his own head and drew a finger across his throat in the stop-talking-at-once signal. Then he tapped his earphones. But Aaron had no intention of switching to CUE just then.

"You want respect for *that*, Phantom? Respect for bein' a pile of dog crap that walks and talks and wears a mask?"

"What do I have to do, Sunset Scott, to win your respect?"

Aaron started to answer, then stopped, aware of the dead seriousness that weighted the Phantom's every word. It came filtering through the phone lines like a psychic presence, palpable inside the broadcast booth. Aaron knew that he was just working *shtick* here, making radio patter to build up his courage, and drive away his fear.

The guy on the other end was not.

"Do I have to pay a visit to someone close to you? Is that what it takes to win your respect at this point, Sunset Scott?"

Aaron had no doubt about the seriousness now. He could feel the sweat beneath his earphones and the pounding of his heart, like a muffled drum machine inside his chest. Negotiations had reached a very critical stage, at the eleventh hour of a high-stakes game. Every point counted now. Every card laid on the table was a matter of life, or death.

He did not have to look up to know that the others were watching him from behind their glass walls. He could feel the nervous energy galvanizing the entire station.

"I'm ready for you, man."

He thought of the recently purchased SIG P220, still in its box at home in a closet, useless because he hadn't learned how to shoot it yet.

"I wasn't ready the last time. I admit that. But I'm ready now, man—for what*ever* you want."

"We could put that to the test, Sunset Scott."

At this point, Aaron should have started to backpedal, and he knew it. He should have started cutting deals, making amends, smoothing the Phantom down of darkness till he smiled. He could feel Jerry willing him to start cooling it. If he looked up, he could probably see Jerry kneeling behind the glass wall now, praying for him to switch to CUE.

"How do we put this to the test, Phantom? You gonna take off your mask and show me your ugly face? Make me gag to death on my own vomit? You know, everybody, I don't think any of you stupid listeners out there have any idea just *how* ugly our mysterious masked friend, the Phantom, really is! I mean, I only saw the back of his damn head! And *that* was so ugly, he shouldn't just wear a mask! He should wear a goddamn lead *shield!* He's so ugly, he's radioactive-ugly!"

"I didn't call you to indulge your twisted—"

"He's so damn ugly, I can hardly even *describe* it for you, everybody! But it's sort of like if you *burned* somethin' in the microwave, okay? Then you lost it behind the fridge for six months? Then your dog or somebody else digs it out, and it's all covered with *roaches?* Roach-ugly! *That's* how ugly the Phantom's head is! It's *roach*—"

"No one wants to hear this childish—"

"*Roach*-ugly!"

"I'll talk to you later, Sunset—"

"*Puke*-ugly!"

"*Shut up!*"

"*Hair*ball-ugly!"

"*SHUT UP!*"

"Wino-moons-a-passing-bus-full-of-nuns-ugly!"

The voice on the other end fell silent, leaving only the sound of Aaron's laughter braying into the microphone. After he laughed himself out, the air turned truly dead and empty, with a sinister quiet to it, like the stillness that follows a gunshot.

"You'll pay for this, Sunset Scott."

The dial tone began to buzz, filling the air with menace.

Aaron snapped it off.

"And there he goes, everybody! The Man with the Mask! Totally blown away by the Man with the Mouth! The Phantom just couldn't *take* it any longer! And you know why? Because here, *live*, on KRAS FM, 108.5—Sunset Scott in the Morning, all mornin' long—we went boldly where no shock jock has ever gone before. We cranked it to the max and went—"

Aaron flipped on the echo filter.

"BEHIND THE MASK!"

He flipped it off and leaned sideways into the microphone.

"We went behind the mask and got under his skin! *Yeah!* Right down under his scabby, blotchy, wrinkled, melted, quick-grab-the-Clearasil, call-the-plastic-surgeon, peel-it-off-and-start-all-over-again, *roach*-ugly *skin!* And now, everybody, listen *up!* We're gonna start us a new contest! The Ugly Phantom Creepstakes! All you gotta do is tell us *how* ugly the Phantom really is! 'The Phantom is so ugly, he—' Just fill in the blank! That's all you gotta *do!* Be the ninety-seventh caller to dial 1-800-GOD-AM-I-UGLY and win a total facial makeover at Demolition Dermagraphics, Hair and Nails and Chaos for the Nineties! And now, while you're heatin' up the phone lines, let's break for another commercial, then get back to take more listeners on *live!* Here, at KRAS FM, 108.5! Home of the *roach*-ugly Phantom!"

He slammed in a commercial cassette and leaned back in the chair to catch his breath.

The madness of what he had just done took hold of him then, like the sudden onset of exhaustion after an adrenaline high.

He saw Leah Steinberg, alone in her deli, except for Shirley Landau, and a few customers older than either one of them. He saw Sam, walking alone to her car in the On-Target lot, or across the courtyard of her apartment complex in Studio City.

"That was cute, Aaron," Jerry said. "Real cute."

He came into the booth, leaving the door open.

Aaron did not turn around to look at him.

"You think the listeners liked it, Jerr?"

"Sure."

"You really think so?"

"You'll have the biggest funeral of any corpse in L.A."

29

PRECAUTIONS

Late breakfast was still being served by the time he reached Steinberg's, right after his airshift ended.

Three older men sat at a table, arguing heatedly about something in Russian. Two young Hasidim, with black hats and coats, stood near the counter as Shirley Landau rang up their order of bagels, lox, egg salad, and knishes to go.

"Hi, Aaron," she greeted him. "How are you?"

"Where's Mom?"

"In the kitchen. Making more matzo ball soup."

The kitchen was cramped, with the stove, refrigerator, and cutting table set so close together that only one person could work there efficiently.

Leah looked up from a kettle full of floating matzo balls.

"Aaron! What brings you here so early?"

"Mom, I have to talk to you."

"Now? Aaron, we got customers."

"This is important."

"You're looking terrible, Aaron. You're so thin, like a scarecrow! And you got dark circles under your eyes. You getting enough sleep at night, *bubeleh?*"

"Fuck how much sleep I get!"

"Don't use such talk in front of your mother."

"Sorry. Look, Mom—"

"What's wrong, Aaron?"

"Mom—could you maybe think about, you know, closing up the place for a little while? Taking some time off?"

"Time off? What's this? I got a *deli* to run. I got customers who depend on me. Who's going to feed them if suddenly I lock my doors?"

"Everyone needs some time off—to go places."

"I take two weeks in August, same time every year. I go to Palm Springs and stay at the Desert Mirage. You know this. You used to go with me. You're still invited—God forbid that I should interfere with your plans. But what's with this *meshuggas* of taking time off right now?"

Aaron didn't answer her.

"It's him, isn't it? The one that almost killed you?"

"He didn't almost kill—"

"I know about it, Aaron, even though you never told me. I wouldn't watch it on the news, because I couldn't sit there and look at them carrying out the bodies. But I read about it in the *Times.* Thank God he didn't hurt you! You stay far away from him, Aaron. Don't even *think* about him."

"He called me today."

"*Called* you! Where? At the radio station?"

Aaron nodded.

"And you hung up on him, yes?"

"No. We talked."

Leah dropped her spoon into the kettle, splashing hot broth on the stovetop, where it sizzled in the burner's flames.

"I can't be*lieve* it! I raised such a *schlemiel* for a son? A serial killer almost kills him, then calls at work. And what does my son do? He *takes* the call!"

"He didn't try to hurt me," Aaron said, staring at the floor. "But he might hurt you. There's just you and Shirley here—alone. The police can't help. You need to leave, Mom. You have to get out of town for a while."

He paused.

"You don't know what he's like. You haven't seen him. I *have.* He could come in here anytime—"

"Aaron." She squeezed his arm. "I could *die* anytime, from natural causes. I should live to be a hundred, *alevai.* But I'm not afraid to die. When death comes for me, it comes."

"I'm not talking about natural death!" he shouted, his voice carrying out into the dining room of the deli with such force that even the three Russians stopped their argument.

Leah stared at him.

"There's only one other kind of death—*miesse meshina.*"

Aaron felt a chill pass through him as he heard his mother speak the Yiddish words for a strange, ugly, or unnatural death.

"You're the one who has to worry about a *miesse meshina,* Aaron, if you don't free yourself from this—*dybbuk.*"

The chill grew more intense as he thought of the Phantom, a true *dybbuk,* or demon, if ever there was one.

"And now if you'll excuse me," she said, "I got some matzo ball soup that needs looking after."

She turned back to the kettle, fishing out the spoon, and began to make herself look busier than she actually was.

"I'm driving up to the motion picture retirement home tomorrow, Mom. The one in Woodland Hills?"

"Oh?" Leah said.

"I'm going to find out some more about Mick Grady."

She did not turn around, but she held the spoon motionless above the kettle, broth from the soup rising in front of her like incense.

"I'm going to talk to a guy named Moe Edelstein who used to be some kind of production manager for Panopticon back in the days when Mick Grady worked for them."

"Don't mention that name in here again. Or in my home."

"Why not? What's wrong with saying my own father's name?"

"Because he's *dead!*"

Out in the dining room, the Russians stopped arguing again.

Leah turned around, a frightened look in her eyes.

"He died a *miesse meshina*, your father—a horrible death. I don't want the same thing happening to you! Let go of the past, Aaron. It belongs only to the dead. Let them have it."

Over on Wilcox, Montoya sat behind a desk cluttered with clear cellophane candy wrappers. He looked as if he had not been sleeping well. Lopez, feet propped up on the front of the desk, sat in a chair leaning back from it, hands behind his head, Armani suit jacket tossed over a nearby chair, sleeves rolled up to his elbows—very informal, for him.

"So," Montoya said, "at least you still have your job."

"I'm on probation again."

"But you're still working."

"On what?"

"They left us in charge of the case—in name, anyway."

"And took away all our power to *solve* the son of a bitch!"

"Francisco—"

"They cut off our *cojones* and handed them back to us in a fucking Ziploc bag, saying, 'Have a nice day, *cabrónes!*' "

Lopez whipped his feet off the desk and pitched forward in the chair, bringing his hands down on the desktop with such force that the candy wrappers rattled like leaves in a storm.

"Francisco, *calma ti*—"

"We had him, Rafael! We fucking *had* him!"

"No," Montoya said, "we never had him at all."

"Bullshit! If I'd started shooting a little sooner—"

"You *might* have killed him, and died in the attempt. I'm glad he decided to run when he did."

"Why? You turning *cobarde* on us, Ralph?"

Montoya looked at him quietly, the charge of cowardice hanging in the air like gunsmoke. Lopez held his gaze for another few seconds, then looked away.

"I think you know me better than that, Frank."

"It doesn't matter now. We're fucked."

"The only real difference," Montoya said, unwrapping a piece of hard candy, "is that now we can't do any direct surveillance or proactive intervention—not that we were allowed to do all that much before this, anyway."

"So now we just sit on our asses and wait for him to kill again, and hope that maybe he gets sloppy, or we get lucky."

"We know more about him now, Frank. Knowledge is power."

"What do we know? That he's big, fast, and very good?"

"And very smart. He's working by conscious design."

"So?"

"That tells us a lot. The killings at the Rakehell Club were *not* the work of a crazed serial killer on a rampage—no matter what the news broadcasts say. They were part of a carefully orchestrated performance. He had it all worked out to the very last detail—except for the part where you came running up to the stage, shooting at him, and then got him in the leg later, out in the alley. None of that was in the original script. Everything else was."

"Hold on, Ralph. He didn't plan the meeting. Scott did."

"Aaron Scott taunted him about a meeting—at *our* suggestion. But the Phantom set the time and the place. And he didn't come up with them on the spur of the moment. He's been planning something at the Rakehell Club for quite a while. He would have tried to meet him there eventually, one way or the other, whether Scott suggested it first or not."

"You think he's that many moves ahead of us?"

"Yes. We have to try to get inside his head now, see if we can figure out his grand design, jump a few moves ahead of him—or at least catch up."

Lopez frowned at the idea, shaking his head.

"That's *your* way, Ralph. The big mind game. Catch him in his own trap. It doesn't work for me. I have to *be* there. I want to find him again, and take him down."

"*Cuidado*, Frank. Some things are worth the risk. This isn't, not right now. You're on probation."

"I don't mean prowling the streets, or hanging around Esposito's tit joint, hoping he'll come back to the scene of the crime. But what about Scott's mother? She's a likely target—after what Scott said on the radio today, almost guaranteed."

"True."

"So what's wrong with checking out her place? That little deli she runs over on Fairfax?"

"It's still surveillance, Frank."

"Not of the Phantom!"

"But related to this case. Go ahead and try it. If they catch you at it, you'll find yourself back in uniform, riding a patrol car—or on permanent suspension."

"You want to just wait till he comes after her? Sets fire to her face with one of her own gas burners, then leaves her body in little pieces all over the floor?"

"I don't like it any better than you do."

Lopez looked away, glaring at the wall.

"I can't just sit at a desk and shuffle papers while you try to outguess him, Ralph. It's not my *way!*"

"If you're that anxious to do fieldwork, you could start interviewing plastic surgeons."

Lopez looked up at him. "What?"

"We're dealing with a man whose face and head—perhaps other parts of his body—have been badly disfigured. We don't know whether he was born that way or whether something happened to him. But we can be certain that he's seen a plastic surgeon sometime in the past. He may still be seeing one now."

"If he is, then the doctor's probably covering for him."

"No doubt. But you know when someone's lying, Frank. You're good at that. You also know what kind of patient to describe—his size, the way he moves, the way he talks, what he looks like, even though you've never seen his face."

"All I have to do is talk to every plastic surgeon in L.A.?"

"And in the greater metropolitan area, yes."

"Maybe farther out than that, right? He might have had the work done in San Diego, or San Francisco—even out of state."

"Possibly."

"What happens when, or if, I find this magic doctor?"

Montoya laid an empty candy wrapper alongside the others.

"Then," he said, "it might be time to take a risk."

Aaron squeezed the trigger of the SIG P220. Recoil made the pistol buck in his hands and the first shot missed.

He kept firing, each successive shot kicking harder than the last. The next four shots also missed. The sixth one caught the edge of his shoulder, but he kept coming forward with unstoppable momentum.

Aaron fired again and again. The last three shots went wide. He kept pulling the trigger, but the magazine was empty now and the SIG only clicked in his hands like a toy gun.

The moving paper target rushed up to within several feet of him and stopped, its bullet-riddled margins mute evidence of his poor marksmanship, the black silhouette he was supposed to hit silently mocking him, safe except for an insignificant-looking hole at the far edge of the left shoulder.

The palms of his hands stung from where the SIG's grip had kicked against them, and his ears rang with the shots' loud reports, despite the hearing protection devices he wore like oversize headphones.

He took them off to hear the shooting range instructor.

"—keep it steady. You're lettin' it jump all over the place, like a garden hose on high."

"It's not my fault! It jumps whenever I pull the trigger!"

"That's the recoil. It'll do that every time. You got to correct for it. And when you pull the trigger, you want to *squeeze* her real gentle, just snap off them shots nice and easy—not jerk on it like you're doin'."

"I get mad because I keep missing."

"That just makes you miss even more. But you'll get the hang of it, if you keep practicin'. By the way, you're gonna burn up a lotta bucks, shootin' them nine-millimeter Parabellums. You should be usin' wad-cutters just for target practice."

"I want to use the real thing."

"It's your money."

In the target lane next to them, a young man with ear protectors and goggles opened up full automatic fire with an AK-47, letting off multiple rounds with each burst. Aaron winced as the deafening explosions hammered at his unprotected eardrums. After the firing stopped, he looked up at the moving paper target, still moving, but shot into as many tattered ribbons as the Flying Dutchman's mainsail.

Aaron turned back to the instructor.

"What if the target was a real person, and I hit him like that, just on the shoulder?"

"Depends on whether he's armed or not, and skilled."

"Let's say he's both."

"Then you're dead."

Aaron looked at the AK-47, smoke curling from its muzzle.

"Maybe I should buy one of those."

"That's up to you. AK's sort of hard to carry concealed, unless you wear them baggy gangbanger pants. But you just keep practicin' with that SIG and you'll be all right."

The instructor walked off, obviously bored with the slow progress of a first-timer, and went over to check out a more experienced shooter.

Aaron put his ear protectors back on and ejected the empty magazine from the SIG's grip, replacing it with a loaded one.

Then he pressed the button to start another paper target moving toward him and steadied his gun in a two-handed grip, the way he had seen Lopez do it that night at the Rakehell Club.

Trying to remember to *squeeze* the trigger instead of jerk it, he took careful aim at the moving target and fired.

And missed.

30

COLD STORAGE

The receptionist at the motion picture retirement home—a pleasant, round-faced woman in her fifties—studied the photograph on Aaron's driver's license, then looked up at him.

"Mr. Edelstein doesn't receive many visitors," she said.

"Sorry. Guess I should've called first."

"No, that's not it. He doesn't *mind* receiving visitors. He just doesn't get many."

She handed back his license, along with a folded pamphlet.

"All the family members from his generation are dead. He has a daughter in San Diego and a son somewhere in Hawaii. But they never come to visit. Of course, I'm sure they'll come after it's too late. They always do. That map shows you how to get to the Irving Thalberg section."

"Do I need his room number?"

"No. He'll be waiting in the lobby area. I don't think he knows who you are, but he seems eager to meet you."

* * *

Morris Edelstein wore a brown houndstooth jacket over a white shirt and beige trousers. Once elegant and expensive, the clothes, like their owner, had suffered a sea change.

Edelstein was one of those tall, angular old men, all bony knees and elbows. In his younger years he must have moved fast and spoken even faster. Time had worked its usual deceleration, but he still spoke quickly, with a querulous whine to his words, and his movements tended to be abrupt and jerky.

The room they sat in—long, whitewalled, sparsely furnished with minimalist pieces—looked like a stage set or a backlot mock-up, an illusion designed to hide the reality behind it. Even the sunlight, falling through wide, filter-screened windows, seemed denatured, aseptic, washed pale as the white fluorescent light that came down from ceiling panels.

"Johnny Moffet?" Edelstein asked, leaning forward over his bony knees. "That *alter kocker?* He's still alive?"

"Last time I talked to him, yeah."

"So what's he doing?"

"Still working on the Panopticon lot."

Edelstein snorted derisively, shifting his bony knees.

"Listen, sonny. You can't put one over on me that easy. I may be an AK myself, but I still got a few marbles left. There ain't *been* no Panopticon for almost thirty-five years!"

"I mean Post-Tech Sound Labs, where Panopticon used to be."

"What's Johnny doing there? Working as a sound editor?"

"I think he's more like a dishwasher."

"*Oy gevalt!* Such *tsuris!*" Edelstein shook his head. "But then, Johnny always was a real *schlimazel.* Bad luck followed him around like a nagging wife. And he had gambling troubles. Maybe that's what made him a *schlimazel* in the first place. It sure made him a *schnorrer.* He was always mooching off everyone on the lot. 'Can you spot me ten bucks till payday?' Always."

"Didn't he make good money as an assistant director?"

"Panopticon was no MGM. But he did okay. We all did okay.

There's no trick to making money. *Keeping* the money, that's the trick. Johnny, he liked to play the ponies at Santa Anita. But he was no L.B. Mayer. On his salary, he couldn't afford. It's like these young kids today. They make more money than we ever dreamed of. But it all goes up their nose. Cocaine—or booze, or Vegas. There's always someplace to throw your money away. I hung on to mine. And look what I got for it!"

He gestured at the long, white room and laughed.

"Johnny said you worked with the stuntmen at Panopticon."

"Me? Where the hell did he get that idea? He must be losing *his* marbles. I never was part of the stunt crew! That's a goddamn dangerous job. Falling off a horse, or off a cliff. Jumping from a speeding car onto a moving train—"

"No," Aaron interrupted. "Johnny said you handled *payroll* for the stuntmen. Made sure they got paid."

"Of course! That was part of my job. I did payroll for stuntmen, stand-ins, extras—anyone who stepped in front of the camera, except for lead players and contract players."

Edelstein leaned forward and stared suspiciously at Aaron.

"So what are you? Some auditor for the IRS?"

"No. I do a drive-time radio show."

"Which station?"

"KRAS FM—108.5. Sunset Scott in the Morning."

"Never heard of it. But then, I don't listen to the radio too much these days—except for this canned shit they pipe in here twenty-four hours a day. Muzak? Something like that. I *used* to listen to the radio, though. Christ! Radio was *big* fifty years ago. Even bigger than television is today. No competition from VCRs, shopping malls. Just about the whole damn country tuned in every week to Jack Benny or Edgar Bergen. That's why the big boys at the big studios—guys like Jack Warner and L.B. Mayer—never thought television would catch on. Never thought it could knock out radio. What *schmucks* they turned out to be! But then, Goliath never sees David coming till it's too late, *nu?*"

"About the stuntmen at Panopticon—"

"What's this always stuntmen? You want to quit your radio job and become a stuntman? I'm not the one to ask."

"I wondered if you ever knew a stuntman named Mick Grady?"

"Individual names already! What am I supposed to be? A directory of ex-Panopticon employees?"

"You did payroll for the stuntmen. I thought you might remember him, maybe."

"What's the name again?"

"Mick Grady. Maybe it was Michael Grady on the payroll."

"At Panopticon? Bank of America we weren't. The only time we used formal names was on the credits. But stuntmen didn't get screen credit back then."

"So it would've been Mick Grady."

"Grady. Grady. Sounds Irish. Was he Irish?"

"I don't know. Maybe."

"*May*be? You don't know *bubkes* about this guy and you want *me* to remember his name? Where'd you get it? Out of a hat?"

"He's sort of like—a relative."

"Part of your *mishpocha?* And you told me you were a *landsman!* Said your name was Scott that once was Steinberg. Now all of a sudden you're Irish?"

"A distant relative, by marriage."

"That happens. The Jews and the Irish, they intermarry some. It don't always work out so good. Of course, it don't always work with Jews and Jews, either. It did with me and Sadie, though. Forty-seven years we were married. Already now it's ten years since I lost her."

Edelstein's gaze seemed to move beyond the room they sat in, as if he had suddenly gained brief access to a different time and another place.

A small shiver passed over him, and he began to rub his bony shoulders through the houndstooth jacket.

"Does it feel cold in here to you?" he asked Aaron.

"No."

"You're always cold when you get to be my age. But let me tell you, I think it's on purpose, the way they set the temperature so low in this goddamn place? It's like they're keeping us in cold storage, so when we check out all of a sudden, it don't smell so bad if a few days pass before they notice."

Edelstein laughed, but there was not much heart to it.

"Of course, I guess I shouldn't complain. This place isn't so bad, for what it is. You got to go somewhere when you get too old to be useful. We used to have some real celebrities around here, let me tell you. Mary Astor was with us until a few years back. Most of the big names are gone now. Just the last of us Mohicans, waiting our turn."

Aaron checked his irritation. This wasn't working. He decided to cut things short and get the hell out of there before this lonely old guy unloaded the story of his whole life.

"Well, thanks for—"

"Wait a minute! Wait just a minute. Grady. Mick Grady. *Now* I remember! One of those big, strong Irish guys? Kind that could carry a piano on his back down the street, and the piano player along with it? Looked sort of like Kid Irish from the Bronx? Freckles, blue eyes, big laughing mouth?"

"Yeah, I guess so."

"You *guess* so? You never *saw* him before? What kind of *mishpocha* you come from, anyway?"

"It's been—a long time."

"I remember Mick. Not that he stood out from the crowd much. He did some stunts for us, and worked as an extra some, and even as a stand-in once in a while, when we had an actor his size—which wasn't often, let me tell you. But, you know, those stuntmen all sort of blur together when you look back at them. They all seemed to be big, tough, daredevil types. I saw that they got paid, but Christ, we didn't pay them much—not for risking their necks like that. And what money they got they spent on booze and broads and ponies. They were like a bunch of kids on a Saturday afternoon. Life was just one long party. I'll bet not one of them ever saved a dime—Mick Grady included."

"Mick Grady didn't have time to save much money. I heard he died in some kind of accident."

Edelstein frowned, trying to remember.

"We lost a few that way. One of the occupational hazards of the business. But Mick? I don't recall— Wait a minute! You're right. He *did* have an accident. A fatal one."

"A *miesse meshina?*" Aaron asked.

"A real *miesse meshina*—God forbid it should happen to us!"

"Did you see it?"

"No. It didn't happen on the lot. It happened out on location. They were doing another B-Western. What else? The title of the picture was—I'm not sure I can remember. We're only talking thirty-five years ago . . . Wait a minute. *Bad Men of the Badlands.* That's it! *Bad Men of the Badlands.* A real piece of *schlock.* They all were. Anyway, they were out there filming it near Lone Pine. Where else?"

"Where's Lone Pine? Arizona?"

"Ari*zona?* It's right here in California! Not far from Death Valley and the Nevada border and Mount Whitney. You never heard of Lone Pine?"

"No."

"A sleepy little Sierra foothill town. One of the few places that hasn't changed much in all these years. There's some rock formations outside of town called the Alabama Hills. They look like the backdrop for every B-Western movie and television series ever made. That's because all of them were shot there—every last one. But that's not all that's been shot at Lone Pine. They did *Gunga Din* there, and *High Sierra*, and *How The West Was Won.* Christ, when you think about it, almost everything was shot near Lone Pine—except maybe *Ben Hur* and *South Pacific.* They *still* shoot movies there."

"About Mick Grady's accident—"

"I was getting to that. Anyway, they're out there shooting near Lone Pine and we get a long-distance call from the assistant director— Could have even been Johnny Moffet. Who knows? We get this call saying one of the stuntmen has had an accident, a bad one, and they need us to send out a replacement right away. I'm sorry to say this, because I know he was your relative, but we saw stuntmen sort of like interchangeable parts back in those days. If you lost one, you just put in another."

"I understand," Aaron said.

"Maybe they *still* see them like that, if some of the rumors I hear about these new big-budget action pictures are true. Anyway, I remember that now. It was definitely Mick Grady. I had to take care of all the paperwork. But it wasn't so bad in Mick's case because he wasn't married. If a married stuntman bought it on some film, I had to cash out the rest of what was coming to him and send it to his widow as a kind of death benefit payout. There was nothing like accident insurance back then—not for stuntmen. I think Mick was going with some girl when he died, some waitress at a deli. Most of the stuntmen had more than one sweetie. But this girl of Mick's was just a girlfriend, not a wife, so we didn't have to pay her nothing."

Aaron looked away, down the length of the white room, where a nurse's aide walked across the tile floor, moving gracefully, without apparent effort, like a figure from a dream.

When he could trust himself to look back at Edelstein, he asked, "How did the accident happen?"

"You're asking the wrong man. I wasn't there."

"You heard about it."

"Of course. But you don't always hear the truth in a case like that. Truth gets mixed up with rumor."

"What did the rumors say?"

"It was some kind of fire. One of those scenes where they burn down a cabin or a saloon or a schoolhouse. That's what the script usually called for in a B-Western. What they really did was build a kind of lean-to shack and have the special effects guy set it on fire. You can't tell what kind of building it's supposed to be once it gets burning—not in a B-Western, anyway. Then they'd have stuntmen run into the building, or run out of it, or maybe jump off it while it's collapsing."

"Did you have them catch fire, the way they do today?"

"We didn't have the technology for that. And the audience wasn't as jaded. It was exciting enough to see some guy rush into a burning building then come out a few minutes later, coughing on smoke. It was dangerous, too. With the stuntman inside, the building could collapse before it was supposed to, trapping him in there with no way out."

"Was that what happened to Mick?"

"Look, sonny, I *told* you I wasn't there, all right? I don't *know* what happened. So don't be a *nudzh* about it!"

"Is anyone still around who might remember?"

"The actors are all dead. Director's dead, too. Old Sparky Weiner. Now *that* was a real—" Edelstein paused, then simply said, "Sparky had a drinking problem and a hell of a temper. They both caught up with him in the end."

"You said Johnny Moffet was the assistant director—"

"I said he *might* have been, for all I know. But you already talked to him. And he told you nothing. So sue me! I'm wrong. Maybe Johnny wasn't the AD on that shoot."

"But when I asked him, it wasn't like he didn't know about it. It was more like he just didn't want to talk."

"No wonder! You're the only one that wants to keep stirring up all this old *chozzerai.*"

"You're sure no one else was there who's still alive?"

"Naw. They're all gone. There's not even— Wait a minute. *He* might know. He must've been there during the shoot. He was always there, that *putz.* But he won't do you much good if you're in a big hurry. Because you'll have to drive all the way out to Lone Pine just to talk to the bastard."

Aaron leaned forward. "Who?"

"Tex Lassiter. He was a freelance wrangler back then."

"A what?"

"Wrangler. The *schmo* that handles the animals on a shoot. These days that can mean anything. Spiders. Birds. Monkeys. Snakes. Back then, on B-Westerns, it meant mostly horses."

"This guy Tex lives out in Lone Pine?"

"Always lived there. He was a real-life, working cowboy in his younger years—until he found out that movie companies pay better than ranches. It was convenient having someone like Tex already up there on location, even if he *was* a *putz.* Whenever we needed to send a B-Western unit to Lone Pine, all we had to do was call Tex ahead of time, and when we got there the horses would be waiting for us, saddled up and ready to go. He took care of feed, water, stabling—"

"Was he there when Mick—had his accident?"

"Probably. Even if he wasn't, he *heard* about it. Something happens in a town that small, a *schmuck* who's lived there as long as Tex always knows about it."

"You think he'll remember?"

"Who knows? If he's lost his marbles, he won't remember how to get to the bathroom. But, you know, it's sort of funny. When you reach my age, you don't have such a good memory for what happened just last week. But thirty-five years ago! *That* comes back like an instant replay. Like what you asked about today. It's been years since I even thought of Mick Grady. Now I can see him there big as life—laughing, joking, lending ten bucks to that *schnorrer*, Johnny Moffet."

Edelstein stopped and looked at Aaron, who had turned away.

"This relative of yours. You were close?"

"No. It's just been—a long time. That's all."

Edelstein nodded, his gaze drifting away from Aaron.

"Sometimes the years, they make it worse. Everyone tells you it gets better with time. But that's shit. After I lost Sadie, they all said to me, 'Keep on *schleppin'*, Moe! It'll get better!' You know what? It got worse. At first the shock of losing her kept me from feeling the loss. But then, after you get over the shock, *that's* when you feel the loss. You never get over that. Am I making sense?"

Aaron said nothing. In a corridor at the far end of the room, a door opened, followed by loud voices.

Then the door slammed shut, its closing a solitary, echoing sound that carried down the length of the room.

"You have his address?"

Edelstein snapped out of his introspection. "What?"

"An address for Tex Lassiter."

"Who needs one? Just ask for Tex. It's a small town."

"Should I call first?"

"Did you call *me?* Tex isn't much for the phone, unless it's to talk money. But just go. Drive up there sometime. It's a nice drive. A nice town. Maybe you'll stay a few days. See the sights. Who knows if you'll find what you're looking for. But it's worth the drive."

"Thanks for your help," Aaron said, getting up to go.

Edelstein took out a battered wallet, its leather cracked and torn, faded with sweat and age. He thumbed through it.

"Somewhere here— *Nu,* an AK at my age, you would expect me to carry pictures of my grandkids, right? Never have. Greedy little *pishers!* Who wants to look at them? But my Sadie . . . Now that's another— Ah!"

He produced a worn photograph of an older woman staring into the camera with a somber expression, her face heavier than Leah Steinberg's, but not unlike his Aunt Miriam's.

"She's very pretty, Mr. Edelstein."

"Pretty? She was more than that. An angel my Sadie was."

"I appreciate your help, but I've got to get going—"

"She never lost her temper. Can you believe that? Me, I'm *always* losing mine. *Still,* at my age! She would never *nudzh* me about it. But once in a while she would say, 'Morris—' "

Aaron took his leave, his own footsteps following him across the emptiness of the long, white room.

31

MEAT LOCKER

It had begun to rain by the time Aaron picked up Sam at the On-Target studios—not a real rain, more of a light mist, accompanied by fog blown in from the sea.

Sam's heels clicked sharply on wet asphalt as she walked across the parking lot and got into the Porsche, bringing with her smells of perfume and stale newsroom cigarette smoke.

Aaron made a 180-degree turn and headed for the exit.

Behind them, another pair of headlights came on in the fog.

"A great night to go out," he said, squinting through the windshield. "You can hardly see in all this shit."

"Gripe, gripe!" She poked him in the side. "You just want— Ouch! What the hell is *that?*"

"Bulletproof underwear."

"Aaron, what have you got *on?*"

She pulled back his leather jacket to reveal the SIG P220 stuck in his waistband, metal grip extending along his side.

"Oh, for God's sake— I can't be*lieve* this!"

"What do you think I bought it for?" he asked, heading west on Sunset, toward the Strip. "To keep under my pillow?"

"Aaron, put it away. Now."

"Hell, no."

"Aaron, this is not some action movie! If a cop stops you and sees that in your pants, we could both wind up in jail!"

"Don't worry. They all know me at the Hollywood station by now. We'll get the best cells in the house."

"Aaron! I'm not joking! Put it away!"

"I bought this gun for a reason. It's not like I *want* to use it, okay? But if I have to, I'm ready."

"You know how to shoot it?"

"I went to a target range. I took some lessons."

"God, this is so sick—"

"You should carry yours, too. That's why we bought it."

"I am not taking a *gun* in my purse."

"You feel safer with that?"

He nodded at the video camera in a leather case that she carried on her lap, On-Target logo engraved in the grain.

"That's for cover. I told everyone we were going to some clubs on the Strip to get interviews for a piece on young Hollywood at night. Certain people got very nosy about it, like they didn't believe me. So I decided to take this along."

"Which certain people?"

"Bonnie Redfield, for one."

"I thought she hated my guts."

"She does. But she was all smiles tonight—and *very* nosy. 'So where are you and Aaron going?' "

"You should use that to take some shots inside this place."

"They don't allow video cameras. Or handguns."

They stopped at a red light in the fog, pale and ghostly as a watercolor wash. The light changed to green and they moved on, a pair of headlights trailing them through the fog like twin suns in a milk white sky.

They drove in silence, interrupted every five seconds by the swish of wipers across the glass.

"Want to drive to Lone Pine with me?" Aaron asked.

"Where's that?"

He told her.

"What for?"

He told her that, too, leaving out nothing—including the parts about reading his mother's letter, and talking to Johnny Moffet and Moe Edelstein.

Sam was silent for several seconds after he finished, watching the wipers flick across the glass. Then she reached over and touched him lightly on the cheek.

"Aaron, I'm sorry. I never knew that about your father."

"Yeah, well, it's not something I talk about much."

"You told me he was dead. But I thought that happened when you were older. You never told me that he died in some kind of horrible accident—"

"I just learned the details myself. That's why I want to go up to Lone Pine and find out some more from this Lassiter guy. You want to come with me or not?"

"Are you just going to take off from your radio show?"

"I'll probably do it this weekend. Drive up Friday afternoon, then drive back Sunday. You don't have to come."

She watched the wipers scraping across the glass.

"What will you find there that you don't already know?"

"I'm not sure. Maybe I'll find out where he's buried. Or maybe I'll meet someone who knows more about him, or has a picture of him. Hell, *I* don't know what I'll find! I just want to go up there and talk to Tex Lassiter. That's all."

"Okay, Aaron. I'll go with you."

They moved through the fog-enshrouded city, past irregular blobs of buildings, almost indistinguishable in the mist. The light rain continued to come down, spotting the windshield in the five seconds between the wipers' ministrations, but doing nothing to wash away the fog. Other cars' headlights drifted past them like spectral lanterns.

As they drew near the Strip, illuminated billboards glowed down at them through the mist, lettering indecipherable.

"Are we getting close?" Aaron asked.

"Almost. Just a few more blocks."

"We'll probably miss it in this goddamn fog."

"It's hard to miss. There's a large white neon sign—"

"Sounds like you hang out there, Sam."

"You should talk! *Mis*ter Rakehell Club charter member!"

"That's just a place for old guys to get their rocks off."

"This is where Generation-Xers do the same thing."

"No shit? Just point me at the good stuff, then."

"Aaron, I've never been there before. I've *heard* about the Meat Locker from other people. This is my first time."

"Women always say that."

As they made their way up the Strip, a white neon sign began to materialize from the fog, like bleached bones shining through a snowstorm: THE MEAT LOCKER, in large stick letters, and in smaller letters below that, A PRIVATE CLUB.

"Where's the valet parking?" Aaron asked.

"That's only for guests."

"What the fuck are we supposed to be?"

"Celebrity guests, Aaron. The kind who show up in *People.* Not you. Not me. We get to park on the street, along with the rest of the guys."

"There's no goddamn parking on the street!" Aaron said. "Even if there was, you couldn't see it in this fucking fog!"

"Then we'll just have to turn off on a side street and park up in the hills somewhere. You're the one who lives in this part of town, Aaron. You should know what to do."

"I don't go out in fog like this!"

He nosed the Porsche up a narrow side street that carried them into the lower levels of the Hollywood Hills, only partway up the mountainside, but high enough to look down on the blurred neon lights of the Strip. The walls of the houses on either side of the road hemmed in the Porsche, almost touching it, stray tendrils of fog drifting across stucco surfaces like wisps of white smoke. Lights from the upper stories shone down on them, glowing like smudged stars in the mist.

When he finally found a space that wasn't in front of someone's garage door, Aaron pulled up the Porsche and parked it as close as possible without taking off paint.

They sat and listened to the cooling motor tick and ping.

"Jesus! We could've parked at my place and walked down."

As they got out of the car, they felt the light rain misting their faces, damp and cold.

"You bring an umbrella?" Aaron asked.

"No," she said.

"Shit!"

"At least it washes away the smog."

"Fuck it. I'll take smog any day."

Aaron set his car alarm, traffic noise rising from Sunset at higher than normal volume.

As he looked up, he noticed the headlights in the fog.

They winked out the moment he saw them, fading into the fog like the cathode-ray tube of a switched-off television set.

"What the fuck was that?" he asked.

"What's wrong now, Aaron?"

"There!" He pointed to where the headlights had been.

"I can't see a thing."

"*Something* was there. Just a few seconds ago. I saw it!"

"What?"

"Headlights. When I noticed them, they went out."

"Probably someone coming home. What's *wrong* with you?"

"Nothing. I'm cool. I'm just glad I got this."

He touched the SIG beneath his black leather jacket.

Sam folded her arms. "*That* has to go."

"The only place it's goin' is down there with me."

"Aaron, they *search* people before they let them into this club! If they find that on you—and they will—then they'll just kick you out. If you're going to act this way, we might as well save ourselves the trouble and go home now."

"How do you know so much about this place?"

"Because people who've been there have *told* me! I asked around at On-Target. It's called doing your homework. Are you going to put that thing away or not?"

"No. I brought it with me for a reason."

She turned back to the Porsche.

"Sam—"

"Would you please unlock this door for me? I'm going to wait here while you walk down there and get thrown out on your ass. If you're not back in fifteen minutes, I'm calling a cab."

"All right, all *right!*"

He walked over to the Porsche's trunk and unlocked it.

"This is so fucking stupid—" he muttered.

"It certainly is."

"I mean it's fuckin' stupid to buy a gun that cost sixteen hundred fuckin' bucks—"

He tossed the SIG into the trunk and slammed down the lid.

"—then leave it locked up in your trunk when you're on your way to meet a fuckin' serial killer!"

The last words seemed to echo back from a nearby wall.

"Aaron, keep it down. Sounds carry in the fog."

"Well, ex*cuse* me!"

He started down the steep side street that led to the Strip, moving ahead of her into the fog. Their footsteps echoed off the pavement in alternating rhythms. A streetlight, dim as a candle, glimmered in the mist.

Something big seemed to be taking shape in the fog ahead of them, larger than any person of ordinary size.

Aaron slowed down his own pace, unsure of what he saw—whether it was moving toward him, or just standing still.

I could kill you before they knew what was happening.

He heard the Phantom whispering to him again at the Rakehell Club, and felt a chill come over him that had nothing to do with the fog or the light rain falling on his face.

He was sorry now that he had listened to Sam. If he ran back to where the Porsche was parked, it would still take another few seconds to open the trunk, get out the gun—

Bright light burst from inside the fog, cutting through it like a laser beam. Aaron stepped back, shielding his eyes from the light, reaching inside his leather jacket for where the gun should be, finding nothing there but his belt.

"Who the fuck's out there?" he shouted into the fog.

No one answered at first.

Then a woman's voice said, "Sure as hell can't use that."

"Want me to turn off the sound?" asked a man's voice.

"For now, yeah."

Aaron stepped forward, into the light. As he did so, it resolved itself from a hazy supernova into a more familiar video camera light. The cameraman was operating with a shoulder brace for the camera and the video light on top of that. Bonnie Redfield stood beside him, gripping a handheld microphone.

"Bonnie!" Sam cried. "What are you doing here?"

"Just following my nose."

"That must be easy," Aaron said, "even in the fog."

"Aaron," Sam said, "keep out of this."

"I've got a gun." Bonnie patted her purse. "Fuck with me tonight, Scott, and they'll have to *carry* your ass out of here."

"See?" he whispered to Sam. "She has one!"

"Bonnie," Sam said, "we were just going to have dinner. You're welcome to join us—"

"Don't bullshit me, Samantha. You're going to the Meat Locker, and dinner's not what they eat down there. I don't know who you plan to see or what you're after, but I'll bet my favorite vibrator it's got something to do with the Phantom. And if anything breaks on that story, it's *mine.*"

"So it's your story, Bonnie. Is that the way it works?"

"Come on, Sam," Aaron said. "Let's go. If she wants to follow us that bad—fuck it, just let her."

He took Sam's arm and pulled her down the street, toward Sunset, her head still turned back in Bonnie's direction.

"The only thing I want from you, asshole," Bonnie called after him, "is for you to lead me to the Phantom!"

Behind them, the portable video light, reduced to a diffused glare again, moved down the hillside slowly and steadily.

"Aaron! Slow down!"

"You want to lose her or not?"

"I don't want to break an ankle doing it!"

They came out on Sunset in the heart of the fog.

Voices and cars passed by them, barely seen, like shadows in the mist. Still holding on to Sam, Aaron started to cross Sunset, no clue as to where the cars were, or how fast they were coming, except for the sound of tires hissing on wet pavement, the rush of metal as they sped by.

"Aaron! The crosswalk's back there!"

"If we cross here, we'll lose her."

"Aaron!"

A van bore down on them out of the fog, applying its brakes at the last minute as the driver saw them emerge from the mist.

He came to a stop within a few feet of hitting them.

"Asshole!" Aaron kicked the bumper, denting it.

The driver of the van leaned on his horn, shaking his fist at them through tinted glass.

They crossed the rest of the way in the fog. More horns honked at them. Another set of brakes squealed to a stop.

As they gained the curb, Sam dug her nails into Aaron's wrist, forcing him to let go of her hand.

"Hey! What the fuck—"

She stared at him, raindrops beading her face.

"If you *ever* do that to me again, Aaron—"

"I wanted to ditch that bitch. And we did. Look!"

He pointed to the other side of the street, where the portable video light burned like a beacon beside the crosswalk.

"I don't *care* if she follows us, Aaron! They won't let her into the club with all that shit, anyway. They probably won't even let *us* in!"

She turned and headed for the entrance. As Aaron followed her, he could see the groups of people—most of them in their twenties, more men than women—arranged casually but self-consciously in front of the Meat Locker, like extras from a grunge-art movie shot somewhere in Seattle. The fashion styles ranged from basic black leather to basic black rubber, with lots of jewelry piercing the fabric, or the skin, or both. Hair came in every color that could shock or startle, shining through the fog with radioactive intensity. The only look that seemed more popular than hair of many colors was total baldness, skin scraped to a Yul Brynner sheen, radical and serene, with tattoos burned into the back or sides like designer logos.

The guy doing guard duty at the head of the line was the usual bouncer with muscle and attitude, skimpy leather vest open over a bare chest to show off how many hours a day he spent at the gym and how many steroids he took to expand a mortal frame to the staggering dimensions of a comic book superhero. The fine rain gleamed on chiseled pecs and abs. His small eyes narrowed to lizardlike slits as he watched Sam approach, blond hair limp in the mist, Aaron hanging back behind her.

"I'm Samantha Collier, with On-Target News."

"Media's got to be cleared with management."

"I'm not here to get pictures or interview anyone."

"Who's he supposed to be?"

"I'm Aaron Scott. KRAS FM. Sunset Scott in the Morning."

"Sunset Scott!" someone called from the side. "Hey, man!"

Aaron nodded to acknowledge him, then stopped when he saw that the asshole was just putting him on.

"Sunset Scott," the bouncer said. "One of those old sixties guys? Plays tunes for other old sixties guys?"

"Give me a break, man. I was still in grade school when the sixties ended. You're thinkin' of Demolition Dave, the guy who does Groovin' with the Oldies on that other shit station."

The bouncer stared at them through his lizard slits.

"We just want to see it happen," Sam said, giving him her best smile, damp blond hair clinging to her cheeks. "Please?"

The bouncer snorted, then tilted his head to one side.

"Security check's that way."

Beneath a projecting edge of the roof—still outside, but out of the rain—a bouncer with less spectacular bodywork and a girl with spiked raspberry hair ran metal-detecting wands over Aaron's and Sam's bodies, each matched with the right gender, just like at the police station. They passed the wands over every part of their bodies, especially the genitals, and made Aaron show them his keys and a pocketknife.

Inside, it was the standard mix—hard rock with enough force to rearrange your chromosomes, cigarette smoke that seemed to have been packed in amber, and lighting low enough to simulate the extremes of legal blindness. Lights of different colors, like thin fluorescent tubes, were inlaid along recessed tracks in the high ceiling. Red, blue, purple, green, chartreuse, magenta, they stretched out in networks overhead, shining down on the festivities below like neon meteor trails in a plaster sky.

The crowding was intense, yet everyone, despite the density, seemed to have his or her assigned space. And they seemed to move hardly at all, as if their positions had been preordained. Moving past them was like winding your way through a forest of mannequins in some basement back room of a major department store.

The music, the darkness, the stasis, the neon meteor-tracks in the ceiling—all of it proved so disorienting for Aaron that he lost Sam within seconds of stepping inside.

"Sam?"

He turned to find her, and bumped into one of the customers posing as statues. The guy had on sunglasses that reflected the room in miniature.

"Sorry, man," Aaron apologized, backing off.

The guy nodded—one quick, jerky shake of the head that could have meant *That's cool* or *Fuck you*, or nothing at all.

"Sam!" he called out for her.

But there was no fighting the power of the sound system that drove the hard rock relentlessly into his brain. His shout did not even register. For all the good it did, he might have been mouthing the words. He couldn't see anything—just statues and darkness and smoke.

He turned again, and someone bumped into him. He looked down into flat dark eyes in a pale white face, limp dark hair framing it like seaweed clinging to a bleached skull.

"Want a piece of God?" she asked, holding out her hand.

Aaron drew back from her. "You talkin' to *me?*"

She held out a syringe and hypodermic needle, the disposable plastic kind you see in the doctor's office.

"Heroin's God," she said. "Here."

Her breath, wafting up into Aaron's face, had a foul, wasted odor to it, as if she had just been vomiting refuse and trying to swallow it back down again as fast as it came up.

Aaron backed farther off, bumping into another statue.

He turned to apologize, but the statue had already moved.

A hand grabbed his wrist and he jumped slightly, thinking that the girl with the vomit breath and syringe had come back.

But it was Sam, looking small and blond among the statues.

"Come on," she said. "We've got to go to the Deep Freeze."

"What the fuck is that?"

"The most private part of the club."

"I thought the whole place was private!"

"The Deep Freeze is ultimate privacy." She pulled on his hand. "This way. We've got to go through Virtual Video first."

"Speaking of that—" He turned around, holding tight to her hand, looking for the video light and the cameraman and Bonnie Redfield. "What happened to your friend?"

"They stopped her outside. I knew they would. Come *on.*"

They wound their way through the statues and the smoke, past more celebrants bearing deities in syringes, the music assaulting them from the darkness all the while like some physical but invisible force. He leaned down to Sam and put his lips next to her ear and shouted.

Even so, she could barely hear him.

"*What?*"

"How do we *find* him in all this shit?"

"We don't. We let him find us. He knows we're here."

He wanted to ask her what made her so sure about that, but they entered Virtual Video just then, and other things began to occupy his attention.

The room, larger than the one they had just left, but with a lower ceiling, held four walls of seventy-inch television screens, four to a wall, sixteen in all. The darkness of the other room dissolved into a flat, white light that seemed to come from the ceiling and the floor and the oversize images themselves, filling up the big screens.

The images looked to Aaron like cheap porno—badly lighted, poorly framed, crudely shot—the kind of shit they offer at ten tapes for a buck in the back pages of third-rate tit magazines.

Then he looked at the screens again, and at the room itself, and realized that these weren't tapes at all, but live feeds coming from video cameras trained on couples and solitary performers spread out in various positions and combinations across the deep pile carpeting. Cameramen and camerawomen—amateurs all, club members, fun-seekers—turned camcorders on the couples and singles, zooming in for closeups, pulling back for long shots, panning for effect, as the spirit and the movements moved them. The screens along all four walls reflected this frenzied hyperactivity in multiple, fragmented, repetitive images of full-color, big-screen virtual unreality.

Gaping vulva filled one screen, finger on the clitoris, like a giant homage to a Stone Age fertility goddess. On another screen a couple humped with the pounding regularity of an oil well pump, his cock sliding in and out, her legs drawing up around him, moans and groans amplified in stereophonic sound. A woman's mouth was fixed to another woman's breast in close-up on another screen, lips and tongue attacking the erect, dark-colored nipple, teeth biting it now and then, or stretching it out from the breast then letting it snap back into place. Another screen zoomed in for a close-up of a vagina being penetrated slowly by an oversize, heavily veined cock, the bright red labia gripping it like clenched muscles as it forced its way in, inch by inch.

Aaron looked down from the big screen to find the real couple doing the real thing on that one. It took a few seconds' worth of scanning the semiclothed and naked bodies scattered across the carpeted floor before he located the stars of the penetration close-up. A small girl with short blond hair, arms thrown back over her head, large pink areolas shiny with sweat, moaned softly to herself as a bald guy with sharply defined muscles and tattoos and pierced body parts shoved his huge cock inside her with all the patience and steady, unwavering determination of a core sample drill operator.

Aaron stared at the real thing, then looked up at the huge, big-screen close-up, then back down at the actual rutting couple, then switching back and forth from reality to hyperreality, his mouth open in benumbed fascination.

"Hi! You want to do it?"

Startled, he looked over to see a thin girl with short red hair and a sharp, beaklike nose staring at him through blue eyes that glowed like twin rheostats. In one hand she carried a camcorder attached to a feeder cord. The only clothes she had on, a pair of pink nylon panties, had soaked through at the crotch. Her nipples looked bright red and inflamed, protruding over an inch from her small breasts, as if someone had been working on them long and relentlessly.

Aaron, atypically, was at a loss for words.

"Uh—sorry. I'm, like, uh, with someone—"

He grabbed Sam's arm for reassurance.

"I *mean*, you guys want to do it together? So I can shoot you while you're doin' it? And if you want to add somebody else or switch around later, that's cool."

"Thanks," Sam said. "But we're here to meet someone.

The girl blinked at them through her glow-in-the-dark blue eyes with genuine confusion and just a trace of hostility.

"Why even come here if you don't want to do it?"

Sam, guiding Aaron, moved them through Virtual Video, stepping carefully around—and, in a few cases, over—the prone bodies that blocked their way. A single male, lying flat on his back, small cock in hand, rigidly erect and pointing at the low ceiling, ejaculated a mother lode of semen straight up into the air where it dropped backward and down onto his belly.

"Whoa!" someone cried out. "Old Faithful!"

"Jesus!" Aaron said, sticking close to Sam as they passed the scene of the eruption. "Any of that shit land on you?"

"I dodged."

Leaving Virtual Video behind, they found themselves in the Deep Freeze, the *sanctum sanctorum* of the Meat Locker.

Entering, they passed through a metal detector similar to those used at airport security checkpoints. A man dressed in black stood on either side of the metal detector, looking less bulked-up but far more dangerous than the pinup boy outside.

Here, in the most private room of a very private club, where the super celebrities of the evening usually congregated, they might have expected more sex, even wilder than what they had seen in Virtual Video. But they found instead more syringes and more heroin, along with a connoisseur's pharmacopeia of exotic designer drugs, as if the lower animal pleasures of copulation had given way to the more refined delights of hard-core addiction.

The rich and famous, and their hangers-on, lounged about the room on oversize satin pillows, bathed in a low blue light of the kind that might follow a nuclear reactor meltdown. Some mainlined heroin with religious solemnity, scrutinizing pockmarked forearms for one more place to slip the needle in. Others ingested designer drugs like manna from an outlaw chemist's heaven. The dealers handling these drugs were not the usual scrofulous types, oozing out of shadows to slap an unmarked packet into someone's hand. They looked more like distributors' reps for a natural foods vitamin company—soft-faced young men, explaining their products in even softer voices. The designer drugs bore distinctive names on colored packages. Ecstasy, Seventh Heaven, and Nirvana, for the spiritually inclined. Chaos, Terminator, and Black Talon for those eager to encounter the pleasures of the dark side.

Aaron, looking around the room, recognized several faces.

"Christ," he said to Sam, "is that who I think it is?"

"Yes."

"And her, too? And him?"

"Yes."

"All the fuckin' money they make," he continued, lowering his voice, "and the only thing they can think of—"

Sam nudged him in the ribs. "Look."

"Where?"

"Over there."

Clustered around a satin pillow, like acolytes attending the avatar, a group of the poor and obscure watched their favorite rich and famous renegade embrace the experience of designer drugs. One of the faithful, even at that distance, wore the unmistakable strung-out long hair of the fallen angel who had jumped Aaron that night with the other two, and had fled from him another night into an alley, to vanish with the Phantom.

"That's *him!*"

"Don't point, Aaron. Let's just go over there."

As they did, the fallen angel opened his mouth to laugh at some piece of wit from the drug-taking celebrity, revealing his bad teeth beneath the low blue light.

"I want to talk to you, man," Aaron said.

The fallen angel jerked his head up in Aaron's direction, frightened eyes taking in him and Sam, then turned back as suddenly to the celebrity in ecstasy. He had been sitting on the floor, watching the show, legs crossed beneath him. Now he got up into a kind of half crouch and began to move sideways around the outside of the circle, like a long-haired spider, one shoulder raised higher than the other, as if expecting a blow.

Aaron came over and grabbed him by the shoulder.

"Look, fuck-face. I want to *talk* to you, okay?"

"Back off!" the fallen angel croaked, voice slightly damaged by drug use or some kind of congenital defect.

Uneasy murmurs rippled through the celebrity's circle.

A pair of black-clad security guards materialized out of nowhere and moved swiftly toward them.

Aaron let go of the fallen angel's shoulder, sharp and bony beneath the fabric of a cheap black polyester jacket.

"I don't want to hurt you, man. I just want to talk."

"Outside," he croaked.

"Outside where?"

The security guards came up to them then, not touching anyone, but moving inside their space barriers, threatening them without lifting a finger or making a sound.

"We got a problem here?" asked one of the guards.

The fallen angel shook his head no.

"We were just on our way outside," Aaron said.

"You do that," said the other guard.

The fallen angel rose from his half crouch to a full standing position, shoulders hunched. As Aaron and Sam turned to follow him across the Deep Freeze toward an exit door, a cry broke out from the luxuriating celebrity on the satin pillow.

"*Ahhhhhhh!*" he screamed, grabbing his head in both hands and rocking back and forth like a dervish in holy ecstasy.

The circle of the faithful widened, and began to move back.

"Watch him," Aaron heard one guard mutter to the other. "He gets any worse, you take him outside fast. Nobody fucks on us in here like that, *capish?*"

Aaron and Sam followed the fallen angel out an exit door at the back of the Deep Freeze and found themselves in an alley obscured by fog and misting rain. They could hear traffic noises from either end, but all they could see inside the alley was the indistinct form of the fallen angel. He turned to them, long hair and bad teeth blurring out of focus in the fog.

"What you want with *me?*" he croaked at them.

"I don't want any part of you," Aaron said, stepping toward him. "I want your friend. The dude with the shaved head and the little tuft of red hair? You know. The Phantom."

The fallen angel smiled, not a pretty sight with his bad teeth. Then he gave a low growl that could have been a laugh.

"He ain't the Phantom, man."

"Sure. Where do I find him?"

"That the only reason you came here tonight?"

"No other. Where is he?"

"He don't hardly ever come here."

Aaron glanced at Sam, who shrugged her shoulders.

"Cool. So where does he hang most of the time?"

"At the warehouses, the ones where they do the parties."

"Where's that?"

"You never been to a flyer party?"

"No."

"They change around a lot. The flyer tells you where—"

"I know what they are. You got a flyer on you?"

He hesitated, then dug out a wadded-up piece of paper from his pocket and handed it to Aaron, who unfolded it and squinted as he tried to read in the dim, foggy light of the alley.

"This is where he's going to be next?"

The fallen angel nodded. "Tomorrow night."

"You sure?"

He nodded again.

"You better not be lyin' to me about this, man."

Aaron folded up the paper, more neatly this time, then took out his wallet to put it away. As he opened the wallet, the large amount of folding money he carried was clearly visible, even in the half-light of the fog.

"Give it here."

He looked up to see a .38 snub-nosed revolver in the fallen angel's right hand, the black hole of its muzzle pointing straight at his own chest. The other hand was stretched out toward Aaron, waiting for the wallet.

"Are you out of your fuckin'—"

"I ain't got time for this, dude. Hand it over."

His eyes flicked nervously from side to side, as if expecting someone to step out of the fog.

Aaron stared at the barrel of the revolver, blue steel beaded with clear drops of falling rain.

"Give it to me alive or I take it from you dead, mama."

"*Give* it to him, Aaron," Sam said, her voice trembling.

Aaron reached out and dropped the wallet in his hand.

"Fuck you," he added.

The fallen angel croaked out a laugh, then raised the gun.

"Hey, what the fuck? I gave you the fuckin' wallet!"

The fallen angel grinned, revealing his bad teeth.

"He's gonna kill you sooner or later. And his way's harder than mine. Besides, my way don't leave witnesses."

"You fucking son of a bitch—"

Aaron's voice closed off as he watched him start to squeeze the trigger. He turned his head and shut his eyes.

The gun went off with a deafening roar at close range.

Sam screamed beside him.

Aaron's body jerked in anticipation of the bullet's impact.

But it never came. Sam screamed again—a strangled, sickened

note to it this time. Aaron opened his eyes. The fallen angel's body arched backward in front of him, revolver flying out of his right hand, wallet dropping from his left. A dark red hole in his chest about the size of a quarter seemed to expand suddenly, mushrooming like an alien growth inside his body, pumping out quarts of blood as he fell. The back of his head smacked the concrete surface of the alley with the muted crack of breaking bones. He lay where he fell, perfectly still except for the blood gushing from the hole in his chest and forming pools on both sides of his body.

"Get your wallet back from him. Then get out of here."

They turned, nerves still shattered, to see Lopez put his nine-millimeter Beretta back in its holster.

"Thanks," Aaron whispered.

"I said get the hell *out* of here!"

They both flinched at the hard anger in Lopez's voice.

"Neither one of you has *any* business being here in the first place. Two amateurs playing cops and robbers—"

"Isn't anyone going to help him?" Sam asked, still staring at the motionless body of the fallen angel, which now seemed to float on top of a small lake of blood.

"He's gone," Lopez said. "You better get going, too, unless you want to spend the rest of the night at the station house, answering questions."

They started down the alley, moving deeper into the fog.

"Aaron," Lopez called after him.

Aaron stopped and looked back.

"Quit trying to find him."

32

PRIME CUTS

Excited babble carried through the fog from outside the Meat Locker's main entrance as word of the shooting passed from person to person.

Waiting for the light to change, Aaron and Sam could hear sirens in the distance, making their way toward the Strip.

The supernova of the portable video light burst through the fog again, seeking them out in the rain and the darkness, fixing them near the crosswalk. Sam turned her head from its glare. Aaron stared defiantly into the burning eye.

"Thought you gave us the slip, huh?"

Bonnie Redfield's voice cut through the fog and the babble outside the Meat Locker and the sirens screaming down Sunset as she and the cameraman moved in on them.

"We're here in front of the Meat Locker on the Sunset Strip," Bonnie spoke into her handheld microphone, "with Aaron Scott, aka

Sunset Scott, shock jock for KRAS FM, and Samantha Collier, field reporter for On-Target News."

Bonnie stepped aside to let the cameraman get a close-up.

"Aaron, did you meet with the Phantom in the Meat Locker?"

He stared at her hair, wreathed in fog like a Gorgon's.

"No comment."

"People outside the Meat Locker right now are saying that the Phantom just killed a club member. They say that member's body is cut up in pieces and scattered across the alley in back of the club. Do you know anything about this?"

"No comment, babe."

She flipped him the finger, out of camera range.

"Samantha Collier, can you confirm or deny any of this?"

Sam stared into the camera lens as she answered, looking her cool and unflappable field reporter best, despite the fact that she had been trembling as they walked out of the alley.

"We didn't meet with the Phantom, Bonnie. And the club member who was killed—if he *is* a member—wasn't killed by the Phantom and his body wasn't cut to pieces. He was a robbery suspect shot by someone working for the LAPD."

"Can you give us any more information about that?"

"Not at this—"

"Look, Bonnie," Aaron cut in, "I said no comment. That means no fuckin' *comment, okay?*"

"Keep the sound on?" the cameraman asked.

"Yes!" Bonnie snapped. "Is there some *reason* you don't want to talk with us about this, Sunset Scott? Is there maybe some kind of *deal* you made with the Phantom?"

"Fuck you, you bug-eyed bitch!"

Aaron grabbed Sam's hand and pulled her across Sunset. He could hear Bonnie giving instructions to the cameraman as they started after them.

"Keep it turned on no matter *what* that asshole says! We can always edit out all his shit later."

Aaron and Sam made it to the other side just as the light turned red. Bonnie and her cameraman were about one-third of the way across when the traffic on the Strip kicked into high gear again. Cars and vans shot past them, slowing down momentarily to gape at the light and the camera, but not stopping. Angry horns blared through the fog.

"Oh, my God!" Sam cried. "That car almost hit her!"

"Probably a television critic."

"Aaron! It's not funny!"

"She's a big girl. She can take care of herself. Come on, Sam. Let's get going before the light changes again."

They made slow progress back up the steep street to the place where Aaron's black Porsche was parked. Sam kept stopping every few feet to catch her breath.

"You okay?" he asked, when they finally reached it.

She nodded, then went over to the wall of a nearby house and leaned against it, one hand on the stucco surface, the other clutching her stomach. She coughed. A drop of clear rainwater fell from the tip of her nose.

"Hey!" He rushed over to her. "What's wrong? Want me to drive you to an emergency room?"

She shook her head. "I'm okay."

"Okay, my ass! What's *wrong*, Sam?"

She looked up at him, tears like raindrops on her lashes.

"Everyone keeps dying, Aaron. Everything's turning into blood. How many more before this is over?"

She grabbed hold of him suddenly and buried her head in his chest. He could feel her body shaking and the heat of her tears as she sobbed against him.

He put his arms around her, displacing raindrops on the back of her leather coat. His lips touched her rain-damp hair.

"It's okay, Sam," he said.

The fog seemed to gather around them like rolling smoke from a bonfire of the dead.

"We don't have to keep doing this shit. Lopez is right. It's their job—"

The scream tore through the fog, sweeping over them like a banshee's wail, carrying with it all the naked fear of death a human voice could convey.

Farther down the hillside, where the narrow street began its steep ascent from Sunset, Bonnie and her cameraman labored up the incline, the noise and chaos of the Strip and the Meat Locker fading slowly into the fog behind them.

"He'll be gone when we get there," the cameraman said.

"No, he won't. There's only one way down."

"This road probably connects with Mulholland somewhere—"

"Aaron Scott's too big a prick to take the back way out. He'll come down here in a few minutes, just to put on a fucking macho act. And when he does, we'll be ready for him."

"*I* ain't standin' in the middle of this road when he comes down it like a bat outta hell. You can. I'll stand to the side and film it while he runs you down."

"I hope he tries. If he so much as nudges me with that fucking yuppie Batmobile of his, I'm gonna own his ass *and* his balls. You don't fuck with the media in this town and live."

"Hear that?" The cameraman stopped.

A car's engine strained through the fog.

"Just someone else coming up from the Strip," she said.

They both stepped aside to let the car pass by, a sleek gray Jaguar with wipers on high, fog lights on low.

"Come on," Bonnie said, panting for breath as she started up the slope again. "The higher we get, the harder it'll be for that little prick to turn his car around."

"Don't wait for me. I only got a few tons of gear."

"You camera boys have it so easy. You don't have to talk to anyone. Or get threatened by fucked-up weirdos."

"You got it all wrong, Bonnie. The real crazies come after us. We're the ones taking their picture. That day at the KRAS station? That whacko Scott almost—"

Bonnie stopped and held up her hand. "Listen!"

The sound of footsteps came toward them through the fog, then stopped suddenly, a scuffing of wet pavement.

"Who's that?" Bonnie whispered to her cameraman.

"Maybe he's comin' back down—"

"Sunset Scott!" she shouted into the fog. "Is that you?"

No other sounds came from the fog, although the sense of something there—indisputably there—persisted. Nothing could be seen, but something could certainly be felt.

"People live up here," the cameraman said. "Some guy could be takin' his dog for a walk, takin' out the trash."

"Turn on your light," Bonnie said. "Shine it over there, next to that wall."

He shouldered his camera and reached up to switch on the light. Bonnie stared at the place in the fog about to be illuminated. A blast of music came from the second story of a house across the way as someone cranked up a sound system to the max. Her attention distracted, Bonnie glanced in that direction just when the video light cut through the fog.

The cameraman sucked in his breath. "Sweet Jesus—"

Bonnie heard the soft hissing sound of metal slicing through rain and fog, and turned in time to see a meat cleaver descending upon the cameraman's head.

He tossed the camera away with one hand and raised the other in a futile effort to protect himself. The cleaver sheared through the uplifted hand like a stalk of broccoli and continued down with full force to the top of his bald head, splitting it jaggedly in half, dropping through bone, brains, gristle, and flesh, stopping somewhere below the chin.

Blood burst from the newly opened fissure, spattering Bonnie's own face as she watched in slack-jawed horror.

The black-gloved hand that held the cleaver wrenched it from the split skull, blood falling through the fog and rain.

Aaron broke free from Sam's embrace, running toward the screams. Sam stumbled after him, almost paralyzed by fear.

He could see the bright shaft of video light cutting up through the fog, shadows moving violently in front of it, like silhouettes in a dark cartoon. Before he came any closer, the fog lifted partially, revealing a white stucco wall at the side of the road. A burst of blood hit the wall, spattering it with globs and streaks of intense red, running down the white surface at crazy, twisting, intersecting angles.

Aaron skidded to a stop on the wet pavement, chest heaving, gasping for breath. He stood and watched the blood run down the white wall, starting to blur now as fog dropped over it again. He heard Sam weeping behind him but could not turn and comfort her, could do nothing except stand and stare at the blood flowing down the wall.

"Sunset Scott—"

The whispering voice floated through the fog like the disembodied summons of death itself.

"You wanted to find me, didn't you?"

Aaron turned and grabbed Sam hard by one shoulder, dragging her back up the hill with him, eyes on the large shadow in front of the video light, something in its hand.

"But you didn't expect to find me—like this, did you?"

Aaron heard the pop and tinkle of breaking glass. The video light went out, as if stepped on by a heavy, booted foot.

Sam continued weeping helplessly, one hand over her mouth, the other held out at an awkward angle as Aaron dragged her with him up the slanting street.

A burst of flame seared the fog, catching hold of something, burning brighter, turning into a small, intense fireball, and with it came a stomach-turning stench, a sickness in the air that Aaron had smelled before and knew too well.

"Here, Sunset Scott. Catch!"

"No!" Aaron cried, dropping Sam's arm, raising his own.

The fireball came hurtling at them through the fog, trailing its sweet-roasted stench as it passed overhead.

It hit something with a hollow, metallic *clunk*.

Aaron saw it burning on the roof of his Porsche.

He moved toward it slowly, gripping Sam's shoulder again, both of them taking the uncertain steps of the stunned and disoriented.

They stopped several feet from the Porsche's trunk, where they could see clearly Bonnie Redfield's severed head, face slashed again and again, beyond recognition, dark hair on fire, like a flare in the rain and the fog.

Sam, past the point of tears, stood and stared at the burning head, her own face rigid.

"Bastard," Aaron whispered. "Fucking *bastard.*"

He took out his keys, hands shaking, found the one for the trunk, opened it, grabbed the SIG automatic, pulled it from its holster, started back down the hill, gun raised before him, gripped in both hands, the way he had seen Lopez do it, the way he had done it himself at the target range.

He moved toward the place in the fog where he had seen the shadow, the point where the burning head had come from.

He heard a squishing sound underfoot, and stopped to look down. He saw that he was standing in a pool of blood deep enough to come up over the thick soles of his Doc Martens. Bonnie Redfield's body parts lay randomly scattered across the blood, like pieces of meat in a rich, tomato-based stew. Over to one side, as the *pièce de résistance*, the cameraman's body rested still as stone, blood from the cloven skull leaking slowly into the sea of red around it.

Aaron turned suddenly, splashing blood up onto his jeans legs, revolving in a slow circle, gun held out in front of him, sweeping through the fog and light rain.

"Where *are* you?" he screamed, voice coming back at him from the walls of close-packed houses on either side of the street.

No whispering voice answered from the fog.

33

PYRE

They were questioned by the police, but not for long. The cops knew what had happened, even before they asked.

At one point Montoya introduced a man about his own age with styled gray hair and a very expensive custom-made suit as Captain E.L. Hammond, chief of the Hollywood Division. Lopez was in the room with them, dark eyes watchful.

"Did this man," Hammond asked, pointing to Lopez, "offer to protect you, or help you in any way tonight?"

"No," Aaron said.

"Did he approach you at any time earlier in the evening?"

"No."

Hammond turned to Sam. "Miss?"

Sam, who had been given a sedative on their arrival at the police station, simply shook her head no.

"After Sergeant Lopez intervened in the robbery attempt, did he ask you any questions about the Phantom?"

"No," Aaron said.

"Is there any reason why you might be reluctant to answer my questions? Any reason having to do with a bribe or a threat of any kind that Sergeant Lopez might have made earlier?"

Aaron laughed out loud.

"Man, we've seen three people *buy* it tonight! You think we're scared of what some fuckin' *cop* says to us?"

Hammond drew in his breath sharply.

He muttered something to Montoya, then left the room.

As Aaron and Sam got ready to leave, Montoya regarded them with a sad, tired look.

"I suppose it wouldn't do any good," he said, "to ask you not to try something like this again, would it?"

"You have the authority to stop us?" Aaron asked.

"No."

"Then it wouldn't do any good."

Montoya held out two pieces of cellophane-wrapped candy.

"Quick energy," he said.

Aaron stared at them, then shook his head.

"If they weren't red, I might say yes."

He wanted to take Sam to a hotel, or to one of her girlfriends' apartments, but she insisted on being driven back home to Studio City. Fog covered the interior courtyard of the apartment complex and obscured the outside stairs leading up to her second-floor unit.

The walk seemed long for both of them.

"It's not smart to stay here tonight, Sam."

"You know anyplace safer?"

She sat down in an armchair in her small living room, looking as if she might not have the energy to rise from it.

He came over and put his hands on her shoulders.

"If you'd just let me take you somewhere—"

"Where? He *knows* where we are, Aaron. If we try to go someplace else, he'll know about that, too."

"He's not supernatural, Sam."

She hugged herself, as if warding off a sudden chill.

"At least you have your gun—"

"I'm not using that, Aaron."

"But at least you *have* it, right?"

"Yes."

He took his hands from her shoulders and turned to leave.

"Aaron?"

He stopped. "Yeah?"

"You want to stay here tonight?"

He smiled at her ruefully.

"Jesus, Sam. Any other time in the whole damn world—"

"You don't have to."

"I *want* to! I'd love to! It's just— I have to go check on my mom. I tried to call her from the police station."

"When?"

"When they were giving you the sedative."

"Oh. She wasn't there?"

"She probably just has her phone off the hook. But I'll feel better if I go check. Know what I mean?"

"Sure."

"And by the time I get all the way over there, to come all the way back here—"

"You don't have to explain, Aaron."

"Could I have a rain check tonight, for some other night?"

"Sure—if I'm still here."

She meant it as a bad joke, because she was tired. But after what they had seen that night, it was no joke. Life itself seemed terribly fragile. Sam looked fragile, too, hunched in her armchair, alone.

The distance from where he finally parked the Porsche in West Hollywood to his mother's apartment building over three blocks away proved the longest, most difficult walk of the night. Fog-shrouded doorways seemed to hide hulking shadows. The fog itself concealed things until you were right on top of them: the way the limit of human vision underwater presents a flat wall of opaque blue until something rushes out of it suddenly—like the gaping jaws of a great white shark.

Aaron made it to the inside stairs of the building, heart pounding hard, breathing constricted. He sprinted up the stairs to his mother's floor, blood pressure squeezing his skull.

He rang her doorbell—three times in quick succession—then started hammering on the door, rattling it in the frame. He heard his mother's voice yelling at him, ordering him to stop. Chains slid back and dead bolts turned. The door opened to reveal the angry, frightened face of Leah Steinberg, looking old and vulnerable, gray hair wound up tight in curlers, faded pink bathrobe held closed at the neck.

"Aaron! You know what *time* it is?"

He nodded. "I tried to call—"

"What happened? Is someone sick? Did someone *die?*"

"I tried to call, but no one—"

"I never answer this late at night. Aaron, what's *wrong?*"

"Want me to tell you—out here? Or can I come in?"

"So come in, already!" She motioned impatiently.

He slipped inside the open door, still feeling the fear—fog-shrouded, obscure—that had followed him from the parking space to the building. He closed the door, locked it, double-locked it, secured the guard chain, before turning to her.

"*Nu?*" she asked, still impatient, but softening as she saw the fear in his eyes, sensed it in his movements.

"I wanted to make sure you were okay—"

"Me? Same as always. What's wrong with you, Aaron?"

"I'm okay."

"O*kay?* Do I look like a *pisher?* You have to get up early to do your radio show, and here you are, still awake, and it's after midnight—Aaron, what *is* it?"

He said nothing.

"You're trying to find him again, aren't you? That monster that tortures and kills people— Aaron, why?"

"Sam and I—"

"*Sam?* You would expose her to something like *this?*"

"It was Sam's idea—"

"Don't give me such *chozzerai!*"

"I'm not! It's true. Sam said I had to find him, before he found me. I thought she was crazy at first."

Leah turned her back on him, clutching at the robe with one hand, pointing to the dining room table with the other.

"Sit down," she said. "You want something to *nosh?*"

He shook his head. "I'm not—"

He stopped. A large china bowl, the size of a soup tureen, sat in the center of the dining room table. It seemed filled with the dark flakes of some exotic, unknown grain. Closer examination revealed a bowl heaped full of ashes. Aaron noticed the charred smell in the air then, the after odor of a burning.

He turned to his mother, who stood with her back to him.

"What the hell is *this?* Did something catch fire?"

"No. I set it on purpose."

"You *what?*"

"I burned them, Aaron."

She turned to face him, eyes dark, lips pale.

"I should have done it a long time ago. They're part of the past. They belong with the dead, not the living."

He looked from her to the bowl of ashes, then back again.

"You burned the letters?"

She stared at him, without answering.

"You *burned* my father's letters! You had no *right* to do that! You had no—"

"I had *every* right," she said, her voice hard as iron.

His eyes filled with tears. "Why?"

"They should have died when he did. I couldn't accept that, not at first. I can now."

"I never even got to *read* them!"

"They weren't written to you. They didn't concern you."

"He was my *father!*"

"He's still your father. Nothing changes that."

"But those letters! They were all I had left of him! All I had to remember him by!"

"They were never part of your life, Aaron, any more than he was. It's better it should stay that way."

Aaron buried his face in his hands.

When he took them away he saw, through blurred vision, the bowl of ashes on the table and his mother, her back to him again, standing at the kitchen sink.

"Try to eat something," she said, over the sound of running water. "It'll do you good."

He walked into the kitchen, shut off the water, grabbed her by the shoulders and turned her around to face him.

"Aaron!" she cried. "I'm your mother!"

He dropped his hands, clenching them into fists.

"Why are you doing this to me? *Why?* You've hidden him from me all these years—like some dirty secret, like some obscene thing no one's ever supposed to mention! And then, when I find out about him by accident—when I learn what his name was, what he did, what he was like—then you take what little I have left to remember him by and you fucking set *fire* to it!"

"Aaron, watch your—"

"Why?"

"Because he's *dead!* I've *told* you this before!"

"It's not good enough anymore!"

She backed away, shrinking before him, as if their roles had become reversed, and he was the parent, she the child.

"You think it's easy for me to remember what happened?" she asked, her voice a whisper. "You think I like putting myself through the shame, the misery? You want me to do it all over again—just so you can have your nice little memories that never happened, of someone you never even *knew?*"

He stood in the kitchen, fists clenched, looking down.

"Nu?" she demanded, voice rising. "Is *that* what you want? To put me through hell again so you can play a game of make-believe? Pretend you had the kind of father you never did? Someone who cared about you, cared about me—"

Her voice broke. She turned away to hide her own tears and, seconds later, turned on the faucet in the kitchen sink again to muffle the sounds of her sobs.

After several minutes of running water and diminishing sobs, and

Aaron still standing there, looking down, saying nothing, she spoke again, her voice raw from the crying.

"The past belongs to the past, Aaron. That's why I had to burn them. It's why you need to forget about them, too. Burn them out of your own mind, pretend you never saw them."

"I'm driving up to Lone Pine tomorrow."

She stood with her back still turned to him, hands gripping the sinkboard, the sound of water rushing from the faucet a steady *obbligato* to the silence.

"I'm leaving tomorrow morning, right after my airshift. Sam's coming with me. She *wants* to come. I'm not forcing her. We're going up there to see some guy named Tex Lassiter."

"Good!" She turned around suddenly, lifting her hands in the air, splashing water on her own face and Aaron's. "*Good!* You want to go to that dirty little town where your own father suffered a *miesse meshina?* Go! Go! You want to *schmooze* with that no-good *proster goy?* Go! Enjoy!"

"Mom—"

"*Riboyne Shel O'lem!*" she cried, invoking God in heaven in Yiddish. "Maybe you'll find what you're looking for! Maybe you can find where they buried what was left of him!"

She stopped, tears in her eyes, face tense, anger beginning to dissipate slowly, like scalding steam.

"What exactly did happen to him?" Aaron asked.

"Go ask that *momser*, Tex Lassiter! Let *him* tell you!"

She pushed past him, making her way with quick, jerky steps to the dining table, where she scooped up a handful of charred ashes from the tureen-sized china bowl.

"Here! Take this with you!"

She walked back to him and shoved the ashes forward, dropping them into his outstretched hand. They felt wet and sticky, damp from the moisture of her own undried hand.

"Treasure it like a keepsake! Because it's all you'll ever find in Lone Pine! Nothing but the ashes of the dead!"

34

ACCIDENT

He picked up Sam after his airshift ended and they made just one stop, for lunch at a fast-food place near Lancaster, some seventy miles outside of L.A. Even so, it was late in the afternoon, sun slanting down across the dry, open land of the Mojave Desert, before they came within view of the eastern escarpment of the Sierra Nevada, rising before them like the ramparts of the gods, and at the mountain's feet, the small, unassuming town of Lone Pine, California.

Aaron drove slowly down the short main street—the only street of any size—checking out the bait shops, gun stores, Western wear outfitters, motels, coffee shops, and occasional highway markers showing how many miles to the Mount Whitney Portal or the mountain town of Bishop. They stopped at a gas station, the old-fashioned kind, with red pumps and no signs differentiating full service from self-service, or telling you to pay the cashier first before pumping gas. The attendant who served them was a tall, rangy kid with a Dodgers cap on backwards.

"Tex?"

"Yeah," Aaron said. "Tex Lassiter. Where do I find him?"

"You guys movie people?"

"Not exactly."

"People that interviews movie people?"

"Sort of, I guess. Yeah."

"Them's the kind usually wants to find Tex."

"Great. Where do *I* find him?"

"High Sierra."

"Up in the mountains?"

The kid grinned, wiping down the Porsche's windshield.

"Tex don't go into the mountains much. No bars up that way. High Sierra's a restaurant, right here on Main."

He pointed several stoplights down the street.

"You can see it right over there, if you squint."

"Think he'll be there now?" Aaron asked.

The kid nodded at the setting sun, turning purple-gold behind the austere, rock-bound face of the Sierras.

"He's already there, this time of day. And once he gets set, he ain't likely to move soon."

Aaron parked the Porsche in a gravel lot beneath a large white sign advertising Best Chicken and Burgers in Lone Pine. The other vehicles on either side, and throughout the lot, all seemed to be pickup trucks, some with rear window stickers supporting the NRA and gun racks holding shotguns.

"Some town," Sam said.

"This is where the real West begins, ma'am."

Inside, through a wood frame door with a Howdy-Stranger-Come-On-In sign hanging behind the glass, they found a room divided into an eating area with tables and red leather booths and, at the back, a long bar with a brass rail and redwood barstools. Two families sat at the tables. Everyone else was at the bar. All the men wore cowboy hats, even when seated.

"They've almost got enough for a *minyan.*"

"Shut up, Aaron! They can hear you."

"Nobody in this place knows what a *minyan* is."

They found Tex Lassiter at one end of the bar, laughing and trading cheap shots with a bearded grizzly of a man to one side of him and a young woman behind the bar who looked as if she had been born hard and mean.

"Get you guys somethin'?" she asked, frowning at them.

"Yeah," Aaron said. "I'm looking for Tex Lassiter."

Lassiter, a lighted cheroot in one hand and a shot glass of clear tequila in front of him, shifted his bony face sideways slightly and looked up at Aaron from under the brim of a soiled white Stetson.

"And who might you be?" he asked.

"Aaron Scott. You don't know me. I drove up from L.A.—"

"Friend," Lassiter interrupted, grinning at him with a mouth full of small, stained teeth, "I knowed you was from down there in La-La-Land minute I set eyes on you. Got it writ all over your face, and down deep where the sun don't shine."

The bearded guy sitting next to him and the woman behind the bar laughed themselves silly over that one.

Lassiter did a slow survey of Aaron's faded jeans, black sweatshirt, leather jacket, and black Doc Martens.

"You look like someone as might owe me money, or maybe someone *I* owe money to. If it's the first, you're welcome to sit down. Might even buy you a drink with some of your own goddamn money. But if you're the second, I might have to shoot you and make it look like it was a accident."

The guy beside him snorted into a frosted mug of beer.

Sam moved back, giving Aaron a glance that implied now was a good time to get out of there and just forget about it.

"I'd like to ask you some questions," Aaron said.

Lassiter turned his back on him and downed the tequila.

"I ain't interested," he said, "in no shit-ass questions."

He slid the empty tequila glass across the hardwood surface of the bar, toward the woman standing on the other side.

"Set me up another'n, gal."

Aaron leaned down and spoke beneath the Stetson brim.

"I want to ask some questions about Mick Grady."

Lassiter paused slightly in the process of raising the cheroot. The cigar hovered in midair, halfway between the ashtray and his mouth, tendrils of smoke curling up from its ashen tip. He held it there for several seconds, then put it between his teeth, puffing out clouds of strong tobacco smoke.

"How might it be that you knowed Mick Grady? You ain't near old enough. And you don't seem to be his type of man."

"He was my father."

Lassiter turned and looked at him, cigar clenched tight between his stained teeth.

Aaron could feel the others staring at him along the bar, and even from the two tables farther out in the room.

"Mick was a good man," Lassiter said, "goddamn good. Never knowed he had himself a son. Never heard as he was married."

"He wasn't."

The hard-faced woman behind the bar put down another shot glass of clear tequila in front of Lassiter. Aaron took out what he thought would cover it and handed her the bill.

"It ain't that much," she said.

"So it's a tip, okay?"

She took it from him without smiling.

"I can pay for my own goddamn liquor," Lassiter said.

"Sure. But I've got a lot of questions about Mick Grady and they said you could answer them. Besides, we haven't had anything to eat since this morning in Lancaster."

"This here your wife?"

"A friend," Sam said.

Lassiter tipped his Stetson with tobacco-stained fingers.

"Always glad to meet another friend of Mick's. Maybe we ought to move someplace else where you two can eat."

He called to the hard-faced woman behind the bar.

"Dusty! We'll take the table underneath the puma head."

He turned back to Aaron and gave him a slow, ugly grin.

"Mick Grady's son. Ain't that a kick in the ass? Almost as good as Mick comin' back from the dead himself."

* * *

The wild mountain cat's stuffed head snarled down at them from the wall, fangs bared, as they settled around a table on the other side of the room.

"By God," Lassiter said, "I've *seen* you before."

Sam stiffened as he pointed a callused finger at her.

"On the TV, that's where," he continued. "One of them news shows from L.A. we get up here on cable. Bull's-Eye News?"

"On-Target News," Sam said.

He snapped his fingers. "Bingo!"

A dark-skinned kid with dark hair and eyes came over to the table and put down a glass of water at each place setting.

"I want some ice in mine, boy," Lassiter said.

The kid glanced nervously at him. "*Señor?*"

"I want ice in my goddamn water! *Ice!*"

"*Lo siento, pero—*"

"Don't talk that crap to me! Speak English!"

"*Hielo, por favor,*" Aaron said quietly.

"*Sí, señor.*" The kid nodded. "*Gracias.*"

Lassiter watched him hurry away from the table.

Then he asked Aaron, "You speak Mexican, huh?"

"Just a little restaurant Spanish."

"You know," Lassiter said, leaning over the table, as if sharing a confidence, "it makes me kinda sick to hear someone speak a foreign language, right here in these United States of America, just like it was good as English. Brave men has fought and died, left their bones on enemy soil, just so's we'd have the right to speak English. And then to have to sit here and listen to some mud-faced kid talk that shit language at you—I guess you voted *against* Prop 187, huh?"

"I'm not into politics. I want to know about Mick Grady."

"Your ma never talked much about him?"

"I told you. They were never married."

"So you did." Lassiter grinned. "Sounds like ol' Mick. Sowed his wild oats, but didn't stay for the harvest."

Sam glanced at Aaron to see how he was taking this, but his face seemed blank.

"Who put you onto me, anyways?" Lassiter asked.

"Moe Edelstein. He used to work for Panopticon—"

"*I* know who Moe Edelstein was. That kike!"

Aaron did react to that, but Lassiter seemed not to notice.

"That was always the thing I hated most about ol' Hollyweird—havin' to work with all them goddamn Jew boys. Always playin' like they was your good buddy, then stabbin' you in the back just to make a extra stinkin' buck—"

"My mother's Jewish," Aaron said, his voice low.

Lassiter's bushy eyebrows rose in genuine surprise.

"Was she now? I never knowed as Mick took much of a interest in Jew gals. He sure as hell didn't cotton to sheenies much in general! Course, I heard as how them Jew gals can turn mighty lively on you, once you get 'em in bed—"

Aaron's hand clenched into a fist, but Sam spoke first.

"He *said* his mother was Jewish. So why do you keep talking that way? Are you totally stupid? Or just an asshole?"

Lassiter's eyes narrowed beneath the soiled Stetson brim.

Even Aaron turned to her. "Easy, Sam."

Lassiter bared his stained teeth in a shit-eating grin.

"Well now, I guess a man *had* oughta be careful the way he talks about some other boy's momma. No offense meant, son."

Aaron stared at him and said nothing.

"Funny, though. I never woulda took you for a Jew boy. Too tall, for one thing. Guess you get that from Mick. Not that I'm anti-Jew or nothin'. Hell, I worked with hundreds of them Jew bastards over the years. Just never met one I could trust. To be truthful, Mick felt pretty much the same way. It's one of the reasons why him and ol' Sparky Weiner never did get along. And some folks might add as *that's* why Mick finally had his accident—the one that killed him."

Aaron leaned forward, Lassiter's anti-Semitism, for the moment, forgotten.

"Moe Edelstein mentioned him. Who was he, Sparky Weiner?"

"Real name was Leo. Leopold Weiner. We called him Sparky 'cause he was always blowin' off at someone about somethin'. One of them ornery ol' fightin' cusses, like Ford, Hathaway, Preminger. A real hard-ass type director. Had himself a bit of a drinkin' problem, too, just like Jack Ford, although Sparky didn't need no drink to get himself goin' good. Not that I got anything against drink, mind you."

Lassiter lifted his shot glass, as if to illustrate.

"But Sparky, he was just plain mean. Real pushy, even for a Jew boy. Always drivin' the crew to come in ahead of schedule and under budget—which they did, too, most of the time. But there's always some on any crew as just can't take that kind of bullshit layin' down. And Mick Grady, he was one of 'em. He'd tell ol' Spark just what to do with that high horse attitude of his, and ol' Spark'd come right back at him, threaten to throw Mick's ass off the set and kick it up one side of Sunset and down th'other, and then Mick, he'd challenge ol' Spark to put his money where his mouth was and settle it like a man, and, by God, the thunder would roar and the lightnin' would flash!"

"They got into fistfights on the set?" Aaron asked.

"Hell, no! Ol' Spark, bein' a Jew boy, didn't have the balls for that. Sometimes he'd fire Mick right on the spot, then hire him back a few days later, or have some other Jew boy do it for him on the sly to save face. You could *feel* the tension anytime them two was on the same set. Got real bad the last time they worked together. Last time Mick ever worked with anybody. They was out here in Lone Pine, shootin' on location for some ol' horse opry or other. Can't recollect the title—"

"*Bad Men of the Badlands,*" Aaron volunteered.

"By God, that's right! How the hell'd you know that?"

"Moe Edelstein told me."

"Figures. Somebody prob'ly jewed him out of a dime on that shoot. Jew boys never forget it when *they're* the ones lose money. Anyways, feelin's was runnin' high on both sides—Mick snappin' at Spark, ol' Spark snappin' at Mick. Then the accident— But I reckon you know all about that."

"No," Aaron said, "I don't."

"Didn't your ma never tell you *nothin'* about your pa?"

"She never even told me his name."

Lassiter puffed out a cloud of cigar smoke and watched as it drifted up past the snarling puma head above them.

"Well, then. Story's mighty familiar around these parts. Reckon most anyone else could tell you about it, same as me."

"Were you there when it happened?"

"Hell, yes, I was there!"

"Then I want to hear about it from you."

Lassiter took up a shot glass of tequila and drained it in one quick swallow, tilting his head to knock it back. Then he set the glass down carefully, as if it might break.

"They was shootin' a fire scene, out in th'Alabama Hills. They always did fire scenes out thataway, 'cause there ain't nothin' else could ever catch fire in that goddamn rock pile, 'cept what a man built on purpose to burn. They had this mock-up of a prospector's cabin that the prop boys made for 'em—nothin' but scrap lumber nailed together any ol' which way, but it looked real enough in black-'n'-white. Mick was s'posed to be one of the good guys as gets caught inside the place and comes staggerin' out at the last minute, wavin' his white hat, coughin' on smoke, just as the whole shebang goes up in a big ball of fire. Special effects boys had a gasoline bottle bomb rigged up inside—except it was more like a gallon jug with a fuse and a timer, so they could blow it just as Mick come outside. That's how the goddamn shot was s'posed to work, anyways."

"What went wrong?" Aaron asked.

Lassiter looked up at him from beneath the dirty Stetson brim, eyes flat and motionless as a patient snake's.

"Hard to say. Maybe somebody just plain screwed up. Or maybe they had it in for Mick, and made sure it screwed up."

"Somebody like Sparky Weiner?"

"Who knows? Ol' Spark was pissed enough to do somethin' like that, 'specially on that shoot. Whether he had the clout, or the *cojones*, to get it done—well, that's a whole other question. Anyways, the gasoline bomb goes off before it was s'posed to, with Mick still inside. Wasn't no fire station within hollerin' distance, no hose, no buckets, not even a runnin' creek nearby. Nothin' we could do 'cept just stand there and watch it burn—and listen to Mick inside, screamin'."

Sam, unable to look at Aaron, turned to the window that opened out onto Main Street with its limited scattering of electric lights, and beyond that the dark face of the Sierras, and up above the distant stars glittering hard, cruel, and inhuman in a cold night sky stripped clean of L.A. smog.

"When we was finally able to pull him out," Lassiter went on, voice somewhat hoarse, muted by horrors past, "he was still alive. He was a fighter, Mick was, by God. Hangin' on to life like a buckin' bronc at a rodeo. But the shape he was in when we brung him out—Good God Almighty."

Lassiter looked up suddenly, and Sam was almost certain she could see tears in the eyes of that hard, ugly old man.

"On account of the fact that he was your pa," he said, speaking directly to Aaron, "I won't tell you just what he looked like. But it was somethin' you wouldn't want to see happen to no human bein'—not even no low-down sidewinder like ol' Sparky Weiner. We got him to the hospital soon's we could, him screamin' in pain the whole way. Not much of a hospital in Lone Pine today, even less of a one back then. They done what they could for him. But it weren't much."

"Did he—" Aaron cleared his throat. "Did he die soon?"

"He was still alive later on that night."

"How do you know?"

" 'Cause I stopped by to see him."

Lassiter drew his lips back from his stained teeth, as if the memory still brought on revulsion.

"They had him all wrapped up in bandages, and the blood had soaked right through 'em, and the stink of the burnin' was even worse than it was earlier on, and they had them goddamn tubes hangin' out of him ever' which way—"

"Intravenous catheters?" Sam asked.

"The same. It was a mighty sorrowful sight. He could barely talk by then. Tried to tell me somethin' about somebody back in L.A.—I guess that woulda been your ma."

"Yeah," Aaron said. "I guess."

"Went back the next day to check up on him, see how he was a-comin' along, and he was gone."

"He died—during the night?"

Lassiter nodded, Stetson waving like a tarnished fan.

"Someone come and took the body away. Buried it, I guess. Maybe in the ol' cemetery outside of town."

"And that was it?"

"Not hardly. No, sirree."

Aaron looked up, his own eyes wet with tears by now.

" 'Bout two weeks later, while ol' Sparky Weiner was still kickin' ever'one's butt to finish up *Bad Men of the Badlands* ahead of schedule and under budget, strange things started happenin' on the set. Notes was left for people, 'specially ol' Spark—notes that didn't make no goddamn sense. Then, one day, this ol' dog as had took to hangin' around the set turned up with his throat tore open, layin' in a pool of his own blood. Then, the next day, ol' Spark checked in his guild card, too. 'Cept he didn't go near as peaceable as the dog."

A brief silence followed, until Aaron broke it.

"What happened?"

"Ol' Spark used to bunk at the Rodeo Motel. It's been tore down for over thirty years now, but it used to be the place Panopticon always put up their people 'cause it was so goddamn cheap. They found ol' Spark in his room, layin' real still on his double-wide bed. Seems somebody had set fire to his head. Turned it into one big baked raisin."

"Didn't anyone hear his screams?" Aaron asked.

"I guess they thought he was on another'n of his benders."

"Why didn't he try to get up," Sam asked, "and get to the bathroom, and put out the flames?"

"Seems someone done cut off his feet—hands, too."

Sam turned away from the table.

"Who did it?" Aaron asked.

"Nobody knew then. Nobody knows now. Oh, there was lots of rumors. How ol' Spark didn't pay off the hit men he hired to take care of Mick, so they started leavin' subtle hints, like the dog with his throat slit, and when Spark didn't take the hints, they made him eat the same medicine they give Mick. But them's just rumors. Can't put no stock in 'em."

Aaron leaned forward. "Who do *you* think killed him?"

Lassiter did not answer right away. He struck a match, flame sputtering sharply in the silence, and relighted the cheroot that had gone out, gray ashes dropping from the cigar tip to the table below like fragments falling out of the past.

"Who killed ol' Spark? Someone with a powerful lot o' hate in his heart. Nothin' quite as bad as that ever happened in these parts again—although it was the last time Panopticon ever come up to do a location shoot, I can tell you that. Whole damn studio closed down not too long after. Those of us as lived here kept gettin' them strange little notes for the better part of a year. Sometimes, we'd get more than just a note."

Lassiter glanced out the window at the dark sky and the distant stars and the rock-faced Sierras.

"Once, I was out at my place on the edge of town. I admit I'd been doin' some drinkin' that night, but I didn't have the D.T.'s, nothin' like that. I hear a sound out back."

Lassiter's voice dropped so low they had to strain to hear.

"First I thought it was just the drink, and didn't pay it no mind. Then it come again. Scratchin' sounds, like someone tryin' to get in the back way. I call out, 'Who's there?' and no one answers. So I grab my ol' twelve-gauge Remington and head out that way. Then somethin' starts laughin' at me through the door—a low, dark, evil kind of laugh, as God is my judge. And I don't even wait to hear no more. I just level the Remington, and pull both triggers. Blew a hole through my goddamn back door. Tore the screen door right off the porch. I rush outside, heart pumpin' like a old-time threshin' machine, and I find blood on the ground, and I know I hit *some*thin'. And then I find more blood, a whole shitload of it, and my best horse, a sweet brood mare, with her head cut almost clean off, and a message written in her blood on the side of my own goddamn house, the blood runnin' off the ends of the words like the titles they got in these horror pictures all them young punks like to go watch."

"What did the message say?" Aaron asked softly.

"It don't matter now. It just plain don't matter at all."

"What did it *say?*" Aaron insisted.

"I said, it don't matter!"

"It matters to me. It matters a hell of a lot."

Lassiter's eyes narrowed beneath the Stetson.

"Back off, boy. You hear?"

"I have a right to know—"

With quick, awkward movements Lassiter dropped his right hand below the table, then brought it up again, holding a wide-bladed hunting knife, the kind used to gut a deer.

"My God!" Sam shrank back into her chair.

"You don't have the right to know *shit!*" Lassiter hissed at Aaron, rolling the knife in his hand slightly so that the overhead lights flashed off the polished steel.

"Come on now, Tex!" Dusty called from over by the bar. "Put that thing away before someone gets hurt."

Chairs scraped back across the hardwood floor as members of the two families got up to leave.

"I don't know who the hell you really are," Lassiter said, pointing at Aaron with the knife, moving it forward slightly. "You say you're Mick's son. Maybe you is, maybe you ain't."

Aaron sat with his eyes on the knife, perfectly still.

"Maybe you're part of what happened to Mick, and ol' Spark," Lassiter went on, emphasizing his words with the knife. "Maybe that's why you come up here. To take care of me the way they once took care of them."

"I came up here to ask—"

"Well, you asked your questions and you got your answers. Now git! The both of you! And don't come back no more! 'Less you want your throat slit the way they done my brood mare!"

Sam got to her feet, in no need of a second request.

"Come on, Aaron," she said. "Let's go."

PART FOUR

REALITY

35

WAREHOUSE

The masked face looked out at them, eyes dark, fathomless, the white surface of the mask itself vague and unfocused, like an image disappearing within the mind's eye.

The LAPD sketch artist, a young man with receding blond hair, glanced at the photographic blowup hanging on the rack in front of him, then turned back to his computer screen and typed in another series of keystroke commands.

"Not a bad shot," Lopez said, "considering where you were standing when you took it—at the back of Esposito's tit bar."

"It was the best I could do at the time," Montoya agreed.

"You ever tell Scott that's why I didn't try to take out the Phantom from the back of that room? Because you wanted to wait and snap his ID photo first?"

"No," Montoya said. "He doesn't need to know that."

They watched as Ron Taylor, the sketch artist, typed in his commands, stroke by stroke, creating a computer graphics portrait in full color and three dimensions. The colors burned into the CRT screen, like something etched in acid, more intense than life itself.

"Shit," Lopez muttered, leaning closer. "Is *that* what he looks like behind the mask?"

Montoya stared at the image with Buddha-like impassivity.

"It's one possible version," Taylor said. "There's others."

"Worse than this?" Lopez asked.

"Not necessarily. An alternative sketch might show a normal face—like yours, or mine. Anybody's face."

"How could it? This guy's face is a fucking war zone."

"That's the way *you* think it looks, Sergeant. You and Lieutenant Montoya. That's what I'm going on here."

He pointed at the screen, the horror staring back from it.

"But masks are weird."

Taylor leaned back in his chair, hands behind his head.

"I moonlight a little, doing computer graphics for movies. I know some guys who do special effects and makeup work. They tell me you can get just about anything you want with a mask. You can use latex and shit to build up different facial contours *from inside the mask.* So it looks like it's your own face, but it's not. It's just the mask."

"This doesn't look like a normal mask," Montoya said, "the kind that could contain latex implants. It almost looks like a film that's been sprayed on."

"Which is just what it might be," Taylor agreed. "You can buy a type of over-the-counter spray in any drugstore that creates an artificial skin, like a huge spray-on Band-Aid. Then, if you wanted to alter your face *beneath* that, you'd have to apply the latex to your own skin instead of the inside of the mask. It'd be a little more work each time, but not for someone as smart as this dirtbag's supposed to be."

Lopez turned from the stark computer image to Montoya.

"You want me to stop checking out plastic surgeons?"

"Why?"

"Doesn't seem much point to it, if Ron's right about makeup behind the mask. He could look like anybody."

"But I don't think he does."

Montoya looked at the screen and its heart-stopping image.

"Could you print out some copies of that for us, Ron?"

"No problem. Planning to show it on television?"

"Possibly."

"Better run one of those disclaimers: contains material some viewers may find offensive."

"No shit," Lopez said.

Taylor shrugged. "But if you're right and this is even *sort of* what he looks like, hey. You'll get a quick positive ID. He ever goes to the market, or even steps outside his front door for the paper, somebody's gonna *notice* a face like that."

After the sketch artist left the room, Lopez put on his Armani suit jacket and straightened his silk tie.

"Going out to interview more surgeons?" Montoya asked.

"Isn't that what I'm supposed to do?"

"Yes. But I'd like you to check out this one first."

Montoya took a piece of paper from his shirt pocket.

"I should have thought of him sooner. I don't know why I didn't. He's worked in the Hollywood area for years, at Angel of Refuge, the private hospital on Sunset that always takes more than its fair share of need-based admissions."

"The ones without insurance or money?"

"Yes. Dr. Harold Portis is a plastic surgeon by training, but he doesn't cater to the Beverly Hills crowd."

"Not a tit job and liposuction man?"

"Not at all. His interests are the chronically disfigured and deformed. His work with such patients extends well beyond surgery, carrying over into rehabilitation and adjustments to the social challenges of deformity—especially facial deformity."

"Sounds like the Elephant Man's doctor."

"He was profiled recently in the *L.A. Times Magazine.* I read the article, then forgot all about it. I should have sent you there first."

"Want me to show him our computer sketch?"

"Yes."

"All the cases he sees, you think he'll remember this one?"

Montoya glanced at the sketch before handing it to Lopez.

"How could he not?"

* * *

"NOBODY GETS OUT OF HERE ALIVE-IVE-IVE-IVE-IVE!"

The mock warning, amplified by eight-foot-high speakers, spiked with squealing feedback, reverberated throughout the massive confines of the warehouse in downtown Los Angeles, close to the welter of railroad tracks that once served the now-decaying industrial center. The building, abandoned by its foreign investor-owner, had been taken over tonight by renegade promoters of an outlaw rave, a spur-of-the-moment blowout thrown together quickly to elude notice of the police, its very existence kept a closely guarded secret, passed through word of mouth, publicized furtively by crudely printed flyers handed out to those already in the know, or posted obscurely where they might be seen by those who might want to know.

Limited equipment, much of it stolen, had been brought in for tonight only: speakers, CD player, several strobe lights, a handful of spots with colored gels, beams cutting upward through naked steel girders overhead.

Bodies filled the close-packed room, most of them young, with black clothing, colored hair, pierced skin. Some moved to the techno music pushing out from the speakers, but this wasn't a one-night disco or a makeshift teenage dance club. It was more like a postapocalyptic colosseum, sealed by stone gray walls.

Aaron and Sam stood at the back of the restless crowd, near double fire doors that served as the only exit, open now to the night. New arrivals continued to pour in through the open doors, creatures of the night, drawn by the music and the lights and the smell of the mob. No security guards stood watch. This wasn't a private club, like the Meat Locker. This was an underground party, a loading zone where anything could happen.

Sam cast a sidelong glance at the latest arrivals. She could see the outlines of guns beneath their jackets and within the folds of baggy pants. Aaron was probably carrying, too, for all she knew—that damn thing he bought in the gun shop. She wanted to get the hell out of here, before someone got shot. She had never wanted to come here in the first place.

They had argued about it on their way back from Lone Pine.

"How do you know he'll even *be* there?" she asked.

Aaron stared straight ahead, eyes fixed on lonely U.S. 395, dropping south into the night, drawing them back to Mojave, then to Lancaster, then L.A.

"Because that's where he said he hangs out."

"Who said?"

"That kid with the bad teeth and the long hair. The one that Lopez shot, out in back of the Meat Locker."

"Some source. How do you know the party's tonight?"

"Raves always happen now, on weekends."

"We could've stayed over one night in Lone Pine."

"I could tell how much you loved it."

"I hated it! I especially hated that drunken, dirty cowboy, Tex whoever-the-hell-he-was! But maybe we could've gone out to the cemetery—"

"No." Aaron cut her off. "My father's not there, Sam. His body was probably dumped by the side of the road for the coyotes to take care of. Or maybe *he* buried him in a shallow grave somewhere, out in the desert."

"Who?"

Aaron's fingers tightened on the steering wheel.

"The Phantom."

"Are you crazy? If the Phantom killed your father over thirty-five years ago—

"I know. That's the one problem. But maybe he just *looks* young. Maybe it's part of his disguise, like the mask itself."

"What are you *talking* about, Aaron?"

"We'll find out tonight. Because this is when his luck finally runs out. This is when *he* dies."

On that note they returned to L.A., and drove down to the industrial district and found the address where they stood now, at the back of the waiting crowd—waiting themselves for the arrival of a round-faced murderer with his head shaved bald except for a red forelock, appearing for one night only, here, at the warehouse, without the mask.

Someone bumped into Sam, sloshing her hair and neck with cheap, yeasty-smelling beer. Someone else laughed. The kid who splashed her pushed his way on through the crowd, without bothering to apologize or even look back.

"Asshole!" she muttered after him, then, turning to Aaron, shouting to be heard above the pounding techno. "When are we *leaving* this place?"

"You heard the man. Nobody gets out of here alive."

"Very funny! *You* didn't have some lower life-form just spill beer all over you!"

"Point him out to me, babe. I'll make him pay for it."

He patted the holstered SIG beneath his leather jacket.

"Great! Then I can have blood mixed in with the beer."

This last comment was lost in a stunning blast of techno, moving like a force field through the packed revelers, some of them already high on bad wine or cheap backyard pot, others cruising the internal stratosphere at thirty-five thousand feet on fine-cut Turkish heroin or custom-made designer drugs, all of them plugged into the main current, waiting impatiently for the beginning of the main event.

Their attention was fixed on a raised platform in the center of the warehouse's vast interior. Sam, drawing her arms in close to keep from getting bumped again, assumed that the crowd was waiting for a rock group to appear on the platform, some kind of local, scruffy, low-rent alternative band.

But music wasn't the main event. Music was nothing more than the stimulus, the counterpoint, the aural analog.

The spectacle was the main event.

People began climbing onto the crude stage, girls in their mid-to-late teens, some in their early twenties, pushed up by members of the crowd, helped up by hands extended to them from girls already on the platform. They had short and long hair, skin of different colors, bodies lush, thin, and indifferent, limbs loose and awkward from drink and drugs.

One girl peeled off her top to the roar of the crowd, breasts small and frail-looking at that distance, diminished further by the blinking strobe lights and the heat haze shimmering off the agitated, chanting crowd.

"OFF! OFF! OFF! OFF! OFF! OFF—"

The other girls followed her lead, pulling off their T-shirts and sweatshirts and tank tops, flashing breasts that seemed mostly insignificant amid the mounting frenzy of response.

The guy that passed for a DJ grabbed the microphone.

"NOBODY GETS OUT OF HERE ALIVE-IVE-IVE-IVE-IVE-IVE-IVE—"

The crowd ate it up. People climbed on top of other people's shoulders, human scaffolding in the making, just to get a better view of the amateur topless parade. Girls posed and pranced, playing to the crowd. People—mostly guys, but not all—lifted their arms, raising and lowering them in synchronization with the rhythm of the chant.

"OFF! OFF! OFF! OFF—"

People started throwing money up onto the stage. Dollar bills. Five-dollar bills. Tens. Twenties. Bundles of bills. The girls scrambled to pick them up, fighting for possession, stuffing them into the waistbands of their jeans, shaking their breasts at the crowd in response.

The bigger the payoff, the bigger the shake.

Some of the girls started stepping off the platform, down onto the shoulders of the big-bill tossers. Other girls still onstage began stripping off their jeans, then their underwear, if they wore any. The crowd redoubled its chanting frenzy. Bills flew thicker than ever, arcing up through strobe lights onto the stage. The girls caught them in their hands, scooped them up from the stage floor, locked them tight between clenched teeth.

A group of guys farther back from the platform, behind the big-bill tossers, began moving forward, pushing their way through the crowd like a flying wedge, cutting a V-shaped swath toward the center of the action. These weren't the types likely to toss even small bills, or loose change. They had the uncut, unwashed roughness of dark alleys and dark spaces beneath freeway overpasses, of burned-out tenement buildings and graffiti-scarred housing projects ringing with screams and gunshots in the middle of the night.

The crowd, as if sensing this, gave way before them.

When they reached the platform, the ones in front climbed up onto the stage floor, using the shoulders of the crowd as stepping-stones. Most of the girls onstage, realizing what was happening, started to abandon ship. They leaped onto the shoulders or into the arms of willing rescuers in the crowd below, naked skin shining beneath strobe lights and colored lights—smoke and chaos and drifting bills—their screams washed out by the rhythmic chanting of the crowd.

One girl was left onstage, alone.

She had pale skin, dark eyes, curling dark hair cascading down her naked back. Her body appeared soft and vulnerable beneath the flashing, colored lights. She backed away, into the center of the stage, as the first of the motley wedge swarmed up onto the platform and moved toward her.

By the time she had the presence of mind to turn and jump, it was too late. Three of the rougher beasts had come in behind her and cut off her escape. As they grabbed hold of her, she screamed. But the throbbing techno smothered it in a rush of noise. They lifted her body high above the platform, gleaming white and sacrificial against the colored, flashing chaos.

The crowd shifted its chant, increasing the volume.

"RAPE! RAPE! RAPE! RAPE—"

The members of the motley wedge, most of them onstage by now, threw her down, and let fantasy engage reality.

The girl's face twisted like a mask of agony as the first one forced his way into her. She writhed in the rough hands that held her down, and tried to break free, but there was no way to do it, and no place to go.

She looked out toward the crowd, as if in entreaty.

But the crowd held no saviors that night.

Sam turned away, unable to watch the gang rape continue, and saw more violence on the verge of becoming, only a few steps to her right, not far from the open exit doors.

Two kids—one short, heavy, an ex–high school fullback run to fat, the other thin, wiry, tough, and quick—stood face-to-face, deep into one of those says-who-fuck-you standoffs, both of them on something, eyes wild with glazed light.

"*Fuck* you, man! You spilled *beer* on my fuckin' *shoes!*"

"Don't accuse me of nothin' I didn't do, fuckhead!"

"Aw, man, I mean, just *fuck* you, okay?"

"You shut your fuckin' mouth!"

"Fuck you, asshole!"

"You fuckin' shit—"

It escalated to shoves, then jumped into overdrive.

The thin kid pulled out a cheap automatic and shot the fat one point-blank in the chest. Blood from the exit wound in his back spattered revelers standing behind him. Chants turned into screams. The fat kid vomited, then crumpled to the stained cement of the warehouse floor, clutching his chest with both hands, blood leaking through his fingers, mouth opening and closing like that of a landed fish.

The crowd panicked and rushed for the exit doors, pushing others ahead of them down to the floor, trampling them underfoot, the gang rape on the platform totally forgotten now, old violence overtaken by new.

Sam grabbed Aaron's arm, fingers digging into his flesh.

"Let's get *out* of here!"

More shots rang out above the screaming crowd and pounding techno. Other partygoers drew their own guns and started to exchange fire. Aaron, pulling Sam with him, pushed his way through the crowd toward the exit doors, almost getting both of them crushed against the wall before the mass momentum swept them out of the warehouse and into the waiting night.

They kept moving, screams and gunshots echoing behind them.

"*Aar*on!"

Sam jerked hard on the arm that dragged her forward.

"The car's *that* way!"

He nodded, eyes dull with ebbing panic.

As they turned toward the car, he stopped, reached beneath his black leather jacket, came up with the SIG, burnished steel glinting in a nearby streetlight's glow.

Sam, unable to believe it, thought that he was planning to go back inside the warehouse and join in the shooting frenzy.

"Aaron, have you lost your *mind?*"

"Him!"

He pointed with the gun to a running man, one among many, fleeing the chaos of the warehouse. But this one stood out from the others—tall, heavily built, black clothes masking him like a shadow in the darkness of the inner-city night, head shaved bald, except for a forelock dyed bright red.

"Yo!" Aaron called out. "Phantom! Freeze!"

The running man slowed down without stopping, glanced in Aaron's direction, saw him standing there, SIG gripped in both hands, pointed straight at him, and began to run again, flat out this time, even faster than before.

"*Freeze*, asshole!"

Aaron pulled the trigger. The SIG bucked in his hands.

The gunshot slammed into Sam's ears with a physical impact, driving out the more distant screams and gunshots—displacing everything except an empty, lifeless silence.

"Aaron!" she started to scream, but she could not even hear the sound of her own voice, just the silence.

He glanced at her, at panicked revelers rushing past on either side, at his moving target, unmarked by the ill-aimed shot.

He went after him, running into the jagged urban night, just in time to see his quarry disappear around the corner of a corrugated iron wall.

Aaron followed, and found himself in a maze of crisscrossing railroad tracks. He forced himself to slow down, knowing that a false step here could lead to a headlong fall and a fractured bone, or worse. He hopped from tie to tie, jumping iron rails, clearing gravel beds, while the running man steadily widened the gap between them, as if he had done this many times before, and knew his way into the night.

The sounds from the distant warehouse seemed to fade off into darkness, replaced by the scraping of gravel underfoot, the labored wheezing of his own breath, the heavy pounding of a helicopter overhead, searchlight shining down on the warehouse, rotors chopping into the night sky. Aaron looked up for any trains that might be coming on the tracks they now crossed. But he saw nothing, except more warehouses, dark alleys, orange sodium vapor streetlights—and ahead of him, the running man, vanishing into deeper darkness.

Aaron pushed ahead, leaping recklessly over rails and ties, scattering gravel with his feet, the gun in his hand dragging it down like a lead weight.

They entered a kind of courtyard—the running man in front, Aaron gaining ground behind—enclosed by the back walls of four warehouses, the open space around them filled with empty storage drums, some turned over, others stacked in rows and levels like cans in a supermarket display.

The running man stopped suddenly, pivoted, kicked out with his right foot, knocking loose a storage drum from the bottom row of a stack, bringing down the whole structure, empty drums banging and clattering as they bounced off each other and rolled toward Aaron like boulders in a metal avalanche.

He had to stop and jump out of the way, dodging loose drums as they tumbled down on him. One banged him hard on the shin, almost pitching him headfirst over the barrel rim. He stumbled back, raising the SIG, gripping it again with both hands.

"*Freeze!*" he cried, voice rising above the rolling drums.

The running man turned and started to run again.

Aaron lowered his gun on the target.

A flying drum crossed his field of vision as he squeezed the trigger. The SIG bucked and roared in his hands, waves of sound bouncing off falling drums and warehouse walls. The bullet hit a drum rim and ricocheted off it, hit another and bounced off that, each time with a metallic whine, skittering from drum to drum like a pinball out of hell. It veered off the last one and shattered a window high in the back wall of a warehouse, sending down shards of smog-blackened glass that cracked and tinkled like a shower of dirty crystal rain.

The running man came to a stop, back turned to Aaron.

He came up on him with the gun, breathing hard.

"Turn around—*slow.*"

The dark figure turned, a large knife in one hand.

Reflected light flashed off polished steel.

He rushed Aaron.

"I'll shoot! I'll blow your fuckin' head off!"

His voice rang against the backs of warehouse walls.

The running man stopped, stumbled, caught himself with one hand before hitting the ground, pushed up and regained his footing, knife still balanced in the other hand.

"*Drop* the knife!"

It fell to the gravel with a crackling sound.

"Once again," Aaron said, trying to keep his hands steady as he moved in closer, "but without the mask this time."

The other stared back at him, hands hanging loose, one clenched into a fist, bald head pale beneath the bright red forelock. His shoulders rose and fell evenly, as if he kept in condition for something like this. His face looked young—smooth, bland, unlined, very young.

"You fuckin' talkin' to *me?*"

The voice was young, too, high-pitched, petulant.

"Decided to drop the radio whisper?" Aaron asked, bringing the gun's muzzle in until it rested only a few inches from his face. "Good. It always sounded fake."

"Fuck you, man!"

"No, fuck *you!*"

He shoved the gun forward.

The other stumbled back, small eyes dark with alarm.

"You killed a lot of people, Phantom.

The other raised his lip in a kind of smile then, revealing the dark red gum line Aaron had first seen beneath the Porsche's headlights on that night when all three attacked him.

Man, I am the mask!

"One of those people you killed was my father. Mick Grady. He died hard, years ago. But now, Phantom, it's *your* turn."

"*No!*" he cried. "You got it *wrong!* I ain't *him!*"

Aaron hesitated, finger still on the trigger, only a slight pull, the gentlest of squeezes, necessary to send the full weight of a nine-millimeter bullet smashing into the terrified face in front of him.

"I *work* for him! I *used* to work—"

"You're him," Aaron said, needing to believe it. "You called me that first day at the radio station. Then later, that night, you and your two punk friends—"

"We *all* fuckin' worked for him!" Fear twisted his voice tighter, sending a thin line of spit dribbling over his lip and down his chin. "We were fuckin' scared *not* to!"

The gun heavy in his hands, almost a sentient thing, begging to be fired, Aaron began to realize slowly, like someone perceiving a dark form in darkness, that what he was hearing now, blurred by fear, might be the truth.

But he said, "You're lying."

Aaron moved the gun in closer.

"You were everywhere. That night in the alley, after you killed Lance Trebizond in his broadcast booth—"

"I didn't *do* that! *He* did!"

"You followed me to my place, to Sam's place—"

"I was fuckin' *forced* to!"

"—then to the Rakehell Club—"

"That was *him!*"

"Then, that night when you and your punk friends stopped my car, and you said to me, 'Man, I *am* the'—"

"I was talkin' *shit!*"

Aaron began to feel the fabric of certainty tearing apart.

"You working for him here, tonight?"

"You're the one came here lookin' for *me!* I don't want nothin' to *do* with him! Or you! Jabar's inside because of you. Eddie's fuckin' *dead.* I'm next!"

"You got that right," Aaron said, more to himself than the other, still wanting to pull the trigger, but uncertain now.

Against that uncertainty, the other made his move.

He unclenched his fist and threw a handful of dirt and gravel into Aaron's face, blinding him.

Aaron fell back, grabbing with one hand at his eyes. He could hear the other scrambling in the gravel for his knife. Pointing the gun at that sound, he fired blind—literally blind, eyes weeping tears, squeezed shut in pain. The SIG's recoil numbed his hand. Waves of deafening sound jumped back at him. He heard a cry of shock, or pain, followed by the sound of footsteps on gravel, running away.

"Stop! I'll fuckin' *shoot!*"

But he couldn't see to shoot, couldn't even hear the footsteps anymore—just the sound of sirens on distant streets, like screams in the night, heading for the warehouse.

He staggered forward, blind. The night world came back to him in pieces, through blurred tears and debris. Back walls of warehouses swam overhead. He looked for the one who still might be the Phantom, and might not be, but was going to die for it anyway, because *someone* was going to die tonight. Someone was going to pay for the lives already taken, the pain already caused.

He caught a glimpse of him, like a fragment from a dream, disappearing down an alley. He ran forward, still half-blinded, his own breathing heavy off the sides of the alley, along with the pounding of his feet on concrete, gun gripped hard in one hand like a talisman.

Up ahead, the runner broke from the alley.

"Stop!" Aaron screamed.

But he kept running, down a narrow side street that cut across the warehouse district. The sound of a speeding car echoed through the lethal night. Aaron ran faster, lungs burning, as headlights flashed suddenly onto the side street.

Aaron raised the gun, getting ready to fire.

The runner crossed the street in an effort to beat the car.

The rust-colored compact accelerated—whether because the driver did not see the running man, or because he did. Flesh and metal met in the middle of the street. The car was small, but going fast. The impact snapped him in half, the sound of his breaking spine audible to Aaron as he stood at the mouth of the alley, watching. The man flew across the hood, smashed into the windshield, starring the safety glass, and flipped up into the air, like a diver going backward through his routine. Blood burst from his mouth, spraying in all directions as he spun above the street, lighter than air for several gravity-defying moments before dropping back down to the blacktop, and splitting open like a sack of groceries.

36

CARETAKER

Dr. Harold Portis looked up from the papers on his desk, expecting to see an admissions nurse standing in the doorway to his office, coming back to report that the visitor who wanted to see him had been sent away with an acceptable excuse.

What he saw instead was a tall man in his late twenties with dark skin and eyes, and sharp, hawklike features.

"I'm afraid I can't see anyone right now," Portis said, summoning all his medical authority. "I have to prepare for surgery in less than an hour."

"This won't take long," Lopez said.

"You don't understand. I *can't* see anyone right now. I *won't* see anyone. If you're not going to cooperate with me, I'm afraid I'll have to ring security."

He reached for the phone, to show he wasn't bluffing.

Lopez took out his LAPD badge and showed it to Portis, whose hand, in the process of pushing a button on his speakerphone, went limp and returned reluctantly to the desktop.

"What's this all about?" he asked.

"I'm Sergeant Frank Lopez, Homicide, Hollywood Division. I'd like to ask you a few questions."

"Concerning?"

"One of your patients."

"Which one?"

"If I knew that, I wouldn't have to ask the questions."

Lopez pulled out a chair in front of Portis's desk.

"Mind if I sit down?"

"I thought you said this wasn't going to take long."

"It won't."

Lopez took his seat in no apparent hurry, adjusting his shirt cuffs beneath the Armani jacket.

Portis cleared his throat. "It's not that I dislike giving interviews. In fact, I've given a great many—"

"I know. I read some of them."

"And I'm certainly not bothered by talking to the police."

"Everybody says that, but nobody means it."

"Well, *I* mean it, Sergeant—"

"Lopez."

"Sergeant Lopez. But I do appreciate some kind of advance notice. Is there any reason you couldn't have called first?"

"This is sort of a last-minute thing. I'd like to show you something and get your opinion of it."

He opened a thin briefcase, took out the computer sketch, and leaned across the desk, handing it to Portis.

Lopez did not expect any obvious reaction. Doctors, like cops, are trained to mask their emotions. Even so, Portis's eyes widened and his nostrils dilated slightly. He stared at the sketch longer than necessary, as if buying time.

"You've shown this to other plastic surgeons?"

"A few."

"May I ask what this is regarding?"

"We're trying to catch a serial killer. These types usually pick up station house nicknames. This one named himself. The Phantom. He wears a mask. His *modus operandi* involves torture, burning, extreme mutilation—all while the victim's still alive. Maybe you've heard about him?"

"It sounds vaguely familiar."

"The sketch you have there"—Lopez nodded at it—"is a good guess as to what he looks like behind the mask. Someone with a face like that would have trouble passing for normal in the outside world. He might come to a place like this, to see what you could do for him."

"Angel of Refuge does *not* harbor criminals, Sergeant."

"I understand. But you do see patients like this?"

"Not often. Here at Angel of Refuge we specialize in the treatment and rehabilitation of patients with facial deformities. But *these* deformities are—extreme."

"What would cause something like that? Bad genetics?"

Portis shook his head, studying the sketch again.

"This face shows deep tissue loss, resulting in severe contracture, scarring, and necrosis. The result of an accident, yes, but not a genetic one."

"What kind of accident?"

"That's hard to say, Sergeant, on the basis of a speculative sketch, and absent any kind of patient history—"

"But if you had to make a guess?"

"Third-degree burns, caused by chemicals of some kind—acids, corrosives—complicated by improper nursing care and asepsis, resulting in serious infection. Whoever survived something like this would be lucky to be alive. He could look forward to a semi-invalid existence, with great difficulty in simple feeding and communication, to say nothing of the psychological burden of having to live with a face like—that."

"Could it be fixed through plastic surgery?"

"That depends. Even partial reconstruction could require dozens of operations, possibly hundreds. Recovery would be very slow, extending over years, and very painful. And even after all that time and suffering, the finished product wouldn't look like anything that you or I might call normal."

"He'd have to be a very determined patient?"

Portis leaned back, as if withdrawing into the past.

"I've worked with deformed patients for many years now, Sergeant. People with injuries far less serious than the kind depicted here too often lose their self-esteem, even their will to live, along with their former appearance. The face may be nothing more than a mask for the soul, but you'd be surprised how much it matters when we lose that mask. Some patients, after suffering a severe facial deformity, take it as a kind of judgment on themselves and their lives. They know they could help make things better, but they choose not to . . ."

Portis looked up, very much back in the present.

"I really don't see why you're questioning me about this, Sergeant. A man with this kind of damage would be doing well to get by on a day-to-day basis. He's not a likely suspect for the commission of multiple murders, in my opinion."

"He may not look anything like this, Doctor. We're just guessing. Like you said, it's a speculative sketch."

"But you think he looks like this, behind his mask?"

"That's right."

"I hope you'll forgive my saying this, Sergeant, but I find that kind of thinking highly offensive. I admit to a certain prejudice here. My years of treating deformed patients has led me to see them as no different than anyone else, except for some superficial irregularities. I resent the way society demonizes the deformed—the way you, the LAPD, are demonizing the deformed. You're hunting a murderer with a mask, and your first assumption is that he must be deformed."

"Most people wear masks for a reason, Doctor."

"To hide their identities, more often than not. You don't *know* that this man you're looking for is deformed. You just assume that he is. I don't like that, Sergeant."

Lopez nodded at the sketch, covered by Portis's hand.

"You've never seen anyone who looks like that before?"

"No."

"He never even stopped by for a quick consultation?"

"Certainly not. I would have remembered."

"Do you mind hanging on to it for us?"

"Why?"

"In case he shows up later—here, or somewhere else."

"*If* this is your murderer, he's not likely to come here, Sergeant. Angel of Refuge is a high-profile hospital."

"You're probably right, but would you mind, anyway?"

After Lopez left, Dr. Harold Portis, in no hurry to scrub for surgery, sat and stared at the sketch.

37

TOKEN

Out the sixteenth-floor windows of KRAS FM, the sun sank through smog like dying fire at the world's end.

"And we got *more* of the *hottest* stopless hits! And we got mo' *money!* Just *givin'* it up, here on KRAS FM, 108.5, with Drive-Time Dave, the flash with the cash! But first, it's time for another up-to-the-minute, Drive-Time Dave traffic report, with Sexy Shalonda! Shalonda, baby! What's happenin'?"

"We're over the westbound 101 at Sherman Oaks, Drive-Time Dave, and things are just slammin' out here—"

Drive-Time Dave, aka Dave Emory, worked his airshift in a cramped booth at the far end of the hallway, next to Lance Trebizond's old booth, scrubbed clean of all blood now, fumigated to remove even the faintest trace of burned human flesh.

Aaron's booth at the other end, the largest in the studio, was never in use at this time of day—usually.

Alonzo Gore stopped and poked his hair-heavy head inside.

"Man, I just finished settin' up my own shit for tomorrow. What are *you* still doin', dickin' around this place?"

"Checkin' sound effects. You mind?"

"Hey, man, no problemo! Just don't go workaholic on us."

"No chance of that."

"Stay cool, man! Later."

Aaron nodded without looking up. He tossed the tape he was holding onto the console deck and glanced at the incoming call buttons, alight with song requests for Drive-Time Dave. He wouldn't mind working the afternoon airshift himself. He might even volunteer to work Lance's old evening shift. They had some fill-in from Seattle doing it now, but the guy was a hopeless dickhead and everyone knew it, even the guy himself. Besides, working an airshift would make the night go faster.

After last night, he wanted them all to go fast.

He saw the kid with the shaved head and the dyed forelock again, the SIG shoved in his face, screaming at him.

You got it wrong! *I ain't* him!

Then his shattered body, leaking blood across the blacktop.

"Hey, man! Scope this one out!"

Alonzo was back inside the booth with his massive head of hair, and a large red, white, and blue box in his arms.

"I thought you left," Aaron said.

"I thought so, too! But no, I gotta be your goddamn gofer today. Special delivery, man, from fuckin' FedEx!"

"When did this come in?"

"Just now. Delivery guy laid it on me on my way out. I signed for the fucker. Hey, don't thank me or nothin'!"

"I won't. It's probably just a shitload of demo tapes from some wanna-be in Bakersfield."

"So why don't you open it up and *see?*"

"You open it up."

Aaron turned back to the cart machine.

"Man, where's your normal fuckin' curiosity? I can't *stand* to get a package and not open it!"

"Be my guest."

"Here, man. Here's my X-Acto knife. *Open* the fucker!"

Aaron sighed and took the knife from him. He slit open the tape that sealed the package, sharp blade hissing like a snake as it cut through plastic and cardboard.

"If this *is* demo tapes, I'm gonna make *you* listen to 'em."

"That's cool," Alonzo said. "I'll sell 'em to the asshole that works the night shift. That fucker's so desperate, he'll run anything. Last night he was down to old traffic reports and emergency broadcast announcements."

Aaron lifted the lid to reveal a box stuffed full of wadded-up newspapers. He started to take them out. Most were *L.A. Times* pages, but at least one came from the *Lone Pine Sentinel.* He stopped, the crumpled page in his hand.

"Hey, man!" Alonzo said, peering over his shoulder. "Looks like someone sent you a *real* present. The expensive kind!"

Holding the crumpled page of the *Lone Pine Sentinel,* Aaron felt a coldness grip him from inside. He threw away the page and continued to remove more packing from the box, the muscles in his face hard and fixed.

"All right!" Alonzo said. "It looks like—"

The smell hit them, rising through the dry, acrid odor of newsprint. Someone had tried to cover it up with disinfectant, but this kind of smell didn't cover well: heavy, rotten, slightly sweet, with the stench of burning about it, not unlike the atmosphere of Lance Trebizond's broadcast booth the night the Phantom paid him a visit.

Aaron started ripping out the wadded-up newspaper pages with a furious, almost demented energy, throwing them around his booth. Some pages bore rust-colored stains, and some, as he dug deeper into the box, were bloodred.

Alonzo's face paled beneath his stacked-up head of hair.

The last page came out with a sucking sound, like a leech being pried loose from a living body. But what lay beneath the page was no longer alive, and had not been for some time.

It had been hacked at with a finely honed, sharp-bladed instrument—both eyes gouged out, the nose sliced off, lips cut back to reveal stained, grinning teeth. What skin remained had been set on fire and burned to a charcoal crisp, peeling back from the skull like the skin of a roasted onion. It would have been unrecognizable—a charred, anonymous, mutilated death's-head—had it not been for the stained white Stetson tilted at a jaunty angle atop the skull, identifying it as having belonged to Tex Lassiter, late of Lone Pine, California.

Alonzo Gore backed off, eyes wide. "Shit, man—"

He clapped a hand over his mouth and bolted from the booth.

Aaron stood there, staring at the thing in the box.

He felt no revulsion, no fear—nothing except a kind of deadened exhaustion, as if he had been expecting this, or something like it, one more step on the way he had to walk to wherever he was going.

Jerry edged into the booth, head turned to one side, barely glancing at the box, shutting his eyes when he thought he saw what was inside it.

"Aaron— Is that what Alonzo—"

"See for yourself."

"No thanks. What— How did the FedEx guy look?"

"Alonzo signed for it. Go ask him."

"Alonzo's in the john right now, puking his guts up."

Jerry moved closer to Aaron, eyes turned from the box.

"Aaron— Who would *do* something like this?"

"Come on, Jerr. You know the answer to that."

Silence followed. Neither wanted to say the name aloud.

Dave Emory stepped inside the booth, eyes frightened.

"Aaron?"

Jerry, glad of a diversion, gave him a hard look.

"Who's running your show, Dave?"

"I'm on a fuckin' twenty-minute set, okay?" He turned to Aaron. "A call just came in for you. I think it's that freak, the one who used to call in during your show? The Phantom?"

The name seemed to echo inside the enclosed booth.

"Anyways, he's too fuckin' weird for me. If you don't want to take it, I'm losin' the son of a—"

He noticed the head in the box then.

"Holy shit!"

Dave began backing toward the door.

"Holy fuckin' *shit!*"

"What line's he on?" Aaron asked.

"Lucky thirteen," Dave whispered, and left.

"Aaron," Jerry said, "don't take it on the air—please."

"Get the fuck outta my booth, Jerr."

Jerry left, closing the glass door quietly behind him.

Aaron picked up the receiver used for taking calls off the air. He found button number thirteen on the lighted panel and punched it hard.

"What the fuck do you want?"

A brief pause followed, then the whispering voice, almost buoyant this time, full of satisfaction with a job well-done.

"You've been a very busy man of late, Sunset Scott. Driving up to Lone Pine, hanging out at warehouse parties—"

"Let's cut the crap, Phantom. Yeah, I got your surprise package. Hah-hah-hah. I especially liked the bit with the hat. That's almost your signature, isn't it, man? The psycho with a sense of humor."

"He was sorry he talked to you, Sunset Scott. Very sorry. He told me so himself. But by then, it was too late."

Aaron held the receiver away, imagining what it must have been like, even for someone as deserving as Tex Lassiter.

When he put it to his head again, the anger took over.

"Listen, you fucking sick freak, I'm *tired* of playing your fucking twisted *games!* I want to get this *over* with!"

"Are we on the air, by any chance?"

"No! This is between you and me, fuckhead!"

"I thought I detected your usual histrionic windup—"

"You killed my *father*, you fucking son of a bitch!"

The Phantom did not respond. For a moment, Aaron thought he had hung up, cutting off the call silently. Then he felt him, *sensed* him, still on the other end, a malignant entity, biding his time, listening.

"You set fire to him, you dirty fucking coward! You left him in agony, more dead than alive. Then you broke into his hospital room at night and finished the job. I want your blood, man. I want your dirty fucking *blood!* I want to *drink* it!"

Silence, then the whispering voice again.

"Tex Lassiter told you all this?"

"He told me the *truth!*"

"He told you part of the truth—the only part he knew."

"That's why you killed him, wasn't it? Because he told the truth— Well, just try and set fire to someone else, okay? 'Cause I'm gonna kill *you!* I swear to God— I'm gonna cut off *your* fuckin' head, and hang it on my fuckin' *wall!*"

Aaron gripped the receiver so hard his arm began to tremble and he had to grab it with his free hand to hold the phone steady against his head.

"It sounds like you want another meeting, Sunset Scott."

"The *last* meeting, fuckhead, because you're gonna *die.*"

The voice on the other end paused for several seconds.

"We don't want it in some public place, like the last time, when your friends the police—"

"This isn't for the police—this is for me, and my father."

Soft laughter began to echo from inside the receiver.

"Go ahead and *laugh*, motherfucker! I'll make you die slow and hard, just the way you made Mick Grady—"

The laughter stopped suddenly, a cold, metallic sound to it, like the closing of a coffin hinge.

"Meet me at—the Panopticon Studios. It's not called that anymore, of course. But you know that, don't you, Sunset Scott? You know all about Johnny Moffet, and Moe Edelstein, and Sparky Weiner—"

Aaron had to swallow hard before he could speak.

"When?"

"It's almost dark now. Full darkness will be here within the hour. Meet me in Studio A. That's the large, redbrick building, the first one on your right as you enter the lot."

"You better not be bullshittin' me, because if you *are*—"

"Have I ever lied to you, Sunset Scott? You'll learn the truth tonight—the whole truth, and nothing but."

38

NIGHT CALL

Sam, working late at On-Target News, had just taken a bite from a vending machine sandwich—part of it dripping down onto a production schedule—when her desk phone rang.

"Shit!" she muttered, wiping at the mess with one hand, picking up the receiver with the other. "Samantha Collier."

"Miss Collier? This is Sergeant Lopez, LAPD Homicide."

She dropped the sandwich and grabbed a pen and paper.

"Yes?"

"Do you know where to reach Aaron Scott right now?"

It caught her off guard. She was expecting news of another Phantom killing—unless it was the Phantom himself that Aaron saw killed last night. But not even Aaron—

"He's probably home by now, or maybe still at KRAS?"

"We tried both places," Lopez said. "He's not picking up at home. The radio station said he left almost an hour ago. We had trouble getting exact details from them. They had an incident there about the time he left."

"What happened?"

"Someone sent him a severed head in a box."

Sam tossed the rest of her sandwich into the wastebasket.

When she could speak again, she asked. "Was it—"

"We think so. He didn't include a return address."

"Is Aaron okay?"

"Probably. But we need to contact him."

"Have you tried his mom's place in West Hollywood?"

"Nobody picks up there either," Lopez said.

"Maybe he stopped somewhere on his way home—"

"If you hear from him, would you let us know?"

"Sure. At the number for the Hollywood station?"

"This is the direct line for Lieutenant Montoya or me."

She wrote it down as he read it to her.

"Sergeant Lopez, what's happened to him?"

"Maybe nothing. We want to be sure."

As she hung up the phone, she thought of Aaron last night, coming back to her through the crowds still fleeing the warehouse, a dazed, disoriented look on his face.

I killed him. But it wasn't him—

Even after she got the full story, and tried to convince him that the accidental death wasn't his fault, he still had that hard, staring look.

He killed my father. I've got to kill him.

Sam stared at the number Lopez had given her. Where was Aaron now? Out trying to find the Phantom?

All their leads were false, or dead.

The Phantom was everywhere, and nowhere.

She picked up the phone and dialed Leah Steinberg's number.

She let it ring fourteen times before hanging up and dialing another number.

"Michelle? Sam. Look, I've got a really big favor to ask— Yeah, I *know* it's not your night to cover the field desk, but this is an emergency—"

* * *

Aaron pulled up in front of the gate to what used to be the Panopticon Studios. It was an old-fashioned piece of black wrought-iron scrollwork with a large ornamental P at the top. Kept open and mostly unnoticed during the day, it was always closed and locked at night.

But not tonight.

The heavy chains securing three padlocks had been cut and the gate pushed open, not all the way, as in the daytime, to let two-way traffic in and out, but wide enough to allow one car on the far right side. The broken windows on the upper floors stared down at Aaron and his black Porsche like blind eyes in a stone face. New graffiti stained the outside walls.

Aaron eased the Porsche through the narrow opening, keeping his eye on the wall and the gate to make sure he didn't scrape.

He wondered, as he drove onto the lot, where the old security guard was who had talked to him that first day he came here. What did Johnny Moffet say the guy's name was? Trask. That was it. Floyd Trask. Maybe the old guy didn't work this late, but they had to have *some*body watching this place at night.

The Porsche's headlights cut through swiftly gathering darkness—the closest thing to twilight in L.A.—illuminating a steel door in a white brick building on the other side of a narrow interior street. He rolled down his window and looked for a redbrick building, formerly Studio A. Everything around him was silent, except for the sound of his own engine.

Something thumped beneath his left front tire, making the car bounce on its shocks. He stopped and opened his door.

A right arm, severed at the shoulder, Smith & Wesson .38 service revolver gripped tight in the dead hand, lay in a wash of blood that spilled out from the arm across the pavement like leaked engine oil. His eyes followed the blood across the driveway to a dark form sprawled against the wall on the other side. He got out and walked over, blood squishing beneath his Doc Martens like the blood he had waded through in the hills above Sunset to find the remains of Bonnie Redfield and her cameraman.

The body, its right arm missing, lay sprawled facedown. Aaron used his foot to push it over onto its back. A slack-jawed face stared up at him through glazed eyes.

Floyd Trask had worked late after all. Or maybe he simply left late, after the front gate was locked, and just happened to notice some guy with a mask trying to cut through the chains with a pair of heavy, sharp-bladed metal shears.

Aaron walked back to the car, blood sucking at his soles.

The smell of blood was pungent inside the car as he turned onto the narrow street, headlights sweeping from a white wall to one composed entirely of red brick.

Studio A.

He stopped halfway down the street, in front of double steel doors, one standing partway open.

As he got out of the car, drops of something wet began to spatter his face and the backs of his hands. He sucked air with a hissing sound and looked up, afraid that some new atrocity was hanging somewhere overhead, dripping blood down on him.

He saw nothing but empty windows in an upper story as rain began to fall out of the darkness masking the sky.

The rain was falling much harder by the time Sam arrived outside Leah Steinberg's apartment building in West Hollywood. She dashed through the downpour, ducking water wings kicked up by passing cars. As she climbed the stairs to the second floor, her soaked blond hair lay flat against her skull.

She rang the doorbell, water dripping from her arm.

No one answered.

She rang again, waited several seconds, rang once more.

Under ordinary circumstances, she would have thought the hell with it and left, maybe slipping a note under the door to say she had stopped by. But there was nothing ordinary about tonight, and the fear that had driven her over here in the first place was edging toward irrational panic.

She doubled up her fist and began pounding on the door.

"Leah!" she called above the heavy thumps rattling the door in its frame. "It's me! Sam! Sam Collier! Aaron's friend!"

She heard a muffled cry from behind the door and put her mouth close to the doorjamb, shouting through it.

"Leah! Open up! *Please!* I need to *talk* to you!"

She heard the sound of a dead bolt lock, then the turning of the doorknob. The door opened a few inches, held in place by a security guard chain.

Sam gasped and drew back.

In the narrow vertical slit of the partially opened door, Leah Steinberg stood with gray hair falling about her pale face, eyes red from crying, and in one hand a long, sharp-edged butcher knife, raised for striking, reflected light flashing off its flat steel blade.

"Leah—" Sam began.

"You alone?" Leah croaked, voice thick with anguish.

Sam nodded. "Yes! I—need to talk with you."

Leah lowered the knife slowly and drew back the guard chain, which squeaked along its track.

She stopped suddenly, raising the knife again.

"Nobody followed you here?"

The fear in Leah's voice, and the terror in her eyes, made Sam turn and look down both sides of the hallway, feeling as she did so a chill cut through her that had nothing to do with her wet clothes or the cold rain falling outside.

She was staring at a shadow near the stairs when Leah reached out and pulled her inside, scaring the hell out of her.

"Don't just stand there!" the old woman cried. "In! In! Even now he could be coming up the stairs from outside!"

She closed the door and turned the dead bolt, put the guard chain back in place, aged fingers trembling.

"Who?" Sam asked, brushing wet hair out of her own eyes. "Who could be coming up the stairs? Aaron?"

Leah covered her face with both hands, dropping the butcher knife, which fell straight down, missing her right foot by inches, sharp point cutting through the carpet and embedding itself solidly in the hardwood floor beneath. It stayed that way, stuck in the floor, standing straight up.

Leah went over and collapsed in a rocking chair near the sofa, moaning softly, face covered by her hands, rocking slowly back and forth.

Sam glanced at the knife, and shivered.

"Leah?" Sam moved toward her. "What's wrong?"

She moaned, chair rocking back and forth like a metronome.

"Where's Aaron? Did something *happen* to him? Leah!"

Leah took her hands from her face and clenched them into fists, eyes squeezed shut, tears dribbling down her cheeks.

"Oh, God! I never wanted it to happen like this!"

"Leah! What *happened?*"

"He—called me here."

"Who? Aaron? Where *is* he?"

"He said—he's going to kill him."

Leah's voice broke into a whimper on the word *kill.*

Sam knelt down beside the rocking chair, bringing her face in close to the frightened older woman.

"Leah, *listen!* Aaron said he's going to kill the Phantom?"

"He's going to *kill* him—"

"Is that where he is now? Has he gone somewhere—"

"He's going to kill my son, my *boychik.*"

Sam got to her feet, stepping back from the rocking chair, the chill that came over her now so cold and deep that it made the earlier one seem like a summer breeze.

She turned away from Leah and saw a large china bowl, in the center of the dining table, filled with what looked like ashes, and beside that a black-and-white snapshot, the oversize kind old Kodaks used to take.

Sam moved slowly, as if in a dream, toward the table with the bowl and the ashes and the photograph. She picked up the photograph, the paper heavy, slick beneath her fingers.

It showed a man and woman standing in front of a stucco bungalow somewhere, palm tree in the distance, a new car's rear end protruding into the frame with fifties fins.

It was L.A. all right, but L.A. of long ago.

The woman's face was obviously that of a young Leah Steinberg, smiling and squinting into the strong California sunlight, full of energy and hope.

The man's face had been torn out of the photograph. He wore the oversize, body-concealing clothes of the fifties, baggy pleated trousers and boxy white shirt open at the neck. Even so, you could see that he was large and well built, left arm around Leah, shirtsleeve rolled up to reveal a heavily muscled forearm, veins standing out beneath dark tanned flesh.

But he had no face.

"I *told* him never to call here! *Never!* And he never has— Never— Until now."

Leah was talking to herself, rocking back and forth.

"Our son— He called him *our* son. That's a lie! He *never* cared for us! Going off to do that picture when I was pregnant and sick— And then—"

Leah looked up with her red-eyed, tear-streaked face.

"You don't know what it was like," she said to Sam.

But Sam was looking at the photograph, staring hard at the blank space where the face should be.

"Sure," Leah said, talking to Sam, but turning away now, staring at the living room wall, as if looking into the darkness of the past. "It was easy to feel sorry for him. Don't you think *I* did? I would've gone up to see him after it happened, if I hadn't been so sick— And if he hadn't been so angry, so full of hate. Like it was *my* fault! It *wasn't!* It was a *miesse meshina.* Only, he didn't die—"

Sam dropped the photograph, as if it burned her fingers.

"At first, I thought he *did* die," Leah said, almost whispering now, her words carrying clearly across the silent, fear-filled room. "At first, for months, there was nothing. Then, one night, he comes back. I was near the end of my eighth month. When I saw him, I almost lost the baby—"

Leah turned to Sam again, hatred in her own eyes now.

"You don't *know* what he looked like! You weren't *there!* He thought— He wanted to be—together again. But you don't under-*stand!* It wasn't possible!"

Leah rose from the rocking chair.

"I sent him away! I told him never to come back!" She drew a ragged breath. *"Don't look at me like that!* You would have done the *same thing!* You didn't *see—*"

She sat back down, leaning forward, chest to her knees, wailing softly, like someone hurt beyond hope of healing.

Sam came toward her, sick with fear.

"Leah. Did he say *where* he was going to meet Aaron?"

"I know!" she cried out to the living room wall. "I shouldn't have taken the money he sent to us— I should have sent it back to him, dead ashes to the dead— But it was *our* money, Aaron's and mine! We needed it. *I* needed it, to buy the shop. We had a *right* to it! After all that had happened, we *deserved—*"

She broke down, unable to go on.

Sam grabbed her and shook her so hard that Leah's head rolled from side to side.

"Where *is* he, Leah?" Sam shouted, her anger driven by fear. "Where is he *now?*"

Sam stopped shaking her and Leah's eyes opened wide, staring with wonder, as if she had just recognized Sam in another world, or another life.

"Angel of Refuge," she whispered.

"Christ." Sam let go of Leah's shoulders and stepped back. "All this time, he's been that close . . ."

Leah nodded, speaking rapidly, staring at the wall again.

"He's always been there, ever since— He never told me. *They* did. But even they couldn't help him, because he wouldn't let them. He didn't *want* to be helped. He wanted things to stay the way they were—as a judgment."

She whispered the last word, lips moving slowly.

A sudden pounding rattled the front door, threatening to tear it loose from the hinges.

Leah let out a wail of despair, hands raised before her.

"Riboyne Shel O'lem!" she cried.

Sam, terrified, held on to Leah. The older woman gripped Sam's forearm with both hands, fingernails digging into flesh.

The knocking continued, louder and more savage than before, falling on the door like the summons of death itself.

Aaron stood inside the open door to Studio A, rain coming down in sheets behind him, hissing on the blacktop outside.

Inside, beyond the rain, water dripped from his black leather jacket onto the concrete floor. The interior was cave-dark, black as a sky without stars, but he could make out certain objects near the open door: storage crates, light stands, rolling racks hung with plastic-covered costumes. He could see the twisted metal where the lock to the double doors had been forced open by brute strength.

He reached beneath his leather jacket, feeling for the SIG as he stared into the silent darkness. He stepped farther inside, feeling with hands and feet for obstacles in his way, turning back often to glance at the partly open door as a measure of how far he had come.

The Phantom had to be inside this darkness, somewhere. He was the one who had forced open the door. He had said he would be here, and whatever he said, he did.

I KEEP MY PROMISES, read the message scrawled across the mirror in the Cinematheque rest room. DO YOU?

He glanced back, surprised to see how far he had come, how small the open door looked now, the backlight of a city sky reflecting off the rain-wet blacktop, the sound of the rain itself a distant, hammering drone.

Behind him, he heard a kind of sighing sound, almost a purring, like someone laughing softly in the darkness.

He turned, heart pounding. Groping for the SIG with an awkward hand, pulling it from beneath his jacket, he fumbled for the safety in the dark.

The sound leaped upward, into a shrieking whistle.

Aaron fired at the sound in the darkness.

The SIG's recoil crashed into his hand. The reverberations sounded like heavy artillery fire, rolling off the walls of the studio, bouncing from floor to ceiling, and back again.

At first he could hear nothing except the deafening echoes of the gunshot, then the shrieking sound rising above him, and with it the flutter of wings. He realized then what it was.

A goddamn dove.

In the distance, the open door slammed shut with a metallic clang that cut through the dying echoes of the gunshot.

Aaron turned back toward it in a true panic, but he could see nothing now. Everything was darkness—and somewhere inside this black box, near the door, away from it, or coming toward him, was the Phantom.

Aaron gave in to his panic and ran for the door.

He didn't get ten steps before tripping over something hard and unyielding, and crashing down onto the concrete floor, banging his knees and hands, knocking the breath from his body, almost losing the SIG.

He stayed there on the floor for several seconds, breath wheezing in and out of his lungs, listening for any sounds other than the bird fluttering overhead or the rain coming down on the studio roof with the dull roar of impending disaster.

He got to his feet, wincing, SIG held in a shaky hand.

Light burst from the darkness like a second sun.

39

MAN OF BLOOD

The two women held on to each other, frightened eyes on the door as the relentless knocking gathered force.

Sam broke free, went over to the butcher knife, yanked it out of the carpet, then turned to the door, knife in one trembling hand, and began to unlock the dead bolt.

"No!" Leah cried, half-rising from the rocker.

Sam cleared the dead bolt, and as she did the door flew open, tearing the guard chain loose from the wood.

She fell back, knife raised in defense.

Frank Lopez entered the room, knuckles of one hand bloody, dark hair gleaming wet, dark eyes hard and angry.

Behind him, Ralph Montoya entered more quietly, collar of his raincoat turned up, quick eyes taking in everything.

"We didn't mean to alarm you," he said, "but we heard voices. When you didn't open right away, we became concerned."

Leah stared blankly at the two detectives, her gaze shifting from one to the other. Then she collapsed back into the rocker and covered her face with her hands.

Montoya turned to Sam. "Did Aaron Scott—"

"The Phantom called her. Here."

Montoya's eyes narrowed.

"You're sure about this?"

"Absolutely."

He turned to Leah, as if preparing to ask a question.

Sam put a hand on his arm. "Not now. I'll explain. She doesn't want to talk about it. She can't."

"Do you know where Aaron Scott is right now?"

"No. Neither does she. But I think if we go to Angel of Refuge Hospital, we may find out."

Lopez, wrapping a handkerchief around his bleeding knuckles, looked up sharply.

"Coincidentally," Montoya said, "that's where we were planning to go next. Do you mind telling us what your interest in Angel of Refuge is?"

"I'll explain."

"Perhaps if you went there with us—"

"Let's go. But we can't leave her here alone."

"Sergeant Lopez? Would you please tell one of the officers downstairs to post a guard up here on the second floor, in front of Mrs. Steinberg's door?"

Montoya turned to Sam.

"Do you think she needs medical attention? A sedative?"

"No. This is just very difficult for her."

"I'm sure you'll explain."

Aaron stared into the blinding glare of the klieg light and raised the SIG, gripping it in both hands, aiming it straight at the radiant white center of the light.

"Don't try to be a hero, Sunset Scott."

It was the same voice he had heard over his headphones so many times before—heard right beside him, in the smoky, mirrored darkness of the Rakehell Club—raised above its familiar whispering level now to carry across the vast interior of Studio A, but still hoarse and strained, muted by damage.

Aaron's hatred for him, for what he had done, suddenly reached a new and terrible intensity, burning through his own fear, turning everything else to ashes.

"You killed my *father!* You're dead meat, asshole!"

He screamed it at him, his own voice echoing inside the cavernous immensity of the studio.

"You don't want to pull that trigger, Sunset Scott. Your clip carries nine rounds, maximum. You've already wasted one. I, on the other hand, can fire 950 rounds per minute. It wouldn't be a fair fight."

"*Fuck* you!"

"Think about it."

Aaron stared up into the light, the gun heavy in his hands.

"So nice of you to come by, on a rainy night like this—"

The Phantom's voice floated down to him from somewhere near the klieg light on a catwalk overhead, but Aaron could not make out anything in the blinding glare.

"—and not bring your friends the police along with you—"

"Nobody's with me. This is just between us."

"Your arms must be getting tired, Sunset Scott, holding the gun like that. Don't you want to put it down?"

Muscle aches radiated along both arms, held out straight in front of him as he aimed at the white light and the mocking voice behind it. But he refused to lower the gun.

"Step out from behind that light, you fucking coward!"

"You don't like the light, do you, Sunset Scott? But you should. The spotlight's on *you.* Isn't that what you want? To be the center of attention, always? The famous Sunset Scott."

The Phantom began a low, mocking laugh that grew harsher, and steadily louder, rising above the drumming of the rain on the studio roof.

Aaron almost pulled the trigger, but it would have been useless. Blinded like this, he might have been able to hit the glass face of the klieg light, if he fired more than once.

He couldn't hit the Phantom.

"Sunset Scott. One false name, and behind that, another. Aaron Scott. And behind that, still another. I wear only *one* mask. And behind that, no name, no face—"

"Shut the fuck up! You piss-poor, third-rate, dickless ham actor! You have more of a face than you left Mick Grady, after you finished with *him!*"

The Phantom's voice dropped its mocking edge.

"It's been a good game, Sunset Scott. You played it hard and, for the most part, fair. But now it's coming to a close."

Aaron heard a creaking overhead.

"We can't keep playing it forever. One of us has to die, and bring this game to an end."

The creaking came again, feet moving across the catwalk.

Aaron tried to follow the sounds with his gun, but he still could not see beyond the blinding light. He glanced to the far side of the studio, where the klieg light's backwash picked out a metal ladder in the shadows, leading up to the catwalk.

"One of us must die, Sunset Scott."

The footsteps stopped, catwalk creaking directly overhead.

"But it's not going to be me. You see, I've already died, once before. And once is more than enough, for this life."

Aaron heard the sharp, metallic click of a grip safety being disengaged for firing.

"Give my regards to your father, Sunset Scott."

They drove through the downpour, and even with the patrol car's wipers on high, they still saw the night world through a shimmering liquid veil, as if all Hollywood—streets, buildings, electric signs—had been submerged, like lost Atlantis, and made a watery grave.

The wipers flicked back and forth with a frantic beat, the loudest sound in a mostly silent car.

Sam had told them what Leah said. Montoya sat quietly, digesting the information. Lopez drove fast down the rain-wet streets, the knuckles of one hand crusted with drying blood.

"What happens," Sam asked, "if we find him there?"

"Chances are we won't," Montoya said. "If we do, get out of the way at once, if that's possible. If not, get down on the floor, and stay there until the shooting stops."

"You're not even going to try and take him alive?"

"He won't let that happen."

"Leah said he lives at the hospital, that he's always lived there. But you can't *live* at a hospital—unless you're dying, or a veteran and the government's paying."

"Or unless you're seriously deformed, and Angel of Refuge takes you in on a charity basis. They maintain a small number of live-in patients that way. He could be doing janitorial work, maybe helping with orderly and nursing duties."

"With or without the mask?"

"Without, of course. His face, shocking as it might be on the street, would actually serve to comfort other deformed patients, like being taken care of by one of their own. The hospital provides a perfect living environment for him. He never has to go out for food, clothing, or medical care."

"Just to murder people."

"That's why he wears the mask. He doesn't want his friends at the hospital to know."

"But they *have* to suspect something."

"Not necessarily. Yesterday, Sergeant Lopez showed a computer-generated sketch of what we think he looks like to Dr. Harold Portis, one of the top plastic surgeons at Angel of Refuge. Now Dr. Portis certainly knows him. He may even have treated him in years past. But when Sergeant Lopez showed him the sketch, Dr. Portis was anything but cooperative. He was unwilling—perhaps unable—to admit that a trusted patient and friend of many years might possibly be the monster on the six o'clock news."

"Leah said he didn't want his face fixed, like some kind of self-punishment. Why didn't this doctor talk him into it?"

" 'Therein the patient must minister to himself.' "

"What's that, the Bible?"

"Shakespeare."

"Do you have a copy of this sketch with you right now?"

"Yes."

"Can I see it?"

"No."

"Why not?"

"You don't want to, Miss Collier."

"Maybe the On-Target News audience does."

"They don't need to see it either."

The patrol car took a hard left, skidding on the rain-slick street. They bounced up onto a cement driveway and came to a stop in front of the admitting entrance to the hospital, the illuminated white letters ANGEL OF REFUGE glowing through the rain and the darkness.

"We're here," Lopez said.

Inside, an uncooperative night nurse—adamant that it was past visiting hours, no matter who the visitors were—yielded at the sight of Lopez's LAPD badge, and his knuckles, cracked open once again, dripping blood onto her countertop.

She told them that Dr. Portis was still in his office.

"But I have to warn you, he's not in a very good mood."

They found Portis standing before a window with his back to them, a cigarette in one hand, watching the rain come down.

He turned as they entered without knocking.

"What's the meaning of this?"

Lopez nodded. "Dr. Portis, you may remember—"

"How did you get past the nurse downstairs?"

"We told her it was an emergency."

"Get out of here! All of you! Now!"

"This is Lieutenant Montoya, my supervisor at the LAPD—"

"I don't care who the hell he is! Get *out!*"

"Someone's life is at risk, doctor."

"I'm calling security."

Portis picked up the phone, pretending to ignore Lopez.

"Miss Collier here is with On-Target News. If you make us go back and get a warrant, it's going to wind up all over the eleven o'clock broadcast. Is that where you want it, Doctor?"

Portis put down the phone.

"What do you want this time?"

"We need to see the room where Mick Grady lives."

Portis stubbed out his cigarette in an ashtray on the desk.

"Why?"

"We have good reason to believe that he's the Phantom."

"That's a *lie!* A damnable, despicable lie! He's an innocent man. The only thing he's guilty of is having suffered a terrible accident—and an almost-unimaginable deformity."

"He's deformed lots of other people. Where's his room?"

"You don't know what you're talking about! He's a hardworking, compassionate human being! He's sent money to a woman he never even married. He's helped her support a son she's never allowed him to see. Do you *know* any of this?"

Lopez started to answer, but Montoya spoke first.

"Doctor, the life of that son is the one that's at risk, even as we speak. I'll have to insist you show us his room."

"Suddenly we're all concerned about the son, are we? What about Mick? Does anyone give a damn about him?"

He looked at each in turn, then walked out of his office.

He led them, by means of a private staff elevator, to a small room at the end of a long corridor in a restricted wing of the hospital's top floor. The moment they entered the wing, Sam noticed the signs of age and disrepair: peeling gray paint on cinder block walls, a line of bare lightbulbs extending down the center of the corridor ceiling, old-hospital smells of sickness, disinfectants, and death. This was the part of the building that time, and money, had forgotten.

As they passed by open doors, several patients came out to stare at them. One, a shirtless, sunken-chested man in his early thirties, had hands instead of arms growing from his shoulders like stunted wings. Another, about ten years younger, clad only in cotton briefs, revealed a face and body covered with bulging, discolored, tumor-like growths.

Portis nodded to each of them, smiling. "Edward. Simon."

Then he spoke to the others, without looking back.

"We have a wide variety of disorders. Thalidomide accidents. Neurofibromatosis. Offensive to some, but to these patients, they form the parameters of their lives. That's what we try to give them here—a chance to live, not just exist."

Portis stopped in front of a locked door. He took out a key ring, found the right one, and fitted it to the lock.

Sam caught her breath as the door opened.

The room was dark, except for the outside light coming through a small, rain-spattered window above a narrow bed, falling on a dark wool blanket and white pillow, ghostly white in that darkness. Portis flipped a switch, and by the light of a single naked overhead bulb, Sam could see the bed with its barred metal headboard, the small desk supporting a television, VCR, and portable radio. A tall metal cabinet took the place of a closet, looking more like a gym locker than an armoire.

"This is his room," Portis said, "the confines of his life. He rarely leaves it."

"A television," Montoya observed, "but no phone."

"This is an older wing. The rooms aren't wired for phones. When patients need to make calls, they use the one out in the lobby on this floor."

"What if they want to make a private call?"

"There's a pay phone outside on the street."

Lopez looked up, catching Montoya's eye, who then said to Portis, "He doesn't seem to have any personal photographs."

"Patients with facial deformities usually don't. Obviously they're not fond of former pictures of themselves, but they don't care much for pictures of people close to them either. You'll also notice the absence of mirrors. The only reflective surfaces are the television screen and the window at night."

Lopez walked over to the metal cabinet and turned the handle. Things rattled inside, but the door remained locked. He took out a small tool that looked like a nail file and raised his dark eyebrows at Montoya, as if seeking permission.

Montoya nodded.

Lopez inserted the tool into the lock and gave it a quick twist. A sharp cracking sound was followed by the turning of the handle and the squeaking of the metal door.

"Hold it right there!" Portis ordered, looking up at the sound. "This is private—"

He stopped as the cabinet door swung all the way open.

Taped to the inside of the door were two pictures: one, a black-and-white close-up of Leah, perhaps enlarged from the damaged snapshot Sam had seen on the dining room table; the other, a publicity still of Aaron, also in black-and-white.

The picture of Leah had been mutilated by two vertical slashes that removed the eyes and the mouth, leaving an image of a dead face—empty, mute, expressionless.

The photograph of Aaron had been cut into various jagged fragments, positioned correctly, but with space between each piece, giving the impression of a face in the act of exploding.

Dark, reddish brown stains smeared the surface of each image, the residue of dried human blood.

"Oh my God," Sam whispered.

"This is a deliberate violation of a patient's right to privacy—" Portis began, then stopped, not sounding convincing anymore, not even to himself.

One of the shelves inside the cabinet contained a roll of electrical tape and a box of surgical gloves. Another shelf held knives and scalpels, scissors and razor blades, sharp-pointed instruments for poking and piercing, some of them crusted with dried blood, others scrupulously clean. In a wide-mouthed, capped glass jar, the top layer of skin from a human face, carefully cut away and peeled back, floated in a formaldehyde solution like a yellowed silken mask.

Sam drew a sharp breath and turned her head away.

At the far end of one shelf, an aerosol can stood apart from the other items, with a label that read:

> COLLODION (PYROXYLIN SOLUTION). WARNING: EXTREMELY INFLAMMABLE. DO NOT USE NEAR OPEN FLAME. AVOID CONTACT WITH EYES.

"What's that?" Lopez asked.

"Collodion's a type of plastic skin," Portis explained. "You apply it with an aerosol propellant. It dries on your own skin to form a kind of spray-on bandage. I can't imagine why Mick would have needed something like that—"

"His mask," Lopez said.

"I beg your pardon?"

But Lopez was studying the contents of the cabinet again.

Butane lighters of different sizes covered one of the lower shelves, along with small plastic bottles of lighter fluid and other inflammable liquids. A medium-sized metal cylinder sat by itself on the bottom shelf, with a label identifying it as liquid nitrogen and warning against improper disposal.

> CAUTION: CORROSIVE CHEMICAL. DO NOT DISPOSE OF DOWN SINK OR STORM DRAINS. REFER TO TOXIC WASTE DISPOSAL UNIT ONLY.

"What did he use this one for, Doc?" Lopez asked, pointing at the liquid nitrogen. "To burn off his warts?"

"I—have no idea." Portis cleared his throat. "But I'm sure there's some reasonable explanation—"

"He used it on several of his victims' faces," Montoya said, "while they were still alive."

"Can you *prove* that, Lieutenant?"

"I think so. In the meantime, this room is off-limits to all patients and hospital staff, including yourself."

"For how long?"

"At least until the forensic team is finished with it."

Lopez slammed the cabinet door, rattling the contents on their metal shelves. He turned to Portis.

"Where is he?"

"I have no idea—"

"You said he spends most of his time in here."

"That's correct."

"He's not here now. Where could he be?"

"I don't have to answer these questions!"

Portis started to leave.

Lopez stepped in front of him, fists clenched at his sides, dark eyes burning with such intensity that Portis backed up.

Montoya raised a hand, ready to intervene.

The last time someone had refused to cooperate in a situation like this, Lopez had picked him up and thrown him out a window. The informant, a small-time bookie, had survived, but Lopez had been placed on suspension without pay for six months.

Tension flowed through the room like a live current.

Portis turned away from Lopez and stared out the rain-streaked window, talking quietly, as if to himself.

"He really doesn't get out much. Most of our resident patients don't. I guess that's a good thing, considering the neighborhood. Not too long ago, Mick had a run-in with a mugger. He went out for a walk and came back with a bullet wound in his right leg."

Lopez glanced at Montoya, who put a finger to his lips.

"He was lucky. It didn't do any permanent damage. We treated him and he healed fast. He's always healed fast—even after his accident. A thing like that would have killed most men . . . Sometimes we let him take one of the delivery vans to pick up materials from a nearby medical supply warehouse. We don't let him *keep* anything for his own use, of course. I have no idea how he got hold of—those."

He gestured vaguely at the cabinet, without turning around.

"Did you send him to the warehouse tonight?" Lopez asked.

"No, we did not."

"Then where do you think he went?"

"I told you! I *don't know!*"

Portis stared hard out the window, into the rain.

"He talked about— He asked me if I remembered some old B-movie studio, Pan—something or other."

"Panopticon?" Sam asked.

"Something like that. I told him not only didn't I remember it, I'd never even *heard* of it. I guess Mick used to work there, before his accident. He said something about stopping by the place, to pay a visit for old times' sake. I didn't think he was talking about going over there to*night*—"

Portis stopped at the sound of sudden footsteps, and turned in time to see Lopez and Sam running from the room, Montoya moving quickly after them.

Aaron fired into the white light, squeezing the trigger four times in rapid succession.

The arc light exploded in a shower of sparks and glass, masking Studio A in darkness once again.

A burst of automatic fire came from the darkened catwalk overhead. Aaron had been ready for this, dropping to the cement floor even as he fired at the light. Now he lay facedown, hands covering his head, an ineffectual gesture against the nine-millimeter bullets bouncing off lights, storage crates, the cement floor itself.

Even above the deafening reverberations of automatic fire, he could hear footsteps moving rapidly across the creaking metal catwalk. Remembering the ladder he had seen, Aaron rose to his knees and tried to track the footsteps in the darkness, following what he heard with the gun held in both hands. He waited until he thought he had a lock, then fired, squeezing off three more shots in a row.

A startled cry of pain and fury rose from the darkness, followed by several short, savage bursts of automatic fire that pinned Aaron down flat to the floor again.

But the firing did not last long. It was followed quickly by the creaking of the metal catwalk, louder this time, more uneven. Aaron rose cautiously, steadying himself with one hand, the other pointing the SIG in the direction where he thought the ladder should be. He waited in the darkness, straining to hear the heavy, thumping sounds of the Phantom's feet as he descended the ladder to the studio floor.

What he heard instead was a whirring sound, like line being fed from a windlass, a great weight attached to its length. Aaron listened as it passed overhead, unable to figure out what the hell it was, until he heard the sound of feet striking cement.

"Shit!" he whispered, and turned toward the sound of the Phantom limping awkwardly across the studio floor.

One of the double doors swung open with an echoing clang.

The rainy night outside, reflecting the lights of the city, gleamed bright as day in the doorway of the pitch-black studio, outlining the Phantom in silhouette as he limped through the lighted rectangle and out into the downpour.

Aaron took aim and started to squeeze the trigger.

And stopped. He did some rapid calculating: one shot for the goddamn dove, four for the klieg light, three more for the Phantom in the dark, one of which must have hit home.

That left him one more bullet, and after that, nothing.

He had another clip, fully loaded, locked in the trunk of his Porsche. But that was outside, across the street, in the pouring rain. If he fired now, and missed, all he had between him and the Phantom was a toy gun, a hand prop.

Rushing forward to get a closer shot, he sprinted across the dark floor. A metal tripod leg caught his own, pitching him headfirst toward the cement. He twisted, falling hard on one leg. When he got up again, he was limping too, hopping on the leg as he came out into the downpour, rain hissing on the blacktop, soaking him to the skin, cold and relentless, like the fury of vengeance itself.

He looked both ways down the street and saw no sign of the Phantom—not that he could see anything in a deluge like this.

Limping across the street, he dug the keys out of his pocket to open the Porsche's trunk and get the loaded clip.

He saw the headlights flash, heard the engine roar, the tires squeal on slick pavement, all in the same instant, as the black delivery van came out of the rain like a monster from the apocalypse, bent on destruction.

He watched openmouthed as the van moved toward him, wipers

flicking back and forth hypnotically, driver's window rolled down, the Phantom aiming an Uzi submachine at him, gripped in one bloody hand, white mask glowing above the wheel like a disembodied death's-head.

Aaron threw himself down behind the Porsche, rolling underneath the chassis as the Phantom opened up with repeated bursts of automatic fire. He heard the shattering of safety glass, the metallic chunk of bullets tearing into the car's body, then the squeal of tires as the van raced down the narrow street, turned, and headed for the lot entrance.

Automatic fire ringing in his ears, he scrambled into the Porsche and slammed the accelerator to the floor.

The car zoomed forward like a greased bullet, forcing Aaron to fishtail wildly on the first turn. He was moving at close to maximum speed when he came up on the entrance gate and saw, through bullet-starred glass, that someone had pulled it shut. He jumped on the brakes and turned hard right, coming to an earsplitting, sideways stop just inches from the iron bars of the closed gate.

As he grabbed hold of the rain-slick bars, pulling the gate open slowly, like a dancer in an underwater ballet, he heard the growl of a heavy engine, the skidding of tires, and looked up to see the black van, misty as an apparition, gliding down the street into the darkness and the rain.

40

BEHIND THE MASK

Aaron followed the Phantom right through a red light, glancing both ways for oncoming cars—just in time to see one bearing down on him in a stroboscopic blur.

Lopez, the other driver, turned the black-and-white patrol car mere seconds before collision, throwing Sam all the way across the backseat and into the side door.

"Miss Collier," Montoya called above squealing tires as Lopez threw the patrol car into a sudden reverse U-turn, "do you have your seat belt fastened?"

"No," Sam answered, rubbing a bruised shoulder.

"Put it *on.*"

Aaron closed in on the black van, rain falling through his headlights like glass beads, coming up so close behind it that spray from the rear tires blinded him, smearing his bullet-starred windshield with water, dirt, and oil, despite the frantic twitching of the wipers. He stuck his head out the shattered side window to get a clearer view when he saw the van's brake lights flash bright red. Going too fast to stop, or slow down, Aaron jerked left on the steering wheel, cutting out into the lane of oncoming traffic, his bumper clearing the van by inches.

Horns blared and headlights flashed as he hurtled toward a head-on collision with two cars coming at him in the other lane. Still unable to stop, or do anything with his brakes but lose control, he floored the accelerator and cut in front of the slowing van. The driver of the first car panicked and swerved right, jumping up over the sidewalk and into a brick wall.

The car behind it, a cinnamon-colored Camry, veered in the opposite direction, right in front of Aaron's speeding Porsche. Aaron swerved right, back into the oncoming lane, followed by the Phantom in the black van. Lopez, coming up fast in the patrol car, took the same escape route. The driver of the Camry slammed on the brakes and went into a 360-degree skid, turning in endless circles on the rain-slick road.

The Porsche, the van, and the patrol car slid and swerved across the rain-soaked blacktop like berserk bumper cars. The spinning Camry clipped one parked car and smashed broadside into another, blowing out its own back window and spattering the inside of the windshield with blood.

The three skidding vehicles realigned themselves in their original configuration as the Phantom pushed the van's speed to maximum, busting another red light. Aaron kept on top of the black van—not so close he couldn't slow down, but close enough to keep from losing it through some unexpected maneuver.

As if to put that to a test, the Phantom turned right at the next side street without slowing down, taking the corner on two wheels, tires screaming beneath the van's weight. Aaron negotiated the turn with ease, skidding slightly, but regaining traction almost immediately, unlike the patrol car behind him, which slid back and forth across both lanes before Lopez could bring it back under control. Another jolting turn brought them all back onto a main thoroughfare.

As they approached the next major intersection, the light turned green ahead of them. The black van increased its speed. An ancient canary yellow VW bug crossed against the light, directly in front of the van. The Phantom leaned on his horn. The VW, out-of-tune engine strained to the limit, scooted across with unexpected vitality, moving almost but not quite fast enough.

The black van clipped it on the rear as it hurtled past, flattening the driver's head against the windshield, knocking the VW into a sharp turn that sent it straight back in a headlong rush at the Porsche and the patrol car, the dead driver's blood running down the shattered glass.

Aaron skidded out in a left-then-right movement that veered around the careening VW and back into place behind the van, the Porsche responding so smoothly and quickly that the whole thing seemed nothing more than a sudden blurring of the optic nerves. Lopez, without the same flexibility at his command, moved left in an effort to avoid a head-on collision, but still hit the VW broadside.

The subcompact seemed to disintegrate. Sam screamed and leaned forward in the backseat, covering her head with her hands as metal, glass, seat cushions, tires, engine parts, and body parts all struck the front end and windshield of the patrol car, rolling across its roof, bouncing off its sides. Part of the engine block hit the upper-right side of the windshield, sending spiderwebs crackling across the glass.

"Frank," Montoya said, "we have to stop and go back—"

"Fuck it!"

"They could suspend us both for something like this."

"Fuck 'em!"

Lopez hunched over the wheel, dark eyes burning into the rainy night ahead of them, illuminated by only one headlight now.

Montoya unhooked the microphone from the dashboard and raised it to radio for backup in a high-speed pursuit.

"No," Lopez said, without taking his eyes off the road. "I don't want every asshole on patrol jumping in on this."

Montoya replaced the microphone and looked at his partner.

"What *will* you stop for, Frank?"

"*Nada.*"

They had covered most of central Hollywood by now, cutting a jagged course north from the former Panopticon Studios, crossing Melrose, Santa Monica, Fountain, Sunset, Selma, skidding left onto Hollywood Boulevard in a wide-arcing turn, heading west past bright lights and deserted sidewalks, emptied by rain of tourists, sightseers, drug dealers, prostitutes, pimps, and other hard traffic, the inlaid stars on the Walk of Fame glistening with unusual luster on this wet, electric night.

The Nike billboard loomed ahead of them, depicting the young sports icon of the moment, rising up the side of the Taft Building, towering above the boulevard like some god of cool contempt, looking down with disdain on mere mortals below, whether they happened to wear Nikes or not.

Aaron, taking advantage of the wide-open boulevard, moved out and around, pulling into the oncoming lane, right beside the black van. He glanced at the white mask above the steering wheel, turning toward him now, muzzle of the Uzi rising into view. With a sudden wrench of his own steering wheel, he pulled into the van, metal colliding with a horrible grinding noise, sparks popping and trailing along the blacktop.

The black van and the black Porsche began to weave back and forth across the boulevard, locked in a mad embrace, the one-eyed patrol car tracking them from behind, rain coming down like a hemorrhaging of heaven. Aaron jerked harder to the right on his steering wheel, just as the Phantom released the grip on his own wheel to aim the Uzi and open fire. The van lost control and veered right, bouncing up onto the sidewalk, smashing through a guard chain, into a parking lot, skidding to a rubber-burning stop just before its front end hit the side of a building directly beneath the giant Nike sign.

Aaron drove his Porsche through a rushing gutter, up onto the sidewalk, across the parking lot, and straight into the back of the van, ramming it against the side of the building, locking it solidly in place. The Porsche fell apart under the impact. Both doors buckled shut, trapping Aaron inside the car.

The Phantom staggered out of the van, right side dark with blood, gloved hand dripping blood as it gripped the Uzi. The dark eyes in the white mask looked down at Aaron, locked inside the Porsche. He pressed himself back against the front seat, unable to run, or hide.

The dark eyes held him, like an animal under the vivisector's knife, staring at him through the rain and the shattered glass of the Porsche's windshield, Nike billboard rising into the darkness above them.

He raised the Uzi, and fired—but not at Aaron.

The burst was aimed at the black-and-white patrol car, splashing through the flooded gutter into the parking lot, solitary headlight burning like a cyclopean eye.

Automatic fire began to stitch random bullet holes across the surface of the windshield.

"Get *down!*" Montoya shouted, turning to the backseat and shoving Sam into the cramped floor space below.

The sounds of shattering glass, screeching tires, and the crash itself overwhelmed all other sounds.

The Phantom kept firing at the oncoming patrol car, bullets turning the windshield to chipped ice, tearing chunks from the hood, blowing out the last headlight, and the tire below it.

The car lost all control, skidding wildly to the left, away from the van and the Porsche, and the Phantom standing in front of them, like Ajax at the ships.

Aaron, beneath the hammering bursts of the Uzi, had managed to crawl out of the Porsche through a shattered side window and work his way back to the trunk without being seen, the Phantom's attention entirely on the oncoming car. But the trunk, like the doors, had locked shut, buckled tight by the impact.

He grabbed the SIG with its one bullet and rushed up to the Phantom, shoving the gun in his face.

"Drop it!" he shouted above the exploding rounds.

The Phantom lifted his finger from the trigger.

The patrol car flipped over on the driver's side, skidding across the wet parking lot, sparks flying out from beneath it, breaking through another guard chain and out onto the sidewalk, before crashing headfirst into a glass display window, shards coming down in an endless fall of crystal, bouncing off hood and roof, tinkling gently on the rain-soaked pavement.

"*Drop* it!" Aaron repeated, moving the gun in closer.

Dark eyes glanced at him from within the mask.

Lopez, body lanced with pain, twisted sideways in his seat belt, trying to unfasten it. He shook his head to clear his eyes and mouth of broken glass. Then he felt something wet falling down on him—something that, unlike the rain, had both warmth and aroma to it, a cloying, coppery smell. He looked upward, to his right, in the lop-sided interior.

Montoya hung from his seat belt, expression calm, Buddha-like, as always, but fixed forever this time, eyes glazed with the inward contemplation of death, a small bullet hole in his forehead leaking scattered trickles of blood, the exit wound in the back of his skull gushing like an artesian spring.

Lopez reached up a hand and touched the lifeless body.

"Rafael?" he called softly.

He unfastened his own seat belt and twisted toward the backseat, gritting his teeth against the pain. Sam lay on the floor behind him, curled up in a ball.

He heard her groan.

"You all right?" he asked.

She looked up, blood spilling from a broken nose.

"What did— Is everyone—dead?"

"I'm not. How about you?"

"Okay."

"You sure?"

She nodded, more blood spilling down her chin.

"Stay there. Right where you are. I'll be back."

"What about Aaron?" she called up after him.

"That's what I'm going to find out."

As he climbed up past Montoya's body, on his way to the broken side window that was his only exit, he stopped and looked into the empty eyes of his former partner.

Outside, rainwater rushed down the gutter, flowing into a storm drain with a hollow, echoing sound.

"*Adiós, compañero,*" he whispered.

Aaron stood with the gun in both hands, muzzle inches from the

Phantom's masked face, huge gloved hand still gripping the Uzi, blood dripping from it onto the wet pavement of the parking lot, deliquescing in the rain.

"Just drop it," Aaron said, "right on the fucking ground."

The Phantom stared at him from behind the mask.

It looked different close up—filmy, as before, but harder now, and translucent, hinting at discolored granulations beneath its pale surface, like mountains and valleys seen from the air, obscured by mist and drifting clouds.

He hung on to the Uzi, making no move to let it go.

"Look, asshole. I know you can count, okay? So can I. This thing carries nine. I used up eight. That means I only have one left. But that's all I need at this distance. So why don't you stop shitting around and just—"

The shot rang out in the parking lot, startling Aaron, making him jump back. The Phantom jerked, as if taking an invisible blow. He brought up the Uzi, swifter than thought, and began firing. Other shots, single fire, but in rapid succession, continued beneath the bursts of automatic fire.

Aaron, still stunned, looked up to see Lopez running toward the Phantom, the way he had that night at the Rakehell Club, Beretta gripped in both hands, firing round after round, eyes dark with a hatred that outharrowed madness itself.

The first burst hit Lopez on the left shoulder, bringing him to a stumbling stop, still firing, but up into the air now. The next burst caught him full in the chest, lifting him up off the rain-wet pavement, turning him halfway around, dropping him shapelessly onto the hard surface of the parking lot, blood flowing from his wounds in chest and back, right hand twitching convulsively, firing the Beretta one last, useless time.

"*Drop it!* Or I'll blow your fuckin' *head* off!"

Aaron shoved the gun into the Phantom's face, next to his left eye. The muzzle of the automatic scraped against the mask, a hard, scaly overgrowth, like crusted exudate, with dark discolorations swirling beneath its pallid surface.

He released his grip on the Uzi.

It clattered onto the wet pavement.

The Phantom leaned forward, grabbing his right side.

"Son of a bitch," Aaron muttered, glancing at Lopez's body lying sprawled in the rain. "You fucking son of a *bitch!*"

He turned back to the Phantom, tears from his own eyes mixing with the rain on his face. Still holding the SIG with one hand, he raised the other and began to pull at the tough plastic surface of the mask.

"Who *are* you behind this fucking thing, anyway?"

The collodion started to tear loose with a ripping sound.

"You'll have to pull harder, Sunset Scott," he whispered.

Aaron clawed at the mask, tugging on the stubborn, resistant substance, unable to make it give way. He yanked hard, hissing through his teeth, wrestling with it, as if locked in mortal struggle with the mask itself and everything it stood for: the blood, the murders, the stalking nighttime horror, the sense of personal vengeance for someone else's death.

A sudden tearing sound cut through the rain, like the ripping of real skin on a broken body. The unexpected release of tension made Aaron stumble back, catching his balance with an awkward spreading of his arms, the SIG still clutched in one hand, mask in the other. Fresh gouts of blood smeared the inside of the spray-on plastic, matched by new blood on the Phantom's face where the mask had pulled loose from the skin.

But the blood was the least of it.

Aaron stared in horror at the face in front of him, his own mouth dropping open slowly, filling with rain. His right hand began to shake so badly he almost lost the gun, as if he had no further use for it and knew that he could not kill what stood before him in the darkness and the rain.

With his mask, the Phantom had seemed almost supernatural.

Without it, he looked inhuman.

A true death's-head stared back at him, dark eyes in a skull without a soul, covered in place of skin with a black, rotting excrescence, shaded by swaths of red and purple, dark colors all. Everything human had been burned away: ears, nose, hair, the roundness of cheeks and chin, most of the lips, upper and lower, leaving long, yellowish teeth that grinned obscenely, like the fangs of a centuries-dead vampire dug up from beneath the moldering earth, brought back to life by unholy incantations.

Aaron gagged, choking on his own vomit as he tried to hold it back, bringing up the gun, gripping it hard with his other hand to steady himself, to give some balance to a reeling world.

"One of us has to die," he whispered hoarsely.

He leveled the gun at the grinning death's-head.

"This time, it's you."

He started to squeeze the trigger.

"Aaron! *Wait!*"

He stopped, hearing Sam's voice calling to him through the heavy rain and the distant wail of police sirens, howling like a wolf pack on the hunt.

He glanced back, keeping the gun on the obscenity before him, and saw Sam staggering through the rain, blood spotting her face, her white silk shirt, purse gripped hard in one hand, as if it contained the things that mattered.

"Sam!" he shouted at her. "Get back!"

"You can't do this, Aaron! He's your *father!*"

The whole world seemed to slip just then, tilting the wrong way on its axis, things going in reverse rather than forward, dropped objects rising instead of falling, reality becoming illusion, and all truth a lie.

"No," he whispered, then louder. "*NO!*"

This wasn't his father. It wasn't even human. It was some twisted thing that had *murdered* his father.

"Don't kill him, Aaron! He's Mick Grady!"

If anyone else but Sam had said that, it would have been a joke, cruel and hateful. But Sam knew about Mick Grady, one of the few people who did.

Why would *she* say something like that?

The gun wavered in his hands. He had trouble keeping it level, aimed at the grinning, blackened thing before him. The burned head itself started to shift and bob, moving from side to side like something that wouldn't stay still. It began to melt, as if dissolving beneath the steady, merciless downpour.

He knew he was crying then, salt water blending with rain.

The knee slammed up into his groin, driving breath from his body in a strangled gasp, doubling him over with pain. Fingers like steel gripped his gun arm, bending it backward, threatening to break it in half at the elbow. He jerked on the trigger, firing his last shot, but it went high into the night sky, past the sports god on the lighted Nike billboard.

He let go of the SIG, heard it clatter down below.

Another hand chopped him on the back of the neck, causing pain to jolt through his entire body this time. He dropped to the wet pavement, scraping his hands and face. Then he felt himself being picked up, lifted bodily off the pavement, his own face brought in close to the grinning, monstrous skull, more cold and inhuman than any mask could ever be.

"You're *not* my father," Aaron whispered.

"No longer, no. Now I am your judge, come to bring judgment on you, and all the others. But I *was* your father, once, before they destroyed me."

He heard Sam's halting steps through the falling rain, and the distant sirens, the wolf pack closing for the kill.

"And once, you were my son, or could have been, before they destroyed you. Before *she* destroyed you, by giving you a Jew name, and a Jew heart, and a Jew tongue to lash the world with."

He could hear Sam's labored breathing now as the rain fell into his eyes, staring up at the dark eyes that regarded him from the depths of that skull without a soul.

"Do you under*stand* what she did? You could have been everything Mick Grady wanted to be, but was not, before he died. The Jews always held me back, little Aaron. And when they couldn't hold me any longer, they did me in. They set fire to my heart, my hopes and dreams, and burned them to bloody ashes. You *do* understand that much, don't you?"

"Aaron!" Sam called again, her voice distorted in the rain, drifting into his consciousness like something from a dream.

"You could have done it, little Aaron. You had enough of the Grady Irish in you. I had my hopes as you grew up, even though *she* kept me from you. But then she poisoned you, turned you into a complete and utter Jew. You became one of them, and they let you prosper. You grew rich, and lordly, and famous, in your own way—all the things Mick Grady could never be. And when I called your hateful radio show, to test the measure of your poisoned Jew heart, you scorned me, boy. You brought the judgment down on your own head, little Aaron."

Holding Aaron in one steel-hard hand, he drew a knife with the other, its blade long and broad and sharp as a razor's edge, rainwater dribbling down its shining surface.

He brought it in close to Aaron's face.

Then it disappeared, a flash of polished steel, as Sam grabbed his arm, pulling back the knife.

"Wait!" she cried, blood from her broken nose staining her teeth. "He doesn't know—"

The Phantom turned his face toward her.

She closed her eyes and lowered her own face.

"He doesn't mean to hurt you. But he doesn't understand—"

She looked up, forcing herself to open her eyes.

He jerked his arm free and struck her hard on the side of her face with the heel of his hand. She screamed as she fell, collapsing onto the pavement, purse sliding from her grip.

"Fucking *bastard!*"

Aaron began to struggle with him, feet slipping awkwardly on wet pavement as he heard the mocking laughter once again—coming in through his headphones, echoing inside the darkness of Studio A—inflaming his rage, driving it into madness.

In the heat of the useless struggle he saw it, and stopped.

Lopez had pushed himself up to a semiseated position, leaning on one bent arm, the other lifting the Beretta with a palsied hand, fresh blood spilling from his wounds, his mouth, nose, ears, even his eyes, a veritable man of blood, raising himself from the dead for this, his final effort.

The Phantom lifted Aaron by the neck and hurled him into a brick wall, the back of his head cracking against it. He slid down the wall, head scraping across bricks, the world breaking up into contrasting colors, as he watched the Phantom limp over to where Lopez sat shaking on the pavement and kick the Beretta out of his hand, then kick him again, hard in his blood-soaked chest, knocking him flat to his back. The long gleaming knife still in his hand, he raised one heavy, booted foot and brought it down on Lopez's face, crushing it into the wet pavement, the sound of breaking bones sharp and clear above the hissing of the rain and the whining of police sirens.

He limped back toward Aaron, one foot trailing blood.

"Now," he said, "*he* has no face."

He leaned over suddenly and brought Aaron back to his feet, locking him again in the steel-hard grip, moving the knife in so close that Aaron could smell the wet metal.

"Your face needs work, too, little Aaron."

He placed the pointed blade against his cheek.

Aaron tried to turn away, pricking himself instead, a thin line of blood trickling down his cheek.

"Like father, like—son."

On the last word he cut down, slicing open Aaron's cheek.

Aaron gasped, in shock first, then pain, blood rushing down his neck, spilling warm inside his shirt.

"But it doesn't matter much what your face looks like, does it? In your kind of work, the voice is everything. So maybe we should start with that. Yes, maybe it would be better if we started by cutting out that lying Jew tongue."

Aaron opened his mouth to scream for help, then clamped it shut when he saw the knife coming at him again, wet with his own blood. He turned his head to one side, preferring to take it on the other cheek instead. He saw the Capitol Records Building in the distance, glowing brightly, blurred by tears of helplessness and abject terror.

The Phantom forced his head back around and brought the knife in until the point touched his lips.

"Be a good boy, little Aaron, and open your mouth."

He kept his mouth shut tight, breathing through his nose, warm breath misting the steel blade.

The knife jerked once, slashing through Aaron's upper lip and into his left nostril, cutting that open, too.

Blood burst inside his nose and mouth, making him cough and lean over as he spit it out onto the wet pavement, the pain sinking deep into his face.

"That's what happens to bad boys. Now *open your mouth.*"

Aaron raised his head, blood pulsing from nose and lip, and looked up into the pitiless, grinning skull.

Sobbing, he opened his mouth.

The Phantom brought the knife in toward it.

The blade jerked again, but all the way up this time, into the night sky as the Phantom's arm convulsed and the shot exploded at close range, deafening Aaron, the stench of cordite stinging his slit nostril, burning his eyes.

He turned and saw Sam, blood on her face, Heckler & Koch automatic clutched in both hands, a hard look in her eyes as she pulled the trigger again.

That one missed, cutting wide through the rain.

Squeeze! Aaron wanted to shout at her. *Don't jerk!*

But she couldn't have heard him, eyes fixed on the Phantom.

Raising the knife, he came after her.

She fired again, HK bucking in her hands, but she hit him again that time, slowing him down, not stopping him. He kept coming toward her, knife raised high, a grinning skull on a bleeding body, lumbering through the rain, worse than any nightmare she had ever awakened screaming from as a kid—

She fired again.

One of them hit him in the chest. Blood bubbled up from his black sweatshirt, spilling down his body.

She fired again.

The bullet struck the top of his skull, blowing it off, charred fragments scattering in the rain.

And still he came forward, blood and rain running down his body, mingling together in some kind of terrible ablution.

Locking on his face, she fired again, and again.

The center of the skull imploded, taking one eye with it, leaving the other attached and staring at her through the rain and the darkness and the blood.

She fired again and heard the hollow click of an empty gun.

He came down on her, huge body falling forward, blocking out the electric lights, the reflections off the rain-wet boulevard. She screamed and tried to get out of the way, but he knocked her flat to the pavement, crushing her body with his, long knife still clutched in a hard, unmoving hand.

Aaron staggered toward them, face on fire, his own blood dripping into pools of standing water. Both bodies lay still, Sam's beneath the Phantom's. He grabbed hold of the massive, black-clothed body, the pain in his own face forgotten, fresh blood leaking from his slit lip and nose as he struggled to turn the Phantom's body aside, to lift it off Sam.

Like most stuntmen— Tall, good-lookin'—

He heard the voices again as he pulled at the ruined body—

One of those big, strong Irish guys? —big laughing mouth?

—sobbing for breath as he strained to roll it over—

—a good man . . . Never knowed he had himself a son.

Sam opened her eyes to raindrops falling in them, pounding on her face, driving the pain of her broken nose deep into her skull. She tried to sit up, and groaned at the other pains throughout her body, as if a semi truck had slammed her into a stone wall. Sirens wailed in her ears, somewhere on Hollywood Boulevard, approaching fast. Close by, she heard an uneven thumping sound, like someone hitting something, beating on it with slow, steady, relentless blows.

She turned toward the sound, and saw Aaron bent low over the Phantom's corpse, raising his right arm, bringing it down, raising it again—grunting hard with each effort. She tried to get up, and failed. She started to call to him.

The sirens caught her attention again. She watched in numb

fascination as flashing turret lights, reflected in windows across the boulevard, grew larger and steadily brighter—

A patrol car rolled into the parking lot. Doors opened. Armed officers got out. Turret lights bounced off the van and the Porsche, off Lopez's dead body, and the Phantom's.

She turned again to look for Aaron, but he was gone.

Moishe Levitsky sat in his cab parked on Yucca Street, one block up from Hollywood Boulevard, trying to figure out all the police activity down there. You had to be careful with cops. Sometimes you could get good fares from things like street corner busts. Then sometimes they wanted you to drive for free. Emergency transport. Who needed that?

He was still trying to decide whether to go down and check it out in person or hang here and let it come to him, when he heard a metallic tapping on his side window.

He turned—and drew back.

The black bore of a Beretta automatic pressed up against the rain-streaked glass. And the face above the gun—*Bozha moy!* This one must have just held up a 7-Eleven, and tried to escape by diving headfirst through the front window. His face looked cut to ribbons, blood all over it. Even on the barrel of the gun there was blood.

He tapped on the glass again, hard enough to crack it.

"All *right!*" Moishe cried, rolling down the window, squinting into the rain. "What do you want?"

"Get the fuck outta there."

"What? You crazy?"

Aaron fired, blowing out the window on the other side.

"Riboyne Shel O'lem," Moishe breathed, face pale.

"Out. Leave the keys in the ignition."

Moishe got out, holding the door for Aaron, who slipped inside, bent over almost double, gun in one hand, the other holding his stomach, as if he had been shot.

"It's yours. Enjoy. But I still got payments—"

The cab took off with a squeal of rubber.

* * *

The uniformed officers posted out in front of Leah Steinberg's apartment building in West Hollywood, and up on the second floor, not far from her front door, had all departed at once after receiving word of the events on Hollywood Boulevard, leaving no one to witness the arrival of a yellow cab, lighted roof display glowing in the rain, engine idling as the driver got out and hobbled his way up the outside stairs, bent over like someone old and feeble, or very ill.

Aaron crawled up the inside stairs with the hunched gait of an elderly woman, stopping in front of Leah's apartment, ringing the doorbell, pounding on the door.

"Mom!" he croaked.

"Aaron?" He heard his mother's voice. "Is that you?"

"Open *up!*"

The door opened, a narrow crack, then all the way.

"Aaron! My God!"

She reached out for him.

"Your face! What *happened?*"

He barged inside, knocking her hand away, still bent over as he shuffled toward the dining room table.

"Aaron! What's *wrong?* Talk to me!"

He stopped, looked back at her, gasping for breath, wounds breaking open, leaking fresh blood onto the carpet.

"It's been a *long* time," he said.

Then he started to laugh—high-pitched, jarring, unreal.

He pulled it out from beneath his leather jacket, slippery in both hands, and plopped it down inside the china bowl, scattering ashes all over the polished tabletop.

"But he's back *home!*"

Leah Steinberg screamed, raising both hands before her face, unable to look away, looking still as she moved back from it, into the living room wall, trying to push her way even beyond that, pinned struggling against the wall, screaming.

Burned, shattered, mostly obliterated, like a piece of monstrous abstract sculpture, carved from the heart of death itself, it sat on the ashes in the china bowl and stared back at her, what had once been the head of the Phantom, who had once upon a time been Mick Grady.

41

BROADCAST

Ready when you are."

"Okay, Alonzo. Stand by."

Alonzo Gore flashed a thumbs-up at Jerry Deel, who smiled nervously in return, then stepped outside the broadcast booth to where Charles J. Davis waited for him in the glassed-in hallway.

The clock on the console inside the booth read 4:59:23 A.M.

"Let's just say he *does* show up for this morning's show—"

"Jerry, you're looking for trouble in all the wrong places. Right now not even the police know where—"

The door banged open at the end of the hallway.

They both looked up, appalled by what they saw.

The blood had dried reddish black on the cuts to his face.

"Aaron—" Jerry began, then stopped.

He still carried the Beretta, and still walked with a limp.

"Who the fuck is *that?*"

He pointed with the Beretta to Alonzo inside the booth, pushing

PLAY on the cart machine, starting up the intro tape for the Sunset Scott in the Morning Show.

Chuck stepped forward, blocking Aaron's way.

"Aaron," he said, eyeing the gun, "you shouldn't be—"

"I *said*, who the fuck's runnin' my fuckin' *show* in there?"

"That's Alonzo," Jerry said quickly. "You remember—"

"Tell him to get the fuck outta there, Jerr."

Aaron pounded on the soundproof glass of the booth.

"Yo, Alonzo!"

Alonzo turned at the sound, eyes widening beneath his massive head of hair. He gave Aaron a tentative thumbs-up.

"Get the fuck outta my fuckin' chair, you asshole!"

"Aaron," Jerry said. "He's doing your shift this morning."

"The fuck he is— *I'm* doin' it!"

"Aaron, you're too late. It's already started."

The intro tape echoed from the speakers in the hallway.

"—nastiest shock jock in all L.A.!"

"Get him outta there, Jerr."

"Aaron, it's *too late.*"

"—the only true terrorist of the airwaves! The Man with the Mouth! Sunset Scott!"

Aaron fired the Beretta, blowing a hole in the soundproof glass wall, cracks radiating out from it in a fast-spreading web. The bullet struck the clock on the console, sending up a shower of sparks, stopping time in its tracks.

Alonzo leaped from the chair, ripping off his headphones, stumbling out into the hallway, hands raised above his head.

"Jesus fuckin' Christ, man! I'm outta here! Don't shoot, man! *Jesus!* I'm *outta* here!"

He edged past Aaron, flattening himself against the wall.

Aaron glanced at the shattered clock, then turned to Jerry.

"Now it's not too late," he said.

He limped inside the booth, took a seat in front of the console, put on his headphones, adjusted the volume, potting up the sound just a little, switched from CUE to BROADCAST, and leaned in close to the Electro-Voice RE-20 microphone, Beretta still in one hand, the wounds on his face breaking open again, leaking fresh blood, as he started to speak.

Chuck and Jerry stood watching, immobile.

"Okay, everybody! Dig the shit outta your ears and listen up! 'Cause we're cuttin' straight to the fuckin' chase—"

Chuck and Jerry snapped out of their immobility.

"That's right, everybody! You just heard me say fuck and shit over the radio, and that is a very heavyweight, major-league, all-star, license-revoking FCC violation! That's why right now my station manager and my fuckin' producer are shittin' hot shit in their undies. But fuck 'em! This broadcast is gonna be like nothin' *they* ever heard, like nothin' *you* ever heard, like nothin' the fuckin' *FCC* ever heard! Still with me? Any of you assholes out there are into history, you better warm up your tape machines and get ready to record, 'cause, man, this is gonna be *so* fuckin' historical—"

Aaron turned and glanced over his shoulder.

He saw Jerry on the phone, and Chuck farther down the hallway, talking to one of the security guards.

He had to hurry. He wouldn't have long to do this.

"—'cause what you're gonna hear now, right this minute, is *no more lies!* No more fuckin' bullshit on KRAS FM, 108.— Hold it right there! That's *just* what I'm talkin' about! Who gives a shit if I say the station ID? Fuck it! It's all a lie! This isn't KRAS FM! This is *me*, Sunset Scott! Except that's a lie, too! My name isn't Sunset Scott. It's Aaron Scott. But that's *another* fuckin' lie! Because my *real* name—my *mother's* name—is Steinberg. So I'm really Aaron Steinberg. How do you like *that*, all you fuckin' neo-Nazi skinheads out there?"

He looked up again and saw men with special helmets and padded vests—LAPD SWAT Team members—talking to Chuck beyond the door at the end of the hallway, right next to the control room that contained the master switch for the transmitter.

They'd cut his power next. He didn't have long at all.

"But even *that's* not my real name. Aaron Steinberg. It's just *another* fuckin' lie! It's *all* a bunch of fuckin' lies, day in, day out—"

He looked up and saw one of the SWAT Team members moving through the door at the end of the hallway, rifle in his hands.

He turned back to the console, determined not to look that way again. The light seemed to fade around him, leaving only an intense, white-hot beam—not unlike the klieg light in Studio A—focusing on the console in front of him, with its familiar buttons, switches, slide faders.

Everything else slipped into darkness.

"But this is where the bullshit ends, my friends. Because right now, for whatever time we have left—"

He gripped the neck of the microphone with one hand.

"—you're gonna hear somethin' new, somethin' different—"

The Beretta rested easily in his other hand.

"—the truth—"

He heard voices in the hallway, outside the broadcast booth.

"—no more lies—"

He leaned in closer to the microphone.

"—just the truth—"

He tightened his grip on the Beretta.

"—the truth, and nothing but—"